A Wizard's Dark Trap!

The uwagi was suddenly rigid, shoulders flung back, the ghastly features straining upwards, howling at the clouded sky, the taloned hands opening and then clenching as the body shuddered and seemed to shift, another image imposed over its brutish form: the shape of a Jesseryte warrior, the veil of his helmet thrown back to reveal a face, indistinct, beastly and human, both, that smiled malign mockery.

Calandryll stared, seeing the form of the Jesseryte imposed on the flickering shape of the uwagi, one then the other, dream-like, like the shifting, darting movements of a fish glimpsed through rippling, sunlit water.

He braced himself, favoring his bruised leg, the straightsword extended, knowing beyond doubt what—*who!*—possessed the were-thing.

And Rhythamun chuckled and said, "A tidy trap, no? Use that blade and you die, leaving me the victory. Do not use it, and my pets rend you limb from limb. You've seen their work, I think—shall you enjoy that fate? No matter, for I take the day. The day and the Arcanum, both, with all the world to follow when I raise Tharn. And for you, suffering beyond your imagination."

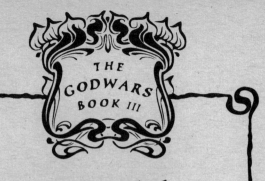

THE
GODWARS
BOOK III

Wild Magic

Angus Wells

BANTAM BOOKS
NEW YORK · TORONTO · LONDON · SYDNEY · AUCKLAND

WILD MAGIC
A Bantam Book / June 1993

Map by Claudia Carlson

ISBN 0-553-29130-0

Published simultaneously in the United States and Canada

Bantam Books are published by Bantam Books, a division of Bantam Doubleday Dell Publishing Group, Inc. Its trademark, consisting of the words "Bantam Books" and the portrayal of a rooster, is Registered in U.S. Patent and Trademark Office and in other countries. Marca Registrada. Bantam Books, 1540 Broadway, New York, New York 10036.

PRINTED IN THE UNITED STATES OF AMERICA

OPM   0 9 8 7 6 5 4 3 2 1

For Carole Blake . . .
Is she not pure gold . . . ?

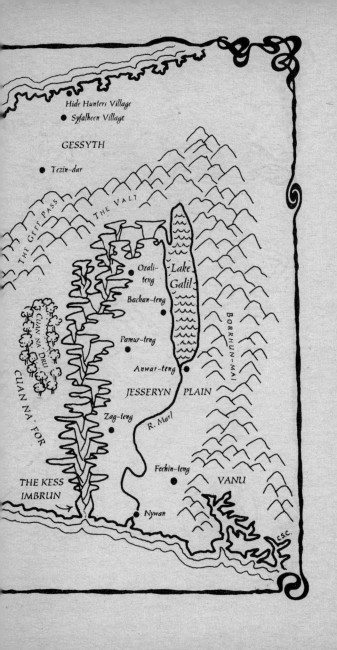

Hide Hunters Village
Sysalheen Village

GESSYTH

Tezin-dar

THE GEFF PASS
THE VALT

Ozali-teng
Lake Galil

Bachan-teng

CUAN NA'DRU

Pamur-teng

CUAN NA'FOR

Anwar-teng

BORRHUN-MAI

JESSERYN PLAIN

Zag-teng

R. Marl

THE KESS
IMBRUN

Fechin-teng

VANU

Nywan

C.S.C.

1

WHEN she saw the riders approaching, she felt genuinely thankful, for her own sake, as if she were truly lost. She watched them, crouched in the grass, until she was certain they were not clansmen, then rose, waving and calling.

They came toward her at a canter: a beautiful woman, whose flaxen hair streamed out, glinting in the morning sun, mounted on a grey horse; a dark-skinned Kern astride a big black stallion, his hair black and bound in a long tail, his eyes hard and blue as he sighted her; a younger man, tanned dark, but Lyssian to judge by his features and the sun-bleached mane that he wore in the Kernish style, his expression puzzled.

She ran toward them and they slowed, eyeing her curiously, hands lightly touching their swordhilts, glancing round as if anticipating some trick, wary of ambush.

"Praise all the gods you've come," she cried. "My name is Cennaire."

Calandryll stared, torn between surprise and sus-

picion, wondering how she came here, and in equal
measure how she could appear so lovely. Hair tangled and dusted with tares fell in raven folds about
a dirt-smudged face, that discoloration seeming
only to emphasize the lush redness of her full lips,
her great brown eyes. She wore traveling gear of
soft brown leather, disheveled and stained, the tunic loose, so that as she approached he saw full
breasts outlined against her dirtied shirt, long legs
beneath the breeks. He thought her the loveliest
woman he had ever seen. He reined his horse to a
halt and bowed from the saddle, letting go his
swordhilt: he perceived no danger. He smiled as he
dismounted, ignoring Bracht's warning grunt, the
open suspicion in Katya's grey eyes.

"Cennaire?" He moved a pace toward her. "I am
Calandryll."

Cennaire repeated his name, softly, scarcely needing to feign the relief she felt at finding her long-
sought quarry. So this was Calandryll den Karynth,
this muscular young man. From Anomius's description she had anticipated something else—a fop-
pish princeling, an effete scholar—but this man had
the look of a freesword, hard and lean as the blade
he wore, his movements gracefully economic as he
came closer. His eyes were brown and concerned,
his hair a ponytailed mane of sun-bleached gold:
he was handsome. She made a faint moaning sound
and went to him, throwing herself against him,
his brown leathern shirt warm against her cheek,
redolent of sweat and horseflesh, the arms he put
around her comforting, his very presence after so
long alone in this wilderness—after what she had
witnessed—reassuring. It was easy to play her part.

Calandryll held her, not sure what else to do,
murmuring soft comforts as he felt her tremble
against his chest, wondering that sunlight could

strike such sparks from hair so black, aware that
his companions dismounted now, still wary.

"How came you here?"

Cennaire raised her head from the refuge of
Calandryll's chest, looking to the speaker. Shirt and
breeks of soft black leather, jet hair drawn back
from a hawkish face in which eyes of a startling
blue surveyed her impassively, a falchion of
Kernish style sheathed on the narrow waist: this
must be Bracht. And the woman, her hair near silver, her eyes grey and grave, clad in a shirt of fine
mail and breeks that emphasized the length and
shapeliness of her legs, that must be the Vanu
woman, Katya. Her right hand, like Bracht's,
touched lightly on the hilt of her sword, that a
gently curved saber.

Cennaire drew in a rasping breath and moved a
little back from Calandryll's embrace, sensing
without needing to look into his eyes that he re-
gretted that loss of contact. Rapidly, almost bab-
bling, she blurted out the bones of the story
Anomius had suggested, fleshing that skeleton
with embellishments of her own.

She was, she told them, a Kand, formerly possessed of some wealth, that invested in partnership
with a Lyssian trader out of Gannshold. She had
looked to protect her investment with her presence, she said, and so gone out with the caravan,
circuiting the western quadrant of Cuan na'For.
They had journeyed peacefully, until they came to
the Kess Imbrun, moving eastward, and were attacked by raiders come south out of the Jesseryn
Plain. She affected a shudder here, and essayed a
tear, letting her voice trail away as she spoke of the
running fight and how she became separated from
her companions, who must now surely be dead.

When she was done with her tale she sighed and

sniffed and asked if she might moisten her lips. Calandryll passed her his canteen and she drank, watching their faces.

Calandryll, she thought, was disposed to believe her without undue questioning. Of Bracht, she was less sure; and of Katya, not at all. She thought it did not much matter: these were honorable folk, and would hardly leave her abandoned. Nor did they have spare mounts, to give her one and send her on her way. She thought they must surely take her with them, which was exactly as Anomius desired. And, if she was to free herself of the ugly little wizard's domination, what she desired. Still, as she passed the canteen back and smiled her thanks, she thought on the trump she held, and chose to play it.

"Burash!" she said as Bracht eyed her quizzically, Katya enigmatically. "That alone was horrible—to see so many die. But then . . ."

She thought on what she had seen and had no need of dramatic artifice to shiver, to lower her voice to a horrified whisper, the sentence tailing off.

"Then?" Bracht demanded.

"Dera!" Calandryll protested. "Can you not see she's distraught? Hungry, too, no doubt."

"I am," Cennaire agreed, lying, "but I'll tell your friend my tale first."

Calandryll made a sound pitched somewhere between agreement and irritation, and she smiled at him, thinking fleetingly of how easy it was to mold a man's emotions. Or some men's, she corrected herself—Bracht appeared impervious. Because, she decided, he loved the Vanu woman, that notion giving rise to another: what was it like to command such love? She pushed those brief musings away and told the truth, entire and unadorned.

"My horse died nearby," she said huskily, "and I came here. I thought I was saved when a rider approached, but something . . . I cannot say what, for I did not properly understand it . . . prompted me to caution. I sensed evil in him . . . a malign aura . . . and hid myself. As well I did, for I was right."

She paused, frowning as she relived the experience. She had all their attention now.

"He lit a fire and brought meat from his saddlebags. I watched him eat. Burash, it was ghastly! He roasted pieces of a man and ate them!"

Calandryll said, "Rhythamun!" The single word was invested with massive loathing. Katya's full lips pressed tight together, thinned with revulsion. Bracht spat his contempt and said, "Go on."

Cennaire wiped her mouth as if to rid herself of some unpleasant taste, the movement instinctive, her own revulsion real. "I was afraid," she continued, still telling only the truth. "Afraid that he should sense my presence and afraid to flee, lest he see me. I remained hidden in the grass, watching. I could think of nothing else to do."

"How did he look?" demanded Bracht curtly. "Describe him."

"Sand-haired," she returned, "with a broken nose. His eyes were brown."

The three exchanged confirming glances. Bracht motioned for her to continue.

"He used magic," she said. "It must have been magic, for some time later five Jesseryte warriors came up out of the chasm and he set them to fighting. The air smelled of almonds when he spoke. They fought until only one was left alive and—Rhythamun, did you name him?—healed his wounds. That one threw the bodies into the chasm; the horses jumped on a word. Then . . ." She closed her eyes, shaking her head.

Calandryll placed strong hands on her shoulders, his tanned face grave. "Then what?" he asked, far milder than Bracht's harsh questions.

"That one he possessed!" she gasped. "He chanted some gramarye and the almond scent came strong again. Something passed between them . . . as though flame flowed from his mouth into the Jesseryte. Then the sand-haired man fell down. Oh, Burash!"

She turned toward Calandryll, throwing herself into his arms, pressing her cheek afresh against his chest.

"He—the Jesseryte now—threw the body after the others. Then he took the one remaining horse and went down the trail."

She heard Calandryll say, "The Daggan Vhe. He's gone onto the Jesseryn Plain."

"Aught else?" asked Bracht.

"There was a book," Cennaire said. "It was the only thing he took."

She felt Calandryll stiffen, his voice urgent as he demanded, "Tell us of the book."

She shrugged helplessly, certain now that the thing she had seen was that volume for which Rhythamun would so casually shed blood. Or Anomius.

"It was small," she murmured, "and bound in black. But it seemed to radiate a dreadful power."

Calandryll said, "The Arcanum."

"I know not what it was called," Cennaire lied, "only that he seemed to value it."

"Aye," said Calandryll bitterly. "He values it."

"The warrior whose shape he took," Bracht rasped. "Can you describe him?"

"He was short," she told the Kern. "With bowed legs and oily hair. Armored; he wore a helmet, a veil of metal over his face."

Bracht chopped air with an impatient hand: "You describe every Jesseryte horseman on the Plain. Tell us of his face, that we shall know him."

"You'd go after him?"

For all she knew—anticipated accompanying them—that this should be the way of it, still Cennaire found it easy to put surprise in her question: it seemed an impossible pursuit.

"We must," Calandryll told her, gentler than the Kern. "Can you describe him?"

She shook her head. "Not well—he looked not very different from the others. His face was broad, his eyes slitted." She paused a moment, frowning in genuine concentration. "He wore a mustache, and I think he was young."

"Ahrd!" Bracht snapped. "The god who made the Jesserytes lacked imagination—she describes a thousand of them. More!"

Katya motioned for him to be patient, speaking for the first time. "How long ago was this?" she asked.

Her voice was calm, deliberately soothing in counterpoint to the Kern's urgency. Cennaire smiled wanly: one woman thanking another for her support, and said, "Three days ago."

Bracht's curse rang loud in the warm air. "Three days? Oh, Ahrd, could you not have sped us quicker here?"

More reasonably, Katya gestured at the depths of the Kess Imbrun and asked, "Must he not go down the Daggan Vhe? And then climb the farther wall? Do we ride hard, might we not take him in the chasm? He travels alone, after all."

"Hardly." Bracht shook his head, indicating the massive rift with jutted chin. "The Blood Road's no easy descent; no place to hurry. And below? Down there the rocks are tumbled like a maze, like a forest of stone. No—with such a lead he's the advantage of us. Again."

Katya nodded, accepting his superior knowledge of the terrain, nibbling an instant on her lower lip as she thought.

"And he's taken another's form," Bracht grunted sourly. "Filthy gharan-evur! Ahrd, but every cursed Jesseryte looks alike, and none with any love for strangers. He needs only continue onto the Plain to find refuge."

"I should know him again," Cennaire ventured, "did I but see his face."

Bracht's eyes narrowed at that, and she felt Calandryll tense once more. Katya studied her curiously and she feared she overplayed her hand, affecting a trembling of her lips, a tearful blinking.

"We've no spare horse," Bracht said.

"Shall we leave her here then?" asked Calandryll.

"She knows his face," said Katya.

"She'll slow us." Bracht drove an angry fist against his thigh, teeth gritted in frustration. "Do we bring her with us, one horse must always carry double."

"She's light enough," Calandryll offered. "And once before, we found a stranger on the road. The aid we gave *her* was repaid surely enough." He touched the hilt of his straightsword, reminding Bracht of that encounter with the disguised goddess, Dera.

"She knows his face," Katya repeated. "And as Calandryll says—shall we leave her here?"

"Please, no," cried Cennaire, her fear of abandonment quite genuine.

She would not die. Indeed, she could not since Anomius had removed her heart and locked that still-beating organ in his enchanted pyxis, and while it remained bound by his cantrips she was immortal. Neither hunger nor thirst held meaning for her, the sating of appetite a pleasure only, not a necessity. But did they leave her, then she must surely earn the displeasure of the mage, perhaps suffer his wrath. Did they leave her, surely she could never find opportunity to free herself of his mastery, but remain forever his puppet, to be discarded when her usefulness was done, or be destroyed by those sorcerers who would destroy Anomius. Whether she obeyed her master and brought the Arcanum to him, or found some way, through the quest, to possess her heart once more, she was loath to find herself again alone.

It came to her that she had not known fear since Anomius had excised her heart and made her his revenant, and that these past days, solitary on the grass, the memory of Rhythamun's fell magic hot in her mind, had changed her in ways she did not properly comprehend. She clung tight to Calandryll, willing him to take up her cause.

She heard him say, "We cannot. Dera, Bracht, after all she's seen? How long would she survive alone, on foot?"

"And to bring her to some camp would take days," Katya added. "Rhythamun gaining on us all the while."

"Aye, there's that," the Kern allowed with obvious reluctance.

Cennaire sensed a mellowing, heard Calandryll say, "She can ride with me. Perhaps we can find her a horse on the Jesseryn Plain."

"The Jesserytes are not a hospitable folk," Bracht returned. "They're more likely to slay us than sell us a horse."

"Then we'll steal one," Calandryll declared. "But I'll not leave her here. Remember Dera, Bracht!"

The Kern grunted and fixed Cennaire with cold

blue eyes. "Are you a goddess?" he demanded roughly. "Be that so, I'd welcome revelation."

"I am no goddess," she returned meekly.

Bracht grunted, turning his gaze to Calandryll. "If not a goddess, then perhaps some creation of Rhythamun's, left here in ambush."

Calandryll removed his arms, gesturing at Cennaire, never guessing how close was his question to the truth. "Does she seem the creation of magic? Besides, we've a way to know." He smiled as he drew his sword, assuring her he meant no harm, saying, "Only touch the blade and show my doubting friend you're what you claim."

Cennaire paused, cautious now. She knew not what power the straightsword held, wondering if it would unmask her. It seemed she had little other choice than to obey: refusal equated with revelation. Were she revealed, she decided, she must throw herself on their mercy, tell them of Anomius, and hope to persuade them to alliance. Should that fail, then she would attempt to flee.

Mistaking her reluctance, Calandryll said gently, "No harm shall come to you, of that I'm sure. Only place your hands on the blade."

Had she possessed a beating heart, it would have raced as she fastened her grip carefully about the steel.

Nothing happened and Calandryll said, "You see? Dera's magic vouchsafes her honesty. She's no more than she claims—a luckless refugee."

"No longer luckless, I think," Cennaire murmured as he sheathed the sword.

Bracht grunted his acceptance of her honesty and said, "You're set on bringing her?"

"What else can we do?" came the answer. "Save go back and find the closest camp? That way we grant Rhythamun even more time. And she knows his face—does that not lend her value?"

Bracht nodded reluctantly and looked to Katya. "How say you?"

"That we've little choice but to take her. And she may well prove valuable."

The Kern sighed and shrugged. "So be it then— she comes with us." He returned his gaze to Cennaire. "We ride hard, and into danger. You may well find a death less pleasant in our company than if you remain here."

"I'd accompany you," she said with absolute conviction. "Wherever you go, I'd not pass another day alone here."

"Then we're four." He looked up at the sky, where cloud scudded, driven on the strengthening of the ever-present wind, the sun moved closer to the western horizon. "We'll start down come dawn."

"Not now?" asked Calandryll. "Shall we grant Rhythamun another day?"

Bracht ducked his head. "Do we start down now, night shall find us on the Daggan Vhe. That descent will take two days—at least"—this with a glance in Cennaire's direction—"and the Blood Road's ill-equipped with stopping places. Better we have a full day and rested animals."

"As you say," Calandryll allowed, "but I'd see this fabulous road now."

Bracht grinned then and pointed toward the Kess Imbrun: "There it lies."

Cennaire clung to Calandryll's arm as he walked toward the chasm, risking a brief indulgence in her enhanced senses. Through the mingled odors of musky sweat and horseflesh and leather that emanated from him she caught a welter of scents. She aroused him, she recognized, but also that such feelings confused him, as if they came unexpected, distracting him from the greater purpose of his quest. She smelled determination, as if he struggled to set aside his desire, and wondered if he was a virgin, that thought intriguing. She needed no revenant's skills to tell her he was strong and after that swift investigation, she forced her senses dormant, still unsure what powers these three questers commanded.

The air shimmered on the updraft from the Kess Imbrun, the latening of the day shrouding the farther rim in misty blue haze. The grass of Cuan na'For ran to the very edge, ending abruptly where the ground fell away as if cut by some unimaginably gigantic knife, sheer cliffs falling down vast and smooth into depths masked now by shadow, night already descended there. The immensity of the rift was seductive, beckoning observers, tempting them to take one more step and give themselves over to the emptiness, so much space below it seemed impossible a body should ever find the ground, but float, riding the air currents like the black birds that spiraled beneath them. Unthinking, Cennaire pressed closer against Calandryll's side, and felt his arm encircle her shoulders. She leaned against him as Bracht pointed a little way eastward, where the rimrock was split, a gully cut down through the cliff. Lower, it widened and bled out onto a ledge, broad enough for several horses to pass abreast, running across a buttress around the farther edge of which the trail was lost.

"The Daggan Vhe," Bracht said.

"Dera!" Calandryll's voice was awed as he looked from the trail to the immensity of the Kess Imbrun. "It's vast."

"Aye," returned Bracht, "and not the easiest of rides."

"Which way shall Rhythamun take?" asked Katya, less impressed by the chasm for her familiarity with the mountains of her homeland. "Shall he go east, west, or north?"

"If he moves toward the Borrhun-maj as we believe," Bracht answered, "he'll go a little westward and take the closest trail up."

"With three—now four—days' start," Katya murmured, "and into a land we know little of, save that we shall likely be unwelcome there."

"But with one who knows his Jesseryte face," said Calandryll, his arm still comfortingly about Cennaire's shoulders, his next words alarming her: "And surely there are sorcerers among them. Shall they not discern our purpose, as did the ghost-talkers of Cuan na'For?"

"If the warriors don't kill us first," said Bracht.

"That threat's been ever present." Calandryll grinned. "Shall it halt us now?"

The question was rhetorical and neither Bracht nor Katya deigned to answer, only grinned back and turned away from the great dividing rift.

IT was easy for Cennaire to maintain her role as they lounged about the fire. Whatever magic Calandryll's sword possessed, it had not shown her revenant, and they all three accepted her as a natural woman cast adrift by misfortune. What questions were directed at her, she could readily answer, they being far more concerned with Rhythamun than her past, and she with excuse enough to question them.

Playing her part—though whether for Anomius or herself now, she was not certain—she acted the innocent, gleaning the bones of their story as she pretended hunger and wolfed down meat.

"In Varent den Tarl's form Rhythamun duped us and snatched the book when we thought it safe," Calandryll explained, "using his magic to transport himself from Tezin-dar back to Aldarin. There he took the body of Daven Tyras—the man you saw ensorcell the Jesserytes—and we have chased him since. North across Lysse, and then the length of Cuan na'For. We think he travels to the Borrhun-maj; to the lands beyond."

"Does aught lie beyond?" Cennaire wondered.

Bracht answered that with a curt, barking laugh: "That we shall likely discover, do we live long enough."

"Perhaps Tharn's resting place," Calandryll said, softer. "It's Rhythamun's intent to raise the Mad God, to stand at Tharn's elbow and rule the world."

"I'd thought Tharn and Balatur were both sent into limbo by the First Gods," Cennaire whispered, "banished by their parents for the chaos their warring brought."

"Aye, they were," Calandryll agreed solemnly. "But Yl and Kyta did not slay them, only sent them into the limbo of eternal sleep, their resting places hidden. The Arcanum reveals those places, and Rhythamun already holds the gramaryes of raising. Does he reach his goal, then he'll bring all the world down in chaos."

"And you three quest against him," she murmured, impressed despite herself, "and the Younger Gods themselves come to your aid."

"In Kandahar, Burash saved us from the Chaipaku"—Calandryll nodded—"and brought us swift across the Narrow Sea to Lysse. There, Dera appeared to us; she blessed my blade that it might stand against fell magic. In Cuan na'For, Ahrd saved Bracht from crucifixion, and sped us through the Cuan na'Dru."

"Not quite swift enough," Bracht remarked wryly.

"But closer than we've been ere now." Calandryll smiled at Cennaire. "And with one who knows his face. Perhaps you were put here by the gods to aid us."

She answered his gallantry with a smile of her own, that freezing on her fresh-washed face as a new thought filtered into her mind. Suspicions and fragments of knowledge, both those imparted by Anomius and those picked up on her own quest, came together, and she saw the true enormity of what Rhythamun intended. It alarmed her, for she realized that the sorcerer was bent on the destruction of the world, and that did he succeed in his aim, she, too, was likely doomed. With such power as Tharn would grant him, Rhythamun must surely stand supreme among sorcerers, a madman with ultimate power. Anomius was no less insane, and no less likely to confront Rhythamun—and lose, she thought, for with Tharn's aid, Rhythamun must be omnipotent. What should her fate then be? As Anomius's creation, as his agent, she must surely be condemned with him: did Rhythamun succeed in raising Tharn, then likely she was doomed as certainly as these three.

Her agile mind assessed the dilemma, reaching only one conclusion: that for her own sake she must lend the questers what support she could, for the defeat of Rhythamun was as much in her own interest as theirs, or the world's. After that . . . after that, she must decide again. To take the Arcanum and bring it to Anomius? What then? Should her usefulness not then be ended and she discarded as Anomius took up the same mad game? Perhaps better to give wholehearted aid, and throw herself on the mercy of the Younger Gods when—if!—the

quest was won. Were she to share in that victory,
surely the Younger Gods would forgive her many
past transgressions. She did not, could not, know:
only that for now she was bound to these three,
their quest become hers in a manner she dare not
reveal to them.

Calandryll misinterpreted her silence. "The gods
move mysteriously." He smiled. "Perhaps they did
put you here, but whether or not, it's of no
matter—we found you and now we ride together."

She found cause for hope in that and smiled
afresh, saying, "I think mischance put me here, but
still I'll do all I can to aid you."

"Well said," applauded Calandryll.

Across the fire, Katya smiled and Bracht nodded,
taciturn, and suggested they sleep, mounting a
watch against the possibility that Cennaire's fic-
tional raiders remained in the vicinity.

Katya took the first shift, waking Calandryll to a
night bright with stars, undisturbed by anything
save the distant howling of the wild dogs that
hunted the grasslands. It was warm, the summer
by now well advanced, and he rose, taking up his
bow and walking a little way off from the fire to
hunker down where flame-glow should not hinder
his night vision. In his mind he saw, clear,
Cennaire's face.

Dawn came early, heralded by the myriad small
birds that inhabited the grasslands, their chorus begun while the sun still lay below the eastern horizon. The sky there brightened, lightening to pale
blue as great radiant shafts drove upward from beneath the world's rim. Random billows of cumulus
drifted on the breeze, ethereal islands in the vastness of the sky. The loud chorusing of the birds dis-

persed into individual songs as the avians completed their daily welcome and went about their individual business. Calandryll rose, shaking dew
from his blanket, and scooped handfuls from the
grass to bathe his face before rummaging through
his saddlebags in search of comb and mirror. Bracht
was crouched by the fire, their breakfast cooking,
grinning as he watched Calandryll perform his
careful toilet.

"Handsome as a prince—she'll surely be impressed," he murmured, just loud enough his friend
should hear, the comment eliciting an embarrassed
grin in response. It had been a while since he took
such care of his appearance.

Katya and Cennaire woke, rising and walking a
distance off to perform their own ablutions, the
one limber, the other feigning a degree of stiffness.
Calandryll watched her, his mind no less troubled
by her presence for what little sleep he had managed.

She seemed cheerful enough as she came back to
the fire, which he put down to her relief at finding
herself no longer alone, and he wondered if she
truly comprehended the enormity of the journey
she was about to start. He pushed the thought
aside: without alternatives there was no point to
worrying.

For her part, Cennaire pretended a healthy appetite, consuming the portion of the stew Bracht
handed her with gusto, returning Calandryll's
greeting with a demure smile, nodding obediently
as the Kern advised her she should ride with him.

"My black's the strongest horse," he explained,
"and likely the surest-footed. The Daggan Vhe runs
steep at times, and often narrow. Hold tight to me,
and if you fear the heights, close your eyes."

"I shall," she promised.

Calandryll experienced some small prickling of
resentment that Bracht so casually assumed to
command the raven-haired woman, then silently
cursed himself for such foolishness. What Bracht
said was right, and only sensible; there was no
more in it than concern for safety and speed. He
quelled his momentary jealousy, though he could
not help regretting it would be Bracht's waist her
arms encircled rather than his.

They finished eating and stamped the fire dead,
then saddled the animals and mounted. Gallantly, Calandryll helped Cennaire astride the black
horse, excited despite himself by the contact. Her
skin was soft and smooth, and when she murmured
thanks he bowed as if he were back in the court at
Secca. Then blushed as he saw Katya studying him
speculatively, amusement in her eyes, and hurried
to his own mount.

"Who leads?" he wondered, thinking that Rhythamun might well have left some occult creation behind to ward his back. "What if the way is guarded?"

"In Kandahar, Anomius was weakened by much
use of magic," Bracht returned. "Think you Rhythamun is different?"

"Anomius still found the power to create the go-
lem, and Rhythamun is a greater mage." Calandryll
walked his horse level with the Kern's, touching
the hilt of his sword. "I've this—best I take the
van."

Bracht shrugged and said, "So be it," though his
expression suggested he thought perhaps Calandryll
looked to impress Cennaire with his courage. "But
carefully."

Calandryll nodded and turned the chestnut horse
into the gully, down through shadow to the sunlit
ledge beyond.

From the rimrock the Kess Imbrun had been impressive enough, but now it seemed he stood at the world's edge, infinity yawning below him. To his right, the cliff fell down immense, precipitous walls and massive spines transforming the landscape into a ragged labyrinth of mazed canyons that tumbled chaotically downward, obscuring the river at the chasm's base. The farther cliffs were hidden behind a curtain of bluish mist and birds hung on the air currents, so that it was as though he looked down on the sky itself. His horse fretted, sensing its rider's awed uneasiness, and he urged it left-ward, closer to the reassuring inner rockface. Behind him, he heard the clatter of hooves on the stone floor of the gully, and Bracht's shout.

"What is it?"

He swallowed: it seemed the sheer vastness of the descent clogged his throat. "Naught," he called back. "No danger, only this place."

He walked his horse onward, leaving the others room, and heard Cennaire cry out, Katya's gasp.

"This is the wider part." Bracht's voice was casual; Calandryll wondered if such nonchalance was assumed. "The trail will narrow lower down."

Calandryll went on, across the roof of the buttress that formed the shelf, and found the road turned back past the edge, traversing a sheer, smooth rockface. It was unnervingly narrow there, and he concentrated on the way, not wanting to look leftward, to where the trail dropped off, unaware that he rode with gritted teeth until the muscles of his jaw began to ache. He saw an eagle soar past, on a level, unblinking yellow eyes fixing him for a moment before the great bird dipped a wing and drifted clear. The sun rose higher, filling the chasm with light, the cliffs shining myriad shades of red and brown and yellow, the light growing steadily to finally reveal the thread of blue, distant below, where the river ran. It seemed impossible they should ever reach that goal: Calandryll chose not to think that after that they must climb the farther side.

Down and down they went, along a zigzagging switchback, across ledges scarcely wider than the horses' girth, where they dismounted and led the animals; across more slabby buttresses; through clefts, where the rock walls offered comfort; along shelves that widened a little while before the trail turned again. None spoke: it was as though the enormity of the Kess Imbrun leeched their breath, leaving only concentration and the desire to reach the foot of the rift.

The light faded, shadow pooling below, the air ahead translucent as the sun closed on the western horizon, and from behind, Bracht called, "Best we halt at the next wide place. I'd not attempt this in darkness."

Calandryll nodded without speaking, peering into the rapidly blueing air for sign of some suitable place.

He saw it as they rounded a spur, the way narrow there, but spreading beyond into a ledge of a size large enough to accommodate them all, with room for the horses. "Here?" he suggested, sighing his relief when Bracht voiced agreement.

The platform was reassuringly broad, marked at its farther perimeter by a tall jut of stone around which the Daggan Vhe continued its descent, the edge sharp, but the slope there angled and less sheer than the wall behind. It was a cheerless place, bereft of timber or water, but as good a stopping place as any other they might find; and dusk came fast here, the sun already dropping below the western cliffs.

"We make cold camp this night," Bracht remarked, fetching a hobble from his saddlebags. "Cold food and no fire."

Calandryll nodded in reply, hobbling his own mount, and asked, "Shall the horses be safe?"

"All being well," came the answer, and then the Kern walked to the farther side of the shelf, peering into the shadows that now masked the descending trail.

Calandryll joined him, but there was little to see, only rock that darkened to the color of dried blood, blank night falling beyond. They went back, finding Katya busying herself with the spreading of blankets and cloaks, setting them between the horses and the rimrock.

"Is Vanu much like this?" Bracht asked as he joined her.

"A little." Katya brushed hair that in the gathering night was the color of old silver from her face. "There are some trails like this, but the mountains are higher and the ways mostly wider."

"Ahrd, but I've seen enough of mountains to last me a lifetime," Bracht muttered, his grin belying his morose tone.

"You'll likely see more." The warrior woman smiled at him across the blanket they spread, tossing her head in the direction of the chasm's far side.

"Still, on the Jesseryn Plain we'll ride flat land again." Bracht answered her smile with his own. "Ahrd be praised."

Cennaire went to where Calandryll was bringing food from their packs and asked, "What may I do?"

He passed her dried meat. "Take this, if you will," he said, thrilling as her hands touched his, adding, to conceal his excitement, his embarrassment, "It's poor enough fare, but all we'll manage here."

Cennaire nodded, aware without any use of her preternatural senses that her proximity aroused him. Best, she decided, to play the part of demure maiden. Did he come to love her, better it be naturally, in his own time, and without overmuch encouragement from her. She had no doubt she could ensnare him with her wiles, with artful guile—she had employed such artifice enough before—nor any that he would succumb unwitting, but with the others present such tactics would be dangerous. Bracht, she sensed, was not yet entirely convinced of her honesty, and Katya . . . of Katya, she was uncertain. The Vanu woman had barely spoken with her, and while no disapproval had been expressed, she felt that Katya, for all she had voted in favor of augmenting the party, as yet reserved a measure of her judgment. So she smiled and took the meat and walked away.

Calandryll watched her, admiring the undulation of her hips, the way the rising moon struck silver sparks from her raven hair, thinking that she bore the hardships of the trail without complaint. Nadama, he thought, would never accept this journey with such equanimity. He shook his head, admonishing himself: this was no place to contemplate a woman's charms, no place to think of amorous dalliance.

But later? said an eager voice, deep inside his mind. *Clear of the Kess Imbrun, what then?*

He did not know. He was not sure how Cennaire felt. Perhaps she saw him only as a rough warrior, a freesword welcomed for the aid he gave her, but no more than that. He had little experience of women and the courtly manner he could affect was, were he honest with himself, a defensive camouflage. In truth, he felt like a fumbling boy. Regretting his inexperience, he carried journey bread and cheese to where the others waited.

Bracht and Katya sat side by side on the blankets, Cennaire to the warrior woman's left. He took a place beside her, using his dirk to carve slabs of the hard bread and wedges of the scarcely softer cheese. Bracht cut the cured meat, passing them each a slice, and they began to eat.

Hunger satisfied, they agreed the order of their watch, Bracht taking the first spell. The three questers were tired, less from the physical effort of the descent than the degree of concentration required, and when the cold food was consumed Calandryll and Katya settled down to sleep, huddling close against the falling temperature. Cennaire felt the cold only as an objective sensation, neither was she tired, but she feigned a shiver and a yawn, wrapping herself in Calandryll's borrowed blanket.

"Shall you be warm?" she asked him shyly, amused by his response, her innate vanity flattered by his gallant reply.

"I've my cloak," he declared stoically, "and that's warm enough for me."

"You're kind," she murmured, stretching out, deliberately arranging herself so that she lay close beside him. "My thanks for all your kindness."

"What else should I do?" Calandryll responded, aware that his heart beat faster as he felt her rump press against his thigh. It seemed to him that even through the thickness of the blanket and the cloak he felt her warmth.

He lay down, thinking for a moment to settle an arm about her and draw her closer; thinking then that she might not welcome such a gesture. He wondered what Bracht would do—the Kern had seemed, at least before he met Katya, to hold few reservations where women were concerned. But this was no serving wench, he told himself, no maid to be casually brought to bed. Nor would he,

with his comrades so close, even though he
breathed the scent of her hair, could feel her body
against him: he did his best to dismiss the lascivi-
ous images that filled his mind, willing himself to
sleep.

Beside him, Cennaire pretended slumber, shifting
a little, increasing their contact. For her part it was
as much habit as design. She was not yet ready to
seduce this handsome young man: she was not yet
certain what path she would take, did they succeed
in seizing the Arcanum from Rhythamun, and so
was not yet ready to risk the enmity of his companions. There was, she decided, time aplenty for
such decisions. It appeared impossible they should
overtake the sorcerer in this godforsaken place: she
would bide her time.

With that thought in mind, she allowed herself
to relax into an approximation of sleep, lulled by
the pleasant warmth of Calandryll's body and the
gradual descent of his breathing from a nervous
panting to a steady rhythm.

KATYA woke him with the sky black above and he
rose carefully, not wishing to wake Cennaire, unaware that she was instantly alert to his movements, contemplating joining him, but deciding it
was too obvious a ploy. Instead, she stirred sleepily
and drew the blanket closer about her shoulders as
Calandryll paced across the shelf to the egress of
the trail, leaning against the spine that jutted there,
listening to the silence. The Kess Imbrun was
quiet, the night disturbed only by the occasional
snorting of the horses and the song of the wind. It
blew cold against his face and he wrapped his cloak
across his chest, a hand resting light on the

straightsword's hilt, struggling to resist the memories of Cennaire's body pressed against his.

He was grateful for dawn's arrival, and he went to wake his companions. The sky shone blue as they set to preparing a meager breakfast, and when they were done eating, and the horses fed what little oats remained, they loosed the hobbles and started down once more.

The Blood Road remained vertiginous, the going no easier. Then it seemed they came to the detritus of the chasm, as if whatever force had carved the great rift had left the riven stone piled about the foot. Gullies and canyons spread randomly: Bracht's promised maze. Great slabs of rock tumbled like discarded building blocks, the way winding intricate among shadowed avenues of red stone until, past a boulder large as a house, it ran out onto a stony beach lapped by the river. From the rim of the Kess Imbrun it had seemed no more than a thread, a ribbon of distant blue: no great obstacle. Now Calandryll saw it ran half a league wide, a band of furious energy channeled by the confining rock, murmuring angrily, as though daring them to attempt its crossing. He rode out onto the beach and reined in, sheathing his sword, staring at the water in the dying light.

"Dera! How shall we cross that?" He gestured at the torrent as Bracht and Katya brought their horses alongside.

"There's a ford," the Kern said confidently. "A league or two westward."

Calandryll heeled his mount around, starting in that direction, halted by Bracht's cry: "The morrow's soon enough to find it. We'll camp here this night."

"There's light yet." Calandryll gestured impatiently at the sky, to where the sun painted the rimrock with hues of red. "And every hour we delay grants Rhythamun more time."

"And Rhythamun may well have left some guardian at the ford," came Bracht's response. "And likely dusk will be on us before we find the crossing place. And this river's no thing to attempt in darkness, even be it unguarded. Better we wait for full daylight."

The Kern's tone was amiable but firm, brooking no argument, and Calandryll felt a flash of resentment at that casual assumption of authority. He glanced again skyward. The sun was close on the western rim now, and already the light began to fade. It seemed they sat within the very bowels of the world, and it came to him that dawn must come late to these depths, delaying them still further. For a moment he thought to argue, but Bracht had already dismounted and was helping Cennaire to the ground, and he realized the Kern was right. The river alone was obstacle enough, and if Rhythamun *had* left some guardian behind, it was better met by day's light. He grunted, embarrassed, and swung clear of his saddle, angry with himself for such lack of caution, for he felt it diminished him in Cennaire's eyes, and then angry again that he should find that his first consideration.

He resolved to put all thoughts of the woman from his mind, avoiding her eyes as he turned to Bracht and asked, "Here?" his voice gruff.

"It seems as good a place as any." The Kern nodded. "We've wood for a fire and fresh water aplenty."

In his haste, Calandryll had seen only the watery barrier. Now he looked around, and saw that stands of scrubby bushes and tenuous pines grew among the jumbled stone; grass, too. "Aye," he admitted, "you're right. Dawn is soon enough."

He busied himself unsaddling his horse, and when all three were stripped and watered, he offered to take them where they might graze. He led them to the lushest patch of greenery, though that was poor enough, and tied the hobbles in place. That done, he set to cutting wood, expending his self-directed anger on the timber.

Katya came to join him, her expression unreadable in the rapidly descending twilight. For a moment she studied his face, then said, "You've no need to try so hard, Calandryll."

"What?" He lowered his blade, turning to her.

"I suspect it's less the desire to catch Rhythamun than another that drives you now," she murmured gently. "Cennaire is very lovely."

He was thankful for the shadows: they hid his blush. Still, he said, "I'd grant him no more time than we must."

"I know." Katya ducked her head. "Nor would Bracht, or I. But we know something of his wiles, and to ride headlong into danger can only favor him."

"Aye." He felt his embarrassment grow, for all Katya spoke gently, friend to friend. "I was foolish."

"No more than Bracht, on board the warboat." She laughed softly. "Did you not urge him to patience then?"

He nodded, grateful for her diplomacy, and she continued, "She'll be with us awhile, I think; and I think she looks with favor on you. Do you take a woman's advice, I'd tell you to be yourself. That alone is sufficient."

"Think you so?" he asked eagerly.

"Most surely," Katya replied, smiling now.

"And do you trust her?"

The warrior woman's smile faltered, her lips

pursing an instant. "She has given me no reason to doubt her," she said softly.

"But?"

"I am not sure." Katya shrugged, her mail shirt rustling. "I sense something about her. What, I cannot say; and so will not judge her."

"Surely she is no more than she claims." Calandryll frowned. "I perceive no guile in her."

"I suspect we see her through different eyes." Katya smiled again. "I do not say she is untrustworthy; neither more nor less than what she claims and seems. Only that your vision is . . . enhanced . . . by her beauty."

He thought she might have said *entranced*, and shook his head, less in negation than puzzlement.

"You've no need to impress her," Katya went on, "only be yourself, and let matters take their course."

"Aye." He gathered up the splintered branches, smiling ruefully now. "I'll heed your advice—and thank you for it."

Katya nodded companionably, taking up her own burden, walking beside him as they returned to the beach, where Bracht and Cennaire had spread the blankets and were preparing food.

Soon a cheerful fire drove back the shadows and a stew bubbled over the flames. Calandryll, resolved to heed Katya's words, curbed his desire to impress the raven-haired woman, behaving—as best he could in her intoxicating presence—normally. It was not easy, for his eyes were drawn constantly toward her, marveling at the play of light on her skin and hair, her beauty a temptation to boast of exploits past, to impress her with his feats and his learning. He had never, he knew, felt so drawn to a woman. Nadama paled in comparison, a callow girl whose face he could now hardly recall. He wondered if he was in love; if such emotion could strike so swift. In Bracht's case, yes: the Kern's feelings for Katya had been immediate. He, on the other hand, *was* of different mettle, raised to a more courtly, a more sedate, approach, and such a background made it all the harder for him to understand the fierce attraction he experienced. Confusion once more gripped him, and he fell silent, joining in the conversation in desultory manner.

Cennaire sensed a change in him, and wondered what the Vanu woman had said as they talked among the trees. Something concerning her, she guessed, deciding that as yet she was not entirely trusted by Calandryll's companions. Whatever course she might ultimately choose, she knew she must for now earn their confidence, and so made no attempt to charm Calandryll, but pretended weariness, and a degree of unease that was not entirely feigned.

Indeed, all their talk of Rhythamun rendered her nervous. He appeared a mage of dreadful power and she marveled that these three had survived so long in their pursuit of the wizard. They spoke almost casually of entering a hostile land, of the likelihood of traversing the Jesseryn Plain to whatever lay beyond the Borrhun-maj. They were prepared to face Jesseryte warriors and demons with equal equanimity, trusting in themselves and the benevolence of the Younger Gods: they entertained no doubt but that they go on, no matter the odds against them. Such conviction she found almost frightening. She thought of the magic mirror hidden in her baggage, and wondered how Anomius fared. Did her master fret? Did he wonder where she was? At some opportune time, she thought, she must contact him, but not yet; not while use of the mirror must surely reveal her for his creation.

The night passed slow and she was glad when she
saw the sky above begin to pale and the camp began
to stir, the questers readying for departure with the
efficiency of long practice. The fire was blown to
fresh life and breakfast set to cooking, the horses
saddled while water boiled, Bracht and Calandryll
drawing dirks across their stubbled cheeks as the
two women washed in the icy water of the river. Before the sun's light had reached the lowermost deeps
they were mounted, Cennaire again settled behind
Bracht's saddle, and riding for the promised ford.

The crossing lay a good two leagues to the west,
its presence announced by sullen thunder, in a
curve of the Kess Imbrun where the great rift
broadened, the beach widening before a barrier of
tumbled stone high as the walls of a city.

Calandryll, in the lead, halted, staring awed at
the natural dam, waiting for Bracht to come up.
The hypabyssal blockage rose skyward above him,
the boulders at its foot transforming the riverbed
into a wild terracing of rocky cascades over which
white water foamed, ferocious as it gushed between
the stones. Along the face, spreading in a haze of
silvery gold, a mist rose from the spray, glittering
rainbows arcing as the sun struck the great foun-
tains jetting from high among the boulders.

"The ford lies beyond." Bracht shouted his opinion, leaning from his saddle to put his mouth close
to Calandryll's ear. "Above the rocks."

They climbed awhile, through a shimmering
haze, cloaked against the watery fog that soon engulfed them, the clatter of hooves on stone lost in
the thunder of the cascade, the horses fretting nervously at the sound. Calandryll remained in the
lead, squinting through the mist until he saw an
opening between two enormous stones, indicating
the gap with an outflung arm: to speak in that din-

ning would be useless. He urged the chestnut into the dim-lit pass, the way rising steep there, tortuous and slippery.

He emerged onto a broad shelf, its edge overlapped by the great expanse of water pent behind the dam, the river become more akin to a lake. Calandryll studied the ramparts of the dam with uncertain eyes, waiting as the others aligned themselves beside him. The topmost level of the barricade was wide and smooth as a made road: ten horses might go easily abreast, no more than a finger's depth of water spilling over the stones. But to the one side lay a drop that would send a rider tumbling into the cascades below, and to the other . . . he studied the vast pool, wondering at its depths, and the currents that must surely rage there beneath the surface. The mist hung sparkling above, a spectrum of colors set to dancing by the morning light, beautiful and at the same time eerie, as if spirits pranced there, tempting the unwary. Cautiously, he urged his mount forward.

The horse began to stamp and snort, liking this ford no better than its rider, and Calandryll held a tight rein, his eyes narrowed against the film of moisture that covered his face, dripping from his hair, finding whatever openings his clothing offered to trickle irritatingly down chest and back. The edges of the way were soon lost behind a curtain of swirling colors, and he could see scant feet ahead. It seemed he traversed a way akin to the magical road that had brought him to Tezin-dar, a place where time was without meaning, distance become abstract, the morning filled with the threatening rumble of the torrent below, the strange silence of the lake beside, the aural contrast disorientating. It occurred to him that if Rhythamun left some monstrous creation to ward his trail, here would be a fine place, and thought then to draw his sword, and then thought better of it, deciding it was the wiser course to hold the reins firm against the panicky fretting of his mount.

In that negation of time he had no idea how long the crossing took, and was surprised when suddenly the mist brightened, the shifting colors resolving into a soft golden haze. He wiped his eyes, peering ahead, and saw the gold darken, merging with a reddish-grey, and realized that he could discern shapes, like huge sentinels, waiting.

In a little while they resolved into the primeval detritus of the Kess Imbrun, the great stone blocks that marked the limits of the dam, spreading across the northern beach in welcome announcement of the ford's end. He lifted the roan to a faster pace, the horse responding willingly, and they came out of the mist onto a broad shelf.

Calandryll sprang down and turned to see Bracht emerge from the haze, Cennaire disconsolate behind him, Katya coming after. He went to meet them, giving Cennaire his hand as she slid from the stallion's back. She clung to him a moment, her face against his chest, and he held her awkwardly, watching as Bracht and Katya dismounted. Then she stepped back, smiling faintly, and said, "I thought that road would never end."

"Nor I," he returned, studying her face, unsure whether he felt relief or reluctance that she let him go.

"Ahrd, but that was a wet crossing." Bracht's voice interrupted his contemplation. "Do we find timber and get a fire started before night finds us?"

Calandryll looked about. The sun hung low in the western quadrant now, not far off its setting, and he realized that the fording of the river had taken the better part of the day. A breeze drifted

cool down the chasm and he shivered, the involun-
tary motion prompting Cennaire to ape him. Katya
bent, wringing out her long hair; Bracht, who appeared not much discomforted, pointed toward the
northern cliffs.

"Likely we'll find the makings there. Do you
take Cennaire a while, and I'll go ahead."

"What of Rhythamun?" Calandryll asked.

"Did he plan aught, I think we'd know ere now."
Bracht shook his head, sending droplets flying. "I
think we're safe enough here."

Not waiting for an answer, he swung astride the
black horse. Katya followed him into the saddle.
Calandryll shrugged and mounted, reaching down
to help Cennaire clamber up behind him. For all he
was damp, and not a little miserable, it was a pleasant sensation to feel her arms encircle his waist,
her body pressed against his back. He thought to
voice some gallantry, but all he found was, "We'll
build a fire soon enough, and then be dry."

"Thank the gods," came her response: that she
was wet afforded her no physical discomfort, but
her vanity was offended. And she thought it wiser
to pretend a degree of suitable dejection, so she
contented herself with holding him, pressing hard
against his back. As he turned his mount after
Katya's grey, he could not see her smile.

Like the southern bank, this side of the Kess
Imbrun was a labyrinth of tumbled rock and the sun
was almost set before they came to a place where
the boulders formed a circle that afforded shelter
from the strengthening wind. Bushes grew there,
sufficient that they could build a fire, and forage for
the horses. They cut branches enough to construct a
hearty blaze and Bracht and Calandryll delicately
withdrew, rubbing down the animals while the two
women shed their wet clothing in privacy.

The evening grew chill as the sun set, darkness layering the chasm, the rumbling of the torrent below them a murmur dulled by distance and the intervening canyons, the lake invisible behind the sheltering stones as they set food to cooking, aware that their supplies dwindled and they must soon hunt, or ride hungry.

"We've enough for two days more," Bracht declared, fetching out falchion and dirk to wipe the blades, "do we eat sparingly."

Calandryll drew a rag over his own weapons, applied a whetstone to the edges, testing his work with a thumb. "The Jesserytes surely eat," he remarked. "There must be game we can hunt down on the Plain."

"Which must delay us." Katya glanced upward, at the looming darkness of the cliffs. "Rhythamun has surely reached the rim by now."

"And likely taken his place among the Jesserytes," said Bracht somberly, "save they recognize him as gharan-evur."

"Your folk did not." Calandryll slid his sword home in its scabbard. "Dera, but this pursuit is like the finding of a single straw in a haystack. Even though we've one who knows his face."

He looked to Cennaire as he spoke, and she smiled gravely. "I shall not forget that face," she murmured, shuddering at the memory. "Do I but see him, I shall know him."

"That," Bracht said with a sardonic grin, "is the easy part. Bringing you to him, the hard."

"Still, we've found his trail thus far." Katya stretched bare arms toward the fire, her tone thoughtful. "And that has been no easy thing. Does Horul aid us as have Burash and Dera, then we've another godly ally in our quest."

Bracht shrugged diffidently, making no comment. Calandryll said, "Perhaps the Younger Gods design it so," not sure whether he spoke from conviction or the need for optimism. Certainly it seemed a monumental labor to hunt down a single man in the unknown country of the Jesseryn Plain. "I pray it be so," he added.

"And I." Bracht chuckled, his lean face hawkish in the fire's glow, "For the gods know, we need all the aid we can muster."

Cennaire glanced surreptitiously from one face to another, marveling at the determination of these three. She was not much given to admiration—her experiences in the bordels of Kharasul, as a courtesan in Nhur-jabal, had taught her more of misprizement than respect—but now, she admitted with surprise, she could not help but feel a grudging admiration for the singularity of their purpose, for their courage. Did she, she wondered, develop some notion of morality in their company? A conscience, even? Could that be so, given her revenancy?

Her contemplative mood went unnoticed, or they assumed she was wearied by the journey, and soon it was agreed they sleep, Calandryll taking the first watch.

He had little thought of danger: it seemed, as Bracht had said, that Rhythamun was confident enough he left no traps behind him, nor did it seem likely they should encounter hostile Jesserytes in this place.

How wrong he was, he discovered when something whistled out of the darkness, wrapping around him so that his arms were pinned, his legs entangled, and all he could do was cry out once as he toppled sideways, crashing hard against a stunted pine before he thudded down.

2

CALANDRYLL heard Bracht shout, and in the same instant saw figures dart from the shadows, running past him, one halting to kneel beside him, settling a cold hand about his throat, the other displaying a knife, the steel gleaming briefly in the moonlight. He thought to die then, but the blade was tapped warningly against his cheek as the hand tightened on his windpipe, threatening to choke him, and the wielder made a guttural hushing sound, cautioning him to silence.

He could offer no resistance. Whatever had felled him now bound him firm, and the strangling hand denied him the air with which to vent a cry. Such would, he realized despairingly, have been useless anyway: he heard the sounds of brief protest, but no hint of battle, and knew that his comrades were taken as swiftly as he had fallen. Uselessly, he cursed himself for failing in his watchman's duty.

Then the hand let go his throat and he felt his legs loosed. He was snatched unceremoniously upright, spun round before he had opportunity to identify his captor, and shoved toward the glow of the fire. Bracht, Katya, and Cennaire lay beside the deceptively cheerful blaze, like animals trussed for slaughter. Around them stood figures clad in dark armor, their faces masked behind veils of woven mail. Like executioners, Calandryll thought.

A kick sent him down, gasping as he struck the ground, stretched beside Bracht. The Kern's eyes were closed, but his chest rose and fell against the bonds encircling his body. Calandryll saw that they were some manner of throwing device—long leather cords weighted at their ends with small metal balls. He looked across the supine Kern and saw that Katya and Cennaire were similarly entangled, though both the women were conscious. Katya's expression was angry, her grey eyes stormy in the fire's light; Cennaire appeared confused and thoughtful. He assumed she wondered what fate awaited her and said, "Did they plan to slay us, it would be done by now."

He intended to reassure her: he could not know she thought of snapping her bonds and fleeing. He was about to speak again, but a boot drove the air from his lungs, and a hand gestured for him to be silent. He groaned and turned his gaze to his captors.

Nine of them stood there, what expressions their faces might have held masked by the concealing veils. He studied them, seeing conical helmets from under which dangled ringlets of oiled hair, dark as the armor they wore. Breastplates covered their chests, rerebraces and vambraces their arms, gauntlets their hands, cuisses and greaves their legs, all black save where the fireglow was reflected, red as blood. Wide belts circled their tassets, each holding two scabbards, one for the deep-curved swords they wore, the other for the wide-bladed knives. They were menacing figures, the more so for their silent contemplation.

Calandryll wondered what thoughts passed behind the veils. Those curtains were cut with eye holes, but he could read no expressions there: it was as if nine automatons regarded him, creatures of metal standing in judgment.

Then one spoke, a few harsh words, and the captives were hauled to their feet, their legs unbound. Bracht groaned, swaying dizzily, and two men—Jesserytes, Calandryll assumed—took his arms, supporting him until he steadied himself, shaking his head and blinking.

"Ahrd! Are we taken? I heard you shout . . ."

The Jesserytes' leader spoke again, clearly ordering the Kern to silence. Bracht spat, the gobbet landing between the man's boots. He laughed, as if he approved such defiance, and barked another order, pointing toward the cliff, then touching a hand to Bracht's lips, withdrawing it to make a slicing motion across his throat that was clear indication of his meaning. A further burst of curt orders set leathern gags in the prisoners' mouths, and the Jesseryte pointed again at the cliff, then beckoned and strode away.

Five warriors formed about the prisoners, shoving them roughly after, and the remaining three loosed the horses from their hobbles, bringing up the rear.

It was an ominously silent procession. None spoke, and their passage was marked only by the creak of leather, the slow clopping of hooves, as they clambered among the rocks, moving, Calandryll assumed, toward the north foot of the Daggan Vhe. He drew some measure of hope from that, small solace, but all he had. He had spoken instinctively to Cennaire, looking to reassure a woman he assumed was terrified, but now saw the truth of his statement: did the Jesserytes intend to slay intruders in their land, they would surely have killed them where they lay. No less, was Rhythamun numbered among the faceless warriors, he would surely have destroyed the questers on sight. For some reason he did not comprehend, they were kept alive. For subsequent execution? For reasons obscure to any save the Jesserytes? He did not know, but that they *were* alive allowed a degree of optimism.

He clung to that thought as he stumbled, awkward with tight-bound arms, through the rock-strewn shadows.

In a while they reached a ledge where small, caparisoned horses stood tethered, tended by a single warrior who barked a greeting as the Jesserytes' leader approached. It was answered in the same incomprehensible tongue and the guard brought one animal forward, dropping on hands and knees that the leader might use his back for a mounting step. Another guttural exclamation had the captives disarmed and slung roughly astride their own mounts with wrists lashed to the saddle horns, thongs binding ankles to stirrups. Cennaire was tossed astride Katya's grey, behind the warrior woman, a cord passed about both their waists. The Jesserytes mounted, a man taking up the reins of each larger horse, another falling into station immediately behind, and they started across the ledge.

Calandryll wondered if their captors knew the way so well they dared attempt the trail by darkness, or if their night vision was unusually developed. Whichever, they moved at a brisk pace through the maze of gullies and basal canyons spread about the foot of this northern wall of the

Kess Imbrun, trotting where the way allowed, holding to a fast walk where the road climbed.

In time it rose clear of the lower convolutions
and the elevation allowed the moon to light the
way. The lunar disk was fattened and the night was
clear, cloudless: Calandryll saw the ribbon of the
Blood Road winding precipitously ahead, an unnerving path for a man with bound arms. He
clenched his teeth against the threat of panic, telling himself these strange and silent men were
not—at least, not yet—ready to see him die. Even
so, it was a disconcerting prospect that he sought
to combat by studying them closer.

Their armor, he saw, was polished jet, marked on
chest and back with yellow symbols. Some form of
clan insignia, he guessed, for the leader wore the
same sign, though his back also bore another
marking—of rank, presumably—and the cloths that
dressed the little horses were similarly decorated.

He forced himself to relax in the saddle, knees
firm against the chestnut gelding's ribs as it dutifully followed the smaller animal ahead. The
Jesseryte beasts were not much larger than ponies,
but surefooted, taking the dizzying trail without
hesitation, climbing steadily upward, as if they traversed some gentle gradient rather than a road that
before long dropped away on one side or the other
into a moonlit infinity. Their hooves clattered a
busy counterpoint to the sighing song of the night
wind, rising above the grumbling of the cascades,
those soon enough lost in the distance. There were
no other sounds. The masked men said nothing;
nor, under threat of blows, did the captives protest,
only rode, each in turn wondering where they
went, and why.

❖   ❖   ❖

CENNAIRE, pressed hard against Katya's back, thought again of snapping her bonds and flinging herself clear of the grey horse, and again discarded the notion. In part it was from fear of bringing the horse down with her, both tumbling over the precipice that loomed scant feet to her right. She was confident the fall would not—*could* not—kill her, but by no means so sure she would escape injury. Without a living heart to animate her body, she knew she must defy death, but it remained possible her bones would break, and the thought of lying broken, perhaps helpless, in the depths of the Kess Imbrun was an idea unappealing as the thought of what such a descent must do to her beauty. Equally, such action must end her alliance with the questers, and so it was better, she decided, to continue in her role of mortal woman, to act the helpless prisoner and see what the future held.

Did things come to such a pass, she could free herself later. For now, she would wait.

BRACHT, his head still ringing from the blow that had felled him, thought mostly of holding his seat: the black stallion afforded him concern enough he had little room for much else. The horse resented the indignity of a lead rein, snatching against the leathers and snorting irritably, ears flattened back and head tossing whenever the halter slackened. The Kern did his best to calm the beast, urging it on with knees and soft murmurings, aware that did it succeed in breaking free it would certainly attack the smaller animals ahead and behind, and in the process no less certainly find its way over the road's rim.

He did not think the Jesserytes would let him live—the hostility of the horseclans of Cuan na'For

and the folk of the Jesseryn Plain was ogygian,
long-rooted in times past, a matter of tradition. He
assumed they were taken alive only that their
deaths might be prolonged, an amusement for their
captors. All he had heard of the people of the Forbidden Country suggested that—that they were
little more than beasts, savages who pleasured
themselves with the torture of prisoners. That, or
the transformation of captives into slaves, which
was the worse option—involuntarily, he shuddered
at the thought: male slaves were gelded.

He bit hard on the thong that gagged him, abruptly aware of the pressure of his saddle between his
thighs, chancing a swift glance back, to where
Katya was led, behind him. She was no woman to
accept slavery, to allow herself to become the play-
thing of some Jesseryte lordling—she would die,
rather.

That thought, and the simple determination that
while he yet lived he must not give up hope of defeating Rhythamun, held him back from the alternative he would have taken had he been alone.
Were he alone, he would have given the stallion its
head, urged the great horse to vent its anger, and
taken a Jesseryte or two over the cliff with him. Instead, he sought to calm the beast, the sullen
pounding in his skull resolving into sullen anger.

For now he would cling to life.

For her part, Katya rode confused. She knew nothing of the Jesserytes save what she had heard from
Bracht, and none of that promising. Yet the strange
warriors, for all their treatment of the prisoners
was brusque, had offered no real harm. They had
come out of the night so suddenly, so silently, they
seemed, in their dark armor, like ghosts. She had

heard Bracht's shout and woken with hand on
swordhilt—only to find her arms pinioned before
the saber had chance to clear the scabbard, her legs
an eyeblink after. She had seen Bracht come to his
feet and fall in the same moment, thinking at first
an arrow took him—such thought horrifying—then
seeing that he was bound by the curious throwing
ropes that whirled and whistled from the shadows.
A gauntleted hand had clubbed him down when he
struggled to rise, but that had been all: there had
been no further violence offered.

She wondered why she—why all of them—lived
still. Everything Bracht had told her of the
Jesserytes suggested they slew intruders on sight,
yet these appeared bent on taking them captive.
Why?

A possible answer chilled her: because Rhythamun
had ordered it so.

Because the mage had found himself in some elevated station in his new form, and sent minions
to ward his back, with orders to take his pursuers
alive. Such would likely be his way: to gloat before
commanding their execution.

Yet, were that the way of it, surely questions
must arise. Surely Rhythamun must justify his
knowledge—and how else could he know he was
pursued, save through magic? In which case, she
told herself, as calmly as she was able, he must
reveal himself for a wizard. Would whatever sorcerers the Jesserytes bred accept him so readily? Were
her suspicion correct, yes. In which case, the quest
was ended, Rhythamun victorious.

She bit hard against her gag, seeking calm against
the despair that threatened to overwhelm her. She
must not give in! She must hold to the vows made
in Vanu and Tezin-dar, and while she still lived,

cling to what tenuous fragments of hope yet existed.

So it was that each of them, in their own fashion,
chose to live on, to cling to hope until that precious commodity should be finally expended, as
the procession wound its way up the Daggan Vhe.

They climbed through what was left of the night,
the sky above paling toward dawn before a halt was
called, on a massive ledge where a wide-mouthed
cavern ran back into the cliff's wall.

The Jesserytes' leader walked his mount into the
cave and dismounted, his men not following until
he barked an order, then swinging down, bustling
about with the economic efficiency of a well-
disciplined band entering a familiar refuge. Calandryll watched, puzzled and intrigued, as the ponies
were led in, tethered to one side, fodder obviously
stored against such visitation piled in mangers of
rock. Two men built a fire, fetching kindling and
cut logs from niches in the cave walls, and others
brought provisions from similar caches. Flambeaux
were lit, their flames joining with the fire to illu-
minate the interior. One man remained watchful
beside each prisoner, waiting stoically until their
leader issued another order that had the bonds
about the captives' ankles freed, the thongs binding
them to the saddle horns loosed. They were still
confined by short lengths of leather around their
wrists, dismounting awkwardly to find themselves
pushed into the cave. Men took their horses, and it
came to Calandryll that the Jesserytes were somewhat awed by the larger animals, Bracht's stallion
in particular, for their silence was broken by anxious mutterings when the beast whickered irritably
and began to plunge against the reins.

Bracht turned back then, his sullen face abruptly anxious as the black horse threatened to fight loose, to plunge over the cliff. A warrior blocked his way, hand raised to halt the Kern, who mouthed a muffled curse, his eyes flashing angry as the stallion's. Calandryll feared he would be clubbed down anew, but a word from the Jesseryte chieftain—if such he was—set the man aside, allowing Bracht to go to the stallion, murmuring soothingly through his gag, taking the reins and leading the horse after the others.

The stallion continued to fret somewhat, seeming vexed by the presence of the smaller animals, and Bracht kept up his mumblings until the beast calmed, allowing him to pass the reins back to a Jesseryte.

Relieved, Calandryll looked about the cave, seeing it was not entirely natural, but enlarged by men, as if used as a staging post. The fire burned in a crude hearth, its smoke carried away up a rocky chimney; a grotto, part natural and part man-made, stabled the animals, stout poles penning them secure; to one side a spring bled water into a bowl. The place was dry, warm, and smelled of horseflesh and salted meat, as if regularly used. From that, and the pace they had taken, he calculated they were midway up the north face of the Kess Imbrun. He waited to see what the Jesserytes intended.

No harm, it seemed; at least, not yet. The leader walked bowlegged toward the captives, loosing the latches of his helmet. He removed the bowl and shook his head, freeing a tangle of blue-black ringlets, studying them slowly. His eyes were fulvous, tawny as a cat's, and narrow, slanted above high cheekbones, a prominent nose. Thin lips slashed his lower face, bracketed by a curving mustache. It

was a cruel face, without any expression Calandryll
was able to interpret.

The man touched his chest and said, "Temchen,"
then beckoned one of his men, speaking briefly in
his own language.

The gags were removed and the leader tapped his
breastplate again, repeating, "Temchen."

Calandryll licked his lips, sensing that the man
announced his name. He said, "Temchen?" gesturing with bound hands at the Jesseryte.

The man nodded, saying, "Ai, Temchen," then
jabbed a finger toward Calandryll, saying something in the Jesseryte tongue that Calandryll assumed was a demand for his own name.

For a moment he thought to conceal his identity,
wondering if such revelation should result in death.
It seemed unlikely: were these warriors sent by
Rhythamun, either they knew who their captives
were, or would find out soon enough. Perhaps, by
giving his name, he might learn something, even
were it that he was taken by the warlock's allies.
He raised his hands, touching his chest in turn, and
said, "Calandryll."

Temchen ducked his head: "Kah-lan-drill."

His tongue found its way around the syllables
with difficulty, no easier around the others' names.

"Brak." This with a stare Calandryll thought
speculative, a gesture toward the cavern's mouth,
as if Temchen pointed southward, a babble of inde-
cipherable sounds.

Bracht shrugged and Temchen tapped his chest,
pointed at himself, then touched his swordhilt,
pantomiming combat. Bracht grinned tightly and
said, "Aye, we fight you. Give me back my blade
and I'll fight you now."

The Jesseryte's eyes narrowed, hearing the hostility in the Kern's tone, then laughed, calling some-

thing to his men that was answered with chuckles and catcalls. Calandryll said, "For Dera's sake, Bracht! Would you provoke him?"

"I'd as soon die now as see myself unmanned," the Kern muttered, falling silent as Temchen turned to Katya.

The Jesseryte seemed awed by the Vanu woman's flaxen hair. He touched it as she spoke her name, fingering it as though it were rare silk, or precious metal.

"Cat-ee-ah." He stroked her hair a moment, reluctant, it seemed, to leave it go. "Sen-air."

He was far less interested in Cennaire. Likely, Calandryll thought, because the Kand woman was much closer to his own kind in coloration: Katya was a rarity.

He ended his inspection with a nod, more guttural words, and turned away, going to the fire, where meat roasted and dough sizzled on a skillet. The captives were ushered forward, motioned to settle themselves against the cave wall, the Jesserytes interposed before the exit. No further attention was paid them, save when food and water were passed them, each receiving a slab of greasy meat and a cake of unleavened bread.

They ate in silence, the three hungry, Cennaire feigning an appetite, as the arc of sky visible beyond the mouth grew brighter, the opalescence of early dawn giving steady way to sunwashed blue. When they were done, the Jesserytes bound their ankles again, and passed loops around their chests, pinning their arms. The tying, for all the cords were firm, was not ungentle, and when they were secured each was draped with a blanket, and Temchen performed another little pantomime, indicating they should sleep.

The Jesserytes set a watch, two men, while the

rest bedded down, and the cavern grew silent, save
for the snuffling of the horses, contented now, and
the snoring humans. Calandryll lay between Bracht
and Katya, no more able than they to sleep for the
confusion of thoughts, doubts, bewilderment, that
raced through his mind. Thinking to avoid a blow,
he waited until he was confident the Jesserytes
slumbered soundly, then wormed his face close to
Bracht's.

"They cannot intend to slay us," he whispered.
"And I doubt they're Rhythamun's men."

"You think not?" Bracht's voice was low in answer, sharp with an undercurrent of tension.

"How can they? Were we for execution, why feed
us? Why bring us here? And Rhythamun? Temchen
showed no expression when he learned our
names—did he go about Rhythamun's business,
surely he'd have shown triumph then."

"I'll grant they're not likely allied with the sorcerer," Bracht allowed. "But for the rest . . . Execution is not the worst fate."

"How so?"

The Kern's teeth gritted a moment, then: "The
Jesserytes take slaves. Male slaves are gelded."

Calandryll bit back the gasp of horror forming in
his throat. Instinctively, he pressed his legs tight
together, shuddering as horrid chill crept down his
spine. "You're sure of this?" he forced himself to
ask.

Bracht grunted confirmation.

"Even so." He licked his lips, his mouth abruptly
dry. "We live still."

"Gelded? You call that living?"

"Even so, we've hope. Why did they come after
us? Surely there must be some reason for that?"

"They planned to raid into Cuan na'For. As did

the band that attacked Cennaire's caravan. They found easier prey."

"Think you it can be so simple?"

"I think I am taken by barbarians who unman their slaves. I think Katya is a great prize—you saw that strutting whoreson finger her."

"I grant he found her exceptional. But still . . ." Calandryll paused, the ugly churning deep in his stomach that Bracht's blunt announcement had begun worked its way ominously lower. It was an effort to calm that horrid trepidation, to impose some measure of logic. "But still it may be they *were* sent, though by some other agency."

Bracht snorted softly, dubiously.

"Perhaps some Jesseryte sorcerer sensed our presence," Calandryll insisted. "We've spoken before of a design in this, of the Younger Gods lending what aid they can. Perhaps this capture is a part of that; perhaps we are brought to the Jesseryn Plain swifter than had we traveled alone."

He was no longer certain whether he spoke from conviction or the need to reassure himself, and Bracht offered no help. The Kern scowled, noncommittal, saying nothing.

"Do you concede the victory then? Do you grant Rhythamun the fight?"

"I concede I go bound into an unknown land; I concede I'm mightily concerned. For us all. Do we find the opportunity, I say we must escape."

"How?" Calandryll tested his bonds: they held him tight, and how could they escape, here, perched on the wall of Kess Imbrun, surrounded by warriors?

"I know not," Bracht replied. "But does the chance arise . . ."

"Aye. Does the chance arise."

He did not think it would: Temchen seemed too

careful a man to let his vigilance waver. It seemed
far more likely they should be brought captive to
whatever destination the Jesseryte rode. But then
. . . perhaps then. But if they did . . . what then?

They would be fugitives in a strange land, pursuing Rhythamun in a form only Cennaire could recognize. There was no longer any magical talisman
to guide them, no longer any one of them familiar
with the country they must traverse. It seemed unlikely, did they escape and flee, that they should
find allies; still less likely they should happen upon
their quarry. The odds seemed suddenly weighted
against them, fate showing them an unkind face.
Despair threatened and he struggled not to contemplate the fate Bracht outlined, forcing himself to
consider his own words, endeavoring to believe his
own optimism.

It was not easy, *but surely,* he told himself,
*Horul is the god of the Jesserytes, and Horul is kin
to Burash and to Dera, to Ahrd. Surely Horul must
favor this quest, else he, like all the Younger Gods,
see Tharn raised up, himself destroyed. Surely
Horul must league with us, and be that so, then
perhaps there is some measure of divine intervention here. Perhaps Temchen was sent by the equine
god, some indiscernible pattern working to our favor.*

I must believe that, he told himself. *I must not
give in to despair. I must continue to hope.*

That thought lingered as a great weariness possessed him, lulling him so that he did not know he
slept until a boot nudged his ribs and he opened his
eyes on sunlight and a masked face, a Jesseryte
kneeling to strip off the blanket, loose his feet and
arms that he might rise. He stood on command, his
comrades with him, going over to the fire to re-

ceive a bowl of thin porridge, a cake of hard, sweet
bread, a mug of bitter tea sharp with herbs.

That breakfast was taken swiftly and then they
were set back on their horses, gagged and bound in
place again. A man knelt to afford Temchen a
mounting stool, and the Jesseryte once more led
the cavalcade along the Blood Road, upward, climbing briskly toward the sky.

THE sun was not much advanced along its westward path, not yet close to noon, and Calandryll
realized their sojourn in the cavern had been only
a brief respite, likely taken to rest the horses and
men who had spent the night descending this same
steep road. They seemed not to hurry overmuch—
the trail was precipitous, narrow enough in too
many places that undue haste must be dangerous—
but still they progressed at a good pace, as though
Temchen were anxious to reach the rimrock swift
as possible.

Their faces masked by the metal veils, it was impossible to discern expression there, nor did the
Jesseryte physiognomy lend itself to interpretation
when the veils were lifted, when they halted
awhile in the afternoon.

The prisoners were dismounted then, given water and a little food, but there was no more attempt
made to communicate, as if the learning of their
names was all the information Temchen required
of them. Neither did the Jesserytes speak among
themselves, but went about their duties with the
precision of well-drilled soldiery, their tasks sufficiently familiar as to render words unnecessary.
When Calandryll spoke, Temchen glanced his way
and raised a finger to his thin lips; when Bracht replied, a man raised a hand in threat. The Kern,

though clearly galled, fell silent, and Calandryll deemed it the wiser course to follow suit. Katya said nothing, only studied her captors with storm-laden grey eyes; and Cennaire merely waited, not speaking, to discover to where they went.

The food consumed, the gags were replaced, the prisoners remounted and again restrained, and they continued the ascent.

Onward, ever upward, through an afternoon of sunlight that bathed the ramparts of the Kess Imbrun with golden light, the fantastic crenellations shining like great red spires, many-hued, the canyons pooled with misty darkness, or glowing where the sun invaded as if fires burned within their depths. The yellow disk moved across the sky, westering, the crags and buttresses dulling as the light shifted, hurling great shadows eastward. The filling moon hung above the horizon, stars visible as the heavens were transformed from shimmering azure to shades of deepening indigo. The western sky burned crimson-gold awhile, and twilight fell. Calandryll thought they might halt then—knew that did he ride with his comrades alone, they would, for the road was too hazardous to attempt by dusk's light—but Temchen showed no sign of slowing their pace, and he wondered again if the catlike eyes pierced the darkness better than his own.

It was no less unnerving for the experience of the previous night to take that way by darkness. Soon there was only moonglow by which to negotiate the trail, and that deceptive, shadows concealing rocks, the pale silvery radiance tricking the eye, deceitful. Bats once more fluttered, their roosts seemingly located about the midparts of the chasm, and that flocking did nothing to make the going easier. But still the Jesserytes pressed on, climbing, climbing, until it seemed they must rise up to meet the moon along its way and ride in company with the stars.

What haste possessed them? Calandryll wondered. Or was it their habit to travel so, heedless of the sun's passing, as if the night were their domain? Certainly, clad in their beetle-black armor, silent, they seemed akin to nocturnal creatures, and he wondered what motivated them, that musing bringing back Bracht's dire warning.

He fought the unpleasant sensation that thought delivered to his bowels, telling himself that surely, did they view their captives as nothing more than slaves, handily found and taken without undue difficulty, they would not press so hard. Neither could he believe they served Rhythamun—that argument he had put to Bracht, and now, with little else to do save think, he found it the more convincing. But what answers there were to this captivity, to this urgent nighttime journey, he could not surmise.

You will travel far and see things no southern man has seen . . .

He smiled around the gag, cynically, as Reba's words came back, whispered on the night wind, taunting. That, surely, was the truth—what else, from the lips of a spaewife? All she had foretold was come true. His father's anger had driven him from Secca; his own brother proclaimed him outlaw, renegade, patricide. He had known betrayal and found true comrades; had traveled roads no man had trod. She had prophesied danger, and that he had met in quantity. But the ending . . . that she had not scried along the many branching paths of the spaewives' art.

Perhaps—the ugly chill of doubt grew colder— this was the ending. Perhaps Bracht was right, he wrong: they were taken as slaves, to be gelded, the women placed in some Jesseryte harem, a bordel, while Rhythamun continued unhindered, to find Tharn's resting place and raise the Mad God. He shivered, willing himself to calm, to logic, invoking the litany of past experience to quell doubt, to impose hope.

In Kandahar, Sathoman ek'Hennem had threatened the quest, taken him and Bracht prisoner, but they had escaped the rebel lord.

Anomius had used magic against them, but they had eluded his gramaryes.

The Chaipaku had sought their lives, his and Bracht's and Katya's, but thanks to their own skills and the intervention of Burash, the Brotherhood of Assassins was no longer a threat.

They had survived the swamps of Gessyth, evaded the trap Rhythamun set in Tezin-dar.

In Lysse, he had passed within hailing distance of Tobias, who would surely have slain him on the spot had his brother recognized him. But he had not, and they had gone free.

Into Cuan na'For, into the arms of Jehenne ni Larrhyn, who had crucified Bracht, only to see the Kern saved by Ahrd, the Lykard woman slain by Katya.

Dera herself had set an enchantment on his blade; Burash had brought them down his watery ways in safety; Ahrd had shown his benevolence: the Younger Gods themselves stood in alliance with their quest.

How then should it fail?

Because, said the cold, mocking voice of the wind, *the Younger Gods are lesser creatures than their elder kin, weaker than their predecessors. Have they, themselves, not spoken of their limitations? Have they not told you they may do only so much, and no more? Shall that be enough?*

Surely, he said.

Think you so? asked the wind. *Did Burash bring you swift enough to Lysse that you found Rhythamun there? No, you were too late, the sorcerer was gone on, shape-changed.*

But we found his way. We sundered his alliance with Jehenne. And Dera blessed my sword.

The wind laughed about the moonlit spires, rustling down the canyons, and said, *A small enough gift, that. Nor too soon given. You were delayed there, and Rhythamun still went on, no? Not Dera, not Ahrd could halt him.*

But still they lent us aid.

A skirling then, a taste of dust, like ashes blown contemptuous from a funeral pyre: *Ahrd could not bring you fast enough through his own sacred forest to catch the mage.*

But not so far ahead. And one with us now who knows his face.

The wind paused, turning back on itself, and came again, renewed, vigorous. *Much help that, when you ride a prisoner to your unmanning. When you ride into the unknown country, where men wear masks across their faces and carve off manhood as if the bearer were a beast.*

Into a land where Horul is worshipped! And Horul is a Younger God—he cannot stand by!

Perhaps he cannot; perhaps he will not. But is he strong enough? Rhythamun goes before, drawing ever closer to Tharn. Think you Tharn knows not his salvation approaches, even in his limbo? Even dreaming? Think you he shall not do all he can to aid his savior?

What can he do? The First Gods cast him down—Yl and Kyta, his own progenitors. Shall he break their enchantment?

Does he not already? asked the wind. *His raising*

*calls for blood; blood calls for his raising—is blood
not shed aplenty now? Think on Kandahar, fool!
Think on the rebellion of the Fayne lord, think on
the war the Tyrant presses. Think on your own
brother—Tobias den Karynth, Domm of Secca!—
who builds a navy and argues for war with
Kandahar. How much blood shall spill when that
dream is fulfilled?*

Be it fulfilled! It is not yet.

*Perhaps; or perhaps it is. Perhaps e'en now the
warboats sail from Eryn. Perhaps the Narrow Sea
runs red.*

*Tobias must convince his fellow domms, and in
Cuan na'For Jehenne looked to war, but was
thwarted.*

*A small victory: one little battle in a far greater
combat. And you a captive now, riding virgin to
your fate, while Rhythamun goes on . . . and on . . .
on . . .*

"No! It cannot be!"

The denial came distorted through the gag, a muffled defiance, more moan than shout, but still loud
enough the Jesseryte ahead glanced back, warningly,
the man behind came up, driving a rough hand at
Calandryll's shoulder. The chestnut—the gelding!—
skittered, and its rider grunted, seeking with knees
and bound hands to calm the horse, thinking, startled, that the quest might truly end, for him, did the
animal panic, take him off the road. He blinked, realizing he had dozed in the saddle, that the night
waned and the wind was died away. He saw the sky
brighten in the east, and wondered if he had, truly,
heard that silent voice, or only the pessimistic musing of his own mind.

I must hope, he told himself. *Hope, now, is all I
have. Hope, and faith in the Younger Gods.*

In silence, he voiced a prayer to Dera, to the goddess and all her kin, asking that this capture be part of some design, or that he and his comrades—Cennaire he counted now among that number—be allowed escape. He hoped it was not selfishness to ask they escape entire, whole in all parts: the notion that it might go otherwise was ugly.

He could do no more, not now, only sit his horse and watch the road unfold in day's clean light, the breeze no longer insidious with doubt but merry, a cheerful zephyr redolent of warm earth and grass.

That fact did not, at first, strike him, for the gloom of his nocturnal reverie still dulled him somewhat. But then his nose registered the change, that the hard, dry scent of timeless stone was replaced with hint of growth, and he looked up, past the horseman who led him, and saw the rim of the Kess Imbrun.

The great rift's edge was both welcome and ominous, the one for its marking of a step along the way ended, the other for its announcement of impending fate, of resolution of his fears. He steeled himself, seeing the Daggan Vhe traverse a shelf, wind back, steep and wide, then run out between walls similar to the gully that had begun this journey into captivity. The gelding quickened its pace, urged on by the warrior ahead, willing enough, as though it, like its rider, saw the finish of heights and depths, and welcomed the prospect of flat land once more with equine innocence.

They crossed the shelf and climbed the steepened way, then rode a spell through the twilight imparted by the cleft. It was a broad road there, smooth and gently angled, the walls sheer, the sky a wide blue band above, the sun as yet only hinting along the eastern edge. At the farthest extent of the gully the way rose again, clear sky visible, bright blue and shadowed red meeting on a line.

Calandryll heard Temchen, at the column's head, call out, heard a shouted response. Then the Jesseryte topped the ridge line and was gone from sight. His men seemed to take reassurance from the brief exchange, urging their horses on at a canter. The hooves rang loud on stone, filling the gully with their clatter, and the cavalcade emerged onto the Jesseryn Plain.

Calandryll looked about, eyes widening in amazement. To either side stood man-made walls, great blocks of sandy yellow stone set unmortered one upon the other, high as five men, how thick he could only guess. They ran parallel a way, a funnel down which any seeking ingress to the Kess Imbrun must pass, a killing ground for any climbing the Blood Road. They ended at a barbican, a great squat block of dull yellow that rose above the walls, featureless save for the narrow embrasures cut across its face and the massive gates of metal-studded wood standing open below. Beyond those gates there was only darkness: Temchen waited there, dwarfed by the massy structure.

He raised an arm, beckoning them on. As they came closer, Calandryll experienced a strange chill, for it seemed an atmosphere, an indefinable aura, hung about the place, something beyond its naturally forbidding prospect, greater and more ominous, as if ghosts lingered there, or the smell of recently shed blood. His horse shied, the enthusiasm it had earlier shown gone, and from behind he heard Bracht's stallion whinny a protest. He turned, and saw the black horse plunging against the leading rein, ears flattened, eyes rolling white. The mood communicated and he saw Katya's grey curvet even as his own animal began to dance nervously. Indeed, the Jesserytes' small beasts were no less agitated, their riders grunting irritably and holding them tight-reined, too occupied then to remonstrate with their prisoners' recalcitrant beasts.

It took an effort to drive the horses forward, and as they approached the barbican it seemed to Calandryll the chill grew deeper. He eyed the gates with apprehension, wondering if the charnel odor he caught on the breeze was real, or a figment of his imagination, and knew, though not why, that from the blockhouse emanated a sensation of dread, of insensate horror.

He felt his mouth go dry as he passed between the gates, and then wanted to spit, badly, for it seemed a sour, bilious clot filled his throat. Nor, he saw, were the Jesserytes insensible to the sensation: they fingered swordhilts, shaped warding gestures, veils rustling metallic as heads turned warily from side to side. Only Temchen appeared unmoved, and that, so Calandryll thought, was a result of innate discipline, a grim determination to show no dread. The armored man barked a command, hand chopping air, urging his men on down the tunnel that filled all the center of the fortification.

Calandryll saw gates, dim at the farther end, these closed and barred, and lesser openings to either side, shut off with heavy doors. Overhead were machiolations, and then a band of welcome light, albeit faint, as a door was flung open, Temchen turning aside there, down some inner corridor.

The lesser tunnel gave way to a small bailey, stabling around three sides, more sable-armored warriors standing in postures of expectancy, alert, crook-bladed pikes and curved swords in their hands, as if unsure what they might expect of the reluctant visitors. Archers manned the ramparts, arrows nocked, downward aimed. Temchen dismounted, bowed to a man whose armor was marked with symbols in yellow and silver, who answered in kind and lifted his veil, the better to study the captives.

Calandryll found little in his features to distinguish him from Temchen. Save that he wore a stiff, triangular beard and seemed a few years older, they might be brothers, the elder apparently superior in rank, for it was he who issued the order that brought the captives down from their horses to stand before him, another that had their bonds removed, all save the cords about their wrists, the gags in their mouths.

Temchen spoke their names, indicating them each in turn, and the older man nodded, and conversed briefly with the younger. Then, without further word, he spun on his heel and marched briskly to an inner stairwell. Temchen pointed after him, barking orders that set a guard about the four, motioning them to follow, he bustling past to fall into step with the other as they climbed into the depths of the barbican.

The stairs led to a corridor beneath the roof, banded with light from the embrasures running down its length, the omnipresent sensation of dread somewhat abated here, that relief almost physical, as if a weight were lifted. Calandryll wondered if that easing was a result of the hieroglyphs he saw daubed at intervals along the walls or the censers wafting pungent smoke in the still, dry air, and what it meant. The glyphs, he guessed, were imbued with magic of some manner, and likely the incense, too, though by whom and why remained a mystery. He could only follow his captors as they walked the gallery to a door of black wood, where Temchen and the other man halted, removing their helms before tapping softly, respectfully, Calandryll thought, wondering what awaited within.

A voice responded, presumably granting permission to enter, for Temchen nodded and a guard swung the door wide, standing back as the two Jesseryte chieftains went in, halted, and bowed low.

There followed a murmured conversation and then Temchen beckoned, the guards herding the captives into a chamber longer than it was wide, lit dim save where a circular opening in the ceiling bled light across a rectangular table of black lacquered wood at the center. Backless seats, more stool than chair, were set down both sides of the table, jet as the Jesserytes' armor so that they were near invisible in the shadows that pooled to either side. The walls were no lighter, paneled in some dark wood, unadorned save for more of the strange symbols, those painted in yellow and silver and red that seemed to glow in the dimness.

Calandryll squinted as Temchen and the other man marched forward, bowed again, and motioned for the guards to bring the prisoners closer. The farther end of the chamber lay beyond the limits of the poor illumination, and the guards halted before Calandryll's eyes were able to pierce that gloom.

From out of it came a voice, dry and soft as the rustle of autumn leaves stirred by a breeze, but somehow clear for all it was faint, as if generated by a power that transcended vocalization.

"Welcome," it said, and it seemed the shadows themselves spoke. "I have awaited your coming."

Calandryll started as he realized the words were uttered in the Jesseryte tongue, and that he understood.

3

LAUGHTER then, like the rattle of ancient bells, the timbre occluded by rust—Calandryll wondered if his mind was read, or the startlement on his face. He looked to his companions, seeing he was alone in neither understanding nor surprise: Bracht stared with narrow eyes, suspicious visage, into the shadows; Katya frowned; Cennaire appeared frightened, and he stepped a pace closer, that movement eliciting a warning glance from the elder Jesseryte, a prohibiting grunt from Temchen.

"Easy, easy," said the unseen speaker, startling Calandryll once more. "What harm do they offer me? What harm *can* they offer me?"

The questions were mildly put, seeming empty of threat, albeit massively confident. The bearded man answered, but his words were incomprehensible. Calandryll suspected he protested for the soft voice replied: "Chazali, had they such power surely they'd not allow themselves taken. And be it some ruse, I believe I've the strength to oppose them. I say—loose their bonds, remove those gags that we may converse as civilized folk."

There followed further protest, seemingly quelled by some gesture visible only to the Jesserytes, and the voice again, a hint of steel now evident. "Free them, I tell you. Be you so concerned, then remain and ward me against this mighty danger."

Amusement echoed in the last words and the one named Chazali shook his head, shrugged, and motioned Temchen forward, the two of them loosing the cords about the prisoners' wrists, taking the gags from their mouths. They both stepped back, wary, hands resting light and ready on swordhilts.

"Neither have we need for so many guards," said the voice. "Dismiss your men, but leave whatever things you took from our guests."

"Guests?" Bracht's voice was low, harsh with anger.

"So I trust," came the response from the darkness, "for all the manner of your coming. I crave forgiveness for that indignity and shall, in time, explain the need. For now, though, do you seat yourselves? Will you take wine?"

"No."

Bracht's eyes followed the warrior who stepped forward, swords and saddlebags in his arms, clattering down onto the table. Calandryll saw the tension in his body, knowing the Kern calculated his chances of reaching his falchion, drawing. No less Temchen and Chazali, whose curved blades slid a little way clear of the scabbards, the faint susurration of steel blades against leather akin to the warning hiss of a serpent. He looked to Bracht, a hand half raised, and said, "Be we truly guests, you've much to explain. For now"—this directed at Bracht—"we'll hear you out."

He sat then, willing the angry Kern to follow suit, certain that should fury gain the upper hand they must all die. He was grateful to Katya, who sank onto a chair; to Cennaire, who did the same, her great brown eyes fixed intently on the shadows, as if she saw the hidden speaker. With a grunt of irritation, Bracht did as he was urged, and across the table, Chazali and Temchen took seats.

The guards filed out; the door thudded shut, and for a moment there was silence.

Then silk rustled, soft as gently falling rain, and the speaker stepped within the radius of the light. Calandryll stared, thinking he had seen no living creature so old since the Guardians of Tezin-dar. Hair like polished silver fell in sweeping wings to either side of a face so wrinkled as to resemble ancient leather left long in sun and rain and wind, and of much the same hue. Dark eyes glittered between canalicular lids, striated flesh combining patterns of furrows that radiated outward and downward, deep grooves arcing in parentheses about a sharp, proud nose, descending behind a wispery mustache of the same argental shade as the hair, the mouth thin-lipped and wide, exposing large, yellow teeth as it smiled. The neck—surely gaunt as a turtle's—was hidden beneath the high collar of an elaborate tunic, a green the shade of new spring grass, the shoulders exaggerated, stiffened to extend beyond the deep sleeves. A silver sash bound it narrow at the waist, fastened with a brooch of gold so that the hem flared above loose pantaloons of shimmering jet, tucked into ankle boots of some soft, silvery hide, with toes curled up and back, tipped with little golden points.

So grandiose an outfit seemed somehow at variance with the ancient face, which now expressed an apologetic humor.

"I am named Ochen," he said. "Temchen, you have already met; this other is named Chazali."

Both armored men ducked their heads slightly as their names were spoken, but neither took their eyes off the four, nor their hands from their swords. It was clear to Calandryll that they trusted their unwilling visitors no more than Bracht trusted them. For his own part he felt a great curiosity join his wariness: there seemed no enmity in this venerable creature; though, he thought, that was a thing to be decided later.

"I fear we begin with misunderstanding," Ochen said, settling himself gracefully on the faldstool at the table's head.

"I understand we are taken captive," snapped Bracht. "Brought bound to this keep."

Ochen nodded, his smile fading, his reply voiced grave. "That I shall explain, warrior," he promised. "And when I do, I think you'll see the need for such caution. For now, I'd ask you accept my word that be you dissatisfied with what I tell you, you shall be free to leave—to return whence you came, or go on with whatever help I am able to give. Do you accept?"

"The word of a Jesseryte?" Bracht glowered.

Calandryll said quickly, "We'll hear you out." There seemed little other choice—no other that made sense—and the faint hope of aid, should this mysterious ancient prove a friend.

Ochen ducked his head in thanks and said, "A moment then."

Calandryll watched as he reached forward, drawing the blades and bags laid upon the table toward him. He fingered each item gently, almost reverently, frowning a little as his fingers danced over Cennaire's small satchel, murmuring too soft any could hear the words as he touched Calandryll's straightsword.

"Yours," he remarked, looking into Calandryll's eyes. "The goddess would gift such as you with this."

"A sorcerer!" Bracht snarled. "A Jesseryte sorcerer!"

"That I am," admitted Ochen cheerfully, "and be you who I think, you'll have need of my art where you go."

Bracht's mouth curled scornfully. Calandryll said, "You know who we are?"

"I've some notion." Ochen ended his examination, pushed their gear away. "I and my kind have foreseen your coming."

Calandryll frowned at that and the ancient chuckled. "Think you we've not the art of scrying in this land?" He shook his head, the network of wrinkles deepening a moment. "Perhaps we've hid too long; stood too long apart from the world."

"You stood not apart when your Great Khan looked to invade my land," said Bracht, gruff-voiced. "You stand not apart when you raid Cuan na'For for slaves."

"That myth?" Ochen sighed, exasperation in the sound. "I tell you, friend, we take no slaves."

"Name me not friend," Bracht grunted. "Do you say there was no invasion—attempted, at the least?"

"That, aye," said Ochen, sadly now. "There was a madness in the land then—a part of what I must tell you; a part of the evil you look to halt. Of that, I would speak later; for now, I say to you that the Great Khan was possessed; that he forced his will on all the tengs of the Plain; and that he is long dead. We Jesserytes have no wish to invade Cuan na'For. Horul knows, we've sufficient to occupy us here!"

"And you take no slaves?"

Bracht's tone was dismissive: Ochen sighed again, and said, "Only the tensai stoop so low, and they are godless outcasts. Neither do we copulate with horses; nor geld men; nor force women to go with whom they'd not." He shook his head, his tone soft as if he remonstrated with a child, a thin smile on his lips as he continued: "Listen—there are some in this land who believe you folk of Cuan na'For eat human flesh; that the merchants out of Lysse who come to Nywan hide tails beneath their breeks; that the folk of Vanu are all twice a man's height and thrice as strong, with but a single eye— we've cut ourselves off too long, and such stories grow like weeds fertilized by ignorance."

"Even so," Calandryll interjected, "it was folk from your land who attacked Cennaire's caravan, and slew all save her."

Ochen looked toward the Kand woman, his face inscrutable, the twinkling eyes lost a moment as the furrowed brows hooded. In a swift flow of sound he repeated Calandryll's words to his fellow Jesserytes, and across the table Chazali grunted, Temchen shook his head. "Perhaps . . ." the mage said slowly, his voice carefully neutral, "perhaps there was an outlaw band. Your coming was not scried, Lady. Only these three."

Cennaire held her face impassive, answering his stare with her own, willing herself to stillness even as her senses urged that she flee. Beside her, Calandryll said, "Still, now she is one with us. Save," he turned to Cennaire, "you prefer to return, as this mage has promised you may."

It was a test: of Ochen's intent and Cennaire's purpose. He was not sure what answer he hoped for, but felt a confused relief when the raven-haired woman shook her head and said, "No. Do you allow it, I shall remain with you."

Ochen said, "My word is good. Lady, do you wish to go back, I'll send men with you, across the Daggan Vhe. You shall have a horse and food enough to see you safe."

Again, Cennaire shook her head and murmured, "No."

"So be it." Mottled hands steepled beneath Ochen's chin, his voice musing. "Perhaps that, too, is writ."

Katya spoke for the first time then, grey eyes intent on the sorcerer's face, her tone level, neither accepting nor accusing: "You speak much of scrying, of knowing that we three came. You offer us apologies for the manner in which we were brought here, and promise explanation. But as yet I've heard none."

The hands unfolded, settled flat upon the table. Calandryll saw that the nails were long, and lacquered golden. Ochen met Katya's bold stare and smiled.

"Aye, you speak the truth, and directly. I shall explain, but that must surely take some time, and must perforce involve both Chazali and Temchen. So—do you grant me permission to enhance that gramarye that allows us to converse, that they may understand? It is in my power to give you the tongue of this land."

"More sorcery!" Bracht muttered.

"But mightily useful," Katya said thoughtfully, "if we are to go on."

"You'd let this wizard put his magicks in you?"

Bracht shook his head in vigorous dismissal, his blue eyes wide and wary. Katya met his gaze and said, "I think that if he wished to do so, there is little we might do to prevent him. He has not; neither has he yet offered us harm. Is that not some token of his good faith?"

Calandryll said, "Aye, it would seem so."

Bracht sniffed, grunted, thought a moment, then shrugged. "Perhaps," he allowed, unconvinced.

"What harm in it?" asked Calandryll.

"What harm in any wizard's workings?" answered Bracht. "What other gramaryes might he not work on us?"

"Perhaps I've the answer to your doubt," offered Ochen, and tapped a nail against the hilt of Calandryll's sword. "This blade has power, no? I feel it—the strength of a goddess, of Dera herself, is in this sword. Were I to attempt fell magic, to deceive you, would the blade not reveal my treachery?"

Bracht, Katya, Cennaire, all turned their eyes to Calandryll for answer. He pondered a moment, unsure, then slowly said, "It may be so. Certainly it revealed"—he was about to say "Rhythamun," amended that to—"the creature that possessed Morrach."

Bracht shook his head, not yet willing to forget long-held prejudice, gestured at the glyphs marking the walls. "We sit surrounded by his sortilege," he argued. "Might that not overwhelm even Dera's gift?"

"You flatter me." Ochen chuckled, face crinkling. "I am not so great a mage as to overcome the power of a goddess. And these sigils are for all our protection."

"Test him," suggested Katya. "Surely, if his magic is fell the blade must reveal it."

Still Bracht remained doubtful, but Calandryll nodded, saying, "Aye—do you submit to such proof?"

"Happily," Ochen conceded.

Unthinking, Calandryll reached toward the sword, and a stool fell clattering, his hand halted by Temchen's blade. Dera, but the man was near as fast as Bracht, the curved steel glinting in the circle of sunlight, the edge a razor across his wrist. Chazali, too, was on his feet, sword drawn, raised ready to attack. Bracht was no slower, coming upright swift as a flighted arrow, plunging forward, left hand slapping Temchen's blade aside, the right grasping the falchion's hilt. Calandryll saw hairs, cut from his wrist, drift in the circle of sunlight, Chazali moving to direct a blow at Bracht's head, Katya rising, a storm building in her grey eyes as she, too, readied for battle.

"Stop! Enough!" Ochen's voice was no longer a dry-leafed rustling, but thunder, booming loud, authoritative, brooking no disobedience. "In Horul's name—by the names of all the gods!—are we squabbling children?"

There was such power in his command that the words fell like blows, numbing. Temchen, Chazali, froze. Bracht sprawled across the table, the drawn falchion still in his hand. Calandryll was surprised to see the old man was seated, not on his feet.

"Sit!"

It was a command addressed to the Jesserytes: they obeyed. Bracht was slower, and Calandryll said, "Aye, rest easy," waiting until the Kern sank back, tanned features morose. Katya touched his arm, ducking her head in agreement, urging him to calm. Calandryll glanced toward Temchen and Chazali, to Ochen, who nodded, and drew the straightsword.

He turned the blade to the sorcerer and said, "Do you take it then? In both your hands."

"Be I liar, may the goddess destroy me," said Ochen, and set his hands firm on the steel.

Calandryll studied the gnarled face, concentrated his will, seeking knowledge of the sword. Surely, did Ochen lie, were he false, the blade would know it and show him for a betrayer. He felt nothing: the ancient showed no discomfort. Calandryll said, "I deem him truthful."

"Which is good enough for me," said Katya, adding, softer, "for now, at least."

Ochen let go his hold and Calandryll sheathed the blade, looking to Bracht. The Kern shrugged, not speaking, and Calandryll said, "I say we allow this gramarye."

"Aye," Katya agreed.

Bracht shrugged again, which Calandryll took as acceptance. It did not occur to him to ask Cennaire's opinion, nor did he see the shadow of alarm that passed across her face as he returned his gaze to Ochen and said, "So be it—work this magic."

The ancient smiled and rose, his eyes level with Calandryll's mouth. "I think," he said, smiling, "that you had best seat yourself."

"And hold your sword," Bracht muttered.

"If you wish." Ochen's response was negligent, confident.

Calandryll drew the sword closer, slipping it once more from the scabbard, settling it across his thighs, right hand firm on the hilt, left loose about the edges, and Ochen stepped toward him.

The long-nailed hands were dry and warm as they touched his cheeks, papery. He let them tilt back his head so that he looked into the near-hidden eyes. Ochen spoke, the words in a tongue unknown, and the eyes—a yellow, Calandryll briefly realized, akin to the feline shades that seemed common among the Jesserytes, but brighter, more golden—expanded, glowing, until all else was lost in hues of swirling light. He caught the scent of almonds, and thought an instant of Menelian, in Vishat'yi, then of nothing, for he plunged into the light and it consumed him, filling him.

There was darkness for a moment then, and he shook his head, as does a man waking from sleep, unsure how long the mage had held him, blinking as his vision cleared, seeing Ochen stood back, smiling. He glanced at the sword: straight, edged steel, no hint of magic in it, and looked a question at Bracht, at Katya.

Both shook their heads. The woman said, "There was no sign."

"I felt nothing," he replied, and wondered why she frowned.

Because, he realized with a shock, he used Jesseryte words, and said the same again, in the Envah.

"A most useful gramarye," she murmured. "A gift worth the accepting."

"Then take it," Ochen said, and touched her face.

Calandryll watched, intently, the words the sorcerer spoke no more comprehensible than before, the almond scent as pungent. No light, though, this time, only the small, old man standing over the taller woman, her flaxen hair streamed back as she tilted her head, accepting. It did not take long, no more than a few heartbeats before he released her, and she sat a little while, seeming confused, rubbing at her eyes. Then she smiled and said, "I feel no different."

Like Calandryll, she spoke in the Jesseryte language.

Bracht flinched as Ochen came toward him, body

stiff with tension, distaste writ clear on his lean features, but still he submitted, allowing the mage to instill the gift of tongues.

"Was that so painful?" Ochen asked gently, and Bracht shook his head, answering, "Tak," which in Jesseryte was "no."

The sorcerer went then to Cennaire, who flinched like Bracht, so that Calandryll thought her fearful and said, seeking to reassure her, "There's neither pain nor harm."

He could not know she feared revelation, feared that Ochen must look into the depths of her being and expose her. She thought a moment of resisting—and knew that, too, must reveal her, close to panic then, contemplating flight. To where, though? How far might she get, two armored men across the table, more outside? And the mage close. Menelian she had defeated—would Ochen see that? See the blood on her hands?—but he had contested alone: did she resist this wizard, fight him, might Calandryll not take up that goddess-blessed blade and use it on her? That, she thought, she could not defeat.

Then gentle hands rested warm against her skin. Almost, she clutched the wrists; might, she knew, have snapped them, but Ochen spoke, soft, whispering.

"We each do what we must; play the part assigned us. But fate's road makes many turnings, there are many branches. Fear not, your decision must be later come."

Somehow she knew that she alone of all within the chamber heard him, and felt a calm descend, confident—though she knew not how—that did he pierce the secret lodged beneath her ribs, he would not speak of it. At least, not yet; perhaps never. She forced her trembling body to relax and gave herself up to his magic.

"You see?" Calandryll was smiling at her. "Was it so hard?"

"Tak," she answered. "Jo ke-amrisen," and returned his smile, relieved.

Ochen studied her a moment, inscrutable, then nodded as if satisfied, turning away to resume his seat.

"We may now converse freely," he announced. "Let us properly introduce ourselves, as civilized folk do."

He performed a seated bow, indicating that the four—guests or still prisoners, they were not yet entirely certain—should speak first.

One by one they named themselves in full, which took no great time, and then Ochen said formally, "I am, as you know, Ochen. By full title, I am Ochen Tajen Makusen, of Pamur-teng, home hold of the clan Makusen. I hold the title of wazir—sorcerer and priest of Horul."

He bowed again and Chazali came to his feet, armor rattling, head ducking in ritual greeting, a hand slapping his breastplate in formal salute.

"I am Chazali Nakoti Makusen of the clan Makusen, kiriwashen of Pamur-teng."

Again, he bowed, and resumed his place as Temchen rose, performing the same ritual salute.

"I am Temchen Nakoti Makusen of the clan Makusen. I am kutushen of Pamur-teng."

The titles were unfamiliar, even granted Ochen's gift of comprehension, military ranks as best the four could understand. The kiriwashen was the senior, commander of thousands, the title meant, the kutushen leader of a hundred. Calandryll, diplomatic, asked, "How shall we address you?" even as he wondered what brought officers of such status to a keep that could surely not hold a garrison of more than a century.

"With honored guests it is our custom that the birth-name be used," said Ochen. "Shall that suit?"

Calandryll answered in the affirmative, the tension eased somewhat, but not yet dissipated, trust a promise yet to be grasped firm. Bracht sat silent, his face set in controlled lines, as if he was not yet convinced. Cennaire was thoughtful. Katya appeared better at ease, and asked, "Shall you now explain?"

"As best I may," Ochen returned, and gestured at the glyphs covering the walls. "These, as you surmise, are sigils of gramarye; set to defend us against such prying as my kind command. Within this chamber, none may know what we say or do."

"Why?" Bracht demanded.

Ochen sighed, fingers entwining, his silvered head lowering a moment, as if he collected thoughts, then: "We embark on a lengthy tale. Shall it be told over wine?"

Without awaiting a reply, he nodded to Temchen, who rose and strode to the door, calling out that wine and cups be brought. They waited until a man returned, bearing a tray of lacquered wood that he set down on the table, bowing low and withdrawing. When the door was closed behind him, Temchen took the golden jug and filled the seven porcelain cups with a dark yellow liquid. Calandryll saw that Bracht waited until the Jesserytes had sipped before tasting the vintage; and that his reticence was noticed by Ochen. For his own part, he drank readily enough, not anticipating treachery, and found the wine good, rich, and slightly sweet.

"You know my land as the Forbidden Country." Ochen set down his cup, nodding thanks as Temchen poured another measure. "Few venture here—visitors, wanderers, are discouraged. Those merchants trading out of Lysse—what few Vanu folk come down the coast—are confined in Nywan, the Closed City: we have our reasons for such secrecy. Those reasons are our history and, I ofttimes think, our curse.

"Some claim our land was shaped and we put here by the First Gods. This may be true—I do not know—only that to south and west the Kess Imbrun is a barrier few attempt; our eastern coastline is bleak: little reason for any to make landing. And to the north lies the Borrhun-maj." He paused, sipping wine, wiping delicately at his long mustache. "Beyond those mountains . . . some say the world ends; others claim the First Gods dwell there . . . none know for sure because none go there. That passage, its attempting even, is forbidden on pain of death. Though"—a rueful chuckle—"such edict is hardly needful, the Borrhun-maj being impassable."

"You say it so?" Katya demanded when he paused again.

"I say it so," he confirmed, "even though you'd attempt it."

"You forbid us?" snapped Bracht.

And Ochen raised a hand, mildly gesturing the Kern to silence. "I say that magic of inconceivable power is vested there," he answered. "That layer upon layer of barriers exist. Do you folk of Cuan na'For—folk known for your courage—not avoid the Geff Pass, that place you name Hell Mouth? Do such creatures as inhabit nightmares not dwell therein? I tell you that worse exist in the Borrhun-maj, and that they are no more than gatekeepers."

"Gatekeepers may be avoided," Bracht said, "and monsters slain."

"Oh, that I know. And that you've done as much."

Ochen smiled briefly as the Kern frowned. "Much of what you three have accomplished we wazirs have seen. But I tell you still that such creatures as you encountered in Tezin-dar are as nothing to these."

Now Calandryll frowned, wondering how the ancient mage came by such knowledge of their journeyings. What magicks did the wazirs of the Jesseryn Plain command, that they might know of Tezin-dar?

"Think you that your travails go unnoticed?" Did Ochen read his mind? His expression? "What you have done, what you attempt—that affects the occult fundus. The aethyr is not a thing apart, but a realm that coexists with our mortal plane—and you are known there."

"More riddles!" Bracht reached across the table for the jug. "Must sorcerers always speak in riddles?"

"At times perforce we must," said Ochen, not offended; more amused, it seemed, for all a terrible gravity lay beneath his words, behind his gentle smile. "The aethyr is a hard thing to explain, neither do we who are gifted with the sight, the talent for sorcery, always comprehend that realm—so, aye: betimes we've only riddles to use, not plain words."

"I," said Bracht, "am a plain man."

"Plainly," agreed Ochen, "and you've my word I shall do my best to set this out in simple language. But I crave your indulgence—hear me out and ask what questions you will. My word on honest answers; though not, I fear, always simple."

Bracht was a little mollified by that return and ducked his head, gesturing for the mage to continue.

"For now accept that your quest was noticed," Ochen went on, "that our magicks showed us such disturbance within the occult realm that we guessed a part and saw another. Much, I suspect, as did the mages of Vanu." This with a glance at Katya, who nodded confirmation. "And doubtless others. Though it would seem they saw it unclearly, or chose to do nothing, or were otherwise occupied."

"Menelian said as much!" Calandryll could not help himself: he found trust in this wizened old man burgeoned, and a tremendous curiosity. "In Vishat'yi he said the same."

"He was a sorcerer?" asked Ochen.

"In service to the Tyrant of Kandahar," Calandryll replied, choosing to ignore Bracht's warning grunt. Did Ochen see so much, what reason to attempt concealment? "Busied with civil war."

"Kandahar rises against its Tyrant? Aught else?"

For an instant the narrow eyes blazed golden, alarmed; Calandryll nodded and said, "In Lysse my brother would raise a navy, go to war with Kandahar. In Cuan na'For, Jehenne ni Larrhyn spoke of bellicose alliance, the invasion of Lysse."

"He stirs! All the gods help us, he stirs! Thank Horul you were found!" Ochen grew agitated a moment, calmed himself with visible effort. Across the table, Temchen and Chazali radiated palpable tension, their armor rattling as they shifted uncomfortably, like warhorses sensing impending battle. Then: "Endings and beginnings entwine here, and we had best join all we know together do we dare hope for success."

"You speak of Tharn?" asked Calandryll. "Of the Mad God?"

"None else." Ochen answered with a solemn nod. "But let me seek the start of this thread and spin it out in ways we may all understand. So: the Borrhun-maj is formidably guarded. Vile creatures roam those slopes, and did you avoid them, then still you must face the mountains, which touch the sky and howl with such cold winds as still the blood, even at summer's height. More—there are gramaryes set there by the First Gods, by Yl and Kyta themselves, that none may approach those places where they set their sons, Tharn and Balatur, when the godwars were ended."

"And yet," said Calandryll, "there is a way, no?"

"Aye," said Ochen. "The which—may the gods forgive me—prompts me to wonder if even gods are truly all-knowing. There is a way, were the traveler possessed of such knowledge and such power as to attempt it. And were he mad enough!

"Listen, legend has it that we Jesserytes were set down in this place to ward those approaches—for that reason, and that alone, we cut ourselves off, became the Forbidden Country—that none should find their way to Tharn's resting place. Nor Balatur's, lest that balance brought by the Younger Gods be disturbed and all the world fall down in chaos.

"That trust we have held down all the span of centuries; and well enough, I think. But still, long and long ago, the wazirs of that time perceived such portents as suggested the way was found, or known of, at the least. Then, little could be done—it was scried only that the presence of the book—the Arcanum!—was known, and that one sought it. Who, remained a mystery, and it was believed that Tezin-dar itself was lost in terms both physical and magical."

He broke off, taking more wine, as if needing such fortification. Calandryll said bitterly, "Rhythamun!"

"Is such his name? I had thought none lived so long."

"He changes shape," said Katya. "His presence became known to the holy men of Vanu. He has lived for centuries, taking one body after another. He has the form of a Jesseryte now."

"Horul!" Ochen shook his head. "And you quest after him?"

"He tricked us." Calandryll encompassed Bracht, Katya, with a glance. "We found the way to Tezin-dar—that we might secure the Arcanum and bring it to Vanu, that the holy men might destroy it—but Rhythamun duped us and seized the book. We three have followed him since. We made a vow, to the Guardians of Tezin-dar."

"And now he is on the Jesseryn Plain." Ochen looked to Temchen, Chazali, whose faces sat grim. "And even in his limbo, Tharn senses his coming and lends what aid he may. War in Kandahar, you say? The Domm of Lysse waxing bellicose? Tharn calls for blood and his lust shakes the world."

"Cennaire knows his face—Rhythamun's." Calandryll nodded in the direction of the Kand woman. "Do you lend us your aid, perhaps we may catch him."

"Perhaps." Ochen fixed Cennaire with a hooded stare. "Perhaps it is not so easy."

"You would not aid us?"

The mage turned to Bracht and said, "Warrior, I promise you all the aid it is in my power to command. But that may not be enough. No, wait." The same authority that earlier had stilled sword strokes rang in his voice: Bracht frowned, quenching whatever comment formed. "I have told you that your coming was foreseen, and so it was—that three should enter this land in friendship—but Tharn moves to cloud the aethyr, camouflaging his disciple's purpose, easing the passage of this Rhythamun.

"For that reason were you brought to me bound, gagged—for fear you were not those scried, but agents of that other. This land is closer than most to that limbo the god now occupies—we are not immune to his fell workings"—a bitter laugh interrupted his discourse—"no; though since the Great Khan fell we had thought it so. Aye, Bracht, we looked to invade your land then. Because the Khan was tainted by Tharn's dreaming magicks, and led his clan out from Kesh-teng to conquer all the Plain and bring all the clans under his single rule. For a while he enjoyed success, but then the wazirs of that time, and such clans as escaped the taint, fought him. And won—Kesh-teng exists no longer! It was razed, and only dust remains. We believed such threat could never again bespoil the Plain. But we were wrong—like Kandahar, we fight a war."

Sorrow, and more than a little anger, etched the lines upon his face deeper then, and his voice faltered, as if this announcement pained him beyond speaking. He dropped his head, motioning for Chazali to continue.

The kiriwashen said, "The tengs of Zaq, Fechin, and Bachan form an alliance. Pamur-teng, Ozaliteng, and Anwar-teng stand in opposition. A madness stalks our land: the rebel horde now closes on Anwar-teng."

Anwar, Calandryll realized, meant "the Gate." An ugly suspicion stirred: he asked, "What importance does Anwar-teng have?"

Ochen composed himself with visible effort, taking up the tale again. "With the ending of the Great Khan's tyranny the land was, for some while, in disarray. Families vied for supremacy, outlaw bands roamed at will. Order was restored only when the wazir-narimasu—the greatest of the sorcererpriests—leant their support to the Soto-Imjen, declaring that clan supreme by birth and blood. Even then, that the Soto-Imjen should not wax prideful as had the Great Khan, the clan was required to renounce its ancestral hold and reside in Anwar-teng, sworn to the defense of that place. They took up residence in the holy city, peace reigned . . ." He paused, barked a single, bitter laugh. "Until recently! But I run ahead of my tale—that none should again seek to establish himself supreme, it was decreed that while the Khan should be of the Soto-Imjen, each hold should send representatives— Shendii—to Anwar-teng to sit in the Mahzlen, the Great Council, advised by the wazir-narimasu. Our Khan is now Akija Soto-Imjen, who is but seven years of age. Therefore, a regent was named— Nazichi Ojen-Canusi, of Bachan-teng—which was thought a wise decision until Nazichi declared himself Khan! He looks to establish the Canusi in place of our rightful ruler, and in his support the representatives of Zaq-teng, Fechin-teng, and Bachan-teng withdrew from the Mahzlen. Now the armies of those holds march out in battle array.

"Anwar-teng lies under siege. Do the insurrectionists take that place, then they possess a dreadful threat to hold over those loyal to the Soto-Imjen and the Mahzlen."

"The loyal Shendii would die in battle first," Chazali declared, his voice dour as his face. "Or take their own lives before surrender."

"Whichever," Ochen said, "chaos must surely follow. Do the rebels take Anwar-teng, they will next move against Pamur-teng and Ozali-teng. Such bloodshed must be food and drink to Tharn; and such warfare must render the finding of this Rhythamun mightily difficult."

"Ahrd!" Bracht's voice was soft. "We ride into another war."

"But you say Anwar-teng houses these wazir-narimasu," Calandryll said, "and that they are your most powerful sorcerers. Can they not defeat the attackers?"

"Were it so simple." Ochen spread helpless hands. "But the wazir-narimasu are sworn to peace. Theirs is another duty, and they are bound by such gramaryes as divest them of all power do they turn to warfare. Thus are they helpless in this matter."

Calandryll was about to speak, to put another question, but Bracht forestalled him. "And you," the Kern demanded, "the wazirs like you—are you so bound?"

"No." The old man shook his head. "We may use our talents in hostile manner; though we prefer we should not."

"Save those traitors with the rebellious tengs," Chazali grunted. "Their conscience is not so fine."

"Then why," Bracht began, halting as Ochen once more raised a hand, anticipating the question.

"I'd ride with the loyal armies," the wazir declared, "as would Chazali and Temchen, were there not other matters—likely of greater import. This keep"—he waved a hand, indicating the chamber, the walls beyond—"is manned by one hundred chosen men. By turn and turn about each teng sends a century to guard the Daggan Vhe. For this turn, it was the task of Pamur-teng, which sent its soldiers honestly. A century of warriors out of Pamur-teng occupied this keep—all are dead now. Slain by fell wizardry.

"Your coming, as I have told you, was scried. A messenger was sent, to alert the kutushen here that you might be met and brought to me. No word came back, and with my art I saw slaughter done. It was obscure—clouded by Tharn's design, I believe!—but of such a magnitude that Chazali deemed it wise to come here. We found only corpses; a keep held by occult creatures."

"Rhythamun warded his back!" gasped Calandryll.

"So it would seem." Ochen spoke gravely. "There were such creatures in possession as took all my power to defeat, and not a few lives."

"They slew fifty of my warriors," Chazali added, grim-voiced. "And my men do not die easily."

"But Rhythamun was recently shape-shifted," Katya protested, looking from kiriwashen to wazir. "And that must surely weaken him. How was it possible he could raise such things?"

"It is my belief," Ochen replied in somber tones, "that as he draws closer to Tharn, so his strength waxes. No less, as all the world—or so it seems— turns warward, so does the Mad God's dreaming power increase. The disciple feeds his master and the master strengthens the disciple. Close as this land is to Tharn's limbo, the war we fight must greatly aid him."

"And make our way harder," Bracht offered.

"Wait, please." Questions swarmed in Calandryll's mind, like troubled bees, fast buzzing, so that it was difficult to find the words that might dispel his growing alarm. It seemed a pressure built within the confines of his skull, a dull ache starting there, and he rubbed at his temples, frowning. "Cennaire saw Rhythamun take the form of a Jesseryte warrior, saw him summon men across the Daggan Vhe. They must have come from here, no? So it must be the body of a warrior out of Pamur-teng he possesses. Shall you not know him, then?"

Ochen might have shrugged—beneath the wide-spread shoulders of his tunic it was hard to tell— and answered bluntly, sadly, "The men we found were riven, butchered like meat: they were beyond recognizing one from the other. And this Rhythamun did not linger—I'd know—but traveled on about his filthy purpose."

"To the Borrhun-maj?" Calandryll stared at the seamed face, wondering why his head pounded so. "Or to some other place?"

Before Ochen had chance to reply, Bracht spoke: "Shall this war not slow him? If he wears the body of a warrior out of Pamur-teng, then must he not find himself ranked with others? Forced to play a part?"

"Perhaps. But that shall be no great hardship, nor much hindrance. Does he but play the part of simple warrior, then he must find himself marching northward—to the relief of Anwar-teng—and that is the direction he seeks, is it not?"

Bracht mouthed a curse, scowling reluctant agreement. Katya frowned and asked, "Shall your fellow sorcerers not scry him for what he is, and employ their powers to thwart him?"

"It may be so," Ochen replied. "I pray it be so! But I fear the god he seeks to raise will strengthen those magicks with which he conceals himself. He may well defeat such scrying; defeat their power, even."

"Then when the army of Pamur-teng joins with the others," asked the warrior woman, "shall there not then be sufficient wazirs as shall know him and defeat him?"

"Then, aye," Ochen conceded. "But then he shall stand even closer to his master, his strength duly augmented. And in the midst of battle it cannot be difficult for him to elude pursuit. And it is entirely possible those wazirs of the hostile tengs might aid him, should he go to them."

"Knowing what he is?" Katya's eyes grew wide, aghast at the notion. "Knowing what he would do?"

"They move against Anwar-teng," Ochen said slowly, "and that alone is a madness surely born of

Tharn's influence. Be they seduced by the god, then perhaps . . . aye, they might."

Storm built afresh in the grey eyes; it seemed, almost, lightning flashed there as Katya shook her head in horrified denial, frightened acceptance. "Is all the world gone mad?" she whispered.

"Perhaps," came the sorcerer-priest's answer, "save for a few still sane. See you now why I set these protections about us?"

Katya nodded; Calandryll fought the throbbing pain inside his head to say: "All roads, it seems, lead to Anwar-teng. Why?"

Ochen paused, his expression troubled. Calandryll heard the soft intake of Temchen's breath, saw Chazali's impassive features stiffen, and guessed he struck to the heart of the matter. He waited, shafts of stabbing pain behind his eyes, as the mage looked to the kiriwashen, to the kutushen, wishing he knew better how to read those inscrutable visages, for he sensed hesitation, a heartbeat of doubt, as though this were a matter they would prefer be left alone. He saw Chazali incline his head a fraction—granting permission? Agreeing whatever unseen question he read in Ochen's look? Calandryll was unsure. In a voice calmer than he felt, he said, pressing, "Truth was promised between us, an honest exchange."

"Aye." Ochen turned to face him, solemn. "That was so, and truth you shall have—though none others beyond our lands, and none too many here, have ever been granted this revelation.

"The Borrhun-maj is but one entryway to that limbo where the Mad God lies. Anwar-teng guards another."

4

THE sun had shifted westward as they spoke,
the light entering from the circular opening in
the roof no longer a vertical column pooling over
the angles of the table, but slanted now, limning
Ochen with dramatic intensity. His silver hair glittered, the lines mapping his ancient face deepened,
emphasizing the gravity of his expression. Calandryll stared at him, struck momentarily dumb,
numbed by the import of the aged sorcerer's announcement. The drumming ache within his skull
grew worse and he closed his eyes an instant
against the pain. Motes of dust danced in the light;
silence hung heavy in the chamber. It was Katya
who broke it, her voice somber.

"If Anwar-teng is a gateway . . . if Rhythamun
should reach it . . ."

She broke off, eyes wide, fearful. Bracht took up
the stream of her thought, his voice harsh: "He's
won! And he might well change his shape again,
ensuring he stands on the victor's side. Rebel or

loyal . . . Ahrd! It can make little difference to him.
He needs but enter the city."

"And reach the gate."

Katya spoke softly, awed, and it seemed to
Calandryll her words came muffled, slow as the so-
norous beat of a distant drum, pounding against his
senses, each syllable striking a fresh spark of agony.
He thought his skull must burst and stretched his
jaw to fashion a response that came out a strangled
moan. The pain consumed him, and he felt his
muscles gripped with a strange torpor, his vision
clouding, as if blood vessels burst behind his eyes,
so that faces, the sunlight, blurred into a misty red.
He fought a terrible lassitude, despondent thoughts
filling his head. He had believed they found valuable allies in their quest, such men as could speed
their passage across the Jesseryn Plain, bring them
to Rhythamun. With Ochen's aid and all the might
of Chazali's warriors at their back it had seemed
they had at last an advantage, such as could grant
them the upper hand in that ultimate confrontation. Now all that was dashed, the tables, so it
seemed, once more turned in favor of their quarry.
For all the Younger Gods gave what help they
could, still there seemed a greater design worked to
hinder them, to advance Rhythamun on his way.
With hostile armies marching, Anwar-teng besieged, how could they hope to find the warlock?
How prevent him broaching the gate? Once more
the odds seemed impossible, too great to dare hope.
For a dismal while he thought perhaps they had
better concede the victory—there seemed scant
likelihood now of thwarting Rhythamun's foul intent.

He struggled against the assailing doubts and it
was as though he battled with hot and bloody fog,
tendrils of awful despair swirling, mocking, reas-

sembling even as he sought to drive them off. The
chamber dimmed before his eyes, Ochen's face no
longer lit but lost, all become ensanguined, miasmic, hopeless, and he trapped there, a helpless fly
in some painful psychic web.

He groaned, starting, as he became aware of a
hand upon his shoulder, firm, that touch like a
rope thrown to a drowning man, faint words cutting through the pain.

"What ails you?"

He heard Bracht's voice as if from a great distance
and shook his head, unable to form an answer, feeling sweat cold down his back, the aching pressure
of tight-clenched teeth, overwhelming despair.

"Gramaryes."

That was Ochen's voice, faint as a whisper, followed by light and the indistinct mumble of words
in a tongue unfamiliar. The bloody fog dissipated
and his vision cleared, sharpened, until he saw the
mage on his feet, hands moving in strange, intricate patterns, seeming to paint sigils on the empty
air. The scent of almonds wafted sweet and he was
unsure whether he truly saw streamers of crimson
brume dull and fade, or if that was merely an
imposition of a mind that demanded physical explanation of the inexplicable. He watched with
tear-blurred eyes as the sorcerer completed his incantation, clapped his hands three times, and resumed his seat.

"I should have foreseen this cunning. He left
more than monsters behind." Ochen drew the wine
jug closer, filled Calandryll's cup, pressed shaking
hands about the porcelain. "For those who stand
close to the occult, he left other devices. But gone
now; from this chamber, at least, and soon from all
the keep."

Calandryll held the cup in both his hands, wondering at the effort it took to raise so slight an object to his lips. He drained the wine in rapid gulps, not speaking until all was gone.

"Dera, what say you? That I am easy prey to his magicks?"

Ochen studied him awhile, thoughtfully. "I say that some stand closer to the aethyr than others; that in some there is a . . . power . . . that may be used. Sometimes against them."

"Menelian discerned as much," Bracht murmured, a steadying hand on Calandryll's shoulder, concern in his eyes.

Calandryll looked to the Kern, to Ochen, and reached for the jug, his grip firmer now as he poured. "I am no sorcerer," he argued.

"No—you are no sorcerer," the wizard said, agreeing. "But still there is that in you that might make you such. The talent is raw, I think, and you've not the knack of its usage, but you stand close to the aethyr."

"And thus I am vulnerable?" Calandryll wiped wine from his lips and barked a sour laugh, frightened. "Do you say that? That Rhythamun may better cast his spells on me than on my comrades? What does that make me, then? A lodestone to his fell magicks? Perhaps a threat to those about me?"

"Perhaps," said Ochen bluntly, "but listen—this blade"—he tapped the sheathed straightsword— "what is it? A sword in most hands, and no more, to be used for good or ill—that depends on the wielder. Your goddess blessed it, gifted it with that power you know it holds, and that power that rests in you is much the same."

"Save that Rhythamun's gramaryes touch me deeper, it would seem." Still his voice was harsh, edged with doubt. "Does that not render me a danger?"

"It need not." Ochen shook his head, speaking calmly. "Aware, you are forewarned, armed against his trickery."

"But why now?" Calandryll demanded. "Ere now I've stood closer to him, faced his creations even, but not felt that . . ."

He shuddered, remembering skull-bursting pressure, the cloying sensation of dread and despair, of hopelessness. Ochen waved a hand and said, "Because he waxes stronger; because he draws closer to Tharn. Because the Mad God grows stronger. Because"—a smile now, incongruously mischievous—"the god fears such as you."

Calandryll gasped, wine dribbling unnoticed down his chin. "Why should Tharn fear me?" he muttered. "Why am I singled out?"

"I think because of that power," Ochen replied. "And you are not singled out—I suspect the god fears all who move against him."

"But surely he rests in limbo." The notion that Tharn should be aware of his existence was frightening: to oppose a man, albeit a warlock of dreadful strength, was one thing; to believe that he opposed, directly, a god was an entirely—daunting!—concept. "How can he know of me? Of us?"

He turned, encompassing Bracht and Katya with his gaze, seeing their faces stern, Cennaire's beyond no less grave.

"I do not think that gods sleep as men do, nor is their dreaming harmless." Ochen's tunic shifted, rustling; perhaps he shrugged. "We speak of matters that have occupied the wazir-narimasu for centuries, and I am too humble a mage to pretend full knowledge of such affairs, but I suspect that just as Tharn is aware of those who seek to raise him, so is he aware of those who stand against that end. Perhaps not of you, personally, but in the way that a dog—forgive me—is aware of the fleas that roam its hide."

"So now," said Bracht softly, "we face an enemy greater even than Rhythamun."

"Have you not all down your road?" The slitted eyes turned on the Kern. "Has your way not always been opposed?"

"By men," Bracht said. "Sometimes by creatures of the occult."

"And you have overcome those obstacles." Ochen nodded, confirming his own observation. "Neither have you faltered."

"We had not thought to face the god himself," Calandryll murmured. "Rhythamun, aye. But the Mad God himself?"

"Shall you turn back then?" Ochen wondered. "My promise remains—safe passage across the Kess Imbrun."

"No!"

The denial was voiced unthinking, echoed by Bracht and Katya. The Kern said, "We've come too far."

Ochen chuckled, the sound musical, and clapped his hands in approval. "Perhaps it shall not come to that," he said. "Perhaps we shall halt this Rhythamun before he reaches Anwar-teng. Or"—an afterthought—"the Borrhun-maj."

"We?" asked Bracht.

"Of course." The silvered head fragmented shards of brilliance as it nodded. "Did you think to go on alone? What aid is ours to give, you shall have in full measure."

Across the table, their faces shadowed now, Chazali and Temchen grunted their agreement.

"I propose," said Ochen, "that we quit this place as soon we may. Do I employ myself, I can banish the last of Rhythamun's gramaryes ere long, and then we may proceed to Pamur-teng. The warriors march by now, but there may be news; if not, then we go on to join the armies."

"At Anwar-teng?" Calandryll wondered.

"There they march," Ochen confirmed. "There, I think, Rhythamun must surely go."

"And should he avoid the hold? Make for the Borrhun-maj?"

"Anwar-teng is closer, its defenses made by men, not gods." Ochen stroked a moment at his mustache, musing. "Does he go past the hold, then I shall know—and we shall pursue him."

"The wazir-narimasu," offered Katya, "shall they not deny him access to this gateway?"

"As best they may," Ochen replied, "but theirs is a way of peace, and I fear this close to Tharn, Rhythamun may find the strength to overcome them."

"How is this gate so easily broached?" Bracht clenched a fist, opened it, frustrated.

Ochen sighed and said, "Anwar-teng was built to guard the gate, to conceal it. The secret has been ever close-kept, and few know of its existence—the wazir-narimasu, the clan sorcerers, none others ere now. Until I deemed it needful neither Chazali nor Temchen thought Anwar-teng more than the hold of the Soto-Imjen, of the Mahzlen. It was never thought any should be so crazed as to seek entry, and so the wazir-narimasu look to prevent exit rather than ingress."

"Shall Rhythamun know it?"

Calandryll clutched straw, snatched from him by Ochen's solemn answer: "I think he must. Even does he not already, then I think Tharn will find a way to alert him."

"Ahrd!" Bracht's hand was fisted again, crashing angrily against the table's top, wine jug and cups

rattling, the action eliciting grunts of disapproval
from the two armored officers. "Does all favor the
gharan-evur?"

Ochen's brows rose, but he offered no reply.
Katya said, "He must yet reach the teng; enter to
reach the gate. What chance have we of overtaking
him?"

"Some." Ochen's voice remained solemn. He
turned to Temchen: "Do you find us a chart?"

The kutushen nodded and rose, disappearing into
the shadows that filled the farther reaches of the
chamber. There was the sound of wood scraping, a
cover lifted and replaced, and Temchen returned to
the table, spreading a scroll within the radius of the
sunlight, weighting the corners with cups as all
rose, clustering round as Chazali indicated the
map, his guttural voice identifying the places
marked thereon.

"The Kess Imbrun; we are here." A blunt nail
tapped, moving on a line, northward. "This is
Pamur-teng; this, Anwar-teng."

Ochen's spell did not extend to comprehension of
the written word, but as Chazali pointed to each
hold, Calandryll saw that Pamur-teng and Ozali-
teng stood much on a line, the tengs of Zaq and
Fechin to the east, above and below, hostile
Bachan-teng a little south of the lake, closest to the
besieged city. He asked, "How far to Pamur-teng?"

"Thirty days do we ride hard," advised Chazali.
"To Anwar-teng, another thirty. Far slower at the
army's pace."

"The armies march now?" Calandryll stared at
the map, willing himself to recall the lessons in
strategy, tactics, he had suffered long ago in Secca,
thinking them then no more than vaguely interesting historical studies.

"They do," the kiriwashen confirmed.

Calandryll peered, frowning, and touched a finger to the dot that marked the site of Bachan-teng. "This hold will come out to block them, no?" he asked. "You'll meet in battle?"

"You've the grasp of it." Chazali smiled grim approval, nodding. "Aye, they'll likely act as rearguard. They've already warriors about Anwar-teng's walls, though it's the others that form the main force."

"Shall Pamur-teng and Ozali-teng march together?" Calandryll looked from chart to dark, stern face. "Or look to divide the opposing army?"

Now Chazali barked laughter, glancing at Temchen, at Ochen. "He's the gift of strategy besides whatever else," he applauded. To Calandryll, "The warriors of the clan Tessana will march north out of Ozali-teng, to the southern shore of Lake Galil; our Makusen make directly for Anwar-teng—aye, we look to divide and weaken the enemy."

"But still these others lay siege." Calandryll set a finger to the marking of Anwar-teng. "And Rhythamun will likely hold the shape of a Makusen warrior until it serves him better to take another."

"That, or go on alone," grunted Bracht. "To Anwar-teng, and there steal another's form."

"Aye." Calandryll nodded absently. "But for now he's likely served best by the shape he has. Do we ride hard, perhaps . . ."

"We can do little else," said Katya.

"We can overtake the army," Chazali declared, and looked to Cennaire. "Perhaps then you might recognize him."

The Kand woman ducked her raven head, not speaking, her lovely face grave.

"Still no easy task," Bracht murmured. "To find one man in an army? Of how many?"

"Thousands," said Chazali. "Three thousand from Pamur-teng alone."

Bracht said, "Shall it be possible?"

"I've sight beyond my eyes," said Ochen. "I've known something of his magicks, and that must make it the easier to recognize him, even does he look to guise himself with occult means."

"It seems," Calandryll declared, still studying the chart, "that for now all we can do is chase the army; and hope. How long before we may leave?"

The mage succeeded in shaping his wrinkles in an expression of apology. "To cleanse this keep of all the befouling gramaryes will take another day, at least," he murmured.

Calandryll frowned. Bracht waved an irritable hand: "No sooner? Ahrd, can we not leave now? Must we grant him more time?"

"This keep must be manned," said Chazali. "That duty belongs to Pamur-teng, and the clan Makusen does not renege its promises. Nor will I leave men in a post cursed by fell sorcery."

Voice and face were firm, brooking no argument; Bracht shrugged, muttering an inarticulate oath. Katya suggested, "Might some not go on?"

"That would be . . . unwise." Ochen pointed a golden nail at Calandryll. "I've the feeling Rhytha-mun may know now of your coming—at least sus-pect it—and perhaps leave . . . hindrances . . . along his way. You'll travel safer in my company, but I've a duty to my clan—Temchen remains here with his century and I'd not leave him prey to occult crea-tions. So, no—I fear you must curb your impa-tience."

"Before, you gave us leave to go," said Bracht. "Would you now halt us?"

"Horul, but I'd heard you folk of Cuan na'For were headstrong." Potential insult was defused by the sorcerer's smile, his friendly tone. "You'd travel an unknown land, strangers, unescorted? Hostile armies on the march? And roving bands of tensai? How far should you get, think you?"

"We've come thus far," snapped the Kern, "and traveled stranger lands than this."

It was difficult, Calandryll realized, for him to forget long-held prejudices. The self-imposed isolation of the Jesserytes, all the tales told of them, still rendered them suspicious in Bracht's eyes: for all the friendship shown, trust was not yet entire. He smiled and said diplomatically, "That's true, but always aided by friends along the way—Yssym in Gessyth, Menelian in Kandahar, the drachomanii in Cuan na'For. We should not forget that, Bracht. Nor spurn the advice of newfound allies."

"Likely Ochen speaks true," added Katya, laying a hand on the Kern's arm. "And likely we shall travel the faster in his company."

Bracht looked, for an instant, as if he would argue, but then he shrugged, essaying a somewhat embarrassed smile. "Aye, perhaps you're right," he admitted, bowing his conciliation. "Forgive me."

"We'd none of us delay longer than we must," said Ochen. "But nor would we leave clan brothers in jeopardy."

That reasoning was such as Bracht understood: he nodded, murmuring further apologies.

"I think," said the mage, his voice mild, "that we must all accustom ourselves to unforeseen alliances. The Mad God threatens us all, and that should make us comrades, no?"

"It should," Calandryll said firmly.

"Aye," said Bracht. Then grinned, adding, "But still I'd see us on our way as soon as we may."

"Then best," returned Ochen, himself smiling, "that I commence my task. Do you go with Chazali, and he'll show you your quarters."

"And feed you," said the kiriwashen. "Or would you bathe first?"

Katya and Cennaire said, "Bathe"; Calandryll and Bracht said, "Eat." And Chazali laughed; for the first time, Calandryll realized, the simple sound rendering the impassive visage suddenly friendly, confirming the bond that formed between them.

"I suggest," said the Jesseryte, "that we defer to the women. Do I show you to your quarters and then to the bathhouse?"

Calandryll bowed, gesturing that Chazali lead on.

THE chambers assigned them were spartan, little more than cells built into an inner wall, each with a narrow window, shuttered but lacking glass, that afforded a view down into an inner courtyard, across to the keep's ramparts. Each contained a single bed, alcoves cut into the sandy-colored stone of the walls, a washstand, a locker; nothing more. The uncarpeted floors, the walls, the ceilings, and the doors were marked with Ochen's magical sigils, the paint not yet completely dry. They left their gear inside and followed Chazali to the bathhouse.

The corridors and halls they traversed were dim-lit, painted with more glyphs, the armored figures of Makusen warriors parting before the kiriwashen, observing the strangers with slanted, incurious eyes. The bathhouse itself was on the lowest level, a wide, low-roofed hall misty with steam from the huge tubs set into the floor. There were no windows, the sole illumination a series of fat yellow candles set on sconces along the walls, those painted with yet more sigils.

Chazali ushered them inside, hesitating a moment as if wary of offending guests, and said, "I am unfamiliar with your customs. Do you bathe together, or alone?"

Bracht grinned at Katya, not speaking, and Calandryll thought the Vanu woman blushed, though in the dimness it was hard to tell. He found himself wondering how Cennaire would react did he suggest they bathe together, and what it would be like to share a tub with her, his own cheeks warming at the thought's excitement. He fought the temptation, saying, "Alone," in a voice gone suddenly gruff, so that Bracht's grin turned from Katya to him and he felt the flush suffuse his cheeks the more.

Chazali ducked his head and strode halfway down the hall, near lost in mist and shadow, reaching out to draw a screen from the wall, a cunningly articulated construction of lacquered wood that extended across the room, hiding one tub from another. Turning to the women, he said courteously, "Do you remain here, then. When you are finished, a man will bring you to your quarters." To the men, he said, "Do you come with me," and led them back through the door, along a corridor to another entrance.

He left them and they stripped, sliding gratefully into the tub, finding it deep, and filled with water close to boiling. From beyond the dividing partition came the sound of splashing and the low murmur of voices, reminding Calandryll that only that thin screen stood between him and the naked Cennaire: excitement returned.

"Such modesty." Bracht's voice was deliberately grave. "I commend you."

The water's heat was such that his skin was already red, the Kern's face indistinct behind the rising steam. He was grateful for that as he muttered, "I'd not embarrass her. Or Katya."

Bracht's answer was a loud laugh. Calandryll blushed deeper and said, "Katya advised me not to press too hard."

"I suspect you'd not find her unwilling," came the reply. "I saw her face as we spoke and she had eyes only for you, save when Ochen addressed her directly. I believe you find favor there."

Calandryll sought a suitable response, but found none, contenting himself with a noncommittal grunt as he wondered if Bracht spoke true, or merely bantered with him. He hoped it was the truth, albeit he was unsure what steps he should take were it so.

"Still, we shall have time enough, it seems," the Kern remarked, deliberately casual. "A night, another day, in this place—what might happen?"

"Likely nothing," returned Calandryll, sharper than he intended, aware embarrassment lent an edge of irritation that Bracht cheerfully ignored.

"And then days—and long nights—on the road to Pamur-teng."

"The which applies in equal measure to you and Katya."

"Ah, but we made a vow," said Bracht, quite unabashed. "While you suffer no such stricture. Only temptation."

"Not long ago you spoke for sending her back," Calandryll declared.

"Aye." The bantering tone departed, the Kern's voice become serious. "And I would still, save you appear fixed on bringing her."

"She knows Rhythamun's face," he replied.

"Ochen seems confident enough of recognizing him," Bracht countered. "And should he take another's form . . . what use is she then? Save she warms your blankets along the way, I say she's bag-gage."

Calandryll felt irritation grow—the more for the accuracy of the Kern's words: with Ochen for ally, Cennaire did seem supernumerary; but still he was loath to bid her farewell. He hid ire and confusion behind a lathering of soap and vigorous scrubbing.

"Well?" Bracht insisted.

Forced to respond, Calandryll shrugged soapy shoulders. "Does it not seem strange we found her there, at the Daggan Vhe?" he asked. "And she ob-server to Rhythamun's taking of another shape? Perhaps there was a design in that."

"Perhaps," Bracht allowed.

"And still all we agreed there stands," Calandryll went on, not certain whether he spoke to convince the Kern or himself, only that he wished Cennaire to remain. "The Jesserytes would bring her across the Kess Imbrun, but what then? Must she cross Cuan na'For alone?"

"Aye, there's that," admitted Bracht.

Calandryll pounced on the reluctance in his friend's voice. "Think you she could make such a journey?" he demanded. "A solitary woman? Help-less? Would you condemn her to that?"

"Ahrd!" Bracht grunted. "I concede the argu-ment—she stays, and I'll say no more. Save"—he chuckled lewdly—"that you, being under no vow, follow my advice."

"Perhaps I shall," Calandryll muttered, and sank beneath the water as the Kern laughed again and said, "It would do you good . . ."

". . . like a young stallion with . . ."

Calandryll submerged again.

". . . mare," he heard as he broke surface, reply-ing more coolly than he intended, "I'd not name her mare."

Bracht heard the indignation in his voice and said, "My friend, I only jest. No, she's certainly no mare; and do you bed her or not, that's between the two of you, and none other."

Mollified, Calandryll nodded.

"So, I'll not speak of it again." Bracht tossed soap away and sank himself awhile. "Now, do we drag ourselves from this cooking pot before our blood boils?"

Benches were set along the walls and they rested there awhile, cooling, discussing all they had learned, all that lay ahead.

"We've at least a destination now," Calandryll remarked, "albeit an army stands betwixt it and us."

"That may well delay Rhythamun in equal measure," Bracht grunted, toweling his long hair, "and we've allies to speed our passage."

Calandryll turned his head, studying the Kern with a grin. "Your tune changes," he said. "Are the Jesserytes no longer monsters?"

"It would seem not," Bracht answered with a shrug, a somewhat shamefaced smile. "Ahrd, but I grew up with tales of their depravity—which now appear no more than that: tales—and that's a hard burden to shed. But I learn, you see? I learn to trust sorcerers, so should I not trust those who offer aid? Perhaps there *is* a design in this; perhaps Horul sent these Makusen to aid us."

"Aye, perhaps." Calandryll's murmured response was thoughtful.

Bracht chuckled: "With all we face, best hope it's so. For now, however, I hope to fill my belly. So, do we find the dining hall?"

As if reminded they had eaten nothing since the morning, Calandryll's stomach rumbled. "Aye," he agreed.

Dressed, they found a man waiting outside the bathhouse, half-armored, his manner deferential as if they now occupied a new status, no longer captives but respected guests. He bowed, murmuring that they should follow him, and brought them through the shadowy corridors to their quarters, politely explaining that such outfits as were more suitable to the company of wazir and kiriwashen were prepared for them.

Within his cell, Calandryll found candles burning, lighting the simple chamber to a more, to him, normal level, confirming his belief that the Jesserytes possessed such eyes as saw better in the dark than his. He looked about and saw the gear he had tossed carelessly on the bed was now neatly stowed in alcoves and locker, his sword set upright on a stand of dark red wood. On the bed he found clothing of Jesseryte fashion—a shirt of pale blue silk; a wide-shouldered crimson tunic embroidered with a snarling dragon in gold and green that wound sinewy across the chest, an emblem he assumed was that of the Makusen clan sewn in black and silver on the back; loose white trousers; and ankle boots of soft green hide. So grand a costume brought back memories of Secca, and for an instant he recalled that the last time he had dressed in such finery he had hoped to win Nadama den Ecvin, and that her rejection of his suit had sent him out, chagrined, to drown his sorrow and thus encounter Bracht ... that this whole long journey into the unknown had begun there, in that instant he knew Nadama was lost to him. He smiled as he drew on the tunic: her face was blurred now, and when he endeavored to find it, he saw Cennaire's instead. Perhaps, he thought, he should take Bracht's advice; or Katya's, which was to allow events to take their natural course. Bracht's way

was direct, Katya's more subtle; and she was, after
all, a woman. Therefore, he told himself as he
wound a sash of iridescent gold about his waist,
Katya should know best, and he be better advised
to heed her. Aye, he would bide his time and judge
the moment rather than press headlong onward.

He was certain that did he press Cennaire and
she reject him, he would be mightily hurt. Such
pain he would not welcome; and therefore it seemed
the wiser course to wait, to hold back. Cowardice?
he wondered. Or sense? No matter—he felt somewhat less confused, less pressured; or, perhaps, safer.
And as Bracht had said, they faced long days together. He tied the sash and surveyed his splendid
costume, deciding that he cut a rather grand figure.

He moved to buckle on his sword, thinking better of it—likely the Jesserytes would take offense
did a guest come armed to table—but instead took
his dirk concealing the blade beneath the tunic,
grinning as he thought that the innocent who had
fled Secca would never so instinctively seek that
protection.

Still grinning, he quit the room and went to
Bracht's door.

The Kern was dressed no less magnificently, although he was considerably less at ease in the unfamiliar costume. He shifted restlessly, setting the
dark blue silk of his tunic to rustling, tugging at
the silver sash, glancing down at the loose jade-
green trousers.

"Ahrd, but I feel a popinjay," he grumbled.
"Could we not wear civilized clothes?"

"You look most handsome."

Katya emerged from her chamber and Bracht
stopped his fidgeting, jaw dropping as he gaped at
the Vanu woman. She wore a robe of glistening
black, all sewn with twining silver birds, high-

collared, descending to her feet, the tips of silver slippers peeking from beneath the hem. Her flaxen hair was unbound, falling smooth over the gown's shoulders, dramatic contrast to the sable silk, a match to the embroidered birds. She smiled at the Kern's expression, which remained amazed.

"And you . . ." he mumbled. "Ahrd, but I've never . . ."

Katya laughed, waiting. Bracht shook his head, helplessly. Calandryll said, "You look superb," then gaped himself as Cennaire came into the corridor.

Her gown was a reflection of Katya's, shimmering silver, the birds all black and green, her hair a spill of blue-black, falling to the swell of her breasts. Her lips shone red and her eyes were huge, emphasized with kohl, flickering from one to the other, fixing longest on Calandryll.

He bowed, as if once more in his dead father's court, and said, "You are lovely," hearing the words come out hoarse from a mouth gone suddenly dry. Abruptly, he felt awkward, grateful to the armored man who emerged from the shadows, bowing, inviting them to follow him to the dining hall. It was hard to take his eyes from Cennaire's face, exciting to offer her his arm, to feel her hand warm through the silk. He struggled to remember the courtly moves, the conversation, aware of Bracht's muffled chuckle at his back. No words came and he swallowed, cursing himself, his mind gone blank of compliments.

At his side, Cennaire needed no augmented senses to recognize arousal, or embarrassment, and deemed it wisest to affect modesty, murmuring a demure "My thanks. You, too, are splendid," concealing her smile as he cleared his throat, opened

his mouth to reply, thought better of it, and muttered, "Thank you," in a near groan.

To Calandryll, it was almost a relief to enter the
hall and find himself in such company as distracted
him a little from the woman.

The chamber, like all others in the keep, was crepuscular, the flambeaux mounted along the dark-
paneled walls shedding no more than flickering
pools of light, their smoke sweet-scented, mingling
with the odors of roasting meat and wine. There
were windows, but shuttered against the night
now, so that the colorfully garbed Jesserytes who
occupied the five long tables were near ghostly figures, their dark faces lost, as if the bright tunics
themselves were animated, their conversation falling away to a murmur as the guests were escorted
to the farther end of the low-ceilinged room.

There, set at a right angle to the rest, stood a
smaller table, flanked along one side by backless
chairs, allowing the diners there to survey the
chamber. Chazali occupied the central seat, Ochen
and Temchen to either side, the warriors resplendent in outfits of extravagant colors, empty places
between them. Calandryll was unsure if it was a
welcome relief or a disappointment to find himself
located between the wazir and the kiriwashen,
Cennaire to Ochen's right. Katya, too, he noticed,
was placed at the table's farther end, on Temchen's
left, assuming it a Jesseryte custom that the
women should occupy the most remote seats.

"I trust your kitai suit," Chazali inquired. "I had
feared we should find none to fit you."

"Excellently." Calandryll found it easier to converse without the distraction of Cennaire's presence. "You've our thanks for such hospitality."

"We are not"—Chazali smiled, glancing at
Bracht—"entirely barbarous."

"Indeed not," Calandryll agreed as the kiriwashen filled his cup with pale golden wine. "Mystery breeds phantoms, I think—folk tend to fear what they do not know."

Chazali nodded soberly, his face again grave, inscrutable. "I have never met a Lyssian before," he remarked.

"You do not visit Nywan?" Calandryll sensed this was not the time to discuss the war, their quest: the kiriwashen appeared bent on trivial conversation, and he accepted that cue. "Our merchants trade there."

"No." Chazali shook his head. "Nywan is the province of the kembi."

The word, despite Ochen's magic, had no obvious translation, though the note of contempt was clear enough. Calandryll's face expressed his lack of understanding.

"I am kotu," Chazali explained. "Of the warrior caste. Kotu do not dabble in trade, which is the concern of the kembi."

Calandryll nodded, his natural curiosity aroused—there was much to learn of this strange and isolated people. He asked, "Are all here kotu?"

"Save Ochen," said Chazali, "who is wazir."

"And the Shendii?"

"Kotu. The wisest of the kotu, usually the oldest," Chazali explained, and laughed again. "A warrior must survive to learn wisdom, to win the respect of his clan."

"Are there other castes?" Calandryll was intrigued. "Or are all divided between warriors, mages, and merchants?"

"There are the gettu—the farmers," said Chazali, "and the artisans, who are of the machai caste. There are others, but of no account. It is not so in Lysse?"

"No," Calandryll replied, and found himself involved in a lengthy description of his homeland as
men in simple white tunics and yellow pantaloons
served the meal.

It was plain fare, such as soldiers eat, but tasty
enough, and plentiful—the Jesserytes seemed possessed of hearty appetites—and the talk meandered
back and forth, all there learning more of one another's customs and countries. The tengs of the
Jesseryn Plain, Calandryll discovered, were less castles than cities, each containing a population of
many thousands, all linked by birth or marriage or
adoption to one clan. Beyond the walls, the holds
were surrounded by farmland, the gettu living
under the protection of the warrior overlords, while
beyond the arable steadings the country lay wild,
unclaimed by any save the outlaw bands of dispos-
sessed kotu Chazali named, with massive contempt, the tensai. It seemed, to Calandryll, a
society far more rigid than his own, a hierarchy
dominated by the kotu, who in turn were dominated by their kiriwashen and wazirs, the Khan little more than a figurehead, subservient to the
Mahzlen.

It came to him that Chazali was a very powerful
man—indeed, one of the leaders of Pamur-teng—
and that his presence demonstrated the weight he
placed on Ochen's warning. That the kiriwashen
should come himself to the keep indicated the
alarm he felt at thought of the Mad God's awakening. No less was it a further guarantee of true alliance.

"And Anwar-teng," he asked, hoping he broke no
protocol, "is that hold solely the domain of the
Soto-Imjen?"

"Anwar-teng is different," Chazali advised him.

"It is the home of the Soto-Imjen, but also of the Mahzlen and the wazir-narimasu."

"But if the rebels are gone from the Mahzlen . . ." Calandryll paused, choosing his words with infinite care, sensing that he trod delicate ground. "How stand the kotu of Anwar-teng?"

Chazali grunted, staring a moment at his wine cup. Calandryll feared he gave offense, but then the kiriwashen chopped a dismissive gesture and said, "Those who left are tensai. No more than that! They may claim no man's allegiance. Those who follow them are tensai. Worse!"

His voice, guttural by nature, was harsh, like the growl of an outraged hound. Calandryll would have inquired more about the war, the order of march, and the likelihood of the rebel armies broaching the walls of Anwar-teng, but Chazali's tone, his stance, even his expression, which was no longer inscrutable but sharp-edged with fury, disallowed further questioning. He filled his cup, drinking deep, as though to rid his mouth of an unpleasant taste deposited by the condemnation, and afterward concentrated angrily on his plate.

Calandryll thought it more diplomatic to shift the subject, and turned to Ochen.

The wazir, however, was engaged in animated conversation with Cennaire, and Calandryll found himself left awhile in silence, watching them. Dera, but she was beautiful! He studied her animated face, thinking of all the things he might have said to her, all the things he might in the future say, did his tongue not stumble again and the pretty compliments dissolve in gangling awkwardness. He cursed himself afresh for such naive embarrassment, and then she caught his eye and he thought her smile lit the dark room, and he felt his

cheeks grow warm and could not understand why
he had to look away, fumbling for his cup.

He found it, and Chazali's gaze on him, speculative, he thought, though it was difficult to judge.
Less so the raised eyebrows, and not at all the quietly murmured question.

"She belongs to you? I fear these are warrior's
quarters and we've no chambers larger."

"No," Calandryll mumbled. "No matter. She's
not . . . My chamber suits me well."

Chazali, as if seeking to atone for his display of
anger and himself sensing a delicate topic, smiled,
returning his attention to the fruit the serving men
had placed before him.

No more was said, to Calandryll's relief, of war
or women, their talk returning to commonplace
matters, and in a while the meal was ended and
Ochen announced that he would leave them and
continue his magical cleansing of the keep. His departure seemed taken as cue that all should retire,
and Chazali summoned a man to lead the guests to
their quarters.

Cennaire again took Calandryll's arm, and he
found himself murmuring banalities concerning
the food and their hosts, thinking that he babbled,
though she smiled and answered in kind, seeming
not to notice his awkwardness. Indeed, she appeared a trifle withdrawn, as if concerned with her
own thoughts, murmuring a soft "Good night" at
her door and entering the chamber without a backward glance.

Katya was already gone, and Calandryll ignored
Bracht's amused stare, waving a farewell as he
turned into his own cell and closed the latchless
door.

The window revealed a rectangle of star-
brightened sky, the moon close to full, and he

leaned awhile on the sill, aware that the night wind blew cleaner, the tainted aftermath of Rhythamun's magic fading. Even so diminished it was an insult to the senses, to propriety, and he shuddered as he thought of that visitation, of the awful despair that had earlier gripped him, reminded then of Ochen's warning, wondering if his enemy could, indeed, sense his presence, could reach out through the medium of the aethyr to touch him. It was as well, he thought, that the Jesseryte wizard should accompany him, a sentry against Rhythamun's fell sortilege. Then, briefly from across the yard, he caught the scent of almonds, a pale flickering of light that for an instant was shaped in the form of the strange sigils Ochen painted, and guessed that the silver-haired sorcerer went about his magical business, tireless it seemed. The impression of charnel stench faded more, and he yawned and turned away, taking off his unfamiliar clothing and folding it carefully before snuffing the candles and throwing himself gratefully on the bed. He closed his eyes, the image of Cennaire's face clear as sleep took him.

In her own chamber, Cennaire undressed and sat awhile combing her hair absently, lost in troubled thoughts.

That Ochen was a wizard of power, she did not doubt, and wondered if he knew her for revenant. He had said nothing; indeed, throughout the meal he had proven an amusing companion, witty and informative, but still she wondered. Did he recognize her for what she was, why had he not spoken out? He had touched her mind, with his gift of language, and she had thought then to be discovered, but he had seemed, rather, to reassure her. Perhaps he had not seen so deep; perhaps he concealed that

knowledge for reasons of his own. She could not
tell and such lack of certainty unnerved her, rendering her indecisive, for she felt herself surrounded by hazards, her choices leeched off, like a
deer that hears encircling hunters drawing ever
closer, seeing no avenue of escape save headlong
confrontation.

The mirror stood propped within an alcove, and
as she studied her face, she thought of Anomius,
contemplating a summoning, perceiving her master
as another threat to her own safety. Did he wonder
where she was, how she fared? Did he grow impatient? Or was he occupied with the Tyrant's war,
too involved to concern himself with the doings of
his creation? Almost, she spoke the words, but
knowledge of Ochen's presence, awareness of his
power, left them still-born on her tongue. Did she
contact her master, surely the Jesseryte sorcerer
must know it, and how he might then react, she
had no idea. Instead, she completed her toilette,
telling herself she had, anyway, nothing to say, certainly nothing of any great interest to Anomius.
She sighed, setting mirror and comb, both, safely in
her satchel, thinking that she was caught in dilemma.

Did Anomius wax impatient, was it possible he
could find a way to escape the attentions of the Tyrant's sorcerers, return to Nhur-jabal, to wreak
some magic on her living heart? Did he do that,
then she was surely powerless against him. Yet to
assuage his impatience, she must use the mirror
and thus—surely!—reveal herself to Ochen, who
likely would advise Calandryll and the others. And
then . . . then perhaps such magicks as could destroy her should be brought to bear. To act, or not,
both seemed paths fraught with danger: she caught
a lip between her teeth, worrying at the soft flesh,

feeling herself trapped, her choices narrow as her miserable cell.

Patience, she decided finally, and hope—that Anomius was burdened with sufficient as would prevent him both from wondering what she did and returning to Nhur-jabal. Equally, that Ochen's magic had not identified her, would not be used against her. There appeared no other choice but inaction, and while such inertia sat uneasily on her mind, she could perceive no alternative, save flight—which must surely earn Anomius's displeasure.

With that poor comfort, she killed the candles—as would any creature with beating heart—and climbed between the sheets to await the morning.

The night grew older as she lay sleepless, turning thought over thought without finding satisfactory conclusion. Then the soft tapping of knuckles against her chamber's door brought her instantly alert.

For a moment she delayed responding, feigning the confusion of one caught asleep as her mind raced. Calandryll? Certainly he had shown great interest, and great confusion, that night, and in the midst of all her doubts she held the single certainty that he was mightily attracted to her. She had enjoyed the stumbling compliments he paid her, even his innocence, that being a rare commodity in the life she had known, and she wondered if he plucked up the courage to come to her. Another man, one less courteous or perhaps more confident of himself, would not have delayed so long. She smiled, thinking that she would welcome his attentions: he was, after all, a handsome young man. And should he come to love her—that she could ensnare him, she did not doubt: did he spend the night in her arms, the morning must surely find

him love-struck—then she must surely win herself
a powerful ally. Both thoughts excited her; which
the most, she was not sure.

The tapping came again and she ran swift fingers
through her hair, a tongue over her lips, drawing
the sheet modestly over her nudity, and bade her
visitor enter.

She was unable to stifle a gasp of surprise when
the door swung open to reveal Ochen.

"Hush."

The mage raised a warning finger, closing the
door silently behind him, plunging the room into
darkness as Cennaire mouthed a silent, and most
unladylike, curse, hoping he took her startlement
for the genuine surprise of a demure woman finding a man entering her sleeping chamber.

"Who is it?" she demanded, endeavoring to pitch
the question somewhere between outrage and
fright, remembering belatedly that mortal folk
lacked her nocturnal vision. "Who are you?"

Soft laughter—mocking?—answered and she
tensed, preparing to fight for her undead life. If
worse had come to worst, then she would seek to
overpower the mage, slay him if she must, and flee
the keep. Anomius would surely be angered, but
still she could likely follow the questers at a distance, which might satisfy her master. Beneath the
thought hung a barely recognized regret, and fleetingly she wished it had been Calandryll who
knocked. She steeled herself, taken once more
aback by Ochen's next words.

"You perceive me well enough, I think. And do
you only utilize those senses I understand your
kind possess, then you'll know I intend no harm.
Do that, and you shall save us both time."

The suggestion was entirely unnecessary: Cennaire had, unthinking, opened all her preternatural

senses, finding fresh cause for confusion in what she learned.

She smelled no threat from Ochen. Curiosity, rather, and a dry amusement as he arranged his overrobe, settling himself on the bed casually as if he visited an old friend. Confidence, too, that persuading her he was warded with spells against attack. She found no indication of desire in him, but nonetheless drew the sheet closer about her, pretending modesty even as she struggled to assemble her bewildered thoughts.

"No harm," he repeated, his gnarled features clear in the darkness. "Nor shall you harm me—as you doubtless sense, I am guarded, and with such cantrips as would defeat even your kind."

His voice was calm and utterly confident; all Cennaire could think of to say was "What do you want?"

"A little of your time, an honest exchange." She saw him smile. "Did you think to conceal what you are from a wazir? The gift of tongues requires that I enter the mind. I saw that power that invests Calandryll, the presence of Ahrd in Bracht's veins—did you believe I'd not see what you are?"

Cennaire frowned. Had she owned a heart, it would race now. She shrugged, saying, "I wondered."

"And wondered, too, what I should do, no? And when I did nothing—said nothing—you hoped you'd gone unrecognized. Eh?"

She nodded, wondering what game he played. That of Anomius, of Rhythamun? Was she fallen into the hands of another ruthless warlock?

It seemed her doubts showed, for Ochen chuckled again and she smelled his amusement, his desire to reassure.

"I'd not see the Mad God risen, be that what you

fear," he murmured. "Nor—for now, at least— would I reveal you, or destroy you."

"For now?" she whispered, not doubting he could make good that veiled threat. "What then do you want?"

"An explanation," he returned. "I'd know why you league with these questers, who know not what you are."

"And then?"

"And then I must decide."

He had no need to add, "Your fate," and Cennaire ran a pink tongue over lips that seemed abruptly emptied of blood. In that instant she was absolutely confident this ancient mage *could* destroy her, and that her existence depended on satisfying him. Her initial impulse was to lie, to concoct some yarn, but Ochen's gentle voice put thoughts of subterfuge aside.

"No Jesseryte band attacked your caravan," he said with absolute certainty. "Neither kotu nor tensai. That was merely a ploy, no? To win the sympathy of those three honest folk? A wizard of great power made you, and my guess is he sent you out after the Arcanum. Do you tell me true, perhaps we shall reach some accommodation. Do you lie—and I shall know it, doubt that not!—then . . ."

A hand, mottled dark with time's spotting, gestured, the movement implicit. Cennaire drew deep breaths, aware that she was firmly snared, trapped in her deceit; that truth appeared the sole avenue of escape. She looked him in the eye and said, "I was taken from the dungeons of Nhur-jabal, in Kandahar, by a warlock named Anomius. He . . . made me what I am . . . he took my heart . . ."

The telling of it, cold and clear, seemed somehow to set the act in starker light, to grant her an awareness, objective, of what had been done to her.

It seemed, perhaps because she felt Ochen radiate sympathy, as much a curse as gift now, and as she spoke she felt resentment of Anomius grow.

She told the ancient sorcerer everything, holding nothing back, and when she was done, it was as if she had enacted some penance, Ochen's response a benediction.

"Such magic is foul," he murmured with disgust. "This Anomius must be a filthy creature to so abuse his talent."

"But still he holds my heart," she said.

"And would you have it back?"

The question was mildly put; it rang in her ears like a clarion. She saw his eyes between the wrinkled, hooded lids, bright, studying her, and said without hesitation, "Aye."

"Why?" he asked bluntly. "As you are, you possess such powers as mortal folk only dream of. As you are, you need not die."

Cennaire paused, wondering if he baited her, or set some subtle trap. She watched his face: it was inscrutable. At last, slowly, she said, "I'd name no man my master, save I choose it be so."

"Calandryll?" His voice was even, empty of expression; she felt his magic as a shield about him, the wafting scent of almonds denying her senses' interpretation.

"Calandryll?" she returned, seeking time, confused.

"He's a comely youth. He's clearly enchanted by you. And I've the feeling you find his attentions not unwelcome."

"No," she admitted, struggling to rally her thoughts. "He is . . . Perhaps . . . But how should he react to what I am?"

Ochen cocked his head, birdlike. "At this moment," he said cheerfully, "I suspect he'd find the notion revolting. Did he learn you go about Anomius's business, he might well use that englamoured blade on you."

"Think you so?" Cennaire asked, injecting the question with more confidence than she felt. "I think perhaps he would not."

"You've a high opinion of him, or of yourself," the mage returned. "Perhaps you speak aright, but did he not, then surely Bracht would seek to slay you."

"I think he could not," she said. "Save you aid him."

"Aye." Ochen chuckled, nodding. "And that I could do. And should, did it come to that—those three are of paramount importance, while you . . . I am not yet sure what part you play."

"Then why let me survive?"

Ochen drew thoughtful fingers through the silver strands of his mustache, observing her awhile with twinkling, enigmatic eyes, and she grew uncomfortable under his scrutiny, feeling herself in some manner judged, wary of the outcome. She was thankful when he answered: "I've my reasons—which need not concern you for the moment."

"And you'll not expose me?"

She spoke as calmly as she was able, utterly confused. Ochen smiled, shook his head, and said, "No, save you force me to it."

"Why not?" she asked again.

And again he replied, "I've my reasons," amplifying a little: "I've the feeling of a design in this. Beyond my comprehension, or yours, for now, but . . . something."

Cennaire's bewilderment increased. Ochen sat silent, as if lost in thought. When he spoke, it was as though a judgment was delivered, though how, or what the sentence might be, she could not tell.

"The time will likely come when you must make a choice. It will likely be a difficult choice—I'd urge you make it wisely."

"I do not understand," she murmured, brow furrowed.

"No," he returned equably, "you'd not. Nor shall until the time arrives. When that day dawns, remember this conversation. And along the road 'twixt now and then, learn."

Cennaire stared at the wrinkled visage, puzzled, wondering if he spoke honestly, or if he hid intentions, designs of his own. Trust was an unfamiliar element in the world she knew, but for now it seemed he offered an alliance of some kind, a measure of safety, and that she snatched eagerly.

"Until that time," she agreed.

"So be it." Ochen rose, smoothing his overrobe. "I bid you good night, then."

"Wait!" She reached out, clutching at his arm, snatching back her hand as the almond scent grew instantly stronger and she sensed the gathering power of his magic, like a blade poised to strike. "What of Anomius? I am commanded to report as opportunity permits, and should he wax impatient . . ."

She fell silent, Ochen completing the sentence for her: "He may decide to prick your heart a little. Aye, there's that; nor would I have him interfere at this juncture." He stroked his wispy beard, lost awhile in thought. "So: contact him. How is that done?"

"I've a mirror," she answered.

The wazir said, "Then use it. But remember that such magic will be known to me, always."

"What shall I tell him?" she asked, bewildered.

Ochen chuckled softly. "What he doubtless wants to hear," he suggested. "That you ride with the questers, north toward the Borrhun-maj. Make no mention of me, neither of Anwar-teng nor the war. Does he wish to know where you are, tell him you find refuge in a keep, among simple warriors who suspect nothing. Think you that shall satisfy him?"

"Aye." Cennaire nodded. "So long as he believes I continue after the Arcanum."

"Which"—Ochen smiled, rising—"you do."

She watched, dumbstruck, as he went to the door, pausing there to glance back. She thought she saw the slitted eyes twinkle as he murmured, "And my apologies—I regret it was not Calandryll who came to you."

The door closed on his laughter; on her bewilderment.

She sat awhile, staring at the wood, her assumptions all in disarray, thrown into turmoil by the wazir's seemingly equanimious acceptance of her condition. She had thought to find sorcerers ever her enemies, save she serve them. Did she, then, serve Ochen in some fashion beyond her fathoming? Was she become part of the quest? Was Ochen friend or enemy? The answers lay beyond her grasp: all she knew for certain was that Anomius still controlled her heart, was still her master in that, but that now, to some extent at least, it seemed she danced to another's tune.

She drew deep breaths, seeking a measure of calm, and when she found it, took out the mirror and began to speak the words of the gramarye.

5

THE sweet scent of almonds filled the chamber,
the smooth silver surface of the mirror changing, swirling, like clear water disturbed by a
thrown pebble, a whirlpool of color forming there,
fading gradually into a darkness that seemed lit by
distant, flickering fires. Cennaire frowned, staring
at the strange image, wondering if somehow, so far
from Kandahar, communication with her master
became impossible, or if Ochen's magicks denied
the contact. She gasped as the image shifted, dis-
torting, revealing for a moment a brazier in which
coals glowed red, then darkness again, a hint of
some night-lit brightness beyond, something splat-
tering against the surface, as though a stone were
tossed back, toward her. Instinctively, she drew
back, seeing whatever had struck the companion
mirror smeared, all black then, then clear again,
Anomius's face filling the disk.

The ugly little sorcerer drew a sleeve across his
mouth, particles of food dislodging, some remain-

ing about his fleshy lips as he peered at her face,
his own irritated as he said, "A moment."

Cennaire saw the mirror obscured once more and
almost laughed as she realized he ate, and in his
haste spat food upon the surface. She quelled the
impulse, waiting.

Then, curtly: "It's been long enough. Where are
you?"

"Across the Kess Imbrun," she replied, "on the
Jesseryn Plain."

"What else lies across the Kess Imbrun?" he
snapped, churlish as ever. "Where exactly?"

"In a Jesseryte fort," she told him. "A keep that
guards the Daggan Vhe."

"With them?" His face came closer, the mirror
again marked by the food he still chewed. "With
Calandryll and the others?"

"Aye," she said. "They found me as you promised, accepted my story. I go with them now."

"And they suspect nothing?" He rubbed a grimy
hand over his mouth, turned away an instant to
spit. Cennaire heard the faint sizzle as the gobbet
struck the brazier. "They trust you?"

"I am not sure," she answered truthfully.
"Calandryll, I think; but Bracht holds reservations,
and Katya, perhaps."

"Perhaps?" The mirror swayed as he reached
aside, settling as he brought a cup to his mouth,
drinking noisily. "How mean you, perhaps?"

"Bracht would have sent me back," she said,
"but Calandryll spoke for me."

Anomius snorted laughter, like a pig, Cennaire
thought, snuffling in dirt. "He takes a fancy?"
asked the warlock. "As I thought one of them
would?"

Cennaire ducked her head, saying, "Aye, he does.
He's a gentle man."

Further laughter answered her words, contemptuous of such definition, and Anomius demanded, "Has he taken you to his bed yet?"

"No," she said, and again, "he's a gentle man."

"He's a man and nothing more," the wizard grunted, dismissive, "but no matter—work those wiles you know so well and it shall come about. Bind him to you."

Cennaire nodded again, not speaking.

"So," Anomius said, "you're with them and trusted; enough at least you shall continue with them, no?"

"Enough," she returned, "aye. Remember that I saw Rhythamun's new face, and that—"

The warlock overrode her words. "Aye, Rhythamun!" he barked. "What of him? What of the book?"

"He travels north, as best we know." She paused a moment, ordering her thoughts, recalling what Ochen allowed she might tell this disgusting little man, what to hold back. "He slew the soldiers of this keep with magic. Calandryll believes he left gramaryes behind, to ward his back, knowing he is pursued."

"And yet they survive?" The sallow face contorted in a frown. "How so?"

Cennaire realized her mistake, extemporized with truth and fiction: "Calandryll possesses a sword, englamoured. He slew the creatures."

"Tell me," Anomius commanded, "of this sword."

"It was enchanted by the goddess Dera," she replied, nervous now, for her master's face grew angry. "In Lysse, they said."

Anomius grunted, a finger probing in his mouth, emerging with a sodden lump that he wiped on his robe. "So the Younger Gods aid them?" he asked thoughtfully.

Cennaire wondered if an element of doubt, of fear even, put the stridency in his voice, and nodded solemn agreement. "They say that Burash brought them across the Narrow Sea, and in Cuan na'For, Bracht was taken prisoner and crucified, but Ahrd drove the nails from his hands and gave him back life. Even brought them through the Cuan na'Dru."

Breath whistled wet from the sorcerer's nostrils and for a while he was silent, his liquescent eyes pensive as he rubbed at his nose. Finally he said, softer, "But they could not halt Rhythamun, the Younger Gods."

Thinking it a question, Cennaire answered, "It would seem not."

"Nor have they halted you." If he heard her response he gave no sign, rather pursuing the train of his own thoughts. "I think they must be weak, or limited in some way. No matter—so long as you continue unhindered about my business."

"I do," she assured him, now, more than ever, unsure whether that was truth or fable.

"And Rhythamun travels northward, eh? Toward the Borrhun-maj?"

"They believe that," she said, dissembling. "That Tharn must lie beyond the mountains."

"How shall they get there? I know no more than any other of the Jesserytes, but they are acknowledged an inhospitable folk. Shall they not turn you back?"

The question took Cennaire by surprise. A woman less versed in dissimulation would likely have let fall the truth then—have shown on her face, or by her reaction, that she hid things—but

Cennaire was practiced in concealment, and retained her calm, though it cost her effort.

"It seems not," she said smoothly. "The people of this keep are friendly enough."

"What people?" Anomius's voice was an abruptly suspicious bark. "Did you not just advise me Rhythamun slew the soldiery there?"

Almost, she was caught then; only her quick wits saved her as she wove an elaboration. "Aye," she said, "that's true. But some escaped to carry word, and others came. By the time they arrived, Calandryll had slain the creatures Rhythamun left, and so the Jesserytes hail him a hero."

Anomius was mollified: Cennaire vented a sigh of relief she hoped went unnoticed. "And you with him?" he demanded.

"I am counted one of them," she agreed, expanding on her fabrication. "Now the Jesserytes offer us aid. They grant us free passage over the Plain."

"Do they know of Rhythamun?" the warlock snapped. "Of the Arcanum? Do they suspect your purpose?"

"No and no," she said, thinking fast, thinking to herself that this sorcerous game grew mightily hazardous, "and again, no. They believe we travel to Vanu—Katya's homeland—which lies within the foothills of the Borrhun-maj. No more than that."

"Good," said Anomius. "But how far ahead is Rhythamun?"

"Some few days," Cennaire returned.

"Then do not linger," ordered the mage.

"Save you bid me quit their company, I must travel at what pace they set," she said. "But they'd not grant him advantage."

"No," he allowed, "likely they'd not. Stay with them, for I still believe they must be the key to

Rhythamun's undoing, and thus most useful tools to my purpose."

He chuckled at that, a horrid, bubbling sound. *And I*, thought Cennaire, *am no more. Only a tool—to be discarded when my usefulness is spent?* Aloud, she asked, "When we find him . . . what then? I think that sword Calandryll bears could slay even me. And that he'd use it, did I attempt to take the book from him."

"Perhaps it could," Anomius agreed carelessly, and favored her with a pride-filled smile, "but think you I fail to see that far ahead?"

"I know not what you think or what you see," she replied honestly.

"Thus are you the servant, and I the master," came the smug response. "But fear not—when the time is right, I shall be there."

"How?" Cennaire made no attempt now to conceal her surprise. "I thought you bound by magicks. Did the Tryant's sorcerers not set enchanted fetters on you?"

"They did, curse them." The unhandsome little man grew uglier as he scowled. "But I shall rid myself of those hindrances ere long."

"How shall you do that?" she asked, hiding sudden alarm behind a veil of flattery. "Are you so mighty a sorcerer?"

"I am," he told her with total, frightening conviction. "And soon these accursed bracelets shall be removed. How need not concern you; only that when I deem the moment right, I shall translate myself to where you are."

Cennaire overcame her alarm, struggling against confusion, seeing only one way his promise might be kept, and that a fascinating thing, for it afforded her speculation of her own. "Through the mirror?"

she asked, carefully adding, "You are truly a great mage."

"Did you doubt it?" he asked vainly. "Aye, through the mirror, do you but show me what it reveals."

"Of all the world's mages," she said, her tone deliberately adulatory, "I think that only you might overcome Rhythamun."

Anomius beamed, preening, basking in her wisely chosen praise. "Aye," he agreed, "and so I shall, when the time comes."

"Where are you now?" she asked, deliberately humble, pandering to his conceit.

"Outside Mherut'yi," he told her, vanity rendering him loquacious. "The town lies under siege, defended by such gramaryes as only I may undo."

"And then?"

"Likely south to take those other bastions Sathoman now holds. Wait!" The mirror was abruptly dark, as if he thrust it into a sleeve. Cennaire heard faint voices, too muffled that she could make out the words. Then Anomius's face returned. "These petty wizards require me," he announced. "Contact me when next you may."

"That may well be difficult," she warned. "We ride out soon and there will likely be little chance to speak unobserved."

She spoke only the truth, albeit her motives were mixed. In such close company as their progress across the Plain must bring, with Ochen in attendance, it would, indeed, be hard to use the mirror unnoticed; but also she sought to buy herself time, to allow an ordering of her thoughts, perhaps even a settlement of her loyalties, but without incurring suspicion or wrath. She watched the mirror, Anomius's face there, puckered in a frown, or a scowl—his visage was such the two were indistinguishable—awaiting his response.

"Aye," he said at last, though reluctantly. "When you may, then."

"I shall," she returned.

He nodded, grunted, and mumbled the words that ended the enchantment, his image fading, replaced a moment by the spectral colors. The almond scent strengthened, then was gone, and the mirror became again only a disk of glass. Cennaire set it aside, not moving, staring at the rectangle of night framed by the window as her mind raced, assessing all she had learned, and how it might be turned to advantage.

She was more than a little frightened, for Anomius was clearly confident he would soon rid himself of the occult confinements that bound him to the Tyrant's service, and were he able to travel at will he might feel no further need of her. Save, she thought, that he must have the mirror's sight to define his location. She knew enough of magic that she was aware a sorcerer might translate himself safely only to a known destination, one he could see or clearly reconstruct in memory.

So, the thought reassuring, he would likely leave her to continue with the questers until such time as they came upon Rhythamun or secured the Arcanum; and that time he could know only through her agency. Until then, did she but placate his impatience, she was safe.

Comforted by that conclusion she turned her mind to those other tidbits of knowledge he had so casually let slip. He had taught her the cantrip of transportation—she had used it before—but it had not until now occurred to her that by that means she was able to translate herself to his chambers in

Nhur-jabal. The notion excited her: her heart, he had told her, lay there, in the pyxis.

Almost, she conjured the image of the room, spoke the words, thinking that did she but go there, she might find her heart and once again own herself, define her allegiances for herself. Common sense stopped her, the half-formed words dying on her tongue. He was not so careless, not so foolish. Vain, undoubtedly; crazed, too. But imbued with a horrid cunning that would surely have prompted him to encompass the pyxis with protective gramaryes. Likely he had placed such enchantments on the box, on the chamber, even, as would destroy her heart did she attempt its removal.

No, that thought accompanied by a bitter curse, that was not the way, save in desperation. Still she must dance to his tune, reliant on his humors as he was on her enforced loyalty. It was an impasse from which she could see no escape but to go on, ostensibly his servant still.

Even so, there was power in knowledge; not yet of much use, but in the future, did she but continue to learn all she could of wizards and wizardry . . . then, perhaps, she might regain her heart, become again her own woman.

What she would do, she did not know. As Ochen had remarked, there were many who would envy those powers she now commanded. She was perhaps immortal, certainly she owned a strength and a stamina beyond mortal imagining, her preternatural senses alone granted her tremendous advantage over human folk, and one gramarye was already hers—might she not learn others?

Outside, a night bird sang, and its call seemed to mock her. She was powerful beyond men's envisioning, and yet still trapped: heartless, she was prepotent; heartless, she was at the mercy of her heart's possessor. She stared blindly at the night sky, all set with stars, the near-full moon westering toward its setting. A bank of silvered cloud drifted leisurely on the wind's idle breath. Men moved along the ramparts: plain, simple men, whose concerns were ordinary. For a moment she envied them, then her nostrils caught the faint odor of almonds and she thought again of Ochen. Another hand on the strings of her destiny? She was not sure; confused by the wazir's promises and warnings, she could not know whether he was friend or foe. His words had implied friendship, rather than enmity; at least an alliance of sorts. But what were his reasons, what his motives? Those remained hidden, inscrutable as the ancient face that revealed only what he chose to show.

She wondered then if she should tell him everything Anomius had said. No doubt he would inquire, and that the warlock believed he should soon be free of magical bonds was dramatic news. But how would Ochen react? Would he destroy the mirror, for fear of its aiding Anomius; and what might Anomius do then? Would Ochen expose her? Fleetingly, she thought of Calandryll, of his reaction, then pushed the thought firmly aside, for it served only to confuse her further and she felt now that she balanced her own survival.

To warn Ochen, or not?

It was a quandary from which only one certainty emerged: she did not want to die.

Whether or not she wished for immortality—whether or not that was possible—she was not sure. But she was certain she was not yet ready to give up her unnatural life.

Therefore, she decided as the sky outside paled to the opalescent grey of heralded dawn, she would continue to play the double game, to tell each mage in turn only so much and no more. She would hold back from Ochen the news that Anomius believed he should soon be freed just as she kept Ochen's existence from Anomius. She would continue in her role of willing servant until such time as she must finally choose her side, hoping along the way to glean more knowledge, to find answers to the dilemma.

It was all she could think of, and she turned from the brightening window, lying back on the bed, closing her eyes in simulation of ordinary sleep.

MORNING delivered no better answers, serving, rather, to muddle her the more.

She heard the keep wake, birds singing, men calling in the Jesseryte tongue, the snort and stamp of exercised horses, the rattle of metal and leather, the ring of hooves and boots. Scents rose in profusion, intoxicating: the sweat of animals and men, fresh dung, woodsmoke, cooking food, the pristine odor of stone overlaid with the aftermath of Ochen's cleansing magic, and still, loud to her senses, the lingering offense of Rhythamun's. She rose and performed her toilette, wondering whether she should dress in the finery of the previous night or the robust leathers worn when she crossed Cuan na'For. The resplendent Jesseryte costume was more to her taste, but she thought it perhaps excessive, and so chose the simpler outfit, likely more acceptable to her . . . She was not sure . . . Companions? Comrades? She cursed, unladylike, angry with herself; for her own confusion, and no less with the men who tugged the strings of her destiny. She laced the leathers and went to lean, idly, on the embrasure's sill, watching the bustle in the yard below, the wash of early morning sunlight over the ramparts, until a knocking on her door distracted her.

She found Katya outside, simply dressed, confirming her own choice of clothing, the Vanu woman smiling a greeting, the suggestion they avail themselves of the bathhouse in privacy. She agreed, wondering if this were some subterfuge, a pretext to questioning. Instead, Katya appeared only friendly, engaging in casual conversation, as though the previous night, Ochen's acceptance of her, confirmed her allegiance, dispelling any doubts the warrior woman might have entertained. She spoke of the quest and Bracht's vow—that seeming mightily strange to Cennaire—and of the journey ahead. In turn, Cennaire constructed a tale of her life in Kandahar, of a brief marriage, tragically ended, that left her with funds sufficient to invest in the imaginary caravan and a desire to see something of the larger world.

Katya laughed at that and said, "That much, at least, is granted you. I think none have gone where we shall travel."

Cennaire laughed back and said, "I wonder if I shall ever see Kandahar again."

Then Katya's face grew solemn and she said, "You might yet go back. It would surely be hard journeying, but likely easier than where we must go."

Cennaire shook her head. "No, I think I could not do that now." She brushed long strands of hair from her face, affecting a degree of embarrassment, that she might watch the flaxen woman from under lowered lashes. "I cannot say exactly why, but I feel . . . destined . . . to go with you."

"Perhaps," said Katya in serious tones, "you are. It would seem a strange coincidence that you came

to the Daggan Vhe at that particular time, that you
should meet us as you did."

Cennaire nodded, busying herself with soap as
she utilized her senses to determine if suspicion
lay behind Katya's musing words. She found none,
only acceptance, a proffered friendship, a trifle
wary, but nonetheless genuine. It seemed then that
her initial assumption had been correct: that
Ochen's approbation was sufficient guarantee of
her probity.

"Perhaps," Katya went on when Cennaire offered
no reply, "the Younger Gods brought you there.
They take a hand in this, as they may, and perhaps
you've a part to play."

"Think you so?" Cennaire had no need to feign
puzzlement. "How might that be?"

"I make no pretense of understanding the workings of the gods," Katya answered. "But that you
were in that particular place, at that particular
time . . ." She shrugged, water streaming from
bronzed shoulders, and smiled mischievously,
"Certainly Calandryll believes it so."

Cennaire lowered her face, pretending modesty,
and said, "He is very handsome. And a prince of
Lysse—I was surprised he is not wed."

"He's a prince no longer, but an outlaw," Katya
replied. "He was in love once, but she wed his
brother."

"And is he still?" Cennaire asked.

"With her?" Katya said. "No."

Cennaire smiled then, and murmured, "Good."

Katya nodded without offering further comment,
instead suggesting that they quit the bath and find
their breakfasts, with which Cennaire agreed, not
wishing to overplay her hand.

They found the hall, Calandryll and Bracht already settled, eating, Ochen and Chazali with

them, greeting the two women courteously as they approached. Cennaire looked toward the wazir, but his wrinkled face remained inscrutable behind its smile, and he went rapidly back to his conversation with the kiriwashen. Katya took a place at Bracht's side, answering the Kern's smile with her own, their voices soft as they spoke, excluding the others. Cennaire favored Calandryll with a demure smile as he drew back a stool, murmuring her thanks, pleasantly amused by the flush that promptly suffused his cheeks.

"We may leave tomorrow," he advised her, struggling to hide the confusion her proximity aroused. "Ochen will have cleansed the keep by then, he says, and we depart at dawn."

Cennaire nodded, accepting the food a servant set before her, eating with pretended appetite as Calandryll made small talk that to his ears sounded clumsy, to hers charming. Her life, her beauty, had put her often enough in the way of compliments and men's boasting, and usually their approach had been direct—the negotiation of a commercial transaction larded with fine words—and she found Calandryll's innocence refreshing. That he had not the least idea she was once a courtesan made little difference: he might well have boasted of his own exploits, which far outweighed the petty feats of her sundry other admirers, but that was not his way. He complimented her, yes, but awkwardly, and honestly, as if quite unaccustomed to the ritual interchanges between men and women, and that she found entirely engaging. She eased his way a little; not too much, for she remembered her part and forwent the myriad tricks and subtleties she might otherwise have employed, but just enough he began to feel more at ease, less embarrassed.

Then, as the plates were cleared, Chazali announced that he would leave them, to find Temchen and check the keep's defenses. The departure of the kiriwashen emptied the dining hall as if on a signal, and Ochen, too, excused himself, leaving the four alone. They might well, Cennaire thought, have taken their ease, enjoyed some degree of leisure before departing on what seemed certain to be a long and hazardous journey, but Bracht suggested they attend their horses and the others offered no protest: they made their way to the stables.

Their animals had been watered and fed, but stood in need of grooming, and it seemed still, from the attitudes of the Jesserytes in the yard, that the larger horses, Bracht's great stallion in particular, were regarded with awe, and more than a little nervousness. The Kern laughed and set promptly to currying the black, crooning endearments that were answered with snickers of contentment, as if man and horse conducted a conversation in some language known only to them.

"I think," Calandryll remarked as he set to work on his chestnut, Cennaire watching from the gate, "that Bracht loves that horse near as much as he does Katya."

"And you?" she asked, the coquetry slipping out unbidden, a habit. "Who commands your affections?"

The stable was shadowy, but she thought he blushed. Certainly, he bent his head closer to the gelding's glossy flank, applying the brush with renewed vigor as he mumbled, "A man's horse is a valuable thing . . . it deserves care."

Cennaire laughed gently, looking to dispel his awkwardness, asking, "Shall you choose a mount for me? I know little of horses."

"Better that Bracht do that," he replied modestly.
"He's a far better judge of horseflesh than I."

She nodded, choosing not to pursue the conversation, content to simply stand and watch, sometimes handing him a tool he needed, aware of his tentative smile as their fingers touched. It was a companionable silence, and for a while she felt herself far younger, the intervening years slipping away so that she could imagine herself a girl again, watching a brother tend their plow horse on the farm she had almost forgotten.

It was a brief enough respite, for soon the grooming was done and Bracht emerged from the black horse's stall with the suggestion they practice their swordplay. Katya and Calandryll agreed readily and they returned, not without difficulty in the maze of crepuscular corridors, to their quarters, to gather up the weapons left there in deference to the Jesserytes' hospitality.

The keep bustled now and they were hard put to gain more than fleeting directions to a yard suitable for sword practice, those men they encountered hurrying about their duties, with little time to spare to call instructions over their shoulders as they trotted briskly on. Consequently, the four found themselves often lost, wandering seemingly deserted corridors lined with closed doors, often devoid of windows, helpless until some other group of busy men was met. The place was unlike any fortress Calandryll had seen, as if constructed of a single vast block of stone through which passages and chambers had been cut, the exterior walls not separate but integral with the interior parts, the courtyards found suddenly, where corridors ended in balconies or windows, or low doors. It reminded him somewhat of an anthill, the Jesserytes its hymenopterous inhabitants.

Their social hierarchy, too, seemed as rigid as the insects', for when the four finally descended a narrow stairway into a yard where warriors clad in mail and leather drilled with swords and hook-bladed pikes, they were turned away.

This was not, they were told by a meticulously polite officer, a training ground suitable for such honored guests. Better—the suggestion couched in terms that brooked no argument—that they find the yard used by the kotu-zen. A man was ordered to bring them there and they followed him along yet more twilit passages to a second yard, this occupied by warriors in the jet armor worn by Chazali and Temchen.

All activity ceased as they entered, abruptly frozen by their presence. Their escort bowed low and barked an explanation that was answered with a grunt and a dismissive wave. He scurried quickly away, leaving them facing an audience of the kotu-zen, whose stance, Calandryll thought, expressed a mixture of curiosity and outrage, as though some protocol was breached.

The warrior to whom their escort had spoken raised his veil and bowed, his tawny eyes carefully impassive as he studied them.

"What service may I render?" he asked.

Bracht slapped his sheathed falchion and said, "We'd unlimber our sword arms."

The kotu-zen's eyes rounded as his gaze encompassed the saber hung on Katya's belt. "The ladies, too?" Surprise lent his voice a roughened edge.

"Aye," Bracht answered cheerfully, grinning in Katya's direction. "This lady wields a blade better than most men."

The comment aroused a murmuring, clearly shocked, among the onlookers, and Calandryll set a warning hand on Bracht's arm.

"Is it not your custom?" he asked.

The kotu-zen shook his head vigorously, his expression suggesting he was torn between horror at so outlandish a notion and the desire to remain polite. "No," he gasped at last. "The women of the kotu do not . . ." He caught himself with visible effort. "They do not indulge in the manly arts."

"Manly?" Bracht shook off Calandryll's restraining hand. "Ahrd, *man*, I'd wager this woman could take any of you."

More familiar now with the Jesseryte's physiognomy, Calandryll saw outrage on the warrior's face. Quickly he said, "In Cuan na'For and in Vanu—from whence my friends come—it is the custom that women bear arms and understand their use. Does this offend, we apologize."

He aped the Jesseryte's bow, awaiting a reaction. The kotu-zen swallowed, clearly taken aback. He seemed to find the idea preposterous. Finally he said, "Such is not our way."

Bracht opened his mouth to argue, but Katya murmured, "I'd not offend our hosts. Best we leave it," stilling his protest.

Now the kotu-zen appeared embarrassed, stroking a gauntleted hand over the oiled mustache he wore. Calandryll smiled, seeking to put the man at ease, and suggested, "Perhaps there is some private yard where we might practice?"

The warrior thought a moment, then nodded, albeit a trifle reluctantly.

"And gear we might borrow?" added Bracht.

Again the kotu-zen nodded, grunting an affirmative, and spun on his heel to snap out brisk orders that sent two men running to fetch jerkins of padded leather, instructing another to conduct the outlanders to a more suitable ward. Calandryll and Bracht shouldered the jerkins, voicing their thanks, and followed their armored guide from the practice yard. Behind him, Calandryll heard someone mutter, "Barbarians," and another, the voice disbelieving, "Their women fight?"

Bracht chuckled, shaking his head in disbelief; Calandryll threw him a warning glance, indicating their guide and gesturing the Kern to silence. These folk did, indeed, seem strange, but they were no less allies—vital allies—and it was as well to honor their customs. *And we,* he thought as they strode more of the dim-lit corridors, *likely seem as odd to them.*

They were brought to a small yard, the sky a rectangle of blue above, the walls high all around, and windowless, as if the place were chosen for its obscurity, that none might witness this breach of etiquette that put blades in the hands of women. Their guide bowed, unspeaking, and left them there.

"Strange folk," Bracht murmured as he tugged on a jerkin. "Do they cosset their women, then?"

"It looks so." Calandryll shrugged. "But while we go among them, we'd best respect their ways."

"Then best hope we go unopposed." Katya laughed. "For are we attacked, I shall likely shock them more."

"Or turn their ways over"—Bracht grinned—"do their women take your example."

Cennaire, whose life was somewhat more attuned to the ways of the Jesserytes, found it not at all odd that women should not fight, and started in surprise when Bracht handed her a thick-padded jerkin.

"You say you've no blade skill?" he queried, and when she shook her head, "then as well you learn a little."

The suggestion alarmed her, for she thought such

practice might well reveal her superior strength, and she hesitated, her pause misinterpreted by Calandryll, who said gallantly, "No harm shall come you."

"And your life perhaps be later saved," added Katya, she, too, thinking Cennaire's reluctance stemmed from some natural delicacy. "Look you, I'll work with you. Best we start with knives, I think."

There seemed no ready escape and Cennaire could only agree. She donned the jerkin, gingerly drawing the dagger sheathed on her waist, thinking that did she forget herself, she could likely cut clear through the leather Katya wore to wound the Vanu woman. Katya, thinking her unnerved by the blade, murmured encouragement, explaining how the weapon should be held, how her feet be placed to balance her weight.

"Forward and up," she advised, pantomiming the move. "Drive the point in below the ribs, toward the heart. Your thumb should rest against the quillon. When you strike, strike from the shoulder, with all your weight behind the blow. Now, try it."

Cennaire obeyed, holding back her full strength, and was surprised to find her thrust deflected, turned aside by a seemingly casual flick of Katya's wrist that sent her arm out to the side, the tip of the flaxen-haired woman's dagger touching lightly on her jerkin.

"No signals," Katya warned. "Your eyes told me of your intention, and your feet. Give no warning of your move. Now, look you . . ."

She proceeded to demonstrate and Cennaire found herself intrigued by the lethal ballet, realizing that strength alone was not enough, and that she might learn much from this tutor. She applied herself, following Katya's instructions, seeing how a movement of the wrist could turn a blow, how a feint could deceive and unbalance an attacker. It was not unlike the learning of dance steps, and at that she had always been adept; equally, it was a matter of anticipating her opponent's intentions, and in that, too, her past life stood her in good stead. Soon she found herself enjoying the lesson, her only concern that she limit herself to what a mortal body might accomplish.

She was barely aware of the clangor of steel on steel as Calandryll and Bracht set to with their swords, intent on Katya, on the intricacies of step and counterstep, attack and parry and riposte, finding it a fascinating game. One, she thought, that might well prove most useful in the uncertain future. It occurred to her that did she but become adept, she would likely be unbeatable: to the advantage of strength she could add those preternatural senses that would allow her to forecast her opponent's moves, and thus few could defeat her. And if they did, what matter? A blade between her ribs could not kill her. She resisted the temptation to experiment, however, intent for now on learning the basic skills of this deadly art without such secret reserves.

Time passed unnoticed, so intent was she on the lesson, until Katya called a halt, smiling. "Enough for now," she cried as Cennaire stood poised to attack again. "You learn fast."

"Sufficient practice and she could be a passable bladeswoman," Bracht said, and Cennaire turned to find the Kern and Calandryll watching, their own weapons sheathed now.

"The gods grant she's no need," said Calandryll, his face grave, as if he feared for her future safety.

"Did I not do well?" she asked.

"Excellently," he replied. "But even so . . ."

He shrugged, then staggered as Bracht slapped him on the back, chuckling. "Ahrd," the Kern declared cheerfully, "do you subscribe to this odd notion of our hosts now?" and Calandryll grinned ruefully, shaking his head.

Katya said, "Were the world not so disordered there'd be no need. But given where we go and who we go against, it's as well Cennaire be able to protect herself."

Calandryll nodded, sobered by that reminder, and they shed their jerkins, returning along barely remembered corridors to the yard where the kotu-zen had drilled.

The sun stood beyond its zenith now and the place was emptied of the black-armored warriors, men in tunics of grey cotton—presumably, Calandryll decided, denoting some lower caste—busily tending an array of weaponry. Fletchers feathered arrows, others worked on mail armor, two grinding wheels filled the air with the shriek of sharpened steel. It seemed the keep readied for the war, though all fell still as the outlanders entered, the grey-clad men watching them in silence, reinforcing the somewhat unnerving feeling that they were, indeed, strangers in this land.

None spoke until Calandryll asked where they should stow the practice gear, and then a man stepped forward, bowing deferentially, offering to take the jerkins, as if so humble a task were beneath the dignity of the four.

"Ahrd, but all this subservience sets my teeth on edge," Bracht muttered in the Envah.

"I think they rank us kotu-zen," Calandryll returned. "And it seems the kotu-zen enjoy such privilege."

The Kern snorted, glancing round at the still-silent onlookers, who appeared to await further in-

structions, or for the departure of the visitors,
before commencing their duties. "I'm more at ease
with the ways of Cuan na'For," he murmured.
"Even Secca was not so formal."

"Still, we're here." Calandryll grinned and
handed the waiting man his jerkin. "And in a foreign land we'd best accept foreign ways."

Bracht grunted, but made no further comment,
merely tossing the padded leathers into the waiting
arms. Katya and Cennaire passed theirs over and
the man scurried off.

"Do we find the dining hall again?" Katya suggested. "I've an appetite."

"Save we lose ourselves in this maze," Bracht
agreed, his earlier good humor a little waned. "The
sooner we take the road, the better."

"Bracht," Katya advised Cennaire with deliberate
solemnity, "is never entirely happy save he sits his
horse awhile each day."

"So Calandryll suggested," Cennaire replied,
smiling.

And was abruptly struck by the odd thought that
she felt at ease with these three, as if they were,
truly, comrades. She held her smile, frozen, as the
concomitant thought came hard on the heels of
that first, instinctive, feeling: that it would be a sad
thing were she forced to slay them.

She drove the notion away, assuming a careless
gaiety, as they quit the yard and found the dining
hall.

The great room was no better lit than before, and
deserted by all save Ochen, who sat alone at the
high table, platters of cold meat, cheeses, and bread
before him, a cup of wine in his age-gnarled hand.

He greeted them cheerfully, motioning them to
the seats on either side, explaining that the midday

meal was taken some time past, the cold cuts left for their delectation.

"I fear," Calandryll said, filling a cup with pale wine, "that we breached some protocol with our sword practice."

The wazir nodded, chuckling. "The kotu-zen are a trifle rigid in their sense of etiquette," he declared. "But no matter; it need not concern you."

"We've much to learn," Calandryll apologized.

"No less do we," said Ochen. "We've closed ourselves away so long our customs stultify somewhat. The notion that a woman should bear a sword is anathema to some here. Yet did you not"—he smiled in Katya's direction, managing to encompass Cennaire in the same look—"I think perhaps Rhythamun should already have won the day."

"And we two be likely slain," Bracht agreed, raising a cup in toast to the warrior woman. "Had Katya not come to our aid in Kharasul, I think the Chaipaku might well have left us dead."

Katya smiled, more intent on the food than flattery. Calandryll said, "Even so, I'd not offend our hosts. Have you time, some outline of your customs would be welcome."

"I've time now," Ochen returned. "The keep is cleansed; better, I've set the walls with occult defenses. Chazali and Temchen look to the physical aspects, so save you've some better way to pass the afternoon . . ."

Calandryll feared Bracht would suggest they put the horses through their paces, and said quickly, giving the Kern no time to speak, "Aye, that would be useful."

"Well then." Ochen topped his cup, sipped, leaning forward with elbows on table. "Some little I think you know already, from Chazali."

"Who is kotu," Calandryll said, nodding. "The warrior caste."

"All here are kotu," Ochen explained. "But even among the kotu there are degrees of rank. Chazali, Temchen—those warriors you encountered this morning—are kotu-zen, who are the highest of the caste."

"And wear the black armor?" asked Calandryll.

"Indeed," said Ochen, his wrinkled face splitting in a deeper smile. "Only the kotu-zen may wear such armor, which in turn is marked with the insignia of their rank and clan. Did my magic allow, I'd invest you with knowledge of our written language. But, sadly, that is beyond my powers."

"The gift of your tongue is great enough." Calandryll returned the wazir's smile. "Who, then, are the men clad in mail and leather?"

"Kotu-anj," said Ochen. "They are usually foot soldiers, though they may ride as need dictates."

"The men I saw, across the Kess Imbrun," Cennaire interjected, "they wore mail and leather. The one Rhythamun . . . took . . . he was so dressed."

"Then he was kotu-anj," Ochen murmured, thoughtful now. "Which must render him the harder to find—the kotu-zen are relatively few in numbers, the kotu-anj many."

Bracht mouthed a curse, met with a rustling of the wazir's tunic as he shrugged, saying, "That shall not prevent our hunting him down, Horul willing. But do we forget Rhythamun and his foul intent for the moment? We can do nothing now—nothing until dawn—so let us speak of more palatable matters."

Calandryll was content enough with that: his curiosity about this strange land was mightily aroused. "The servants," he said, "those men we met in the grey tunics—are they kotu?"

"All here are kotu," Ochen repeated. "These keeps that ward our borders may be manned only by warriors. Hence there are no women, save"—he ducked his head to Katya, Cennaire—"such honored guests as you. Those who serve at table, who perform the more menial duties, are kotu-ji. They aspire to become kotu-anj, but must first prove themselves."

"And the kotu-anj," asked Calandryll, utterly intrigued now by this multilayered society, "do they aspire to become kotu-zen?"

"They cannot," Ochen told him. "The kotu-zen come only from the highborn families. Theirs is a privilege of blood right."

"Ahrd, but you inhabit an odd land." Bracht shook his head, frowning. "In Cuan na'For all men are equal. Or can make themselves so."

Ochen's wrinkles assumed a vaguely apologetic expression. "So it has been down the centuries," he murmured blandly. "I think that perhaps Cuan na'For is a freer land than most, for are Lysse and Kandahar not ordered in similar degrees of rank?"

"The Tyrant rules Kandahar," said Cennaire.

"And the cities of Lysse are ruled by their domms," Calandryll added. "After them, the great families."

"And Vanu?" Ochen asked of Katya. "What of that mysterious land?"

"All are deemed equal," she replied, "and all choose who shall speak for them in our councils, that the voice of every man and woman be heard."

"To each his own," Ochen murmured, seeming a little taken aback by so revolutionary a notion. Then he chuckled: "Horul, but a fresh wind should blow through this land did our women take up such ideas; or the lesser castes."

He appeared to find the idea greatly amusing, for

he sat awhile shaking his head and rocking slightly, his eyes narrowed to slits as his smile grew broader. It seemed to Calandryll he found the notion not without appeal, as if he might even welcome the wind of change.

"And the wazirs?" Calandryll asked. "Where does your caste stand in all of this?"

Ochen sobered a little, though still his smile was wide. "We are privileged above all, I think," he answered, "for any—man or woman—gifted with the occult talent may become wazir, no matter their family's station. The talent is noticeable in childhood and those so gifted are watched carefully, until it is agreed they should train as ki-wazir. Sometimes the gift fades, but those who go on to become wazir are considered equal with the highest of the kotu-zen. Save for the wazir-narimasu, who stand with the Shendii—the greatest of all."

"But still, for all their greatness," Bracht remarked, "unable to defeat these rebels who threaten Anwar-teng."

"So it is," Ochen confirmed. "But look you, did the wazir-narimasu turn to the dark ways their ability to hold closed the gate should be gone, and then . . . Then did Tharn awake, how should they deny the god entry into the world?"

Bracht frowned, swirling wine around his cup, then said, "*If* the Mad God wakes, why should he come back by way of Anwar-teng? Might he not cross the Borrhun-maj? Or do the wazir-narimasu guard that road, too?"

"A good question," Ochen said, grave now, no longer beaming, "and no, the wazir-narimasu do not guard that road. The First Gods set such magicks about the Borrhun-maj that not even Tharn may come that way."

Now Calandryll frowned. "But you believe

Rhythamun might reach Tharn by that route," he said carefully. "Across the mountains or by way of Anwar-teng, you said. How is that possible, be there such wardings and guardians in attendance?"

"I say the crossing of the Borrhun-maj is nigh impossible for any mortal man," replied the wazir slowly. "And the existence of the gate in Anwar-teng is a secret kept close. But . . ." He paused, sighed, his face suddenly ancient beyond even the years etched there. "But . . . Rhythamun has the Arcanum, no? And that book is both guide and guardian—with that, Rhythamun doubtless knows of the gate, *and* holds the means to survive the crossing of the Borrhun-maj."

The import of his words struck deep, like a honed blade. Calandryll swallowed, his next question voiced gruff: "Say you then, does he succeed in reaching either goal—teng or mountains—the day is his?"

Ochen looked into his eyes, at each waiting face, solemnly, and shook his head once, a small movement, suggestive of doubt. "It may be," he said softly, "but not necessarily so. To use the hold's gate, he must first reach Anwar-teng, enter the city. Guised as he is in stolen shape, he can likely do that, but it will not be easy. More likely—does he choose that path—he'll league himself with the rebels, hoping the siege proves successful and he find entry in the confusion. Should he choose to attempt the Borrhun-maj, then still he must travel there, and even bearing the Arcanum I think his progress must be slowed. Horul willing, we shall intercept him ere then."

"And if we do not?" It was Bracht who spoke, blunt as ever: Calandryll sat silent, momentarily awed by the terrifying prospect of failure. "If he remains ahead of us, crosses to . . . whatever lies beyond?"

"Then those who can must go after him," Ochen said. "The crossing alone is not the end of it. Even does he reach Tharn's resting place, still he must work the gramaryes of raising."

"Those who can?" asked Katya. "What mean you by that?"

"That such magicks ward the gates as deny entry to most," the wazir answered. "There have been those of my calling, in the past, who dared the attempt, seeking to destroy the Mad God. Instead, it was they who were destroyed."

Bracht snorted sour laughter; drained his cup. "The odds stack daily higher against us."

"Would you turn back then?" asked Ochen, his voice deceptively mild. "It is not too late."

"All men must die." The Kern stared at the ancient sorcerer as if puzzled, or affronted. Reaching for the decanter, he shook his head. "Is that reason to give up?"

"No," murmured Calandryll, the single negative echoed by Katya, who added, "Think you we should survive?"

"You've encountered a gate before, no?" Ochen met the gaze of her grey eyes with the tawny twinkle of his own. "And lived to tell the tale, no? Did the spaewife in Lysse not speak of three? And in Gessyth, did the Old Ones not say the same? I think perhaps you three in all the world might survive."

"We three?" Calandryll looked to Cennaire, almost reached out to take her hand. "Are we not four now? Five, do you take a part."

"For now, aye." Ochen nodded, agreeing, looking himself toward Cennaire. "It is my belief the Younger Gods brought you four together, and you shall have all the aid I may command. But be it needful you go beyond this world . . . then—there—I cannot know."

"You'll not make the attempt?" demanded Bracht. "Be it needful?"

"All men must die." Ochen succeeded in aping the Kern's earlier expression, even mimicking his tone. "No, I do not tell you I'll not make the attempt. Only that I may not survive it."

"I think perhaps you've the blood of Cuan na'For in your veins." Bracht's teeth flashed white in the gloom, his blue eyes crinkling as he laughed approval of the old man's courage. "Was there insult in my words, I apologize."

"You need not," said Ochen, "but I thank you."

"Likely, then, we three alone; be it necessary." Calandryll turned from the wazir to Cennaire, back. "Shall Cennaire be safe, do we attempt this crossing?"

Ochen looked to the Kand woman, not speaking for a moment. Cennaire met his unfathomable gaze, wondering what thoughts passed behind his furrowed brow, what doubts, what judgments. Then he smiled again and ducked his head, saying: "It may be the three *are* become four. But fear not, the lady Cennaire rides under wardship of the clan Makusen, and shall be safe."

"Perhaps," Calandryll suggested, "it were better she remain in Pamur-teng."

"No!" Cennaire blurted. "I go where you go."

What motivated her then, she was not sure. Whether fear of Anomius's wrath were she left behind, or genuine reluctance to leave Calandryll's side, she did not know; only that, somehow, she must remain with the questers. That above all else; the reasons, could she ever define them, could come later.

"Lady . . . Cennaire." Now Calandryll did take her hand, earnestly. "It may be you cannot go where we must. And surely Pamur-teng must be a safer refuge than the battlefield or the Borrhun-maj."

"I'll not leave you," she returned, fervent in her confusion, willing him to accept.

He squeezed her hand, smiling gently, and said, "If we must go through this gate, or attempt the mountains, either might destroy you. I'd not have that on my conscience."

"Then do not; let it be on mine," she answered, wondering if—as Anomius had once, cynically, suggested—she did indeed grow a conscience. "But still I'd go with you."

His smile brightened, as if some scarcely dared for hope was confirmed by her words. Almost, she felt guilty as he took her other hand and said, "I'd not see you face such hazard. No, this task is ours, as it was scried. You've no need to put your life in jeopardy."

His eyes were alight, yet still grave: she had no need of preternatural senses to know his ardor then, and almost cried out that she had no life to risk, only the hope of becoming again her own woman, free to choose her own course, masterless. She shook her head, seeking the words that might persuade him, frightened of revelation and of failure, no longer certain which she feared most.

Ochen came to her rescue. "Pamur-teng is a long ride distant," he murmured. "Do we reserve such decisions until then?"

Gratefully, Cennaire nodded. Bracht and Katya exchanged glances, partly surprised, partly amused. Calandryll let go her hands, once more blushing as he saw his comrades' speculative stares. Less confidently, he agreed: "Until we reach Pamur-teng."

"Which journey," Bracht opined, "may well prove hazardous enough itself."

"How so?" Calandryll turned to face the Kern. "We ride with Ochen, with Chazali's warriors as escort. Think you the rebels, or these tensai, shall threaten us?"

"The rebels, no." Ochen answered in Bracht's stead. "Perhaps the tensai, do they grow bold enough. But I suspect your comrade thinks of another danger."

Calandryll frowned incomprehension, met with Ochen's bland stare, Bracht's grim chuckle.

"Do you forget the gramaryes Rhythamun leaves behind?" asked the Kern, his visage abruptly serious. "The dire-wolf in the Gann Peaks? His possession of Morrach? The affliction in this keep? Think you he'll not set his trail with similar obstacles?"

"Dera!" Calandryll gasped, nodding, and sighed. "Aye, I'd put those things behind me."

"It may well be," Bracht warned, "that more lie ahead."

6

THE sun was only a little way risen when they
quit the keep, the air offering a chilled reminder that summer aged, ground mist swirling
ethereal about the fetlocks of the horses, a brumous
sea that dulled the steady pounding of their hooves.
Chazali, his jet armor glistening beetle-bright, led
the way, a retinue of fifty kotu-zen in loose formation behind, protective about Calandryll and the
others, Ochen riding with them, the brightest of all
in a brilliant traveling robe of gold and silver. The
Jesseryte warriors were armed with swords and
long, recurved bows, and it seemed to Calandryll
they were a formidable enough force to deter any
save the largest of tensai bands. Of defense against
Rhythamun's magic, he was less confident, remembering Ochen's suggestion that the mysterious
power discerned in him rendered him more vulnerable on the occult plane. Still, he told himself as
they cantered briskly northward, Ochen had also
suggested that forewarned was forearmed, and the
wazir's own power was surely protection against

fell sortilege. Such doubts he relegated to the
hinder part of his mind, concentrating on the way
ahead.

There, the mist began to dissipate, melted by the
climbing sun and the wind, revealing a flat landscape of grass duller than the lush verdancy of
Cuan na'For, as if thirsty. There was no formal
road, but the passage of centuries had eroded the
green for a width of some fifty paces, exposing a
swath of yellowish-brown earth packed hard as
stone by hooves and wheels and tramping feet. It
ran straight for leagues, a ribbon that passed beyond Calandryll's vision, lost in the featurcless blur
of the horizon. Overhead, birds wheeled on the
thermal currents rising from the Kess Imbrun, dark
specks against the steely blue expanse of sky, that
marked to the east by narrow streamers of white
cloud.

There was something indefinably forbidding
about the terrain, a brooding sensation that reminded Calandryll of the unpleasant presentiment
he had felt on approaching the keep. It seemed, almost, that the land waited, aware of their passage,
watching silently like some vast beast, and he shivered involuntarily despite the burgeoning warmth.

"You feel it, too?"

He turned, startled, to find Ochen close by his
side, looking up, the ancient face shaded by the
brim of a fanciful cap, though not so much he
missed the inquiring gleam in the wazir's slitted
eyes.

"I felt . . ." He shrugged, unable to express the
sensation clearly.

"Watched?" the old man asked. "As though hidden eyes are on you?"

Calandryll nodded, glancing swiftly to Bracht and
Katya, riding side by side, apparently unconcerned.

Surely were there anything tangible, the Kern's keen senses would have noticed, but neither one showed any hint of foreboding, only pleasure at the freedom of the open country, of being again ahorse.

"What is it?" he queried, growing nervous, thinking that if Ochen felt it, then it was not an imaginary experience.

"The land is troubled," Ochen called over the steady drumbeat of the hooves. "The aethyr is disturbed. War spills blood, and that is felt in the occult realm. Linked as you are to the aethyr, so you feel the land's bane."

Calandryll frowned. "I've not known such feelings ere now," he shouted. "Save on entering the keep; and that was surely the aftermath of Rhythamun's magicks."

"Moment by moment we draw closer to those portals Tharn may use," Ochen returned. "And that same spilled blood strengthens the god. You feel that, I think."

"Then shall it get worse?" The thought was ugly, disconcerting. "Shall it grow daily stronger?"

"Likely it shall." Ochen's equanimous agreement was alarming. "But doubtless you'll learn to live with it; learn to accommodate it."

Calandryll swallowed, tasting dust on his tongue, and wiped his mouth. "None others seem aware of this."

"They are not," called Ochen. "But they are not invested with that power residing in you."

Calandryll grimaced: did this strange power sorcerers discerned in him offer any advantages, he had yet to find them; so far, it appeared chiefly a disadvantage.

Ochen saw his expression and smiled, albeit a trifle solemnly. "I believe," he declared, "that when the time comes, you'll find that strength a greater boon than bane."

"When the time comes?"

He waited for an answer, but the wazir gave none, only nodded, still smiling, and allowed his mount to drift a little distance away, deliberately precluding further conversation. Calandryll watched him awhile, thinking that Bracht had spoken aright when he complained of the riddles spoken by mages. Even so, the explanation went some little way to easing his discomfort, for it was one thing to feel watched, unaware of the reason, and another to know the cause. He still felt as if invisible eyes bore into his back, but Ochen's words—as likely had been the intention—rendered the experience more bearable and he squared his shoulders, endeavoring to ignore the sensation.

It grew easier as the day grew older, though there was little enough to occupy his attention. The landscape continued monotonous, a flat plain devoid of features other than the brown line of the track that ran ever onward through the grass; the Jesserytes seemed indisposed to conversation, the which, anyway, was difficult at the pace Chazali set; Bracht and Katya appeared lost in their delight at the ride; and Cennaire seemed too occupied with holding her seat to risk the distraction of words. As the hours passed, Calandryll became familiar with the feeling, resisting the impulse to rise in his stirrups to scan the surrounding countryside, settling more easily on his saddle, letting the chestnut gelding match the gait of the accompanying horses.

They halted at noon, where a low well of yellow stone stood beside the trail, and Calandryll found himself seated next to Chazali, the kiriwashen unlatching his face-concealing veil from the downsweeping cheek pieces of his helmet and pushing back the metal that he might eat. Hoping he gave no offense, and intrigued by the custom, Calandryll ventured to ask why the Jesserytes favored such masks.

Chazali swallowed bread, meticulously brushing crumbs from his short beard, and said, "That those we slay shall not take our image with them into the next life," in a tone that suggested the answer was obvious.

He appeared to consider that explanation enough until he caught Calandryll's dubious frown and expanded: "Must I slay a man, he is likely to curse me for it. Does he die with my face in his eyes, his ghost will remember and perhaps come back to haunt me. Is it not so in Lysse?"

"No." Calandryll shook his head. "We believe the dead are gone from this world. Save a necromancer call them back, they go to face Dera's judgment and may not return."

"That is odd," Chazali said, carefully polite. "I had wondered why you rode unmasked."

"Does Horul not judge your dead?" Calandryll wondered.

"When it is their time, aye," answered Chazali, seeming now a little disturbed by the tenor of the conversation. "But these are matters better answered by a wazir—Ochen might explain better than I."

It was clear enough indication of reluctance on the part of the kiriwashen and Calandryll let it go, determining that he would question Ochen later, for that part of him—albeit diminished somewhat by the exigencies of the quest—that remained scholarly hungered for knowledge of the strange people become his allies.

The afternoon passed without event; without, indeed, any change in the terrain or the pace of their passage. The Jesseryte horses, for all they were of lesser stature than the Kernish animals, were hardy beasts, cantering tirelessly onward, devouring the leagues between the well found at noon and that beside which they halted as the sun touched the western horizon.

The moon, a sliver cut now from its fullness, rode above the eastern skyline, the first stars glinting faintly in the blue velvet twilight. The kotuzen, although usually attended by kotu-ji, seemed entirely familiar with the necessities of travel, stringing the horses on a picket line and starting cookfires with taciturn efficiency. A guard was mounted, the bows broken out from their stowage, and food set to cooking. Darkness fell as they began to eat, the night still save for the strengthened wind that rustled, eerily to Calandryll's thinking, through the grass. The familiar stamp and snort of horses, the cheery blaze of the fires, even the silent, sable-armored warriors, were comforting—the sensation of brooding, watchful eyes increased with the coming of the night, as if the darkness coagulated, solidifying beyond the fireglow into a vital, physical presence.

It was the desire to stay that feeling no less than genuine curiosity that prompted Calandryll to engage the wazir in a dialogue.

"These wells," he began, as casually as he was able, "do they mark all the road?"

"Aye." Ochen drew his robe closer about his slender frame, the fantastic embroidery painted crimson by the fires, his gnarled hands lost in the wide sleeves. "Between all the tengs—at least, as often as is possible—the trails are set with wells that riders may find each noon and evening. That"—he chuckled—"was one gift the Great Khan gave us. It was on his order the wells were dug—that his armies might always find water."

"The Great Khan," Calandryll murmured. "You never speak his name."

A hand, the painted nails glinting bright, emerged from the wazir's sleeve to shape a gesture in the empty air as he shook his head. "Nor is it written," he said. "Nor do any of the monuments he built to himself stand still. Such was decreed by the Mahzlen and the wazir-narimasu: that all the Great Khan wrought should be forgotten, never again repeated. When he died, his body was burned and the ashes cast into Lake Galil, that they might be carried out of the land."

Calandryll nodded, feeling the wind stroke his hair. For an instant he thought spectral fingers brushed him, and fought the urge to duck his head. Instead, he settled a hand about the hilt of his sword, finding reassurance in the contact, and said, "I'd not give offense, but I spoke this noonday with Chazali, about the veils worn by your warriors."

He repeated what the kiriwashen had told him, and Ochen bowed his head a moment, then said, "I think your Dera is very different to our Horul, as your land is different to mine. Our lives are different, and perhaps so are our deaths—here we believe that none lives a single life, but several, the number determined by the deeds performed in each existence. When a body dies, the spirit enters Zajan-ma—that place beyond this, where spirits not yet sundered from their worldly existence dwell—and there await rebirth: his, or her, next cycle upon the land. Horul sets each soul a task that the reborn must dispense before they go on. Finally, when the cycle is completed, those souls who have satisfied Horul are granted eternal rest in Haruga-Kita."

"This is very different," Calandryll agreed. "But still I do not understand why it is so important a warrior's face be hidden."

"Because," said Ochen, his voice patient, his expression amused, "there are some spirits that wax vengeful. The Zajan-ma is a place of waiting— think of it as a chamber with many doors, from which a soul sufficiently misguided, sufficiently determined, may flee. So, does that spirit know the face of its body's destroyer, it might seek revenge. Might return to haunt the one who slew its body. Better, then, it does not see the face; and that is why the kotu conceal their faces."

"And yet," Calandryll murmured, "you do not cover your face. But you have told us your magic may be used belligerent."

"This," Ochen returned with massive confidence, "is my final cycle upon the land. Those gifted with the occult talent are in their last existence and need no longer fear the petty vengeances of ghosts."

"What of us?" Calandryll gestured to where Bracht and Katya lay upon their blankets, speaking softly, privately, together; to Cennaire, who sat a little way off, listening to the conversation. "Shall we go to Haruga-Kita, do we die along this road? Or shall we come back?"

Ochen's face grew thoughtful then and for a time he stared at the sparks drifting from the fires. "I do not know," he said at last. "Perhaps you shall each go to your own gods. Or perhaps this is your last life. I know only the beliefs of my own land."

Calandryll thought a moment, then asked: "Are you afraid of dying?"

"Of dying, no," answered Ochen soberly. "Of the manner of it, aye. I am no more immune to pain than any other man, and I should much sooner breathe my last in some comfortable bed, with friendly faces all about me, than, oh, say slain along this road by tensai arrows."

"Think you that is likely?" Mention of the tensai shifted Calandryll's thoughts from the metaphysical to the more immediate dangers of the journey. "Would tensai attack such a band as this?"

"Were theirs large enough," said Ochen, "or hungry enough."

His tone remained cheerful, dismissive of such danger, or philosophical. Calandryll's grip tightened on the hilt of the straightsword, his eyes moving automatically from the wazir's face to the guards pacing the camp's perimeter, the moonlit shadows beyond. Ochen saw his gaze and chuckled.

"Fear not," he said. "At least, not yet. We stand too close to the keep that danger should threaten. Do tensai look to attack, that will come later."

"Later?" Calandryll found poor reassurance in the sorcerer's words. "How much later?"

"Perhaps two days," returned Ochen. "Ere long this flat country breaks up into hills and valleys, better watered than this plain, more fertile. There are villages there, settlements of gettu the tensai find easy prey. Usually, the warriors of Pamur-teng hold the bandits in check, but with this cursed war ..." He paused, his manner become suddenly somber. "I fear the patrols are called to fight, and the tensai thus ride free. Horul! The Mad God thrives on blood and chaos, and it would seem this land of mine descends into that morass."

"Do the gettu not fight?" Calandryll asked.

"The gettu? They are farmers," Ochen said, his tone akin to Chazali's, earlier. Then he shook his head, chuckling, and said, "Forgive me, I forget how little you know these Jesseryte domains. The gettu do not fight because Horul has assigned them the duty of farming, not that of bearing arms. Theirs is to raise crops, cattle—those things farmers do—not to fight; and so they rely on the kotu to defend them. Does that prove impossible, they give the tensai what the tensai demand."

Calandryll pondered that explanation, bemused by so strict a social structure, one that seemed, to him, overly rigid, designed—by the Jesserytes' god, or by the holders of power?—to favor those born into the warrior caste. That whole villages should meekly submit to the depredations of outlaws seemed an affront, an abomination. In Lysse all men were free to bear arms, and what few outlaws existed were soon enough brought to justice either by the city legions or the local inhabitants.

He forbore to question Ochen on that, for fear of giving offense, and asked instead, "And the tensai? Are they assigned their role by Horul? Does the god give them the duty of outlawry?"

Some measure of doubt, of innate disbelief, remained in his voice, for Ochen eyed him a moment, and he was reminded of his tutors in Secca, when he had asked some question that ran withershins to their formal discourse.

He was relieved when the wazir smiled and said, "Two schools of thought exist concerning that. Some claim it so—that Horul makes souls tensai; the other that they are dissatisfied spirits escaped from Zajan-ma to claim what life they can."

"And you?" asked Calandryll. "To which school do you belong?"

"A third," said Ochen blandly. "A very small, dissenting school that allows for doubt. In a nutshell—I do not know."

His wrinkled face contorted in a huge smile, so friendly that Calandryll could do little but return it, laughing as the wazir laughed and added, "And

every hour I spend with you—your comrades—
prompts me to doubt more. I suspect, my friend,
that your presence here will change this land beyond imagining. Look you, even now Chazali ac-
cepts that your women bear arms—an unprecedent
thing!—and that you ride unmasked. He acknowl-
edges you equal to kotu-zen or wazir—and he has
never laid eyes on foreigners before; already you
change his way of thinking! And mine."

This last was said softer, thoughtfully, and
Calandryll inquired, "How so?"

"Your questions." Ochen shrugged, his expression become pensive now. "You prompt me to consider ways of life I had not before thought much
about. You prompt me to wonder why outlanders
come to battle with the Mad God. Why was that
undertaking not given to we Jesserytes? We wazirs,
the wazir-narimasu, all know of Tharn, yet when
this Rhythamun threatens to awake the god, who
comes? An outlawed prince of Lysse; a clansman of
Cuan na'For; a warrior woman out of Vanu."

"Only we three?" Calandryll studied the old
man, turned his eyes toward Cennaire, who rested
silent on her blanket, seemingly intent on the examination of her clothing. "Are we not now augmented?"

Ochen followed the direction of his gaze. "Perhaps," he said. "Certainly I think all have a part to
play. But at the end . . . ?"

He shrugged again, noncommittal, his features
suddenly enigmatic. Calandryll would have questioned him further, but just then Chazali approached, asking that the wazir employ his magic
to guard the camp and Ochen excused himself, going off with the kiriwashen to set warding cantrips
about the perimeters, leaving Calandryll alone.

He looked about, seeing each fire surrounded by

a group of kotu-zen. Sometimes a face would turn, inscrutable, toward the outlanders, but none moved to join them, or engage them in conversation, for all they must have appeared as fabulous to the Jesserytes as did those warriors to them. The fire beside which he sat seemed boundaried by some unspoken, invisible fence, left to those not born on the Jesseryn Plain, Ochen the only one readily willing to bridge the gap established by their different cultures, their mores and beliefs.

Those differences had been emphasized that dawn, as they prepared to depart the keep. Kotu-ji had stood with waiting horses, some even bold—or dutiful—enough that they held the Kernish animals, each beast flanked by a second grey-clad man. As the group approached, those had dropped on hands and knees, human mounting stools for the kotu-zen. Chazali and his warriors had used them unthinking, stepping from yard to back to saddle with the casual assumption of habit. Calandryll had stared at the man kneeling beside his chestnut, and Bracht had scowled and asked, "Why do they so debase themselves?" Fortunately, he had thought to speak in his own tongue, so the precise meaning of his words had gone unknown. But not the import, for Chazali had glanced down from his saddle, and while his expression was hidden by his helmet's veil, the angle of his head, the set of his armored shoulders, had radiated disapproval. In the Jesseryte language Bracht had said, "Get up, man. I need no aid to mount my horse," and the kotu-ji had stared, uncomprehending and, so Calandryll felt, afraid. For his own part he had thought an instant that he might—perhaps should—follow the custom of the land, but it had seemed so great an affront to another living being that he should so use a man that he had beckoned the kotu-ji away, bowing in Chazali's direction and saying, "It is our custom to mount unaided." He had feared then that offense was taken, but Ochen had spoken briefly and softly with the kiriwashen, and Chazali had grunted and barked orders that the kneeling kotu-ji remove themselves, and the outlanders had sprung unhelped astride their animals.

No further mention had been made of the incident, and Chazali had remained courteous, but Calandryll felt the kiriwashen observed them somewhat askance. Difference piled on difference, he thought, and must surely continue so: he prayed their alliance should not be threatened.

"You are pensive."

Cennaire's voice brought him from contemplation and he smiled, turning toward the woman. She sat studying him, fireglow dancing in her raven hair, her dark skin ruddy in the light. Her eyes seemed huge as he looked into them.

"I thought on all the things that separate us from our newfound friends," he murmured. "How different our ways are, and how easy it is to offend them."

Cennaire nodded solemnly, thinking that he looked very young as he frowned; and very handsome. She said, "They are a strange folk, but surely they make allowance for our ways."

"So far, aye," he returned. "But when we reach Pamur-teng, what then? A city will surely impose far greater formality than the trail."

Cennaire shrugged carelessly: a courtesan grew accustomed to difference, to accommodating differing habits, else she did not prosper long. "We shall likely learn their ways as we travel," she suggested, "and in Pamur-teng we must go carefully. Observe, and perhaps change our ways."

Calandryll nodded, then grinned as he ducked his

head in Bracht's direction. "I am not so sure that Bracht will agree," he said.

"Bracht, too, must learn," she responded.

Calandryll shrugged tentative agreement. "We must all learn, I suppose. But even so . . ." He frowned again, shaking his head in rue and reluctance. "I cannot bring myself to use a man as a mounting stool, and that is but one small thing the Jesserytes take for granted."

Cennaire, that morning, had been perfectly willing to use the kotu-ji. It seemed to her that if such were the custom of the land, then it was no more than polite acceptance to follow that custom. She had abstained only because the others had done so. Now she wondered if she should voice such opinions, or if that expression would distance Calandryll. She opted for tact and said mildly, "If that is their way . . ."

Distaste showed on Calandryll's face and she fell silent. He said, "No," firmly, "I cannot use a man so. I cannot agree with that."

"Then in Pamur-teng we had best be on our guard," she said.

"Aye," he agreed. "And likely we shall not remain there long."

Cennaire was uncertain whether he spoke of himself, Bracht and Katya, or of them all, and that doubt troubled her. She could not allow herself interred in the city, but for now could find no sound argument to convince him she should remain with the questers. The only certainty was that she must be present when—if!—they secured the Arcanum. Somehow, therefore, she must find a reason to continue in their company; but what that reason might be, she could not for now decide. Did she seduce him, he might well still insist she remain in Pamur-teng—indeed, would likely feel the greater

need to see her safe, were he finally infatuated—
and that she could not countenance. Somehow she
must find a reason. It came to her that Ochen
might well be helpful in the matter, for it seemed
the enigmatic wazir had his own reasons for keeping her present, and perhaps he would furnish the
justification. Pragmatic, she decided to wait: the
city lay long leagues distant, and before they
reached the teng she trusted she should find a way.

Aloud, she ventured, "We've much to face before
then."

"You heard Ochen speak of the tensai?" Calandryll assumed a reassuring smile, gesturing at the
armored men around the fires. "Likely he is but
cautious—we're well enough protected, I think."

And bandits offer me little harm, thought
Cennaire, affecting a shudder as she played her part
of innocent, favoring him with a nervous look,
saying, "I've encountered such men before, remember."

Calandryll, entirely unaware she lied, smiled gallantly. "No harm shall come you while I live," he
promised. "And all Chazali's warriors stand betwixt you and any tensai so foolish as to attack
us."

For all she acted a role, Cennaire was touched by
his chivalry. Surely he was unlike any man she had
met before, and the thought that she might one day
betray him was a thing she pushed away, a thing
she realized she preferred not to contemplate. It
had been far easier before she met him, when he
had been only a faceless quarry and her purpose
singular.

Now her purpose clouded, as if his presence cast
a stone into the clear water of her intentions, and
she felt herself, in a way, lost, desultory as a rud-
derless vessel blown by contrary winds. Her only

course seemed to be go on, to play her part and wait to see which wind prevailed. It was not a circumstance she welcomed; it was a measure of her dissatisfaction that she allowed it to show on her face, scowling at the fire's merry blaze.

Misinterpreting, Calandryll said, "Surely we're too strong a party bandits will chance attacking. More likely they'll hide from such as we, and seek easier pickings."

"Aye." Swiftly, Cennaire transformed scowl to smile. "I am well protected, sir," she murmured. "And fortunate to have encountered so brave an escort."

Calandryll felt his cheeks grow warm at the compliment, trusting that the fire's light should hide his sudden embarrassment as his tongue tied and foundered for want of some glib response. Cennaire recognized his confusion—that awkwardness, she thought, rendered him all the more charming, for it served to emphasize his innocence, his lack of guile—and she chose to ease him, yawning deliberately, apologizing prettily, and expressing a desire to sleep.

Calandryll agreed readily enough, watching as she drew an unneeded blanket to her chin, her head resting on her saddle, and closed her luminous eyes. She was, he thought, without doubt the loveliest woman he had ever encountered, and possessed of admirable courage. He cursed himself for his clumsiness, wishing his tongue more subtle, that it might better express his feelings; wishing he were able to better define them. For a while, he continued to watch her, assuming her already sleeping, then himself stretched out, drawing up his own blanket.

❖   ❖   ❖

SAVE for the crackling of the fire and the soft sounds of the horses, the night was still. No nocturnal birds sang, nor insects buzzed; there was no hint of predators ranging the darkness. The moon lay yet easterly, silvering drifts of cloud in a sky that spread like a great indigo canopy pricked through with the glitter of stars. It seemed that whatever magicks Ochen set about the camp dulled the sensation of watching eyes, for while he still felt a vague discomfort it was not enough to stave off the demands of weariness: he felt his eyes grow heavy, closing, slumber's embrace welcome.

And then he thought he woke, roused by some summons now echoed into silence. He looked about, and gasped, though when he did he heard no sound, but felt terror grip him, for he looked down on the still and silent form of a fair-haired man he knew to be himself, sleeping soundly. Cennaire lay beside that shape, Bracht and Katya side by side across the fire. He saw the sleeping kotu-zen, recognized Ochen and Chazali, the wazir stirring as if he felt that bodiless observation, the dark shapes of the guards, the horses. It seemed he rose, spectral, spirit and body separated, helpless, for though he willed a return to physical form, he continued to ascend, as if drawn up by some power beyond his understanding or comprehension. Desperately he struggled, and in his struggling saw—if sight was what he used—that he was formless, without material shape.

Panic threatened. He shouted Bracht's name, Katya's, Ochen's, but still no sound emerged and none save the wazir shifted, and that but restlessly, as might a man in dream's grip.

This, though, was no dream, and were it nightmare it was one he knew, instinctively, contained a horrible reality, drawing the essence of his being out from its fleshly shell. He thought then of Rhythamun, and had he possessed his body he would have shuddered, but all he could do was watch the forms of his comrades and allies recede as he rose, upward like a feather or a drift of smoke borne on the faint wind, toward the distant stars.

In moments they were only blurs, indistinct about the pinprick glow of the fires, those lost as the wind, or whatever force carried him, changed his direction, he flotsam on its breath, drifting northward. Or so it seemed, for he watched pass below the flatlands, breaking up into the corrugated terrain promised by Ochen. Fires shone there, distant among wooded hills and watered valleys, and he saw villages, tilled fields, the shapes of sleeping, pastured animals.

He moved faster, gathering speed all the time, the land below blurring, the stars above seeming to shift in their courses, trailing light like blown sparks. He saw a great fertile plain dominated by a massive hold he thought must surely be Pamurteng, standing square, a vastly enlarged sister to the keep, all sparkling with the radiance of myriad lamplit windows, all lost, left behind as he traveled on.

More lights then, thousands, far below, tiny in the distance, and tents, horses, men: he guessed he looked upon an encamped army. And ahead lay another, greater, fires lit along both banks of a river that ran red with their light from a vast, moon-silvered lake. Lake Galil! And that hold beside the water, where the river ran out, must be Anwarteng.

He drew closer, slowing as if contrary forces tugged in opposed directions, permitting him a clearer view.

More than campfires illumined the night, he saw,

for from the great press about the hold, even from
the surface of the lake, where shapes too dark to
define floated, there came streamers of gold and
crimson, incandescent, rising in sparkling, fiery
arcs to crash against the walls of Anwar-teng, to descend beyond the ramparts, in explosions of searing
brilliance. Almost, he thought to hear cries in the
night, or feel the emotions of the folk below. It was
as though tides battered him. Anger, fear, outrage,
hatred, lust and hunger for what the city meant,
what it represented; no less the determination of
those within, solid purpose underscored with fear
of defeat, rapine, and worse.

He felt his soul assaulted then, that terrible out-
wash more than he thought he could bear, and
struggled, as dreaming men do, to return himself to
the normality of sleep. He could not, but briefly,
like a promise shouted from afar, he glimpsed the
sleeping shapes of Bracht and Katya, saw Cennaire,
her hair spread raven-lit about her face, Ochen
starting up from his blanket, pushing silver locks
from a face that creased in a multiplicity of wrinkles, each one a beacon of concern.

Then, helpless, he was dragged onward, over a
bleak wasteland of grey and silent stone like a
sandless desert, toward the wall that bulked massy
ahead, white-dressed, craggy and sharp as dragons'
teeth. He knew that barrier for the Borrhun-maj,
and knew with a dreadful certainty that some thing
beyond it, past its physical limits, within the occult realm, called him, summoned him. Knew, too,
that were his pneuma drawn there it might never
return, that soul and body would be sundered, the
one trapped, the other locked in eternal sleep until
it should waste and die.

He fought the driving pressure of the psychic current and it was akin to swimming against a fearful

tide. The night whispered that he should give in, that he could not resist, that he was weak, too weak to fight a power so much greater than his poor resources, and though he did his utmost, still it was as if his limbs grew lax, his muscles ached and screamed for respite, to drift and let the tide carry him, that he could do no more, only succumb.

He saw the mountains come closer, so high they melded with the sky, the sheen of snow and starlight, moonglow, become one, as if land and heavens coalesced in occult haar, the world ending, giving sway to another place. The fulgent misting shimmered, trembling and glittering with horrid appetite, and he knew in his soul that beyond it lay that limbo where Tharn resided; and that did he pierce that barrier, he should be forever lost, the quest damned, the Mad God free to await his resurrection.

He weakened, tugged onward, driven, and it seemed he heard laughter, confident and mocking, horribly triumphant. He recognized the sound—it was imprinted on his memory. He had heard it before, in Aldarin, when he and Katya had stood in the private chambers of Varent den Tarl and seen the contemptuous shape of Rhythamun appear from the discarded talisman that he, duped and all unwitting, had carried to Tezin-dar that the warlock might seize the Arcanum. Then—in the lost city and in Aldarin, both—he had felt a vast and righteous anger, a conviction wordless and beyond doubting that he had no choice, nor wanted any, save to oppose the chaos the Mad God would wreak on the world. Now that same anger gave him strength, enough he was able to fight the awful psychic current sweeping him toward the argental barrier.

He fought. In the names of all the Younger Gods; in the name of humanity itself. And his progress toward the aethyric haar slowed a little.

But not enough. Still he was drawn and driven, a swimmer caught in the buffeting of occult tides, grown soul-weary beyond physical comprehension. Had he existed then on the mundane plane, his limbs should have been leaden, his lungs aching, his eyes red-weary, his muscles screaming protest and surrender. But he refused that: he fought on.

And still was washed ever closer to the curtain betwixt the worlds of men and dreaming gods. The silver shimmering pulsed, hungry. The laughter increased: a crescendo of victory. It numbed his ears, threatened to drain his waning strength.

Then faltered.

His progress toward the occult barrier slowed. He hung a moment, suspended; with a tremendous effort turned the eyes of his pneuma back from the haar, toward the place of men.

He saw only the bleak, night-black steppe of the northernmost reaches of the Jesseryn Plain, no light there save what the moon and stars cast, lonely.

Then, far off, a beacon. A warm, golden glow like the sun rising through chill mist, calling travelers home, promising warmth and food, friendship and safety.

Like a swimmer treading water, he fixed his gaze on the light, only dimly aware that the laughter faded, more intent on summoning the last reserves of his strength to make the final effort, to go back.

Something, someone, called him. Not in words, but in terms of pure emotion, lending strength to his own outrage, encouraging his efforts, urging him on. It seemed impossible, hopeless, and a seductive whisper from beyond the fog, from some-

where else, told him it was so, that he had best
surrender, or be forever lost. That voice hinted at
reward, at pleasures undreamt of; and dreadful pun-
ishment did he continue to resist. The other, the
voice of the golden light, cried *Lies*, and *Strength*,
and *Courage*, and he struck out, reversing his direction, moving away from the haar, that, like the
laughter, fading irresolute. Had he looked back
then, he would have seen the jagged peaks of the
Borrhun-maj become again no more than mountains, impressive, vast, but only snow-clad stone
now. But he did not look back, too intent on return, feeling himself drawn by different pressures,
benign. The laughter became a memory tinged
with disappointment and frustration, and that lent
him resolve as he felt his passage speeded, his
pneuma winging southward again, steady toward
the light of the beacon.

He crossed the steppe, saw Lake Galil; felt
Anwar-teng beneath him, the hold seeming to em-
anate a gust of warm and comforting wind that
strengthened his passing, like a friendly draught
filling the sails of a homebound ship.

Briefly, he felt psychic hands clutch at him, a
pang of fear replaced by hope as their grip proved
weak, unable to halt him. A sensation of angry disappointment, of malign frustration, radiated from
somewhere, from someone—from Rhythamun!—
far below, and he reveled in that small triumph.

He sped faster and faster, uncaring now, confident again, heady and gleeful with the velocity,
winging steadily closer to the light, to safety.

And halted with an abruptness that left him
dizzy as he hovered, looking down on his supine
body, Ochen beside it—beside *him*—kneeling with
upraised hands, mouth moving in near-silent muttering.

Bracht and Katya and Cennaire crouched close to the wazir; all the camp was awake, Chazali and his warriors watching, grim sentinels, only the guards not intent on the sorcerer and his occult working.

Calandryll descended, reclaiming his corporeal form.

And opened his eyes to see Ochen smiling, shoulders sagging in exhausted relief.

"Horul, but I thought you lost then."

"Ahrd! What happened?"

"Praise all the gods you've returned."

They spoke together, tumbled words, Ochen and Bracht and Katya. Only Cennaire was silent, her eyes huge and awed, studying him with . . . he was not sure . . . anxiety, welcome, reverence? He smiled wanly, opening his mouth to speak, finding it dry, blinking as sweat ran into his eyes. He shivered, feverish a moment, and Bracht carried a cup to his mouth, an arm about his shoulders as the Kern bled water between his lips.

The water was refreshing, the solidity of Bracht's arm a comfort; he rested back against that support, drinking deep, and sighed, a long, shuddering sound.

"What happened?" he asked.

To feel his lips move, to know that cords vibrated in his throat, to be aware of the coolness of the water on his tongue, to hear his own voice again, all were wondrous sensations. No less the fire's warmth, the reality of the hard ground under him, the scents of leather and human skin, horses and woodsmoke. To know himself returned was unimaginable joy: he laughed.

Ochen set hands about his chin then, turning his face—the feel of the dry, warm flesh was in itself a comfort—and stared deep into his eyes. For an instant he felt himself almost lost again, falling into the tawny light of the sorcerer's gaze. But this was not like before—this light was akin to the beacon that had brought him back. He heard the wazir speak, softly, the words arcane, unintelligible.

Then Ochen said, "All is well. No taint remains."

"Taint?" Calandryll thrust abruptly forward, away from Bracht's arm, hearing his voice come harsh. "How say you, taint?"

"I suspect," the wazir said gently, "that our enemy sought to ensnare you. Perhaps to delude and seduce you. But he failed—no ill remains."

Calandryll swallowed, his throat dry again; Bracht proffered the cup, refilled, and he took it, able now to drink unaided. Ochen said, "Do you describe to me what happened and I can better explain it."

Calandryll nodded and told his story.

Ochen listened in grave silence, and when the telling was done said, "Rhythamun waxes ever more powerful—I warned of that, no? He closes on those portals through which Tharn's dreaming comes strong, and the Mad God knows it—reaches out to aid his minion. God and man, both, sought then to draw your pneuma from you, to deliver you into limbo. Had you entered that mist you saw— had you traversed that barrier between the worlds—I doubt you'd have returned."

"Then you've my thanks," Calandryll whispered. "For I'd not the strength to resist."

"But resist you did." Ochen laughed, an accolade, triumphant, his eyes sparkling between the narrow slits of the lids. "I gave you some help, aye; so did the wazir-narimasu of Anwar-teng, but you it was who defeated the enemy's intent."

"I was caught," Calandryll protested. "I was a leaf blown on the wind, no more."

"Much more," said Ochen. "Far more. There's a strength in you that withstands the blandishments of Rhythamun. Even Tharn's wiles! Horul, but they must be chagrined now!"

"You speak of this power in me?" Calandryll frowned, lost. "Was it not that allowed Rhythamun to suck out my pneuma?"

"Aye," said Ochen. "At least, it was your contiguity with the aethyr let him find you, but that same power gave you the strength to fight him—and Tharn—and that's a mighty gift."

"You name it gift?" asked Calandryll. "That a mage such as Rhythamun is able to part my soul from body? That seems more curse to me."

"Were you not so powerful as to resist, aye." Ochen nodded, absently patting Calandryll's shoulder, as might a parent or a pedagogue, explaining. "But you *were* able. Do you not see? No, of course not—forgive me, I assume knowledge you've no way of having. So, listen—most men—those not so gifted—would have been drawn out and forever lost. A 'normal' man, such as Bracht"—this was with an apologetic smile to the Kern—"is armored against such depradation by his very normality. He stands distant enough from the aethyr that he is, in effect, invisible. You, however, stand close—as I told you before—and so Rhythamun is able to find that part of you that exists on the occult plane."

He paused, and Bracht muttered, "Ahrd be thanked that I be normal. I stand with Calandryll on this—it seems more curse than blessing."

"Are the two not often the mutual faces of the same coin?" Ochen said. "The power in you, Calandryll, allows Rhythamun knowledge of you, and that knowledge waxes greater the closer he draws to his master. But equally, that same power grants you the ability to fight him better. Had you not that power, you should have crossed the barrier and been lost—we should now observe a body bereft of its animus, a wasting husk.

"But you possess that power! Horul, do you not see it? You withstood the blandishments of the Mad God! You were able to fight the machinations of Rhythamun!"

"I felt anger," Calandryll said, shrugging. "Anger and disgust at all Tharn stands for. No more than that."

"Which anger and disgust, righteous as they are, afforded you the power to deny the god," said Ochen. "I think that is a very great power."

"When first we saw the Vanu warboat . . ." Bracht spoke slowly, thoughtfully. "When we believed Katya our enemy . . . You called up that tempest to drive her off."

"And in Gash, when we were attacked," now Katya took up the theme, her grey eyes wide and wondering, "then you drove back the canoes. It was as though you summoned up a terrible wind."

"And in Kharasul," Bracht said, "when Xanthese and his Chaipaku looked to slay us . . . As in Gash, you fought like a man possessed."

"Or in fear of his life," said Calandryll.

"The spaewife there—Ellhyn—she said there was a power in you," Bracht murmured. "Do you not remember?"

"Varent's—Rhythamun's—stone." Calandryll shook his head. "That gave me the power."

"That is not what Ellhyn said." Katya studied him with wide, thoughtful eyes. "I recall her words."

There is power in you that you could use without the stone, did you know the way of it.

"So," he admitted, "do I. But even so . . ."

"And in Vishat'yi," Bracht pressed, "Menelian said the same, or so you advised us."

"And did you not bring Burash himself to our aid?" Katya added. "When the Chaipaku would have drowned us?"

Calandryll threw up protesting hands: to fight these arguments was as hard as the struggle against Tharn's summons, Rhythamun's force; harder, for they came from friends.

"So be it," he allowed. "So it is, if you all say so—there's some power in me I cannot understand. Only that it renders me prey to magic. That it enables Rhythamun to find me; to draw me out like some vampire leeching my blood, my soul."

"Against that," Ochen said gently, "there are cantrips of defense that I can teach you, be you willing."

"Willing?" Calandryll hawked bitter laughter. "Should I refuse such gramaryes as relieve me of that fear? I'd sooner go sleepless than bed down each night wondering if I must journey to Tharn's domains."

"And yet," the wazir said, "there's some advantage may be gained from that."

"Advantage?" Calandryll fixed the ancient face with a disbelieving stare, wary of what thoughts lay behind those musing eyes. "I'd sooner keep my soul, Ochen, be it all the same to you."

Ochen smiled, bowing his head. "I'd not see you lose your soul," he declared, his voice earnest, "but I think you able to go where few others may. I am not without occult resources, but even I could not have resisted that tide that swept you along."

"You brought me back," Calandryll said, almost a shout, for he began to sense the direction of the mage's thinking; and liked it not at all. "Had you not used your talent, I'd be lost."

"I tell you again," Ochen said, carefully now, his voice pitched low, insistent, "that it was your power as much as mine that brought you back. Alone, I could not have done it."

"You were aided by the wazir-narimasu. You said as much." Calandryll's response came hoarse, trepidation mounting apace. "Your magic and theirs, you said."

"Nor did I lie," promised the wazir. "But still, had you not that unknown power, ours should not have been sufficient to stand against those forces that looked to destroy you. To destroy the threat you mean to them."

"What say you?" asked Calandryll, softer, almost resigned: he felt sure he would not enjoy the answer.

"That you are better able than any wazir in this land to confront, to observe, Rhythamun," Ochen replied. "I do not pretend to understand how this is so—save it be some gift of the Younger Gods, or some duty imposed on you—only that I believe you may go to, and return from, places none others may."

"I do not understand." Again Calandryll shook his head. "You speak in riddles."

He looked to Bracht for support, and found none, for the Kern, like all of them, was intent on the wazir.

"There is much of riddling in sorcery," Ochen agreed with what Calandryll felt was an altogether unseemly cheerfulness. "It is a riddle in itself, I sometimes think. But heed—you were able to come close to Tharn and yet return. Rhythamun sent you there, to end your threat, and so may you go to him. You've the power for it, and he knows it . . ."

"I'd put my blade in him, were I able," Calandryll snapped.

"Aye." Ochen nodded absently, caught in the flow of his own thoughts. "And perhaps it shall come to that; but edged steel is not the only way to destroy Rhythamun. Could we draw out his pneuma, as he did yours, then so might we ensnare him just as he endeavored to trap you."

Presentiment, trepidation, fear, all came together in unwelcome understanding: Calandryll said, "You'd ask me to hunt him on the occult plane?"

"Only after I've taught you the cantrips of protection," said Ochen. "Only when you're armored with such sortilege as can wholly defend you. And only with the aid of the wazir-narimasu."

"You ask much of me." Calandryll ducked his head, staring at the straightsword that rested, sheathed, beside him; touched the hilt. "I'd face him man to man. But there . . . ?"

"It may be that," Ochen said. "Perhaps you shall face him at sword's point. But were you able to defeat him within the sphere of the aethyr . . . Is it not his defeat you seek?"

Calandryll looked up, feeling himself almost defeated, and nodded: "Aye."

"We speak," said Ochen, "of a future some time distant. There's much you need to learn before such attempt may be safely made. I need teach you the cantrips, the gramaryes . . . until you know them sound, I'll round you with protections. Only when I know you safe, would I ask you attempt the aethyr. And that not until we close on Anwarteng."

"Then round me," Calandryll said wearily, "for I'm mightily tired now, and I'd sleep—be it safe."

"Safe for now," Ochen promised. "He'll not make another attempt this night, and we'll speak again on the morrow."

Calandryll nodded, and lay back. Ochen left him;

Chazali and his watching warriors returned to their blankets; Bracht and Katya murmured reassurances that he answered with a yawn. Cennaire said, "You are very brave," and he smiled, thinking that a wonderful compliment, for he felt very afraid.

7

I T was some comfort that they must stand far
  closer to Anwar-teng before Ochen would ask
him to go voluntarily into that strange bodiless
state, for he felt entirely inadequate to the task,
and not at all eager to again face those malign forces he had felt buffet him. He did not properly
comprehend why that proximity was necessary,
save—as Ochen explained, somewhat vaguely as
they broke their fast and struck camp—that the
power of the wazir-narimasu was limited by the
hostility surrounding the hold, that emotion
strengthening the Mad God's estivatious sendings,
and that without their anchoring support it was too
hazardous an undertaking. It was enough for
Calandryll that the attempt should be delayed. Besides, there was much else to occupy him.

  In the days and nights that followed he was
largely in Ochen's company, to the exclusion of all
other, become once more a scholar, his thirst for
knowledge reawakened, titillated by the recondite
vistas the wazir gradually revealed, no longer ab-

stract but of practical, perhaps even vital, importance.

Tutored by the patient sorcerer, he learned better
to understand the nature of the aethyr, to see that
plane not as some arcane dimension, but as one si-
multaneous with the physical. It was, Ochen ex-
pounded, as though two worlds existed contiguous,
one—the aethyr—invisible to most inhabitants of
the other, only those gifted with the talent able to
perceive the existence of the neighboring plane
through such windows as their thaumaturgical
skills created. Likewise there were doors could be
built, through which the inhabitants of one plane
might enter the other.

"And like any door," he explained one night as
all around them the camp settled to sleep and
Calandryll struggled to hold open weary eyes,
"they may close behind you. Be barred, even,
against your going back. Such is what Rhythamun
attempted."

"And doubtless would again," Calandryll returned around a stifled yawn. "Save this mystic
door be propped open."

"Which it may be," Ochen assured, seeming not
the least tired, so that Calandryll wondered if he
needed sleep at all. "One adept in the sorcerous
arts does that instinctively. But such a level of skill
requires years of tutelage."

Calandryll nodded sleepily, and Ochen chuckled
and said, "Enough for now. Go find your bed, rest—
and we'll speak again come dawn."

That seemed not far off as Calandryll stretched
himself blear-eyed on his blanket, for the moon
was past its zenith and closing on the western horizon. He sighed, luxuriating in the prospect of at
least a few hours' sleep, and looked to where
Cennaire lay, little more than an arm's length from

his makeshift bed. He did not know she watched him from under hooded lids, marveling at all she had heard; only that he was disappointed they had so little opportunity now to speak together.

No more was he able to converse much with Bracht or Katya, for each morning he woke to Ochen's cheerful summons, given barely sufficient time to perform his ablutions and snatch a plate of food before the wazir embarked again on his tutoring.

He learned, slowly, how to recognize those occult pressures that warned of aethyric scrutiny, and to wrap his tongue around the complex syllables of the protective cantrips. Not yet so well that Ochen failed to ward him round with gramaryes each night, nor yet so well that he might defend himself, but enough he began to believe that in time he should be able to master the sortilege, and that was a reassurance. So, too, was his preoccupation with the task, for he practiced dutifully as he rode, and that inured him to the still-present feeling of observation, that now better understood as he learned more about the occult plane and the interaction of aethyr and mundane.

It was both boon and bane, for even as he came to accept that he did, indeed, possess some power unfathomable, some occult talent that would, as time passed and he learned to employ it, stand him in good stead to battle Rhythamun in the realm of the aethyr, so he began to comprehend the enormity of that other world. He had pursued the wizard thinking purely in terms of the physical—that he and his comrades must overtake the sorcerer and face him with naked steel. Now, his knowledge daily broadening, he began to understand that Rhythamun—the *essence*, the animus, of that being—barely existed in physical terms, save what

he stole. Now it came to him that he and his
comrades—for still those prophecies that had
brought them together surely pertained—must confront the warlock on another level. Rhythamun, he
realized, had become over the centuries of his evil
existence a creature of almost purely aethyric energy, his fell powers waxing ever stronger as he
drew ever closer to Tharn. Calandryll began to
doubt that steel alone might end the threat.

That doubt he put to Ochen, and more.

They sat, as had become their custom, a little
way distant from the rest, cloaked against the cooling of the summer as the sky darkened and the fast-
waning moon climbed above a range of low hills.
Timber grew thick along the flanks, leaves that began already to assume the hues of autumn rustling
in the wind that blew soft from the north, the
wells that had daily marked their passage no longer
needed, for little streams plashed down the ridges
to striate the bottomlands with rivers. Chazali had
increased the nightly watch against the possibility
of tensai attack, and for a while each dusk the air
grew pungent with the almond scent of Ochen's
sortilege. On the morrow, so Calandryll understood, they would reach a village, a settlement of
gettu, where there might be news of the war and
the more immediate danger of predatory outlaws.
For now he felt a different concern, outlining his
doubts to the silver-haired mage.

"He can be slain," Ochen said. "Doubt that not,
for no man is truly immortal, and some part of
Rhythamun remains yet in this world. Were it otherwise, he should be a ghost."

"And yet surely he *must* have outlived his mortal span," Calandryll responded. "Is your—forgive
me, for I intend no disrespect—concept of the after-
life correct, then has he not entered your Zajan-ma

as each life terminates? And come back—escaped!—from there?"

"Likely so. Think you the Younger Gods are infallible?" Ochen accepted the suggestion without demur, chuckling. "Were that so, how should such as Rhythamun exist at all? Horul and his kin would surely order the world to their design, and none should ever threaten their dominance. But that is not the way of things—no, it seems to me the gods are bound by some order beyond their breaking; certainly beyond my understanding. Have you not said that Burash and Dera, both, spoke of a design past their changing? I suspect the Younger Gods need men as men need them; that Yl and Kyta, or perhaps even a power beyond them, left behind a structure neither man nor god can alter."

"So?" Calandryll demanded.

"So Rhythamun has attained such knowledge as enables him to shake off the ties that bind other souls in Zajan-ma," said Ochen. "He is ... How shall I put this?. . . a free spirit. He defies the bonds that govern our existence; defies the gods themselves. He returns from Zajan-ma not as a ghost, neither as a reborn soul sent by Horul, but as and by his own agency, escaping the judgment of mine or any other's god. And that is surely an abomination."

"On that," Calandryll said, "we agree. But still it's a metaphysical concern. I ask you again—shall steel prevail against him?"

Ochen thought a moment, then said: "I believe that did you put a blade in his fleshly form, then, aye, you would slay his stolen shape. That blade Dera blessed likely has the power to sever his hold and send his pneuma into the aethyr, where it would likely wander in limbo forever. Unless . . ."

He paused and Calandryll demanded, "Unless?"

"He has such power as could bring him back again," said Ochen.

"Dera!" Calandryll drove clenched fists against the wind, voice harsh and horrified. "You say he is truly immortal! That even be he slain, he will come back. That his threat is ever-present."

"Evil *is* an ever-present threat," Ochen responded. "But were he thus slain, then that part of him that lived on might be hunted down within the aethyr and destroyed. Do you not see? His strength is his weakness—he lusts for domination, for mortal power. Why else should he seek to raise the Mad God? Only because he looks to stand at Tharn's elbow, the god's temporal lieutenant. He loves life too much to leave it—why else prolong his existence? Only because he *cannot* let go his hold on this world of men.

"*That* is his weakness—that love of fleshly being. He is loath to quit this world; too loath, and were his pneuma sundered from his flesh, then he must surely be greatly weakened. Oh, aye, I know he counts his life by long ages, and must certainly be most difficult to destroy, but still it can be done."

"To achieve that victory, we must apprehend him before he has opportunity to use the gate in Anwar-teng," Calandryll said carefully, exploring the tenons of his doubt. "Or before he crosses the Borrhun-maj, no? Do I understand properly everything you have taught me, then to be certain of victory, we must take the Arcanum from him before he gains a portal to Tharn's limbo. And to take the Arcanum from him must surely mean slaying him."

"Aye," said Ochen, face bland and enigmatic in the pale light of the moon. "You put it well, and I think you understand your lessons."

Calandryll nodded brief acknowledgment and said, "And everything you teach me serves to protect *me*. Yet if the scryings I've heard are true, then three must face Rhythamun—Bracht and Katya must stand with me. How shall *they* be protected if we must go into that place beyond the Borrhunmaj?"

Ochen drew golden nails down through the strands of his mustache; tugged a moment on the wisps of his beard. Then: "I do not know."

"You do not know?"

The wazir shook his head; a slight, wary movement.

"Nor if they shall—can!—survive?"

Again that negative movement.

Calandryll stared aghast at his mentor. He was tempted to shout accusations, arguments; he forced himself to calm, to reason, and when he spoke was pleased to hear his voice come even, disciplined.

"Surely, then, you must tutor them as you do me—afford them what defenses you can."

"Were that possible, think you I'd not?" the wazir asked. "I cannot, for they've not the talent. You alone command that power."

"Then I alone must do it," Calandryll said.

"I do not believe that is the way of it," Ochen returned. "A design exists beyond my comprehension and it binds you three to this duty. It may be broken, aye—you've but to turn about, go back . . ."

Calandryll cut him off with an angry gesture. "No! That I'll not countenance; neither my comrades."

"Then you and they have little choice," said Ochen. "Have you?"

"You say they're doomed," Calandryll sighed.

"I say that if Rhythamun is to be defeated, if Tharn is to be denied resurrection," Ochen replied, "then you, all three, must go on. Perhaps . . ." He paused, chewing a moment on the tails of his mustache, thoughtful. "Perhaps even Cennaire must go with you."

"No!" Now Calandryll's voice rose loud in denial, forced quieter by effort of will as he continued: "She's no part in it, save she knows Rhythamun's new face. And save we find him ere he makes that crossing—which must surely render this debate redundant—then there can be no need that she attempt the aethyr."

Ochen's response was an enigmatic shrug, a further stroking of his beard. "What need was there she met you at all?" he asked.

"Chance," answered Calandryll. "Her misfortune."

"Think you so?" the wazir murmured. "Do you not think it a very great stretching of coincidence that in all the vastness of Cuan na'For she should have come to that single place where you and Rhythamun both came?"

It was the selfsame argument Calandryll had used: he shook his head, helplessly. "What else?" he asked, low-voiced, sensing defeat. "Say you she, too, is a part of this design?"

"I think it likely," said Ochen, and Calandryll felt a hesitation before the sorcerer added: "I suspect she's a part to play."

"Defenseless as the others?" The slight hesitation went forgotten. "Mortal and unwarded?"

Almost, Ochen said, "Hardly mortal," but his training was sufficient that he held back the retort, saying instead, "If it be ordained so, then aye."

"I say you no," Calandryll snapped. "I say she remains safe in Pamur-teng. Also that we put all this to Bracht and Katya—grant them the freedom of choice."

"I think you know their choice." Ochen smiled ruefully. "Such folk as those two will not give up. Even be it at price of their lives, their very souls, still they'll go on."

"Aye." Calandryll nodded reluctantly. "But Cennaire?"

"Should be allowed some say in her own destiny," said the wazir. "Let us put all this to them in the morning, and agree to bide by their decisions."

"Dera!" Calandryll shook his head. "I'd thought to meet dangers, but not such as you promise."

"It may still be that we find Rhythamun in time," Ochen said gently, his words designed to reassure. "In mortal guise he can move no faster than mortal's pace. The body he possesses must eat still; sometimes rest. He needs horses still."

"We thought as much as we pursued him across Cuan na'For." Calandryll snorted a bitter laugh. "And he found ways to elude us—he's not the scruples of mortal men."

"Aye." The wazir's wrinkled face puckered, moonlit. "I've thought on that."

"To what conclusion?"

"That speed is of the essence," replied Ochen, "and that Chazali and his warriors must move slower than a small band."

"You say we should abandon the army?" Calandryll demanded.

"I think that the wiser course," said the wazir. "Chazali must travel with foot soldiers, a baggage train, while you and I—the others—may proceed faster do we go alone."

"Save Anwar-teng be fallen," Calandryll said.

"It has not yet." Ochen gestured at the night, as if at some entity beyond the star-pocked darkness. "Had it, the aethyr should ring loud with the event."

A horrible possibility descended on Calandryll, and almost, he offered no response. It seemed easier—at least less frightening—to let the thought pass unvoiced; and yet, he knew, he must examine every avenue, no matter how skeptical, how gloomy. "Which might yet happen," he said. "And if it does, then Rhythamun wins entry to the portal; while we shall surely be denied even access to the hold."

"In such event," said Ochen with such calm as was near irritating, "we shall likely all be slain by the rebels. Save I shall know, does that event occur, and we can avoid the hold—go on directly to the Borrhun-maj."

"Without the aid of the wazir-narimasu?" Calandryll had learned his lessons well: knew now how vital were the high sorcerers to the quest. "With Rhythamun passed through? No, surely does Anwarteng fall, we've lost."

"Is that, as Bracht would likely say," asked Ochen, "good enough reason to admit defeat? I tell you, that while we live, and dare this venture, we've hope still."

"A commodity that seems fast-waning," muttered Calandryll.

"And therefore to be clutched the harder," said Ochen. "Horul, my friend, do we latch ourselves to every doubt that comes to mind, we'd as well surrender now. Would you take that course?"

"No." Calandryll grinned, resolution strengthened by the sorcerer's admonishment. "You know I'd not."

"Then we press on," said Ochen firmly. "Trusting in the Younger Gods to aid us."

"But still advise the others of what may lie ahead," said Calandryll. "And still I'd see Cennaire

ensconced safe in Pamur-teng, for I'm not yet convinced she need go with us farther."

Ochen nodded, glancing a moment to where the
woman lay, wondering if she listened, confident of
her decision. He said, "On that matter we may well
find some answer in Pamur-teng. There are gijans
there—folk you'd name spaewives—who possess
such talents as discern some measure of the future,
and who may likely perceive the patterning of your
destinies better than I. Do we consult one, and you
abide by what she sees?"

Somewhat reluctantly, Calandryll murmured his
agreement.

"Then," said Ochen, "let us take that course.
And meanwhile, take each day as it comes. First,
let us gain Pamur-teng, then onward to Anwar-
teng. Beyond that . . .?"

"The gods, or destiny, or whatever spins out this
web, shall decide," Calandryll allowed. "But—
Dera!—I wish there were fewer strands to it."

Ochen chuckled. "Were men simpler creatures,
and less prone to ambition, then it would be so,"
he said. "But they are not, and it is not; and we've
no choice but to follow the strands."

Calandryll sighed, gesturing his acceptance, and
the wazir began to speak again of occult matters, of
meditations and mantras, the formulation of mental patterns and the abstruse language that opened
the ways into the invisible world.

SLEEP was become a commodity short supplied and
it seemed only moments since Calandryll's head
had touched the hard pillow of his saddle that he
was shaken awake, Ochen kneeling beside him,
proffering a mug of steaming, scented tea. Dew
decked the grass, the sun not yet risen, though the

sky grew light in the east and the fires were fresh-stoked, the kotu-zen saddling their horses in preparation for speedy departure. Calandryll groaned, rubbing dew-moistened hands over sleep-foggy eyes, and took the mug. Ochen waited patiently as he drank, the sweet-flavored liquid helping to dispel the last vestiges of a slumber he had sooner continued.

"They await us," the wazir said. "But Chazali will not long delay."

For a moment, Calandryll did not understand, but then Ochen gestured to where Bracht and Katya, Cennaire, sat beside their fire, and the promises of the past night came back: he nodded and thrust off his blanket, weary head spinning an instant as he rose. He smoothed his rumpled clothes, belted on his sword, and went to take his place beside his comrades.

"This wizardry would seem hard work," Bracht remarked with ruthless good cheer. "Do you sleep at all now?"

More sympathetic, Katya piled a platter with hard bread, meat. Calandryll smiled his thanks, and she said, "There is some matter you'd discuss, so Ochen advises us."

Calandryll nodded, swallowed, and, with Ochen's help, outlined to them his concerns.

When he was done, Bracht shrugged and said, "Have we not for some while now assumed we might likely need to cross the Borrhun-maj? What changes?"

"I stand with Ochen on this," said Katya. "There's some design in what we do, and I see no reason to shift our course."

"You've not felt Tharn's presence as I did." Calandryll looked from one to the other. "Nor have you the gift of Ochen's teaching."

"We've spoken with gods," Katya returned calmly, "and walked roads unknown to men. I say I put my faith in the Younger Gods and, though I cannot comprehend it, this design. I say we go on."

"Aye." Bracht nodded, dew glinting on the jet of his hair, glancing briefly at his hands. "I thought to die when Jehenne nailed me to the tree, but I live still. I never thought to cross the Cuan na'Dru with the Gruagach for guides, but cross the forest we did. Must we, then, venture into some other unknown, so we shall."

Calandryll had anticipated no less, but still he liked it not, for it seemed to him they spoke— bravely—of a place beyond their understanding, of hazards beyond their comprehension. He sought arguments, but even as he searched, Bracht spoke again.

"We talk of future dangers," the Kern said, his pragmatism characteristic, "while we likely face more immediate hazards. Let us do as Ochen suggests—gain Pamur-teng and consult this gijan."

Calandryll sighed, his objections foundered on the rock of their resolution, and looked to Cennaire. "All prophecies have told of three," he said. "You should be safer in Pamur-teng."

Cennaire met his gaze with wide hazel eyes, aware that Ochen studied her as she replied, "Let the gijan decide. Does she bid me remain, then so be it; does she scry the three have become four, then I go with you."

And even does she bid me stay, she thought, *still I must go with you. Or after you, clandestine; for one way or the other our destinies are joined, and do I allow you to go on without me Anomius will surely vent his anger on my heart.*

She saw Ochen duck his head then, smiling a

small and secret smile, as if he approved her response.

Aloud, the wazir said, "Then our course is set. As far as Pamur-teng, at least."

Calandryll shrugged acceptance, denied further opportunity to dissuade by Chazali's shouted orders, hurriedly finishing his breakfast as Bracht kicked the fire dead and all about, the kotu-zen readied for departure. It was difficult to be sorry they chose to face the unknown with him, for, were he honest with himself, he would sooner venture there with comrades such as these at his side than alone. To feel guilty was far easier, and he fell into a somewhat morose silence as he slung his saddle on the chestnut gelding and climbed astride.

More orders from the kiriwashen sent two men ahead of the main party, and as he fell into line, Calandryll called out to Ochen, asking the reason.

Mist, timber, and the slope they descended afforded the wazir time to answer: "We enter the tensai lands now. They scout the way."

Calandryll remembered the fires he had seen burning, likely in these same hills, as his pneuma had been drawn northward, thinking now they might well have been the camp lights of outlaw bands, and a thought came to him. "Why do you not travel the aethyr?" he wondered. "Would your spirit not prove a more reliable guide?"

Ochen's answer was delayed by a thickening of the trees, their mounts forced apart awhile. Then: "Have you not understood? To travel that plane, total concentration is needed. That journeying is done only when the body has nothing else to concern it. For now, I've sufficient to occupy me. Horul knows, I am but a poor horseman, and save I concentrate I shall likely fall off this awkward beast."

Calandryll might have felt chastened, had the
wazir not grinned then, ruefully, and mouthed a
foul curse as his animal faltered where the slope,
emptying of trees, angled steeper, the grass slippery. Instead, he chuckled and cried, "Then I'll not
burden you with more questions. Save one—might
we not this night go out to seek the tensai camps?"

"*We* might not," returned Ochen, "for you are altogether too vulnerable and I'd not lead Rhythamun to you. Now, for Horul's sake, leave me be
lest I come to grief and tumble down."

Before them, the mist rolled back, revealing a
narrow expanse of valley, a river glittering blue-
silver along its length, alders shining golden beside
the water. Beyond, the slope was gentle, spread
with maples and birch, conifers like sentinels along
the ridgetop, black against the azure of the early
morning sky. Chazali's scouts climbed the gradient,
halting among the pines to wave the travelers on,
and Calandryll urged the chestnut across the shallow water, heeling the gelding up the rise.

Over the crest a wide saddleback stretched between two low hills, the timber there cut through
with narrow trails, running down the incline to the
valley beyond. From the vantage point of the ridge,
a clearing was visible at the roadway's foot, timber
cut back alongside a ribbon of sunlit water, smoke
rising in thin streamers, lining the sky's clear blue
with misty grey pennants that swirled and broke
on the wind. They went down the trail, meander-
ing between the trees, emerging on the river, a ford
there, and where it left the water a palisaded village. Chazali's scouts stood their horses between
open gates, men in dun-colored shirts and grubby
breeks standing nervously about them, bowing as
the jet-armored kotu-zen came closer, bowing

deeper as they saw the kiriwashen at the column's head.

Chazali raised a commanding árm, shouting for his men to halt and wait beyond the walls as he rode in through the gates. Ochen followed him, waving the outlanders to come after.

Within, Calandryll saw a collection of rough and ragged huts, all timber-built, with smokeholes in their roofs, small, overhung verandahs about their sides. From among them watched women and children, eyes wide and, he thought, frightened, wary and as ready to flee as the deer in the woods. He thought to see Chazali dismount, and certainly the village menfolk appeared to stand ready to prostrate themselves to receive the kiriwashen's foot. Instead, Chazali waved them back, remaining in his saddle as he unlatched his veil and threw the metal back to reveal his face.

"We do not halt here," he said. "But we shall take supplies, for three days."

A man bowed, as if this were a great honor, though his face was blank, and Calandryll thought that the victualing of the band must surely be a drain on the resources of the village.

The man—the headman, Calandryll supposed— barked brief instructions and folk began to bustle about, fetching sacks and yellow haunches of dried meat that were carried out to the waiting kotu-zen.

"You've news?" Chazali demanded brusquely.

The headman bowed again, refusing to meet the kiriwashen's eyes, and answered, "Three days ago tensai came. They took two cows."

"How many?" asked Chazali.

"There were nineteen came here," the headman told him, "but I think there were more in the hills. They grow stronger."

Chazali grunted, nodded, and said in a somewhat

milder tone, "When the war is finished the patrols
will come back. Do we encounter these outlaws,
meanwhile, they shall die."

"Thank you, Lord." The headman bowed dutifully. "May Horul guide your blade."

"And may he bless your crops," returned
Chazali. Then, without further ado, spun his horse
round and heeled the animal back through the
gates.

He wasted no time on explanations, only dropped
his veil in place and waved his men forward, as if
the village and its problems were beneath his con-
siderations, already dismissed. The scouts were already gone ahead, cantering up the slope, and the
remaining warriors fell into line behind their commander, the outlanders and Ochen at the center of
the column.

They topped the rise and saw a broader valley before them, the trail cutting down through heavy
stands of timber to another river, a second village
twin to the other, tiny in the distance. Calandryll
had thought to halt again there, but Chazali led
them fast to the ford, splashing across in great
sheets of sunlit silver spray as his outriders cantered to meet him, reporting to the kiriwashen
before returning to their stations, Chazali main-
taining his pace as they cantered on. From the
village gate inscrutable Jesseryte faces watched
them go, bland as the sky above. They did not halt
until noon, in a clearing just off the trail.

As had become their custom, Calandryll sat with
Bracht and Katya, Cennaire and Ochen, separate
from the kotu-zen. He was somewhat surprised
when Chazali approached, bowing formally and
asking permission that he might join them. It
seemed entirely unnecessary, but he nonetheless returned formal invitation, for which the kiriwashen

offered equally formal thanks before seating himself.

"The news is not good," he declared, looking from face to face. "The tensai grow bold. They took food from both villages, and the headman of the last believes they number forty men. He thinks they have a camp within a day or two's ride."

Ochen nodded, making no comment. Bracht asked, "Shall you hunt them?"

Chazali's answer was a smile, brief and, Calandryll thought, regretful, accompanied by a shrug. "Not hunt them, no. Our duty is to reach Pamurteng. Do they look to attack us however . . ."

The smile grew fierce, predatory. It seemed to Calandryll he resembled nothing so much then as some great cat, anticipating a killing.

"Ghan-te is little more than a day now," said Ochen, answered with a curt nod.

Calandryll asked, "Ghan-te?"

"A larger steading," the wazir explained. "It has an inn, a temple, a market."

"And perhaps news," Chazali said.

THE settlement lay at the center of a hill-ringed bowl, the slopes all cleared of timber and terraced, streams diverted through sluices and little dams to water the levels where gettu toiled, looking up from their labors to watch the column approach. A wall of tree trunks encompassed the town, rectangular and set at intervals with watchtowers, breached by great gates banded with metal, those opening on a narrow avenue that ran into the center. The outriders had alerted the place to the arrival and folk thronged the avenue and the peripheral streets that crossed it with geometric regularity. A few wore the drab earth tones that appeared the uniform of the farmer, but most were dressed in more lavish outfits, their clothing and its ornamentation suggesting prosperity. They formed a curious audience as Chazali led his party inward, riding proud between buildings of two stories height, with long verandahs and stone chimneys, the woodwork bright-painted, looming tight-packed above the avenue.

The sun was just set, dusk thrusting long shadows over the ground, and lanterns were suspended all down the way, setting the black armor of the kotu-zen to glittering, like the carapaces of huge, exotic beetles. None spoke, only bowed and watched as the kotu-zen rode past stiff-backed, their masked faces set rigidly forward, looking to neither left nor right, but only to their leader, as if casual communication with the inhabitants was beneath them.

Chazali brought them to a plaza, a wide square set with massive flagstones that rang loud under the hooves, walled by four of the largest structures in Ghan-te, two strung with lanterns, one less lit, the third dark. Chazali halted before it, and from its construction, Calandryll deduced this was the garrison formerly occupied by the kotu-anj now called to the war. Facing it across the square was a more welcoming structure, its facade painted a brilliant red, the windows outlined with blue, the verandah hung with vermilion-tinted lanterns. He guessed that was the inn, and the dimmer building alongside a stable. The fourth, boasting an elevated fascia decorated with a black horsehead on a background of gold, was surely the temple.

Chazali sat his horse a moment, surveying the square, then barked a command that brought townsfolk scrambling forward to prostrate themselves that the kotu-zen might step down. Those most eager, Calandryll noticed, were the most expensively accoutred, who appeared to consider it an honor that they be used as footstools. He found a man in an ankle-length robe of silver-threaded green kneeling beside the chestnut, and turned the gelding away, springing down before the figure had time to scrabble on hands and knees to his new position.

The man climbed awkwardly to his feet, frowning, seeming disappointed, then bowed and walked, head lowered, away. Calandryll took the reins and led the gelding over to where the others waited with Ochen. The wazir said, "We sleep here this night," indicating the shadowy bulk of the garrison. "Likely we shall eat in the tavern."

Bracht asked, "And our horses?"

"The stable." Ochen pointed absently to the neighboring building, his eyes wandering to the temple, as if he noted some irregularity.

"I thought only the kotu-zen rode," Calandryll said, and Ochen replied, "Only the kotu-zen may own war-horses. The other castes are allowed asses or mules. Horses are the gift of Horul, creatures special to the god."

He appeared preoccupied, his attention on the temple, and Calandryll asked, "Is aught amiss?"

"I wonder at the priest's absence," the wazir murmured, frowning. "Where is he?"

"Do we see our animals bedded?" Bracht demanded, far less concerned with the missing priest than the comfort of his stallion.

"Once Chazali establishes order." Ochen nodded vaguely, gesturing in the direction of the kotu-zen who moved purposefully about the square, propelled by the kiriwashen's barked commands. Some strode, Calandryll saw, to the tavern, others to the stable, while more entered the garrison building, shouting for lanterns to be brought. It seemed to him they commandeered townsfolk at random, prosperous-looking burghers hurrying to obey with ambiguous alacrity.

"Leave me your horse," he offered, troubled by the wazir's uncharacteristic air of impatience. "I'll see it bedded while you speak with the priest."

"My thanks."

Ochen wasted no time passing the reins, hurrying toward the temple, calling his whereabouts to Chazali. Calandryll took the animal and led it with his own to the stable. The kotu-zen moved in the same direction, though while they left their horses in care of townsfolk clearly anxious to be of service, the outlanders looked to their own, even Cennaire, following their example, applying the brush and ascertaining the manger held fresh hay, the trough clean water.

Those tasks dispensed, they returned to the garrison, lit now, and bustling with activity as the kotu-zen took up occupation. The place was dark and simple as the keep, a warren of dim-lit corridors and chambers filled with the empty scent of desertion, musty and slightly damp. At ground level was a central hall, a kitchen behind, an armory dug below, and a bathhouse. Stairs went up to the second floor, that mostly given over to a single dormitory, individual chambers built around the outer walls. Townsfolk scuttled, lighting fires, airing bedding, bowing nervously as they eyed the strangers with open curiosity, the kotu-zen with a curious mixture of expectation and fear.

Chazali took it upon himself to escort them to their rooms, those humbler, even plainer than the chambers of the keep: walls of bare wood, a single bed, a chest, no more.

"This place was not built with honored guests in

mind," he apologized, "but we shall remain only this night."

He bowed and left them. Bracht said, "Ahrd, but did you see these folk grovel? This is, truly, a strange land."

"And we strangers in it," Calandryll replied, crossing to the window to peer down into the plaza. He saw Ochen leaving the temple, hurrying across the square, the sorcerer's gait, the set of his shoulders, spoke of anxiety and Calandryll felt presentiment stir. The ancient glanced up and saw his face, raising a hand to beckon him down. Presentiment became certainty and Calandryll turned to his companions: "Something's amiss."

Not waiting for any response, he quit the window and went into the corridor, the others hard on his heels as he descended the stairs.

The hall below was lit now, dimly as seemed the Jesseryte custom, a fire started in the hearth. Ochen stood with Chazali by the fire, speaking urgently, both their faces grave. The kiriwashen had removed his helm, but not yet his armor, and one hand clenched and flexed around the hilt of his sword as the other tugged angrily at the oiled triangle of his beard. The outlanders joined them, and even before Ochen spoke, Calandryll sensed his news was not good.

"The priest is dead." The words came flat, intoned as if this were the grossest outrage, an enormity beyond comprehension. "Slain by tensai."

"Here?" Calandryll gestured, encompassing the town.

"Not in Ghan-te." Ochen shook his head, reached to lift strands of disarrayed silver from his face. "In the woodland. He rode to a naming ceremony in that last village—he did not return."

He paused, sighing, and Chazali expanded: "Foresters found his body and brought it here three days agone. It was butchered, they said. As if torn apart by rabid dogs." His voice was harsh, stony as the cold rage burning in his slitted eyes.

"Then likely the tensai lie behind us," Bracht said, "and no threat."

Chazali fixed the Kern with a savage glare. "You do not understand," he snarled, pent rage finding small outlet in the words.

"How should he?" Ochen waved a placatory hand, his voice somber as he said, "Albeit he was of lesser skill, still this priest was of the wazir caste. No tensai would dare harm such as he, for fear of damnation. To slay a priest is to consign oneself to eternal torment; to risk attacking a wazir is to face dangerous magic."

"Still I fail to understand," said Bracht.

Calandryll watched as Ochen looked, grim-faced, to Chazali, comprehension dawning, confirmed by the mage's next words.

"That they dared it—that they succeeded—can mean only one thing: they've magic of their own. Rhythamun's magic! And be that so, we can surely count on ambush ere long."

8

CALANDRYLL studied the two Jesseryte faces, seeing horror writ there, such open expression of outrage somehow lending far greater import to the alarming news. It had been, he knew, rank optimism to think their enemy should let them pass unchallenged. That was not Rhythamun's way, and that the warlock should leave defenses behind him was hardly unexpected; but the rage that lit Chazali's eyes, the repugnance in Ochen's, suggested this was a matter that struck to the core of their beliefs, a thing they had not anticipated, as if their world was shaken by the murder.

"I must advise my men," the kiriwashen growled. "Do we encounter those who slew him . . ."

His smile grew feral. Ochen put a hand to his wrist, the golden nails bright against the jet of the vambrace, and said firmly, "Remember we've a higher duty, friend. And I suspect we shall meet them soon enough, save Horul bring us safely past them."

Ungently, Chazali took his arm from the sorcerer's grip, his lips compressed in a narrow line of rejection. He seemed about to move, to bellow orders that would send his kotu-zen out into the night after the tensai, but Ochen fixed him with a stare and said, "It's my belief you'll have no need to find them. I think it likelier they hunt us, and these are but servants of a larger cause. The murder of a priest is an abomination, aye. But that Rhythamun should go on to raise Tharn, that is far worse."

He spoke softly, but each word was weighted, binding Chazali, and with a frustrated groan the kiriwashen ducked his head in reluctant acknowledgment.

"Aye, you speak aright, though it sits ill with me to let this go unpunished." His head lowered, chin to chest. Then he looked up, squaring his shoulders, and clapped his hands. Silence fell, and in a somber voice he informed the kotu-zen of the slaying. They took it grimly, calling curses on the blasphemers, promising vengeance, grumbling when Chazali repeated Ochen's admonishments, reminding them that their foremost duty was to deliver the questers safe to Pamur-teng.

Katya asked, "Can you be certain Rhythamun took a hand?"

"Who else?" said Ochen, his rhetoric glum. "Only the wazir command such powers as might destroy a man who wards himself with magic; not tensai."

"Then is he close?" she demanded.

"He need not be." Ochen shook his head, and on his face was an expression Calandryll had not seen before: a look, almost, of fear. "I think he likely encountered tensai—perhaps they thought to waylay a solitary traveler." He barked a short, ugly laugh. "I suspect they found him no easy prey. Indeed, I suspect they found themselves the prey; that he possessed them, or sufficient of them to serve his purpose. And that he leaves them behind, guardians of his path."

"Still they are only brigands," Bracht said, sanguine.

"Aye," said Ochen, "but brigands gifted with fell magic, which I like not at all."

"Nor I." The Kern chuckled grimly. "But when a man's only the one path, then he must follow it to the end."

"And we've perhaps more than just your magic at our beck," said Katya. "Remember Calandryll wears a blade that offends our enemy's gramaryes."

"There's that," allowed the wazir, though with little enough conviction.

"Then lose that gloomy visage," suggested Bracht. "We've faced Rhythamun's magic ere now and won through. Likely we shall do so again."

Ochen smiled then, wanly, as if he welcomed the Kern's encouragement but found it ill-placed. Calandryll said, "What choice have we, save to go on? Better we do that in hope, no?"

"Aye." Ochen's smile lightened somewhat as he nodded. "Forgive me, but that a priest should be slain . . . It is an unprecedented thing."

"So," said Calandryll, "is the resurrection of the Mad God."

THE dinner they ate that night, in a tavern emptied of all save their party and the serving folk, was a glum affair, for the slaying of the priest, and all it implied, sat heavy on all their minds. The kotu-zen radiated a palpable discomfort, compounded of disgust and righteous anger and frustration. Were they not sworn to bring the questers to Pamur-teng,

Calandryll was sure they would even then be out in the hills, hunting down the tensai like rabid dogs. No less were the townsfolk disturbed by the murder, looking to the warriors of the hold to which they swore allegiance to bring the killers to justice. The innkeeper and his people served them in wary silence, as though momentarily anticipating an announcement of retribution against the tensai, and though the food was good enough, and the wine served with it palatable, none took pleasure in the meal, and when it was done they quit the tavern to find their beds, leaving behind folk utterly confused by such disruption of accepted order.

For his own part, Calandryll felt mightily uneasy, his mood enhanced by the Jesserytes' ominous reaction. To face armed men was one thing, and none too forbidding with fifty trained warriors in escort. To face creatures of the occult was an unpalatable hazard, but still something he and his comrades had previously overcome. To know that both dangers, conjoined, lay ahead was poor recipe for comfortable sleep, and he lay on his narrow bed staring at the play of light over the boards of the ceiling. It seemed that he grew aware for the first time that he might well die, that Rhythamun might well succeed, and all the long months of the quest count for naught.

The fear he pushed aside, reminding himself that the knowledge of possible death had always been present and that fear alone was insufficient to deter him. That he should consider the possibility of Rhythamun's victory was, he told himself, to grant his adversary an advantage, to open gateways to trepidation, to vacillation: he set doubt aside. And found he was left with anger, which strengthened him, firming his purpose again, so that in time, not knowing his eyes closed, he slept.

He woke to early sunlight and the faint chill of autumn's advent, birds chirruping about the eaves of the garrison, the sounds of a town already awake. He rose without delay, going out to bang impatiently on Bracht's door, which opened on the instant, the Kern buckling his swordbelt, eyeing Calandryll with a small, fierce smile.

"Come," he declared, "let's rouse Katya and Cennaire and break our fast."

Both women were awake and ready, Katya's tanned face grave as she came out into the corridor, the mail of her hauberk rustling softly, a hand upon her sword as if she thought perhaps some monstrous conjuration might momentarily appear. Cennaire seemed calm, though she stepped without preamble or excuse to Calandryll's side, and he, unthinking, set a hand upon her arm, proprietory.

"I fear we bring you into ever greater danger," he murmured as they found their way to the hall. "But be assured that no harm shall come you for lack of my protection."

"I know that," she returned, and in the instant of the saying was aware that it was true: that she had no doubt but that he would lay down his life for her.

Without thinking, without intention of artifice or coquetry, she moved closer to him, so that for a moment their bodies pressed tight. She felt him start, from the corner of her eye saw him glance down, smiling, embarrassed, and then they reached the stairs and moved a little way apart again, though still he held her arm. From the dim-lit hall she saw Ochen watching, his face clear, though his expression was enigmatic and she wondered if he approved, or merely observed, his interest moti-

vated by his own concerns. She could not tell, and
none others appeared aware of the wazir's subtle
observation, settling to table as food was brought
out with the determinedly cheerful air of folk committed to a path from which there could be no
turning.

They ate well, as if this might be their last meal,
their conversation of the way ahead, Ochen and
Chazali, who joined them, speaking of the road and
the settlements along the way. It ran, they said,
northward out of Ghan-te, through forest for several days before emerging at the foot of the great
central plateau that gave the Jesseryte lands the
name of Plain, where lay another town, Ahgra-te.
There were more villages, but for most of its
length, it wound lonely through densely wooded
cordillera that afforded natural advantage to the
tensai.

It was not, Cennaire thought, encouraging information, and she found Calandryll's eyes across the
table. They were grave, his expression resolute,
breaking into a smile as he met her gaze, as if he
sought to reassure her. She answered his smile,
thinking that of all there present she was likely the
least endangered, warded against physical harm by
her very revenancy, and perhaps immune to whatever magic Rhythamun left behind, were it designed to act upon the living only. Almost, she felt
guilty, dropping her gaze to her plate as it came to
her that she might see all these folk slain, she left
. . . she could find no other word save *alive*. And
then that did she succeed in regaining her heart,
should it be better to reclaim it—were some sorcerer such as Ochen able to perform that counter-
ing magic—or only hold it for herself, within the
pyxis, and remain as she was.

The thought was simultaneously intriguing and

confusing. To be again mortal, or continue revenant? To choose the one would be to relinquish all
the powers, all the strengths, afforded by the other.
She had gloried in her newfound senses, in the preternatural awareness they gave her—and yet she
had suppressed all those abilities during the days
spent in company of these questers. And they, mortal flesh and blood, seemed no more caring of danger than was she, as if they accepted their lives
with relish, living them day by day, prepared to
face the unknown she no longer had need to confront. Because, she decided, they devoted themselves to their purpose, to their quest, pursuing a
higher ideal than mere existence.

Once, she would have laughed at that: dismissed
it as foolishness, as mortal frailty. Yet, in their
company, she had ofttimes near forgot her immortality, had learned again to enjoy small things: their
acceptance, Calandryll's smile, the touch of his
hand. Certainly she had forgotten much of her past:
abruptly she wondered how Calandryll would react
did he know she had been a courtesan; did he learn
she went about Anomius's business; did he discover she had slain men in that cause.

"Fear not." Ochen's voice interrupted her musing, and she raised her head, aware that the others
looked toward her. "You've blades and magic, both,
to defend you."

She essayed a smile, quite unable to interpret the
wazir's expression. His tone, the words, suggested
he sought only to reassure a nervous woman. Yet
he knew her for what she was, and so knew that
she, of all there present, had the least need of comforting. Did he then pretend? Or did he, like
Anomius, look to use her for purposes of his own?
She could not decide; still could not entirely understand why he had not exposed her. He had spoken

of her having some part to play in the quest, and that had then suited her own purpose well enough—but what part? On whose behalf?

"Aye," she answered, smiling again. "And as Bracht said—have we not but the single path?"

"Well said," Calandryll applauded.

"Indeed," said Ochen. "And therefore but one direction."

"Which we shall now take." Chazali was entirely unaware of the undercurrent beneath their words. "We depart!"

He shoved his plate aside and rose, his kotu-zen on their feet in the instant, already armored, fixing the final strappings, moving toward the door behind their kiriwashen.

The questers followed. Bracht said, "Ahrd and all the Younger Gods be with us," and Katya smiled at him, touching his cheek and saying, "Are they not?"

The Kern answered with a laugh and a nod, taking her hand as they fell into step behind the Jesserytes, the two of them more like sweethearts going to some country fair than warriors expecting battle.

Cennaire found herself between Calandryll and Ochen, Calandryll's hand once more courtly on her arm. She had rather he took her hand, as Bracht had taken Katya's, but still the slight pressure of his fingers, as if he sought some contact he was not yet ready to openly express, was pleasurable.

Burash, she thought, *I am like a tripsy girl on the arm of her first lover.*

She ventured a sidelong glance, finding it again returned, though this time he did not look away, but smiled at her, an expression in which admiration and regret mingled, as if he would see her safe

from danger, but was nonetheless happy they
should face it together.

And he, she thought, *my swain; nor any less bewildered by this than I.*

Then all became disciplined confusion as they
crossed the square and entered the stable. Townsfolk thronged the plaza, more inside, aiding the
kotu-zen with their horses, stooping that the warriors might mount, Bracht cursing as one particu-
larly determined kembi crawled vigorously to place
his back where the Kern's foot might use it for a
stool, his efforts ended by the black stallion that,
nervous, kicked out, sending the man tumbling.
Bracht chuckled wickedly and swung astride. Katya
was already mounted; Calandryll helped Cennaire
into the saddle and waved a man intent on helping
him away, springing lithe onto the chestnut.

In the plaza, the kotu-zen formed a column.
Chazali raised a hand, brought it down, and they
trotted back along the avenue, lined with townsfolk, toward the gates of Ghan-te, and whatever
awaited them along the road beyond.

The way ran north across the dish of the bowl,
Ghan-te at the center of the declivity, a crossroads
just outside the town, their path climbing the slope
through the terraces to the trees that rimmed the
edge. Chazali sent two men ahead, which Calandryll
thought a measure rendered somewhat redundant
by the murder of the priest: ambush seemed a certainty now, and the forest stretching out before
them as they crested the rise provided ample cover
for any number of attackers, the outriders more
likely to alert the enemy than give warning of their
presence. The woods spread wide and dense, the
road a shaded avenue overhung with branches,
spruce and cedar joining the maples now, thick
enough it was impossible to see any distance into

the forest. An army might have waited there, within bowshot, and still gone unseen.

It was an eerie feeling, and the rustle of the wind through the leaves assumed the aspect of whispering, warning voices reminiscent of the chattering of the Gruagach that patrolled the Cuan na'Dru. But those strange creatures had proven allies, Ahrd's servants and therefore friends, while here there was no sensation of amity, only apprehension. Calandryll told himself they had faced dangers aplenty before, and lived; and then recalled that Ochen had warned their enemy's strength waxed greater as he drew closer to his master. It seemed then that he felt the land again, felt its unhappiness ooze into him, discomforting as sweat that chills in the wind. He looked about, seeing only ominous shadows, the sun not yet high enough to strike through the timber, night there, with all its lurking terrors.

Something moved and he opened his mouth to shout a warning, hand tightening about his swordhilt, seeing the kotu-zen who rode to his right turn veiled faces toward the disturbance, their blades flashing clear of the scabbards, some swinging nocked bows to line. Then a body crashed through the undergrowth, a scut showed white, and a stag started from cover. A warrior barked brief laughter and Calandryll let go a breath he had not known he held, grinning at his own apprehension as the stag, his harem about him, went bounding to safety.

They rode on, safe to a stream where they halted to take their noonday meal, that brief and eaten quickly, bowmen pacing the edges of the makeshift camp, waiting only long enough to rest the animals before commencing their journey.

❖   ❖   ❖

THEY continued on through an afternoon bright with sunlight, the sky a clear and cloudless blue swathe overhead, lighting the timber so that it seemed a little less threatening, as if the radiance dispelled those monsters of imagination's creation, birds fluttering, singing, their chorus a tuneful reassurance.

It was a brief respite.

The day aged, shadows once more lengthening as the sun westered. The road traversed gentler slopes than they had known, the broken country to the south giving sway to a more undulating terrain, the wide trail cut straight for most of its length, curving only where the land occasionally thrust up in timbered drumlins.

Around one such monticule they found the scouts.

Chazali was in the lead, flanked by kotu-zen, riding hard. Abruptly his mount shrilled a protest and tossed its head. The kiriwashen threw up a hand, halting the column. Calandryll had not known he unsheathed his sword, only that it was in hand, on guard as he shouted, "What's amiss?" seeing horses stamping, curvetting where the foremost riders drew up, milling about the edges of the trail.

From ahead came Chazali's bellow, summoning Ochen.

The wazir urged his mount on. Calandryll yelled, "Wait here!" to Cennaire and heeled his chestnut after the sorcerer. Bracht and Katya came with him, heads swinging from side to side as they surveyed the forest, the hillock ahead.

No arrows flew, nor battle shouts, and the Jesseryte horses, war-trained, were quickly calmed, so that an ominous silence fell.

Calandryll's gelding broke the quiet as he followed Ochen around the curve, breath whistling nervous from its flared nostrils, its ears flattening, hooves drumming a staccato tattoo before he fought it still. He felt the animal tremble, himself shudder.

Bracht said, "It smells the blood."

There was much to smell. It spread viscous across the trail, thick with flies that buzzed and rose reluctantly from the gorging, swarming back when none immediately approached. Crows and ravens perched, beaks bloodied, among the trees, cawing protest at the intrusion. Calandryll stared aghast, horrified by the slaughter laid before him.

The body of one of Chazali's scouts lay beside the road, his sable armor no longer black, but colored with the blood that spilled from the gaping rent in his cuirass. His head, still wearing its helm, the face still veiled, lay some distance off, speared on the broken branch of a maple. The second outrider rested on the grass that grew up the flank of the drumlin, the green slick and red now. His right arm was torn from the shoulder, still clutching the sword that protruded from his chest, his head twisted round, crushed down into the stained sward. Their horses lay dead farther along the road, a hideous barrier of severed limbs and dripping entrails, the equine heads placed atop, grinning obscenely at the horrified onlookers.

Calandryll tasted bile sour in his mouth, and spat.

Bracht said, "Ahrd!" softly, and Chazali muttered a curse, masked face turning to Ochen. "What did this?" The kiriwashen's voice was hoarse, metallic, anger and outrage mixed with undisguised horror. "No mortal hand, surely."

"Save fell magic invests it," Ochen said. His face was grave, studying the bloody work. "This is surely Rhythamun's doing."

Calandryll scanned the hillock, the surrounding
timber, seeking sign of movement, warning of ambush. Between his shoulder blades the skin prickled, the sensation of watchful eyes magnified. It
seemed the whole forest quickened, imbued with
malign observers, and he thought to hear the song
of flighted arrows, see he knew not what charge to
the attack. He saw only trees, the black carrion
birds; heard only their raucous protests, the buzz of
the flies.

"Why?" Bracht, too, inspected the landscape,
blue eyes narrowed, cold and angry. "Why this?
Why do they not attack?"

"I think them gone, save perhaps a few concealed
watchers." Ochen sat slumped in his saddle, face
older, sad. "I suspect they play with us—look to
wear us down."

"In Horul's name I swear this shall be avenged."
Chazali spoke through gritted teeth, fury resonant
in his promise. "Have we the opportunity, they
shall answer for this."

"Aye, and you'll have my help," promised
Ochen. "But now, do we attend our lost brethren?
They deserve that much."

Chazali nodded and roared orders that had a pyre
swiftly built, men and horses both committed to
the flames Ochen summoned with his magic, the
scent of almonds brief on the afternoon air, soon replaced with the smell of burning wood, the sickly
odor of roasting flesh. Ochen chanted a prayer,
echoed by the kotu-zen, and in solemn silence they
watched the thick column of smoke rise black into
the sky.

The ceremony was short enough, but still the
day darkened as they went on, the ribbon of azure
visible through the trees seeming itself shaded by
the flames that licked red behind. Dusk ap-

proached, the forest caliginous and menacing again, and none eager to proceed through the night. There was a palpable sense of relief, even from the impassive kotu-zen, when Chazali called Ochen to his side and soon after announced they would make camp.

The chosen site was a clearing to the side of the road, lush grassed, a spring there filling a pool, the surrounding rocks mossy, sufficient space for all the horses and their riders. A guard was instantly mounted, the perimeter of the clearing ringed with watchful men, the animals set to grazing on picket lines, fires—as much for spiritual comfort as cooking—were soon built, and those not designated sentries grouped tight about the flames. Ochen paced slowly between the encircling trees, murmuring softly, leaving in his wake the sweet perfume of his defensive magic. Even so, there were none who relaxed, the kotu-zen making no move to shed their armor, the questers alert, hands stroking absently at swordhilts, and when they sat, it was with sheathed blades across their thighs, ready.

Calandryll found a place beside Cennaire, she shifting instinctively closer, finding comfort in his proximity, for she was disturbed by what she had seen. She no longer felt so confident of surviving this journey, for it came to her that those creatures that had rent armored men like rag dolls could likely rend her as easily. The notion was horrible: she thought she might not die, but live on, in pieces, and that seemed a fate far worse than honest death. She shuddered, staring wide-eyed into the flames, and Calandryll turned toward her, opening his mouth to speak.

Before the words came out a ghastly shrieking filled the night, and she gasped, pressing closer against him.

It began as a bubbling moan, such as a man with riven lungs might make in his dying. It rose, high-pitched, to become a dreadful yammering that rang through the trees, echoing, reverberating to a ghastly crescendo that ended with an abruptness somehow more frightening for the silence that followed.

"Ahrd, but you've strange-sounding wolves in this land."

Bracht's grim humor drew a tight smile from Chazali that froze as a second wail rang out. The kiriwashen rose. There was a third shriek, and a fourth, all from different directions, and then a chorus to chill the blood. It seemed the singing of souls in torment, of things agonized and filled with hatred, the desire to inflict their suffering on others, utterly malevolent.

Chazali's face was blank, held firm by rigid self-discipline alone. Calandryll sprang to his feet, Bracht and Katya with him, all with swords drawn.

"They look to frighten us." Ochen remained seated, hands extended toward the fire.

Bracht's mouth stretched in a sour grin and he said, "They make a passable good attempt," and the wazir nodded and said, "They're not close. Nor likely to break through the cantrips I've set."

"Only *likely*?" asked the Kern.

"This place is ringed with gramaryes they'll find mightily hard to defeat, but"—Ochen shrugged—"I know not what magicks Rhythamun employs, what sorceries he's put in them."

"Can you not seek them out?" asked Calandryll, voice raised to be heard over the horrid yammering.

"That would be unwise." Ochen shook his head. "Do I venture into the aethyr, then my protections here are weakened. And still there remains the danger that Rhythamun might locate your pneuma again."

Calandryll gestured helplessly at the stygian darkness beyond the fires' glow. "His creatures would seem to have found us," he declared. "Shall they not alert their master?"

"In which case," returned Ochen patiently, "I had best remain close, no? And perhaps they've not such communion with him—I think it likely he worked his filthy magicks on these tensai and left them to their task."

"Then you can do nothing?" Calandryll stared around. It seemed the shrieking pierced his ears, drove hammer blows against his skull. He shook his head, suddenly aware that Cennaire had risen and clutched his arm. "We must endure this?"

"I fear so," said Ochen with a composure near to irritating.

Silence fell, hard and sudden, deafening as the awful sounds. Ears remembered the shrieking, its cessation ominous, like the lull preceding a storm, the quiet before attack. It seemed then that the creaking of the timber, the rustle of wind-stirred leaves, presaged some greater assault. The fires crackled; horses snickered; armor rattled as men peered, waiting, anticipating, into the darkness.

"I'll check the animals," Bracht said. "This unnerves them."

"I'll accompany you."

Katya sheathed her saber. Calandryll caught her eye and saw it troubled. He felt sweat run cold down his back, Cennaire's hand tight on his arm.

"I'll speak with my men," said Chazali.

"Tell them my cantrips shall give full warning of attack," said Ochen. "And that I think none shall come."

The kiriwashen frowned. Calandryll said, "Then why this?"

Ochen barked a single, humorless laugh, and answered, "Were they ready to attack, think you they'd give us such warning? No, they look to wear us down. The attack will come later—and unannounced."

Chazali grunted and stalked away. Calandryll set a hand over Cennaire's and forced a smile, his voice to calm. "Ochen is likely right," he said. "So, do we prepare our dinner?"

She answered with a wan twitching of her lips, releasing her grip, though she had rather held him close. She knew herself frightened in a manner she had not experienced since first she had been cast into the dungeons of Nhur-jabal; and comforted in a manner she had never known by his presence. She ducked her head and settled on the grass.

Calandryll sat beside her, studying Ochen as he set a pot to boiling, fresh meat to cooking. "When?" he asked softly.

"Their attack?" The wazir shrugged. "I claim no ability to scry the future, only to guesses; but, by day's light, I think. Rhythamun knows you've a sorcerer for company and so he'll surely know I ward our camp with gramaryes each night. No less that I cannot work such magic as we ride." He raised a hand as Calandryll frowned a question, opened his mouth to voice it. "To maintain a cantrip about so large a group, moving, is more than any save the wazir-narimasu might do; and then difficult, needing more than a single mage. I suspect Rhythamun uses men and magic, both, and so will have instructed his minions to attack us as we ride."

It was scant comfort, and all Calandryll could find by way of answer was a grunt, a weak smile.

He reached for the meat, spitting fat where it hung over the flames, that distraction denied him by Cennaire, who murmured, "Leave that to me. You've surely weightier concerns."

"Than this?" he asked, wincing as the howling started up once more.

"Do you not learn of the occult?" She looked to Ochen as she spoke, rearranging the strips of meat.

"There will be no instruction this night," the wazir said, loud over the screaming. "In that, Rhythamun wins the day."

"A small enough victory," Calandryll retorted, more for Cennaire's sake than any real conviction.

"Aye." Ochen smiled. "And tomorrow . . . ? Perhaps he'll taste defeat."

"Dera willing."

Calandryll spoke sincerely, though he wondered, as the dreadful cacophony climbed to fresh heights, if the Younger Gods took no further hand in this strange war, but left its waging to men. They sat among dense timber—but where was Ahrd? Could the tree god of Cuan na'For not send his byahs to quell the howling, destroy the howlers? Water bubbled from the spring—but where was Burash? Where was Dera? The goddess had spoken of restrictions imposed on her and her godly kin—did the Kess Imbrun mark the limit of their aegis? Were they, perhaps, without power in the Jesseryn Plain? And Horul—what of the Jesserytes' equine god? He must surely side with the questers, but he remained aloof, it seemed; or overwhelmed by the dreaming emanations of Tharn.

Calandryll felt doubt grow with the shrieking. He would have expressed it to Ochen, but conversation was entirely impossible now, drowned under the shrilling that rose up to fill the forest, the night, his mind, and all he could do was wonder, longing to press hands against assaulted ears, but unwilling to seek that escape for fear he should miss the warnings of attack, not entirely convinced by the wazir's reasoning.

It was a dismal night, wearying and fraying nerves, so that when the sky at last paled into dawn's promise and the howling ceased, they broke their fast in silence, saddled horses skittish with fear, and rode grimly north, pushing the animals to the limits of their strength, hoping to outdistance their unseen escorts.

At noon, they halted to rest and eat, grouped about a stream, watering the horses. Bowmen stood in a wary circle around the animals, others bringing food to their companions, that eaten standing, eyes never still, but constantly scanning the minatory woods. The sun stood high and hot, shafts of gold lancing down through the trees, the air heavy, filled with the buzz of insects and the trilling of birds. Then sudden silence.

Bracht shouted, "Ware attack!"

And bird song was replaced with the susurration of arrows.

A horse screamed, a shaft protruding from its flank. A man cursed, lengths of feathered wood jutting from his armor. He snapped them, hurling them aside, peering round with upraised sword, finding no ready target for his anger as the sentries loosed an answering volley at the shapes that darted among the bosky shadows. Another horse shrilled, three shafts embedded in its neck, blood starting from nostrils and mouth as it plunged, lifting the man who held it off his feet, sending him stumbling, then went down on its knees. Five more arrows struck it, and it rolled, kicking on its side, its screaming horrible.

Then silence again, broken only by the faltering

gasps of the stricken horse. Bracht cursed, dragging his stallion after him, the big black horse snorting, eyes rolling as it was hauled closer to the wounded animal. The Kern slapped reins into the hand of the kotu-zen whose mount it was and drove his falchion into the animal's neck, severing the artery there, ending the beast's agony. Unspeaking, blue eyes filled with rage, he snatched back his reins.

Bird song returned: the forest regained a measure of normality, and Bracht said, "They're gone."

Katya, her voice grim, her eyes stormy, said, "Until the next time."

Cennaire, standing shielded by Calandryll, said softly, "I did not think it would be like this."

He stood with blade defensive, smoked meat and hunk of bread forgotten at his feet. "Thought you it would be easy?" Then, embarrassed that he turned his anger in her direction: "Forgive me—Rhythamun's wiles shorten my temper."

She shook her head and smiled a troubled smile. "I chose the way," she said. "You've no need to apologize to me."

She hoped—a fresh concern—that no arrow should strike her. She was confident the shafts afforded her no threat, but that very absence must expose her. She hid her thoughts behind a shudder that Calandryll took for fear.

"We survive," he said gently. "Another victory."

She nodded, sunlight striking blue-black sparks from her hair. Calandryll sheathed his blade, again wondering at her courage, turning away as Chazali roared orders, angered by the attack, and the column mounted, the horseless warrior finding a seat behind a comrade.

The road narrowed, running by the foot of a low ridge, the slope grassy, treeless save for a scattering of pines, the eastern trailside clustered thick with

timber. The width allowed for no more than three
horses to move abreast and attention was focused
mainly on the forested side: it seemed more likely
an attack should come from that direction. Instead,
it came from the ridge.

Had it been mortal, then likely the mounted
archers would have felled the ambushers and the
riders been able to gallop clear. It was not, however, mortal flesh that raced with unhuman speed
down the slope, but something other, perhaps once
quickened by humanity, but now imbued with
Rhythamun's fell sortilege: changed.

It was impossible to define exactly what rendered
them other than human. Easier to see the arrows
that sprouted, ignored, from their chests. Easier to
see them leap, yowling, at the horse carrying the
two kotu-zen. Calandryll gained an impression of
elongated limbs, of distorted bone that thrust out
the jaws, those filled with fangs; of red, mad eyes,
and nails grown into talons. He saw them spring
outward and up, like grey shadows in the sunlight,
smashing the double-mounted men from the saddle, the horse bucking, shrieking as a hand—a
paw?—thrust out, almost casually, an afterthought,
to rip away the windpipe. The horse fell down,
twitching, already dead. The kotu-zen were carried
away, each held tight by one of the creatures, into
the trees.

He heard them scream, the sound contesting
Chazali's bellowed commands, and looked to
Ochen even as the surviving warriors dismounted
and took battle stations.

The wazir sprang from his horse with an agility
that belied his age, running for the trees after the
captives. Calandryll dismounted with the gelding
still plunging terrified under him, sword in hand,
racing after the sorcerer. He was aware of Bracht

and Katya to either side, Ochen a little way ahead, raising a hand and shouting a warning as they came up. There was the smell of almonds, and a burst of brilliant light, silver and gold mingled, overwhelming the shafts of sunlight that pierced the woodland. Ochen spoke, low and rapidly, the words strange, arcane, and the light expanded to envelop the questers, cocooning them in its glow.

"Stay close," the wazir warned, and reverted to the language of the occult.

Beams of gold-veined silver pulsed out, fluid, like airborne water, winding swift among the trees, their piney perfume replaced with the almond scent, the ethereal streamers shimmering, questing deeper and deeper into the forest. Screams then, such as they all had heard that last night, but brief now, abruptly dying.

"Remain within the aegis of my spell." Ochen beckoned them on, currents still pulsing from the globe that contained them, his voice dropping as he added, "But I fear we shall find little enough."

He spoke aright: they followed the nimbi to a small clearing redolent of almonds and burning in equal measure, and found the kotu-zen. Both men were dead, their throats opened, their armor gashed. Of the creatures there was no sign, save tatters of skin, fragments of bone, little pieces of armor and clothing, the brush painted with blood.

Ochen sighed, shaping a sign of blessing over each corpse. "I'd hoped to take one, at least, alive," he murmured. "We could learn much of Rhythamun's magic from them, but he outthought me."

"At least we know they may be slain," said Bracht. "Whatever they are."

"Slain, aye." The wazir snorted, shaking his head, gesturing at the remnants of the creatures. "But only at dreadful risk to whomever they hold."

"How so?" asked Katya. "Your magic destroyed them. After they had killed these warriors, I think."

"Exactly," said Ochen. "*After*. Had these men lived when my magic struck, they'd have suffered the same fate."

Katya frowned a question. Calandryll perceived the thrust of the sorcerer's thinking. "Your magic exploded the creatures," he said, "and had these kotu-zen lived then, they, too, would have been consumed."

"Aye." Ochen nodded. "You see the way of it—whatever gramaryes Rhythamun employed to make these things reacts thus to offensive magic. The fatherless creature counts on that to limit me, may Horul consign him to eternal suffering!"

"I hear more wizardly riddling," Bracht said. "Do you explain in words a simple man might understand?"

"Do these sad monsters take a man," Ochen explained patiently, "then they'll kill him."

"That much," said Bracht, head ducking toward the luckless kotu-zen, "I had understood."

"And you saw the arrows hit?" Ochen asked. "With little enough effect?"

Bracht nodded.

Ochen said, "So magic becomes the best defense—the expected defense. But Rhythamun has countered that, for do I act to protect those his creatures seize by destroying his minions, I slay those held. Thus, he limits me."

"But these men were not destroyed," said Bracht. "Not by your magic."

"They were already dead," returned the wazir, "and so impervious to my sortilege. Magic is a thing that works against the living, a thing of this world, not much designed to work against the dead."

"Ahrd!" Understanding dawned; Bracht's eyes opened wide. "You say that if one of us is taken, your magic shall slay us."

"You've the grasp of it," said Ochen, his voice somber. "Should I attempt the destruction of your captor, I destroy you."

"Why then take these warriors?" Katya asked. "Why not me? Or Bracht, Calandryll?"

"Such creatures as Rhythamun has made of the tensai are not very intelligent." The wazir shrugged, stroked the wispy silver of his long mustache. "Strong, aye. Mightily difficult to slay by any means other than magic. Filled with hate and blood lust. In fact, little better than rabid wolves, and not much more discerning. They attack—they care little whom they take—only that they slay."

"You know something of them?" Calandryll asked. "What they are?"

"A little," said Ochen. "Not much, save what any wazir learns: none in these lands practices such foul magic. Am I right, then they are what we name uwagi. They are men changed by magic into semblance of animals, were-things that answer only to their appetites and their creator. They are very determined and very hard to slay."

"And these are what we face?" asked Bracht.

"I believe it so, aye," said the wazir gravely. "Uwagi and tensai still men yet."

"So—we face brigands." The Kern raised the thumb of his left hand; the index finger: "Were-creatures." The middle finger rose: "Rebellious armies." The next digit: "Rhythamun." The little finger: "And—do we survive all of them—perhaps the Mad God himself."

Ochen nodded soberly. "That would seem the way of it."

"Then let's not delay," said Bracht, his face rigidly solemn. "Such a panoply of enemies awaits us we shall need time to deal with them all."

For a moment Ochen stared blank-faced at the Kern, then his lined features composed into a grin. "Aye," he said. "We'd best hurry, lest they all grow impatient."

Bracht laughed then, and they took up the fallen kotu-zen and carried the bodies back to the road, where Chazali waited.

Another funeral pyre was built, ignited by Ochen's magic, and the corpses given to the cleansing flames.

Calandryll watched the sorcerer-priest perform the rites, aware that each such delay afforded Rhythamun further advantage, thinking that the enemy need not slay him, or Bracht, or Katya, but only take Chazali's men, one by one, slowing them that the warlock find his way, unhindered, to the gate in Anwar-teng, or on to the Borrhun-maj, and work those gramaryes that should raise Tharn and give the world to the Mad God. He curbed his impatience, telling himself that men who had died for the quest deserved those services their beliefs demanded, and waited to ride on.

THAT night the howling came again, the worse for its repetition, the horses fretful, frightened, and sleepless, the humans little better. Immediate fear was set aside, for Ochen ringed the camp with such gramaryes as hung like silken fire among the surrounding trees, glimmering, burning the few arrows that shafted out of the darkness and holding off the uwagi and the tensai, both. But sleep was again impossible, ruptured by the screaming, so that tempers shortened, the kotu-zen growing anxious to confront enemies in honest combat, frustrated, loosing arrows at random into the darkness beyond Ochen's warding occult light. And the questers no less so, aware that their adversary likely suffered no such delay, but pressed on toward his fell goal.

9

THEY rode more wary than ever, swift between the trees, heads swinging ceaselessly in anticipation of ambush, eyes smarting from weariness, tension their constant companion. But no attack came that morning. The sun rose into a blue sky flagged with pennants of high clouds white as driven snow. A breeze blew cool from the north, fresh and scented with pine. Birds sang among the timber. Twice deer leapt across the road, once a huge, tusked boar charged snorting from their path. Toward noonday they came on a village.

Calandryll stared at the silent pastoral scene, calling up those exercises Ochen had taught him to open his senses to awareness of the occult. Immediately he felt the horrid aftermath of fell magic, akin to the sense of dread that had filled the keep on the Kess Imbrun. It seemed then the pine scent the breeze carried was undercut with a charnel reek, a hint of almonds. He drew his sword; saw Ochen frown, squinting at the palisaded huts. The fields stood empty, devoid of animals or toiling gettu. Neither was any sign of movement visible between the open gates; no smoke rose, no dogs barked. There was only stillness, a sense of waiting that prickled at the skin between his shoulders.

"None lives here," the wazir murmured softly, sadly.

They splashed across the stream, the kotu-zen a wall of black armor around the questers as Chazali halted, peering between the gates. He barked a command and five men sprang to the ground, swords drawn, running into the village.

They returned soon enough, to report all dead within. All slaughtered, butchered like the scouts.

Chazali mouthed a curse that was muffled by his veil. The kotu-zen muttered angrily. Ochen said, "They look to unnerve us." Calandryll thought he held his voice controlled.

"Do you perform the rites?" Chazali seemed both enraged and subdued, wrath balanced by the enormity of the massacre, for the first time unsure of himself. "Have we time?"

"We owe them as much." Ochen dismounted, calling over his shoulder for torches to be fashioned. "Albeit briefly."

He walked, chanting, to the gates, arms raised as brands were quickly made, sparks struck. He gestured, and the kotu-zen ran once more among the rude huts, putting them to the torch. The timber was dry: within moments fire began its cleansing work, a roiling tower of black smoke insulting the azure purity of the sky. Calandryll pinched his nostrils against the stink of burning flesh, aware that the oppressive sense of evil magic faded as the wazir ended his incantation. Ochen lowered his arms, his chant dying, and walked wearily back to his horse.

✤   ✤   ✤

THE road climbed after, the terrain no longer a suc-
cession of valleys but a series of tremendous steps,
as though terraced, each gradual ascent leading to a
wide shelf before rising again. Spruce, hemlock,
and larches rose tall and dark, the shadows between them the more menacing for the carnage left
behind, the knowledge that further assaults must
surely wait ahead.

They went on past noon, riding until the pall of
smoke was no longer visible before a halt was
called, and that to rest the animals, for none present had much appetite for food, as if the taint of
the uwagis' work lingered, sour.

"Ahrd," Bracht muttered as he watched the black
stallion forage, "but I think I'd sooner they joined
in battle than this."

"Aye." Calandryll nodded. "This kind of warfare
plays hard on the mind."

"It's as Ochen says," Katya remarked. "They
look to wear us down."

"And succeed," said Bracht. "Shall we sleep this
night, think you?"

The Vanu woman shrugged, sighing, shaking
flaxen hair from her face. Like Bracht's, like
Calandryll's, her eyes were dulled, hollowed by the
dark crescents beneath. Of them all—save Ochen,
who seemed inured by his occult talent—only
Cennaire showed no sign of exhaustion. Her eyes
remained bright, her complexion vital, and
Calandryll, intending a compliment, said, "Adver-
sity favors you, it seems."

"How so?" she asked, instantly cautious.

"Lady," he murmured, smiling, "you appear fresh
as these pines. While we . . ." He chuckled ruefully,
wiping at his eyes.

Alarm grew: Cennaire had not thought that so
small a thing might betray her. Nervous, she

glanced from one to the other, seeing them all
weary, the badges of fatigue stamped clear on their
faces, in their eyes. Deliberately, she let her shoulders slump, her mouth slacken a trifle, and shook
her head.

"You are kind, sir. But"—she shaped a yawn—
"I'd as soon a good night's sleep as any here."

"Perhaps tonight," he said gallantly, echoed by
Bracht's disbelieving snort.

She smiled, hoping it was suitably convincing,
aware that Katya looked her way, the grey gaze
thoughtful, and rubbed at her eyes. She was grateful that Chazali called for them to mount then,
preventing further conversation, further examination. *I must be more careful,* she told herself. *I
must remember to act always ordinary, to show no
sign of what I am.* And beneath that precautionary
consideration ran another thought, an undercurrent
faint as the rustling of the breeze among the timber: that she might sooner tell them everything,
throw herself on their mercy, swear allegiance to
their cause and so terminate this endless subterfuge.

Then, *No!* To do that was to risk too much. To
risk everything; to chance losing all hope of regaining her heart; perhaps to risk death. Certainly
to risk Calandryll's revulsion: she wondered why
that troubled her so.

THE day closed toward evening. The breeze died
away, the pines silent, ominous as the light grew
dusky. Cloud thickened overhead, squadrons of
birds winged roostward. The road widened a little,
and Chazali bellowed over the steady drumbeat of
the hooves that they should find a site soon, halt
for the night.

And from where Ochen rode, behind the kiriwashen, there came a warning shout, a flash of light, silvery gold lanced through with crimson, like darting flame.

Confusion then: arrows that sang from the twilit trees, and the dreadful yammering screams of the uwagi, the shrilling of struck horses. Chazali's breastplate was suddenly decorated with shafts. A horse went down, its rider tumbling, rising with sword in hand, roaring a battle shout as he charged headlong at the trees. Arrows burned, tinder in the fiery light that lashed from Ochen. A racing, howling creature evaporated in a gust of noisome flame. The archers among the kotu-zen loosed answering shots: men screamed and died. Things once men slashed with nails become talons, fangs that thrust from elongated jaws, at men and animals, indiscriminate.

Chazali bellowed, heeling his horse to a charge, curved blade raising high, falling, rising again. A man shrieked, staggering a scant few steps from the shelter of the trees, blood gouting from his riven chest, a sundered arm flapping useless at his side.

In the fading light the shape of fallen pines showed across the road, a barrier too high to jump, bowmen there.

Chazali shouted again, bringing his horse round, hard, back to the road. Red light like serpents' tongues darted from where Ochen stood, and where it struck uwagi died, exploding in eruptions of hideous fire.

Then they were in close, the tensai not altered by Rhythamun's fell magic holding back, the wazir, afraid of destroying friend with foe, forced to concentrate his gramarye on the human, unchanged attackers.

Bracht's falchion shone silver in the magical radiance, hacking down, darting swift as Ochen's bolts, the black stallion shrilling, kicking, deadly as its rider. Katya's saber moved no slower, though she fought her untrained mount even as she struck. Both blades and hooves clove flesh, gore spouting from the howling grey shapes that closed like rabid wolves on the grouping kotu-zen. But with scant effect, as if the changeling creatures lived beyond pain, ignoring wounds that would have felled any mortal thing, driven by Rhythamun's sorcery.

Where Calandryll struggled to control his panicked chestnut, the uwagi carved a path through the kotu-zen. Men were dragged from their mounts; horses fell, screaming. Calandryll's straightsword was lifted, about to fall even as Ochen shouted, "*No!* For Horul's sake—remember, lest you die!"

He remembered: sheathed the blade and drew his dirk instead. Drove the lesser blade into a snarling face that tore itself away, careless of the wound that severed its cheek, returning to the attack even as he struck again. Uselessly: the uwagi crushed against the gelding, the sheer force of its assault sending the animal stumbling, its footing lost. Calandryll caught brief sight of jet armor, a sword that stabbed past him to score a red hole in a chest covered with thick-sprouting hair. Then hands, horribly strong, clutched his wrists and dragged him from the saddle of the falling horse. A blow landed hard on his temple. The gelding's weight pressed down on him. Light burst in his eyes, painful. He thought he shouted; knew vaguely that he was held, hauled from under the horse.

THE fight was brief, more skirmish than battle. The tensai—those yet human—were not enough to stand against Chazali's kotu-zen. Their armor was makeshift, a random assortment of bits and pieces owned when they became outlaw or looted from their victims, their weapons not much better. They were more accustomed to preying on defenseless villagers than trained warriors and they did not last long. The kotu-zen grouped defensive at first, then dismounted and moved out into the trees on foot: those brigands who did not flee were cut down. Eleven of Chazali's men were slain, and five horses. Five tensai were taken alive. Four throats were slit on Chazali's order—the fourth was brought to Ochen, thrown down on his knees before the wazir.

Katya and Bracht pushed urgently through the watching kotu-zen, blades naked in their hands, anger and fear in their eyes.

"Calandryll's taken!" Bracht wiped blood from his falchion; set the point on the tensai's cheek. "Where? Do you tell me, or do I prick out your eyes?"

The Jesseryte warriors murmured approvingly; the outlaw moaned. Blood dribbled from a cut across his forehead, more from a wound on his shoulder. Then a flow from his cheek as the Kern's blade dug deeper. The acrid stench of urine soiled the evening.

"Where?"

Ochen said, "Wait! There's an easier way to this."

"Save I carve out his answers, I see none," Bracht snarled. "And in a while he'll see not at all."

"Trust me," the wazir said. "Put up your blade."

The Kern eyed him a moment. Katya said, "And Cennaire. Where is she?"

"Wait!" Ochen's voice became commanding. He motioned them away. Reluctantly, Bracht sheathed his sword, though his hand remained menacingly on the hilt. Ochen said, "This way lies truth, without subterfuge."

He gestured to Chazali, who took hold of the tensai's unbound hair and yanked the head back. Ochen set a hand under the tensai's chin, raising the man's face. Tears streaked the dirt there, mingling with the blood as the wazir fixed his eyes, tawny gimlets now, on the captive's.

He spoke softly, the words sending the almond scent swirling on the cooling air, his free hand moving to shape sigils, and the prisoner's body went slack, the fear-filled eyes becoming vacant, unfocused.

"He came to us and we thought to take his horse, his armor . . . But we could not . . . He had such power . . . Like a wazir . . . More . . . A wazir-narimasu!"

The man shuddered, spittle flecked his lips; Ochen passed a hand across his face, the perfume of almonds stronger.

"He had power . . . He slew too many of us, nor could we flee him then . . .Only obey him . . . He made uwagi and left us with a duty . . . To halt the followers. Three, he said, outlanders, not Jesserytes . . . Strangers . . . A woman and two men, from the lands beyond . . . He put their faces in the minds of the uwagi . . . We could not disobey . . . The uwagi would have slain us, did we . . . We could not . . . Only obey . . ."

"Where?" Bracht demanded. "Where have they taken Calandryll?"

The tensai shook his head, as best he could with his hair bunched in Chazali's fist. The tendons down his neck stood out; the veins there throbbed; tears and blood mingled down his cheeks; drool streamered from his gaping lips.

"I know not . . . the uwagi obey him . . . Only him."

"He knows no more than that," Ochen said.

"Their camp?" Bracht stared at the wazir. "Shall they not take Calandryll there?"

Unless Calandryll is already dead hung unspoken on the air.

Ochen gestured again and the tensai said, "We've no camp any longer . . . only riding, following you . . . The uwagi were commanded to take him . . . You . . . The Kern or the woman with the pale hair . . . One should be enough, he said . . . Which one, no matter . . . It would end thcn."

"He knows no more."

Ochen glanced at Chazali, nodding, and the kiriwashen drew his knife and severed the tensai's throat.

"Ahrd!" Bracht kicked the twitching body, grief in his cry, frustration. "To horse, then! After them!"

"We'd not catch them." Ochen swept an arm to indicate the forest, the darkened sky. "These woods are too thick, and night comes on."

"I'll not desert him!" Bracht turned toward his horse. "Must I go alone, still I'll go. Katya, are you with me?"

"Wait." The warrior woman set a hand on the Kern's arm, her grip hard, her eyes clouded doubtful, troubled. "Must we go, then aye. But first a word."

"A word?" Bracht shook loose of her hold, set foot to stirrup. "Calandryll's taken, and be we no longer three, then likely Rhythamun takes the day. Takes the world for his master! I say we ride, woods or no, and Ahrd damn the uwagi."

"Wait!" Katya clutched at his shoulder, strong enough to drag him back. The stallion whickered, stamping impatient hooves, yellow teeth snapping at the bit. Katya swung Bracht round, pointing at the Jesserytes. "These folk know the forest better than we. Ochen knows the uwagi better than we. Do we learn what we can, and then decide."

Bracht stood tense, blue eyes locked with grey, his hawkish features planed in furious lines. Katya met his gaze unflinching, and slowly, almost resentfully, his head lowered in acceptance.

"So?" Katya let go the Kern's shoulder, turned to Ochen, Chazali. "What advice have you?"

The metal mask concealing the kiriwashen's face turned toward the wazir, conceding precedence. Ochen scraped painted nails through the strands of his beard. In the dying light his features were graved with apprehension. "Do I seek him with my magic," he said, "then I slay him."

"That much we know," Bracht snapped, "and so must seek him ahorse. On foot, if needs be."

"These woods are no easy place for horsemen," Ochen returned. "And night comes on to render tracking difficult. In Horul's name, my friend! Do you not think I'd be riding now, did I believe we had chance to take him back?"

"You say he's lost?" Bracht shook his head in helpless denial. Katya reached out to take his hand. "We can do nothing?"

"What I must say is hard," Ochen replied. "For me, no less than you. Listen—the uwagi have taken Calandryll, and it may well be that he is already dead . . ."

"*No!*" Bracht shouted his rejection.

"Save," Ochen continued, "that Rhythamun looks to gloat."

"He's that fondness," Katya murmured, a spark of burgeoning hope lighting in her eyes. "In Aldarin, and when he possessed Morrach . . ."

"And such pride may be his weakness," said Ochen. "That he'll seek to sport with Calandryll."

"Sport?" Bracht stepped a pace toward the wazir, his body rigid, fury stark in his eyes, so that Chazali, too, moved a defensive pace forward, halted by Ochen's upraised hand.

"Be it so, then Calandryll perhaps lives still," the wazir said. "Which is likely our only hope. Save . . ."

He paused, frowning, thoughts dancing across the wrinkles that striated his gnarled visage.

"Save?" demanded Bracht.

"He's what tutoring in the occult I was able to give him," Ochen said. "And perhaps his sword, too. Has he his sword still?"

Bracht spun, roughly shouldering the kotu-zen aside as he went to Calandryll's horse. Behind, Chazali shouted, "Calandryll's blade! Did he bear it with him? Do you seek it!"

"I saw the uwagi take him," a warrior said, "and he wore it then. I stabbed the creature when Calandryll held back his blow."

Another said, "His mount went down, but I thought he had the sword still."

Bracht returned: "I found no sign of it."

"Then we've hope." Ochen nodded. "He heard my warning."

"That he may not use his blade?" Bracht gestured helplessly. "You name that hope?"

"Does he use it, then he destroys the uwagi and himself, both," Ochen said slowly, as if he tracked a thought to its source, to its conclusion. "Rhytha-mun is horribly cunning—and daily stronger—and looks to trick us, to beguile us. But . . . Calandryll is no fool, and does he only remember all I've taught him, all we've learned of these foul creatures, then perhaps there remains a chance."

He paused, nodding to himself, as if confirming his own musings. Impatiently, Bracht said, "Do you elaborate?"

The sorcerer nodded more, but this time to the Kern. "Aye," he murmured. "Think on this—does Calandryll retain his sword and his senses, then he knows he can destroy his captors." He raised a hand as Bracht began to protest. "Wait, bear with me a moment—he knows, too, that does he use that blade, he destroys himself."

"Then Rhythamun needs only the sacrifice of his creations," Bracht grunted, "and I suspect he's little enough concern for them. He needs only one to throw itself on Calandryll's blade."

"Save he looks to gloat," said Katya. "And so delays."

"Aye." Ochen's nodding became enthusiastic. "Save he looks to gloat, which I believe may prove his undoing."

"How so?" Bracht demanded. "Even be you right, and the uwagi have not yet slain Calandryll, then still he's captured. Does he defend himself, he dies. You say we cannot go into the forest after him—so Rhythamun has time to gloat. And then slay him. I say we seek him now!"

"I think," said Ochen, "that did the uwagi hear us coming—as undoubtedly they should—that our enemy would forgo his pleasure and have Calandryll slain."

"Ahrd!" Bracht pounded a frustrated fist against his thigh. "You say we lose, no matter what we do."

"No!" Ochen shook his head, his voice gaining a measure of confidence. "I say we've a chance; that Calandryll's a chance. Perhaps even two."

More gently than Bracht, Katya said, "Do you explain?"

Ochen ducked his head in agreement. "But first—Chazali, do you see the fallen cleared away and a fire built? We must halt here awhile. Our dead I shall attend when I may." The kiriwashen nodded and issued the orders, no less intrigued than Bracht or Katya. Ochen continued, "So, does Calandryll yet hold his sword and his wits, he's hope of survival. Rhythamun, does he look to gloat, must travel the aethyr for that pleasure—and on that plane I may be able to delay him. The wazir-narimasu are alerted to Calandryll's presence, and they can likely aid me—together we might slow Rhythamun and win Calandryll a little time."

"Which must surely leave him to the mercies of the uwagi," Bracht said, angry. "Who are commanded to slay him.

Katya touched the Kern's arm, motioning him to patience. "You spoke of two chances," she said.

"Aye," Ochen returned. "You say Cennaire is gone?"

"Cennaire?" Bracht asked, surprised.

"Aye," said Ochen.

"Her horse is there." Katya stabbed a thumb in the direction of the animals milling, still nervous, at the center of the road. "But she? I did not see her body."

"The uwagi took her I suppose," Bracht said, "and slew her. Likely she lies within the trees." He frowned. "A pity—I'd grown to like her. She had courage."

"Without doubt," said Ochen, and turned to Chazali. "Do you ask your men to seek the body of the lady Cennaire?"

The kiriwashen issued fresh orders. Bracht said, "We talk and talk, and hunt corpses. When do we act?"

"When I know what I must know," said Ochen. "Soon, but until then I beg your patience."

The Kern shook his head, looking to Katya. "I've no stomach for this," he declared. "Do we mount and ride in search of Calandryll?"

"And see him slain?" she asked. "No, Bracht, wait. This is not Cuan na'For, that things be simpler. We know Rhythamun stronger here, Tharn stronger—I tell you, we should listen to Ochen."

"Who bids us do nothing," Bracht snarled. "Save leave our comrade to his fate. I'd sooner act!"

"Even so," Katya urged, "wait a little while."

Their argument was interrupted by Chazali.

"The lady Cennaire is not among the dead," the kiriwashen announced. "Her body is neither on the road nor in the trees."

"Then likely she lives still," said Ochen, smiling. "Good."

"What is this?" asked Bracht. "Does Cennaire live, I'm glad. But it seems unlikely. Surely they took her off and she lies within the forest, dead."

"I think not," said Ochen. "I think you should pray to your tree god she survives."

"I do not understand," the Kern said.

"Nor I," said Katya.

"I've not the time to explain," said Ochen. "Only trust me. And Cennaire."

"Cennaire? Ahrd!" Bracht turned away, moving to the stallion. "Riddles and yet more riddles, while Calandryll faces Rhythamun. I ride!"

"No!" Ochen motioned to Chazali. "Trust me!"

The kiriwashen stepped between Bracht and the stallion. The big horse pawed ground, ears flattened back, eyes rolling. Chazali was wary of the beast, but obviously determined to prevent Bracht mounting. Both men touched the hilts of their swords.

Ochen looked to Katya and said, "In Horul's

name! In the name of all the Younger Gods! For
Calandryll's sake, trust me!"

The Vanu woman studied him an instant and
then moved between the Kern and kiriwashen.

"I trust him." She looked into Bracht's eyes,
deep. "For all I like not the way of it, I see no alternative."

"You say we should do nothing?" Disbelief
harshened the Kern's voice. "Stand here while
Calandryll likely dies?"

"Think, Bracht," she urged. "Shall we go blun-
dering through a night-dark wood, our every move
a herald of our coming? Tell the uwagi time runs
out? I think that way we should likely condemn
Calandryll to death. I love him no less than you,
but I suspect our aid is useless now, while Ochen's
magic at his command, and I say that's our chiefest
hope—to trust in his powers, in him."

"In him, perhaps," Bracht allowed. "But this talk
of Cennaire? What part has she to play?"

"I know not." Katya shrugged. "Do we ask
him?"

The night was dark, the moon waned and not yet
reborn, cloud had built, scudding between the land
and the impassive stars. Bracht's face was shadowed, the blue of his eyes hooded between narrowed lids, his lips compressed, frustrated, and
belligerent. For a long moment he stared at Katya's
face, then a slow sigh escaped and his shoulders
slumped, his right hand moving from his swordhilt.

"Think you so, then so be it."

Katya nodded, her teeth flashing, briefly white,
as she smiled. At her back she heard Chazali's low
grunt, sensed the kiriwashen relax. "Let us ask
him," she said.

But it was too late: a fire was already built and
burning, and Ochen squatted before the flames,

staring blank-eyed into the light. His hands were hidden in the wide sleeves of his robe and his body was rigid, only his lips moving to spill out a torrent of muttered syllables, too low, too guttural, to be heard, even were they comprehensible. As he muttered, the scent of almonds wafted.

Bracht mouthed a curse; Katya set a hand upon his shoulder. Chazali, his veil lifted back, came to stand beside them. "Ochen is a great sorcerer," he murmured, "in not very much time he will be wazir-narimasu. As the lady Katya says—trust him, for if any can help, it is he."

"And Cennaire?" Bracht asked. "How shall she help?"

"That I do not understand," Chazali replied. "But if Ochen says she does, then she does."

The Kern blew breath between his teeth. "Would that this world were simpler. Honest sword work, horses, those I understand. But all this sorcery?" He gestured at the wazir, raised his face to the dark and rolling sky. "That remains a mystery."

"I understand it no better than you," said Chazali. "And had I my way, we'd resolve matters as would you—warrior against warrior in honest combat: there's honor in that—but that's not the way of it, eh? Magic lives in this world of ours, and we must live with it. Trust Ochen, my friend, for he can achieve what our blades may not."

"I've little other choice," Bracht murmured, looking to the wazir, who sat immobile, as if the animating spirit had quit his body for another place.

CENNAIRE had sensed the ambush in the same instant Ochen had shouted his warning. She had learned enough from observation, from listening to

Bracht, to Katya, that she utilized her preternatural gifts in defense of the column. Consequently, she had grown aware that the forest fell silent: she could hear only the steady drumming of hooves, the clatter of armor, the sounds of horses and men, not bird song, or the movements of the animals that inhabited the woods. Then Ochen had shouted and she had seen the light of his magic flash out, and in the same instant the flight of arrows, the shapes of the uwagi. She had screamed a warning, but it had gone unheard—or mistaken for a scream of fear—as the attack came. Then all had been confusion, and she had fought for her life as much as any there.

Her horse had panicked, terrified by the weirdling creatures that raced out of the shadows, and she had found herself unseated, dumped unceremoniously on the dirt of the road as all around her men shouted and fought.

She had risen, confused by the tumult, angry enough she felt no fear, and seen the grey manbeasts carving a path toward Calandryll. She had moved, unthinking, in the same direction, pushing limber amid the struggling throng, darting between horses, ducking under swinging blades. A tensai— man, not were-creature—blocked her path, and she had drawn her knife, moving as Katya had taught her to evade his blow, drive her own blade deep into his belly. Gutted, he had moaned, falling forgotten as she pushed on, intent only on reaching Calandryll before the uwagi might slay him.

One, fiercer than its malignant kin, was already close, reaching for him, he lowering his sword on Ochen's shout. Cennaire had stabbed the beast, the knife sinking between its shoulders, and it had snarled and turned on her. She clutched its wrist, turning the talons aside, and snapped the arm, and

the uwagi had only grunted and smashed its arm
back against her, oblivious of the hand—the paw?—
that flapped useless at the limb's end. She was
thrown back then, tumbling, reminded of the were-
men's terrible strength, and found herself amid a
sea of pounding hooves, all confusion and battle
shouts, scuttling undignified to safety. Climbing
once more to her feet in time to see the chestnut
gelding bowled over, Calandryll lifting from the
saddle, a leg trapped as the horse went down. Seen
the uwagi close about him, drag him clear.

She had moved toward him, but before she could
reach him, the creatures had lifted him up and carried him off. And she had gone after them—after
him.

They had run into the forest, and on its edge she
had halted, wondering what she did. They could
rend her, these creations of the occult. She had
seen their filthy work, and entertained no doubt
that they possessed such strength as could tear her
limb from limb, leave her alive still, perhaps condemned to eternal suffering.

She did not know for sure; only that Calandryll
was taken and that senses deeper than those her
revenancy gave her told her to go on, to do what
she could for him. What spoke to her then ran
deeper than blood, than bone, and she did not understand it, nor have the time to consider it.
Anomius's diktat—that the questers must survive
to win the Arcanum, that the ugly little warlock
might take it for his own? That he should grow
wrathful, did she allow Calandryll taken captive,
slain, without she attempted his rescue? That she
might earn the displeasure of the Younger Gods did
she do nothing?

No!

All she knew in that instant was that Calandryll was taken: it did not occur to her to desert him.

She paused only to assess her path, head raised, listening.

She heard the noises the uwagi made, carrying off their burden, the sounds of snapping twigs, the pad of running feet. She smelled them, a lingering, sour odor, sweat and decay mixed with the pine scent of the woodland. She peered into the trees, the night no obstacle to her vision.

Then she began to run, questing anxious, vengeful.

The ground was soft with the underlay of needles, of coarse grass. Thickets of brambles and brush obstructed, ferns crushed sappy under her feet. Branches hung low and thick: she ducked beneath them, or snapped them off uncaring, ignoring the twigs that snagged her hair, sprang sharp against her face. She ran, pursuing, darting around the massive boles of pines, cedars, larches, the dendrous perfumes mingling with the reek of the uwagi, the scents of terrified animals, deer and rabbits and wild hogs that fled the occult abominations, and through all that the single odor of life: Calandryll's. That, she clung to, knowing that while she could taste it on the air he lived still, that the uwagi had not slain him, but bore him away for some reason she did not understand, nor cared to consider; only that so long as she could smell it he lived.

It was enough: she raced on.

And then she slowed, for ahead the sounds of flight had ended.

She moved more cautiously now, taking care where she placed her feet, avoiding obstacles, stalking the obscene hunters. Then halted, pressing tight against the trunk of a pine, driving herself into its shadow, watching, listening.

There was a clearing. Grass grew thick where the encircling trees allowed the sun entry, dark now beneath the clouded nighttime sky, but that no hindrance to her sight. Pines like the walls of a temple ringed the space, and Cennaire was minded of the shrines dedicated to Burash, in Kandahar, where circles of great stone pillars stood about the altar. But no altar here, nor any god, save Tharn made his presence felt; neither priests, unless the uwagi stood in stead.

And Calandryll the sacrifice, for he stood ringed by such creatures as nightmares make, votaries of the Mad God.

Cennaire reached for her knife and found it gone, likely still lodged in the back of the uwagi she had stabbed. No matter: she had other, greater strengths. Silent as a hunting cat she stepped forward, to the very edge of the trees, pausing in their shelter, studying the tableau before her, not certain what she witnessed; no more sure what she should do, what she *could* do.

CALANDRYLL opened his eyes onto darkness, a strange pattern of shifting shades that blended so fast, one with another, that he at first thought he once more traveled the plane of the aethyr. Then he felt pain and realized he traversed a more mundane landscape, a place of night-dark trees, of rustling branches overhanging and brief glimpses of cloudy, moonless sky. His head throbbed; a leg—which, he could not be sure—felt pounded, aching; his arms and his ankles were held as if set with manacles. A smell invaded his nostrils, fetid and foul, like rotting flesh left overlong in the sun:

knowledge returned and he bit back the cry that
threatened to escape his mouth.

He was carried off by the uwagi, held by the creatures and borne through the forest.

Panic threatened and he forced himself to
calm—at least a measure, imposed over the desperate thudding of his heart, the terror that slunk
about the edges of his awareness—and assessed his
situation.

It was a gloomy prospect. Four of the uwagi held
him firm, casually as if they bore a sack at break-
neck speed along trails too wild, too narrow that
mounted warriors might easily follow. The hands
that held him were iron bands, unbreakable: he realized he lacked the strength to fight free. The creatures leapt tree trunks, thickets, or charged
carelessly through. His teeth jarred in his jaw, his
head spun, bouncing. He feared the sheer speed of
their going should kill him, break his neck, or shatter his skull against a stump. The sword hung still
from his belt, a useless, tantalizing weight.

But he lived.

He did not understand why: the changelings
might have slain him, easily, back on the road; or
killed him within the shelter of the timber. But he
lived: it was a straw he clutched avidly.

He had no way of telling where they went, save
deeper into the forest, each loping pace taking
him farther from his comrades, from Ochen, and
Chazali's kotu-zen. He felt horribly alone, defenseless, wondering if perhaps the uwagi carried him
off to some ritual slaughter, a slow and painful
dying. He felt the sword's quillons snag on brambles, tear free, and wondered why they had not
stripped him of the blade. A flash of reason then,
light through the darkness of fear: perhaps they
could not handle the blade. Perhaps the magic Dera

had set in the steel rendered the sword sacrosanct, beyond the touching of such foul things as the uwagi. Was that of aid, hope? He thought on Ochen's warning—if not aid, then perhaps, at least, escape. Did worse come to worst—and the chance present itself—he could destroy his captors with the sword. He would die, but that should surely be a swifter end, and less painful than anything the creatures planned for him. Save if he took that course . . .

. . . The quest ended with him!

Three, always three: every prophecy, every scrying, had spoken of three. It was scribed on his mind: Katya, Bracht, himself—the questers, those ordained to stand against Rhythamun's fell design, against the resurrection of the Mad God. Did one fall, all was lost. The thought filled him with sadness. Not for the loss of his life, for that had been a consideration, even a likelihood, since this quest began, and while he had no wish to die, still he accepted that someday he must. Rather, it was a sadness that after so much travail the quest should be ended, that Rhythamun should win. Anger stirred then, hot, righteous, dispelling sorrow, and he determined to sell himself as dear he might.

Abruptly, he realized that the darkness overhead assumed a different hue, that motion ceased. He gasped as he was dropped carelessly to the ground, the leg on which his horse had rolled throbbing. He grunted a curse that was no less a prayer, and fought upright, hand falling instinctively to his swordhilt.

The blade whispered from the scabbard, defensive, defiant, and he stared, eyes narrowed in an attempt to penetrate the shadows, confused that no attack came. Gradually, his night vision returned and he stared around, wondering what obscene

game was played, what tune his captors plucked on
his taut-strung nerves.

They stood in a circle about him, seven of them,
behind them a ring of high, wind-rustled pines, state-
ly and solemn. The uwagi seemed to wait, leashed
by some imperative beyond his understanding, beyond sword's reach, watching, their breath like the
panting of wolves, or rabid dogs. Indeed, they appeared as much lupine as human, a hideous blending
of characteristics: creatures out of nightmare. They
stood shorter than the Jesserytes they had been, for
their legs were bowed and curiously bent, as if the
bones, the joints, changed shape, and their shoulders
were hunched, massive, extending into unnaturally
long arms that ended in hands like paws, great talons thrusting where once nails had been. Muscle
bulged and corded over their torsos, bursting the
clothing, the armor, they had worn, tatters of cloth
and mail hanging like cerements, like memories of
their forsaken humanity. Tufts of grey hair, coarse
and thick, sprouted from pallid skin, from features
horribly shifted to semblance of animals. Their
brows were low, flattened, ridges of bone extending
over deep-seated eyes that glowed with a red, unholy
fire. Nostrils flared wide above prognathous muz-
zles, the lips stretched back from long fangs, sharp
as daggers, slaver hanging in streamers that swayed
with their panting. One sported a hand that flapped
loose, the arm broken between wrist and elbow. It
showed no more sign of discomfort than the one
that still wore his dirk in its cheek.

They reminded Calandryll of nothing so much as
a wolf pack. No, for irrelevantly he recalled
Bracht's words—that wolves did not attack man-
kind. A pack of hounds, then. Great, foul, ensorcelled hounds, set to the hunt, now waiting . . . On

what? The order to attack? Their master's command?

Aye! Of course—they waited on their creator!

Calandryll turned slowly round, his sword on guard, and as he turned, so the changeling creatures backed away, drawing clear of the blade's threat. His own breathing came deep and urgent, and he could no more deny the fear that stirred than he could the throbbing of his bruised leg—the uwagi waited. Perhaps even some vestiges of humanity remained within their contorted shapes, within their deformed souls, and they feared the blade, themselves feared the death it might bring them. Perhaps he had a chance.

"So, are you afraid?" He lunged at the closest monstrosity; saw it dart back, the circle shifting to hold him at its center without coming in range of a blow. "You fear my sword? You know what it can do?"

The uwagi growled, shuffling, studying him with horrid red eyes, like coals glowing in blackened pits. He felt a little encouraged, and sprang closer, whirling the blade, taking care it should not quite strike. The changelings backed away, circled, pacing, snarling, continuing to hold him within their aegis. He wondered what they might do did he charge them, and raised the straightsword high, feinting an attack.

One spoke, and it was like the rumbling growl of a dog, the words thickened and distorted, spraying drool and fetid breath in equal measure.

"Attack and you die. We die, but you, too. Our master commands—wait."

The creature emphasized its order with a slash of its taloned paw: Calandryll retreated, not yet quite ready to sacrifice himself. He lived yet, and so there was yet hope. Perhaps his comrades would come, would somehow find a way through the forest. Perhaps Chazali's archers would rain shafts on the beast-men; Bracht and Katya, all the surviving kotu-zen, fall on the creatures; Ochen come with his magic.

Then: No, he thought, for he had already seen what Ochen's magic did to these things, and knew that its use must ensure his own death as certainly as if he drove his blade into the mocking, snarling face. Seen, too, how little use plain steel was against them; and the forest was too deep, the way they had come too trackless, that he should be found.

He was trapped: he lowered the sword, waiting, not sure for what, other than death.

It was unnerving, to stand thus surrounded, and he sought a measure of reassurance in the psychic exercises Ochen had taught him, concentrating, focusing his mind, seeking calm. What had the uwagi said? *Our master commands—wait*, and Rhythamun was their undoubted master, but why did he not order his creations to attack?

Save he intended some worse fate than mere death! Calandryll thought then of the terrible pressure that had driven him across the aethyr, of the sense of awful dread as his pneuma had been drawn ever closer to Tharn. That should be a fate infinitely worse, to "live" eternally in the power of the Mad God. His mouth was suddenly dry; his body abruptly chilled. He struggled to retain calm, and low, the words little more than a rumble in his throat, voiced the cantrips that should ward his pneuma, his essential spirit, from kidnap, hold it—he hoped!—firm against occult assault.

And the uwagi that had spoken was suddenly rigid, shoulders flung back, the ghastly features straining upward, howling at the clouded sky, the taloned hands opening and then clenching as the body shuddered and seemed to shift, another image imposed over its brutish form: the shape of a Jesseryte warrior, the veil of his helmet thrown back to reveal a face, indistinct, beastly and human, both, that smiled malign mockery.

Calandryll stared, scenting the odor of almonds mingling with the reek of the creatures, seeing the form of the Jesseryte imposed on the flickering shape of the uwagi, one then the other, dreamlike, like the shifting, darting movements of a fish glimpsed through rippling, sun-lit water.

He braced himself, favoring his bruised leg, the straightsword extended, knowing beyond doubt what—*who!*—possessed the were-thing.

And Rhythamun chuckled and said, "A tidy trap, no? Use that blade and you die, leaving me the victory. Do not use it, and my pets rend you limb from limb. You've seen their work, I think—shall you enjoy that fate? No matter, for I take the day. The day and the Arcanum, both, with all the world to follow when I raise Tharn. And for you, suffering beyond your imagination."

The warlock laughed, or the uwagi laughed, for they both occupied the same temporal space. Calandryll snarled, not now unlike the ferocious growling of the were-beasts, for rage burned in him, and hatred, exiling all fear, all sorrow, leaving only wrath.

"Which do you choose?" Rhythamun asked. "The one death is, perhaps, swifter than the other, but whichever—your quest ends here. In a lonely place, with none to mark where you fall. Does that sit bitter, Calandryll den Karynth? Do you see now how foolish it has been to oppose me; to oppose Tharn's raising."

"*No!*"

It was a challenge and denial, together, and met with mocking laughter. He saw the armored shoulders of the Jesseryte, and the hulking width of the uwagi, shrug.

"No? How say you, no? What shall you do, save die? Die knowing your quest comes to naught, that I am victorious. That in time your allies shall die. The Kern and the Vanu woman, the upstart sorcerer who aids you—all of them! While I go on to raise my master and stand at his right hand, favored. And you? Your body shall lie here, riven by your own sword or by my creations, while your spirit suffers tortures past your comprehension. Yet, at least; though you shall find them soon enough." Again, the horrid laughter, confident and contemptuous. "Was it such a gift your feeble goddess gave you? It seems to me a curse now—the instrument of your death, if so you choose."

"Save I strike you," Calandryll roared. "What then, warlock? Dera set holy magic in this blade, and I think that do I plunge her power into that body you use, then your pneuma shall feel the blow."

The uwagi that was Rhythamun in his Jesseryte form howled horrible mirth. Slaver fell on Calandryll's face, distasteful; ignored as he waited, poised.

"You take lessons in sorcery, eh? Doubtless from the mage who came to your aid before. My pneuma, you say? You think to harm me within the aethyr? You pride yourself, boy. Think you a scant handful of lessons, a smattering of that lore I've studied down the ages, can aid you or harm me? I say you again, no! Strike and discover!"

Calandryll held back, his mind racing, delving frantically into all Ochen had told him, into all the lessons—few enough, Dera knew!—he had received. Aloud, he said, not sure whether he believed his own words, or merely looked to buy more time, "You send your animus into this thing you made—you meld with it—so do I strike it, I strike you. What then, Rhythamun? Are you greater than the Younger Gods?"

"I am," said the shifting thing, with awful conviction. "Ere your blow can land, I shall be gone, and that blade your puking goddess blessed strikes the flesh of my creation—which shall be your destruction, and the ending of your quest. Tharn's blood, boy, you've seen what magic does to these things! You've lost, and all you've done comes to naught. So strike; or do I set them on you? It matters little to me."

"I think you are afraid," Calandryll said.

"Afraid?" The obscene laughter filled the clearing, howling off the trees. "I afraid? Strike, then, fool!"

"Aye!" Calandryll shouted, and sprang to the attack, the blade carving swift at the mocking face.

10

CALANDRYLL was emptied of fear in that moment: the rage that gripped him left no space for any other emotion. He knew only that Rhythamun's animus dwelt in the uwagi, and hoped—trusted to Dera and all her kindred gods—that his blow should land ere the warlock might quit the body. That he would be consumed in the occult devastation was no longer a consideration, a matter of scant importance were he able to slay the sorcerer. Even did the blow serve only to banish Rhythamun's pneuma to the aethyr it might still prove a victory—Pyrrhic, but what matter that, if Ochen, if the wazir-narimasu of Anwar-teng, were able to hunt the warlock there? It seemed a small enough sacrifice, his life against the sorcerer's defeat: he put all his strength into the cut.

And saw, as if time slowed, as if he stepped aside, occult and corporeal existences divided and he become observer of his own actions, the blade swing down, true, at the cranium of the beast that was Rhythamun.

He saw rank terror glint startled in the red eyes; triumph in the tawny Jesseryte orbs. Smelled fear sweat and almonds; heard mocking laughter. Saw the were-form flicker again, no longer possessed, but wholly uwagi; and knew he was defeated, that Rhythamun fled the body faster than his sword fell, and that as edge clove skull he was dead, the triumvirate broken, the quest doomed to failure.

The blade sang down its trajectory, sure as death, unstoppable, carving air that soon should be replaced by bone and brain, and then the explosion of opposed magicks. He saw his death draw remorselessly closer.

And a shape burst from the pines, fleet as flighted arrow, too fast his peripheral vision had chance to discern what moved. He saw the uwagi hurled aside, bowled howling over, the straight-sword crash against empty turf, driving deep, the wrath-filled force of the blow jarring his arms, his shoulders. He snatched it free, hearing the laughter falter, lost under the uwagi's scream as the were-beast was hauled upright, the hands that gripped its throat tugging back the neck as a knee drove against the spine. Time resumed its natural passage then, as the creature was bent, arched over until the horrid sound of snapping bone announced the breaking of its spine. Its scream pitched shrill and abruptly died. Calandryll saw it lifted and flung across the clearing, tumbling three of its kindred monsters like skittles, and then he was grabbed, spun round, and hurled toward the tenuous safety of the trees.

He landed on his face, winded and momentarily stunned, pine needles sharp, pungent, against his mouth. Bewildered, unsteady, he pushed up on hands and knees, retrieved his sword, and clambered to his feet, staggering, dizzy, back to the clearing's edge. And gasped in naked amazement as a second were-beast was felled.

Cennaire?

He wondered momentarily if he dreamed—how could it be Cennaire who stood there?

Yet it was; like a wildcat, furious, moving with a speed, a strength, he could scarce believe, ducking beneath a reaching paw to clutch the arm and snap it, to crush the windpipe and drive a fist against the gaping jaws so hard, so savage, the bones crumpled, lifting the bulky creature to hurl the thing as though it were no more than a weightless rag doll, at its confused companions.

Two of the monsters lay dead then. Others yammered rage and bewilderment. One stood, arms raised, its form flickering, possessed by Rhythamun, the scent of almonds growing stronger.

Calandryll shouted, "Cennaire!" and began to move out of the timber.

The woman shouted, "No, flee! I can hold them!"

And light, eye-searing, burst from the outthrust hands of the thing that was owned by the sorcerer. It struck Cennaire, smashing her down, blackening the grass where she stood as if foul poison sullied the night-dark green. Calandryll thought her surely dead then, but she rose, shaking long hair from her face, and moved once more toward the uwagi.

Calandryll raised his blade, unthinking now, intent only on defending the woman. Four of the uwagi stood before her, while the fifth again raised its arms, though now the eyes looked not at Cennaire, but to where Calandryll came out from the trees.

"In Burash's name!" Cennaire screamed. "Do you get yourself to safety! Leave me, for the gods' sake. For your sake!"

Calandryll shouted, "No," and saw fresh light, bright beyond color, beyond belief, soul-searing, lance from the Rhythamun-uwagi.

It seemed then that an ax collapsed his chest, a garrotte wound about his throat. It seemed his eyes melted in their sockets, that all his limbs shattered. He did not know he fell, for a while knew only a darkness crimsoned by agony, as if all his organs burst and flooded his body with ruptured blood, and a dreadful tugging, like a cord drawn tight about his soul, about his spirit, seeking to drag his pneuma out into the aethyr, into a limbo of eternal suffering. Not knowing he did it, he once more mouthed the gramaryes Ochen had taught him, warding his animus against the occult attack, careless of his body, concerned only that Rhythamun not take his soul. Then he became aware that his mouth clogged, gagging on turf and needles, which mattered little, for he was choking and burning. The scent of almonds was pungent in his nostrils and he knew that he was dying, was killed.

And then he was lifted again and some measure of sense returned, enough that he realized Cennaire held him, her hair soft on his cheek, her arms incredibly strong, carrying him into the trees even as the uwagi howled and all around them the forest flamed, wracked by sorcery.

Trees toppled, felled by the blasts of Rhythamun's sortilege; the night was loud with detonations, the crash of falling timber, the explosion of burning branches, the crackle of burning bushes. He felt himself laid down, softly, and for an instant Cennaire knelt beside him. Her eyes were huge and brown, moist as if she wept, but she smiled and touched his face gently, and said, "Flee! Better you survive than I. I will earn what time I can."

He shook his head, wincing as pain knifed his skull, and mumbled, "I cannot," the words thick on a tongue that felt scorched and befurred.

"You must," she said urgently, putting her mouth close that she might be heard through the thunder of destructive magic. "They'll slay you else, and your quest be ended. Now go!"

He began to ask, "Why?" but she dammed the question with a touch, her fingers gentle, and rose, smiling briefly, and said, "Because. Ask no more; only save yourself. Before those hunters come again."

Then she was gone, running back through the flames and the tumbling trees.

Calandryll rose awkwardly to his feet. The straightsword was still in his hand and he needed rest on it a moment as his head swam, sucking in deep breaths that, to his surprise, came clear and clean down a throat he thought was crushed. He hefted the sword, looking about, to find the way Cennaire had gone. He did not think of flight: that was desertion, betrayal; instead, he went after her.

It was easy enough to locate her, for fire burned where she went, the night air grown thick with the resinous odor of pine smoke, the howling of the uwagi an aural beacon. Sparks smoldered on the leathers he wore, in his hair; his eyes watered, his hurt leg throbbed dully. He stumbled and staggered, dodging falling trunks, going after her.

He was not sure how he survived the devastation Rhythamun hurled at the forest, blindly it seemed, seeking to destroy by sheer overwhelming force what Cennaire had denied his subtlety, what Ochen's tutelage had denied his occult trap. Calandryll knew only that he did, that he lived and that he found the clearing again, and saw Cennaire,

a little way inside the ring of flaming pines, a dead
were-thing at her feet, three others circling her.

The fourth—Rhythamun—stood aloof, uwagi and
Jesseryte warrior simultaneously, reeking of almonds, the man's mouth forming the arcane syllables that shaped the blasts, the other drooling and
shrieking.

Then sudden silence. A pause, an immense stillness, as if the world's turning halted. The flames
consuming the forest sputtered and died; Rhythamun's chanting ceased; the uwagi's howling faded
away.

Soft, clear light, like the lambent radiance of the
sun rising over the horizon at midsummer, or the
perfect clarity of its setting, shone across the sky
above the glade, folding the pines, the grass, within
a dome of brilliance. The almond scent, somehow
softer, gentler, replaced the acrid smell of smoke. A
curse rang loud from the distorted mouth of the
uwagi Rhythamun possessed and the creature's
form shimmered, leeched of its Jesseryte shape, become again only a were-beast, falling to its knees,
paws outthrust, head hanging as if a blow drove it
down.

Inside Calandryll's head a voice without sound
said, *Ward yourself! Get down*, and he dropped,
flat, obeying the command without thought, aware
through that part of his mind still attuned to the
occult that an aura of benign power enveloped him.

Lucent bolts flickered then, lancing down from
the sky, shafts brighter than lightning, dazzling.
They struck the uwagi, and as they touched the
creatures, the were-things exploded. Blinded,
Calandryll yelled, "No!" thinking Cennaire consumed in that destruction, horrified, a void opening
in him, gaping empty. But when his vision cleared
he saw her standing still, swaying as if she strug-

gled against tremendous wind, shaken by the gusting, but living still. Blood soiled her clothing and her hair was wild, one arm flung up to protect her eyes. Of the uwagi, or Rhythamun's animus, there was no trace, only little tatters of skin hung on scorched branches, tiny fragments of hair and clothing draped on burned bushes. But Cennaire lived!

Calandryll rose, limping clear of the sheltering trees, sheathing the straightsword as he went toward her. There was nothing left of the uwagi, nor any lingering hint of magic, save the dead patch of grass were Rhythamun had cast his first spell, the blackened trunks ringing the clearing. The light that had filled the sky was gone, the welkin again cloud-struck, a moody dark.

Cennaire seemed stunned, unaware of his approach until he put his hands upon her shoulders and turned her round to face him. Then she moaned and fell against him, held him with arms that seemed once more soft, no longer imbued with the strength he had felt before. She shuddered, and he stroked her hair, her face, glad beyond dreaming that she survived. She looked up and in her eyes he saw a terrible desperation, a fear. Mistaking it for something else, he said, "They're slain. I know not how, save Ochen intervened, but they are gone."

She trembled against his chest, and he tilted her chin, lowering his face to kiss her, her lips responding eagerly, her body pressing hard, urgently, against him.

When they drew apart, their arms still comforting about each other, she said softly, "I feared you dead. I thought . . ."

Tears glistened in her eyes and he shook his head. "No. I live," he murmured. "Thanks to you."

"Praise all the gods," she whispered.

"But you?" He raised his head, chin tilted to indicate the clearing. "When that magic struck, how did you survive? Ochen said the destruction of the uwagi should destroy the living. Yet—thanks be to Dera!—you live."

She nodded, her eyes clouding, and murmured, "Ochen said their destruction should slay the living."

"I do not understand," he said.

"No." Fear grew in her eyes and she bit a moment at her lower lip. "There is much to be explained."

Again she shuddered, and he held her tight, not understanding. "Do we find the others?" he suggested, thinking that the best reassurance.

For a moment she hesitated, holding him, not wanting to face what now must be told, what could no longer be hidden. Then she said, very softly, forlornly, "Aye. Do we find them and speak of all this."

CALANDRYLL's bruised leg pained him, aching dully as they made their way back toward the road, so that he leaned against Cennaire, letting her help him over obstacles, avoid the hindrance of thickets and brambles, content enough to feel her arm around his waist, his about her shoulders. The forest was very dark now, the night aging toward dawn, and he found it difficult to discern the path, while Cennaire seemed not to hesitate, as if her eyes found the obfuscation no problem.

He wondered at that, and then at all he had witnessed: her strength, the way she had faced and overcome the uwagi, that she was not destroyed with the were-breasts, and had stood immune to Rhythamun's magic.

But neither was I, he thought, *so perhaps whatever gramaryes protected me protected her.*

Perhaps, he thought, *she is chosen by the Younger Gods, and they protect her.*

And yet, had Ochen not said that the magicks
that might destroy the uwagi must also destroy the
living? That had been the trap Rhythamun set, so
why—*how*—had Cennaire lived through that assault?

Her arm was warm where it rested about his
waist. He smelled her hair, the scent of her skin,
could feel the softness of her as he held her; had
tasted the vitality of her lips. And yet . . . How had
she slain the uwagi? How had she found him? How
had she survived?

He did not understand, and when he turned his
face to look at her, to voice the questions, he saw
hers set grim, determined, as if she moved toward
confrontation, not away from a victory. She seemed
. . . he was not sure . . . wary, fatalistic, and he left
the words unsaid, the doubts unsettled, skirling
troublesome about his mind. She had saved his life,
preserved the quest—surely that spoke for itself,
that she had risked her own life for his sake. There
could surely be no doubt of her integrity. He
pushed such thoughts aside, remembering the softness of her lips, her embrace, and without thinking
nuzzled her glossy hair.

Cennaire started at the touch, glancing up, her
eyes troubled. Her mouth curved in a brief smile
and then she looked away, concentrating on the
path. She was afraid—of what must now become
revealed, and of how he might react, how his comrades would react. Perhaps Ochen—who had so far
kept her secret—could sway them, could persuade
them against . . . She was uncertain what they
might do. Look to slay her? Banish her from their

company? Demand the wazir bind her with his magicks? For an instant she contemplated deserting Calandryll, leaving him to make his own way back to the road. Then dismissed the notion: he could barely walk unaided and might lie lost within the forest, or Rhythamun might return in some guise to slay him. That thought she could not bear, so she stifled her fear and pressed on. She would bring him to the road's edge at the least, and then ... Then she would decide. She could leave him there, safe, and follow after. Save then she must trek to Pamur-teng and likely onward to Anwar-teng, and all her gear lay in her saddlebags. Doubtless, did she simply disappear, the mirror Anomius had given her should be discovered, and with it her secret. Then, if she were gone, the questers must surely deem her enemy, and turn against her; and did that come to pass, she could entertain little hope of success, either of satisfying the strictures of her master, or of regaining her heart.

It was an enigma, a mandala, twisting about itself so that each possibility, every consideration, returned to the starting point: that whichever course she chose, she must stand revealed as revenant.

There seemed, in it all, only the one sure fact— that she must return Calandryll to safety and reach whatever decision she must make after she knew him secure.

As chance had it, or fate, or whatever design wove their destinies, the decision was taken from her.

THE night descended into the absolute absence of light that precedes dawn. The forest was utterly

still. Then the sky was filled with grey opalescence, birds began to chorus, announcing the as-
cension of the sun, and the blank etiolation was
transformed. The heavens paled, grey replaced with
soft pink, brightening to silvery gold, hints of
azure. Cennaire heard the searchers long before
Calandryll, and thought again of leaving him. Dismissed the thought as she felt his weight against
her, and went on, toward the sounds. She felt suddenly very weary, leeched of judgment, indecisive,
even careless of her fate. What came would come:
she would see Calandryll safe, and that would be
enough.

Suddenly, bright as the radiance that filled the
sky, she experienced a kind of freedom. She thought
no longer of herself, but only of him. She smiled
and asked, "Do you hear? We come to the road. To
safety."

Calandryll frowned, head cocked, listening, then
nodded and grinned: "Aye, I hear them now."

Then figures came through the trees, Bracht and
Katya, Ochen, Chazali, kotu-zen. Cennaire called,
"Here," and she was surrounded, passing her
limping burden to the Kern and the kiriwashen, the
wazir and the warrior woman either side of her,
questions clammering until she shook her head and
trod wearily toward the road.

Pyres burned there, consuming the slain, the sur-
vivors of the battle moving farther off, upwind, to
where more welcoming fires blazed, giving off the
smell of roasting meat and tea. Ochen caught
Cennaire's eye and smiled wanly, she answering in
kind, helplessly, allowing herself to be carried
along, seeing Calandryll settled on a spread blanket, against a saddle, Ochen kneeling to massage
his damaged leg, murmuring softly, his sorcery
healing.

Katya said, "We feared you slain," her grey eyes wondering.

Bracht looked up from over Ochen's shoulder and said, "What happened? Where were you?"

Calandryll said, "She saved me. Dera, but had she not come . . ." and then halted, staring, puzzled, at the Kand woman, dawn's early light, the company of comrades, reawakening all the questions the night and relief at living still had stifled.

Ochen said, "Do we take tea, and speak? I think the time has come that certain truths be told."

Cennaire glanced round, thinking that she might, even now, flee. Might burst through the ring of curious watchers and escape into the woods. She had fought with uwagi, had lived through occult assault—these mere men could hardly withstand her. Then she met Ochen's gaze, and saw a question in his narrow eyes, and a measure of hope, and she shrugged, filled with careless exhaustion, a lassitude that leeched her of purpose, leaving behind only a numb fatalism, and nodded, seating herself.

Calandryll, looking hard into her eyes, said, "Had Cennaire not come, I should be dead now. Rhythamun set his snares well, and without her aid, he'd have slain me."

His voice was firm, but she saw a question in his eyes and wondered if he did not dredge that authority from a sense of loyalty, from the attraction she sensed he held. She was flattered, smiling her gratitude, albeit wanly, but still felt careless of her fate, in a manner she did not properly understand grateful that it was now taken out of her hands.

"How so?" asked Bracht. "Her?"

"Aye," Calandryll said. "I owe Cennaire my life."

"Ochen sent his magic to your aid," Katya said,

"augmented by the wazir-narimasu. Do you tell us what happened?"

Cennaire sat waiting, irresolute, committed now to revelation, starting when Calandryll reached out to take her hand, answering his smile with hopeless determination, then turning toward Ochen, saying, "Aye, tell it."

"They seized me," said Calandryll, "on Rhythamun's instruction, and took me into the forest . . ."

Cennaire listened as he told the tale, her eyes on his face, aware of the gasps that escaped the others, surprised, all save Ochen, who took up the story:

"I found the wazir-narimasu as I hoped I should, and we brought our power into the aethyr, joined and channeled. Rhythamun's trap was triple set—that the uwagi might slay Calandryll; or he destroy himself by slaying them; or Rhythamun slay him. All that in the physical plane; far worse that Rhythamun leech out his animus, entrap his pneuma in the realms of the aethyr. It was a design of diabolic cunning, and without Cennaire it should have succeeded. She it was saved Calandryll where I, and the wazir-narimasu, should have failed. Without her, Calandryll would now be dead, and his soul ensnared by the warlock, by Tharn. Had she not intervened, your quest would be doomed to failure. What hope remains, you owe to her."

"How," asked Bracht, studying the Kand woman with confusion in his blue eyes, "did she survive that destruction? You say you placed a protection about Calandryll; but she stood alone when your magic struck."

"And how," Katya asked, softer, the beginnings of suspicion in her voice, "did she find Calandryll? You told us pursuit was useless. That we might do nothing, save trust in you and her."

"Aye, so I did," Ochen returned.

"And that magic that destroys the uwagi destroys the living with it," Bracht said. "So how does Cennaire survive?"

"Dera, she saved me!" Calandryll said, defensive, not liking the direction these questions took. "Does the how of it matter? The why of it? She saved me—I owe her my life! Without her I should be slain now, or worse."

Cennaire felt his fingers clutch tighter on her hand, and smiled thanks for his trust. Their eyes met, a hope, a warning, in his that she chose to ignore as she shook her head and said, "Ochen knows how I survived." Then she sighed and asked, "So, wazir, do you tell it, or I?"

Ochen fetched the kettle from the fire, filled cups with tea, and passed them round, his wrinkled face creased deeper as he pondered. When all, waiting, bewildered and impatient, had accepted, he said, "First, understand that I have known since you came into this land what you are, all of you. That is why I league with you—that Rhythamun shall be defeated, that Tharn be not raised, the Arcanum destroyed. I saw in each of your souls the measure of your spirit, the hope and the purpose in you. Those things that cannot be concealed from one who views the aethyr . . ."

"Riddles," Bracht grunted. "Speak plain, Ochen."

The wazir nodded, hesitating. Cennaire extracted her hand from Calandryll's grip, no longer able to wait, wanting only that all be laid open so that she know, for better or for worse, how they—how he!—might view her when the truth was told.

"I am magic's creation," she said quietly. "Anomius made me."

"*Anomius!*" The falchion was suddenly in

Bracht's hand, leveled on her heart as the Kern sprang upright. "You're his creature?"

"Bracht!" Calandryll moved to push the blade aside. "For Dera's sake! For Ahrd's sake! She saved my life."

The Kern shifted balance, away from Calandryll's grasp, the sword still angled at Cennaire's breast. Katya glanced briefly at Ochen and motioned Bracht to wait, though Cennaire saw her own right hand drop to her saber's hilt.

"He made me what I am," she said, her smile become cynical, her eyes fixed on the falchion's point, uncaring. "He took me from the dungeons of Nhur-jabal and cut out my heart."

"We thought him dead," Calandryll murmured softly, looking from Cennaire to Bracht, to Katya and Ochen. Pain lay in his eyes, a rejection of her statement.

"He lives," said Cennaire. "Oh, aye! He lives, and would have the Arcanum for his own. He'd slay Rhythamun for that prize. And all of you, save he believes you shall lead him to the book."

"With you as guide!" Bracht's blade pressed against her jerkin. "I wondered how you came to join us."

"She saved my life," Calandryll repeated helplessly.

The note of sadness in his voice grieved Cennaire. She lowered her eyes to the blade: no threat to her, to what she was, but she could no longer face Calandryll.

"He took my heart and placed it in a box he bound with his gramaryes," she said, gaze locked on the falchion. "I knew not he should do that; nor what he should ask of me. Only that he gave me powers undreamt."

"And made you his creature!"

The falchion cut leather as Bracht drove the sword forward. And gasped as Ochen reached out, taking the blade casually as if it were a twig, the age-mottled hand closing around the razor edges, turning the sword. The scent of almonds joined the fire's smoke; tendons corded along the Kern's arm as he fought the magic that held back his blow. Ochen said, "You cannot defeat such magic, Bracht. Neither mine nor what Anomius has put in her. Sheathe your sword and let us talk like civilized folk, eh?"

"Civilized?" For a while Bracht strained against the wazir's grip, then gave up the unequal struggle and sheathed his blade, anger stark in his blue eyes. "Civilized, you say? That we should listen to this . . . *thing* . . . this revenant? I say use your magic to destroy her now. Ere she follow her creator's commands and take the Arcanum for him."

"I say you should listen," Ochen returned. "All of you."

Bracht raised his arms, spread wide in frustration. "Ahrd, wizard! Whose side do you take?" he cried. "Hers? Anomius's? She condemns herself—use your magicks to end her threat!"

"Did I believe her a threat, do you not think I'd have done that?" Ochen demanded. "I knew her from the first."

"And kept her secret?" Bracht spun round, eyes finding Katya's face, Calandryll's. "I say we fall among traitors—that this sorcerer works his own design, and forfeits our trust."

Calandryll, torn by doubts, bewildered, said, "Do we hear him out, Bracht? I cannot believe him a traitor." And softer, with a hopeless glance at Cennaire, "Or her. She held my blade without harm . . ."

The Kern looked to Katya for support, and she

shrugged, her grey eyes clouded, stormy with doubt.

Ochen said, somewhat irritably now, as if the Kern's hostility drove his patience to its limits, "As Calandryll has told you—she saved his life at risk of her own."

"That he should live to bring her to the Arcanum!" Bracht retorted. "That we three should live to find the book—that she might deliver it to Anomius. For what other reason?"

"Sit down," Ochen said, "and perhaps you shall hear some other reasons. Listen"—as the Kern shook his head, glaring furiously from wazir to Cennaire, to Calandryll and Katya, encompassing them in his outrage, as if their lack of immediate support branded them, too, with the marks of treachery—"do you hear me out, or must I force you?"

Bracht glowered at the ancient. Katya said, "Sit down, Bracht. Ochen is our friend, I believe, and you should hear him out."

The Kern grunted and sat down, tension in the set of shoulders, disbelief writ clear on his face.

"So, first"—Ochen retrieved dropped cups, fastidiously wiping them, setting them orderly aside—"do you truly believe I am your enemy?"

"You hid her secret," Bracht snarled, his angry eyes accusing. "Perhaps you'd have the Arcanum for your own."

Ochen sighed. Katya said slowly, choosing her words with care, "He's offered us only aid, Bracht. Had he not intervened, Rhythamun should surely have entrapped Calandryll within the aethyr. That first time and again now. No less, he could have ordered us slain."

"Save we are destined to find the Arcanum," the Kern snapped back, refusing to be mollified, "and so he needs us. As does Anomius." He turned his face, hard and cold, toward Cennaire. "What orders did he give you, your maker?"

Cennaire flinched beneath that cold contempt. She gave her preternatural senses full rein now—what reason to hide them any longer?—and it seemed the cold morning air crackled with myriad emotions. From Bracht came hostility, an anger bordering on blood lust. In Katya she sensed suspicion mingled with doubt, a wariness, a desire for reason, a willingness to listen. Calandryll was shocked, dismayed, torn between outrage and dejection, bewildered. Ochen was closed to her, save in his calm determination that the discourse continue.

Staring at the fire's flames, she said, "He commanded me to find you. His first intention was that I should slay you, but then he learned of the Arcanum—what it is, the power it holds—and then he told me to bring it to him. To leave you live until the book was found."

"Anomius believed we sought a grimoire." Calandryll spoke, his voice hoarse, the eyes he fixed on Cennaire's face hollow. "How did he learn otherwise?"

Cennaire paused, then shrugged—the path she trod now was irrevocable, there was no turning back—and said, "At first, he did not know. From Menelian, in Vishat'yi, I found you had sailed for Aldarin."

"From Menelian?" Bracht fixed her with a hateful glare. "Menelian aided us. He'd not have betrayed us, save . . . Does he live still?"

Cennaire shook her head. "He looked to slay me with his magicks. I fought for my life . . ."

She held her eyes firm on the fire, not wanting to

see their faces, loath to meet Calandryll's gaze, hearing his gasp of horror.

"You killed him." Bracht's voice was harsh, condemning. "On your master's orders, you slew him."

"I . . ." She shook her head again, filled with a terrible regret. "I had no choice. He allowed me none . . . It was my life or his."

"Your *life*?" Bracht snorted bitter laughter.

"And then?" asked Katya.

"Anomius dispatched me to Lysse, where I picked up your trail. I learned you sought the Arcanum from two Kerns, Gart and Kythan . . ."

"Whom you doubtless also slew," Bracht grunted.

"No." Cennaire gestured a negative. "They were honorable men. I tricked it from them and left them living."

"Are we to believe that?" the Kern demanded.

"Why should she deny it?" asked Katya. "Already she admits to Menelian's murder—why should she halt with Gart and Kythan?"

Bracht sighed and shook his head. Katya said, "How did you find us?"

"Anomius guessed you must move toward the Borrhun-maj," answered Cennaire, dull-voiced. "He sent me to the Kess Imbrun, to the Daggan Vhe, to await you there. Along the way I saw bones—human—and the marks of riders. I came to the chasm and saw Rhythamun . . ." She shuddered at the memory. "The rest you know—it was as I told you."

"Save there were no tensai attacked your caravan," said Bracht, "for there was no caravan. Only you, going about your creator's business. So shall we believe you truly saw Rhythamun?"

"I did!" she declared. "Aye, there was no caravan;

but the rest . . . I saw him feast on human flesh and possess the Jesseryte. All that is true, I swear."

"Doubtless by all the gods' names," Bracht muttered, and turned to Katya. "Do you believe this farrago?"

The Vanu woman looked long at Cennaire, her eyes appraising, then she said, "I believe she saw Rhythamun take Jesseryte form. I believe she slew Menelian, but left Gart and Kythan alive. Beyond that . . ." She opened her hands in a gesture of wonderment. "Whether she leagues with Anomius, to take the Arcanum, I cannot say. Save she *did* aid Calandryll against the uwagi."

"That he might continue the quest!" Bracht shouted. "Obeying her master's commands. For what other reason?"

"I am not sure," Katya replied. "Perhaps Ochen might answer better than I. Or Cennaire herself."

"If we may trust him still," Bracht muttered. "She I trust not at all."

The wazir nodded solemnly, narrow eyes moving from one face to the other. "You've cause enough for doubt," he agreed, "and in face of all you've learned I can ask only your indulgence. I do not seek the Arcanum—no sane man would, save to destroy it—and all I wish is that you succeed. So, how shall I convince you?"

"You might start by telling us why you hid your knowledge of this creature," Bracht said.

"Because I sensed in her a changing," Ochen returned, "a shifting of the patterns that bind all our destinies. Her allegiance shifted from contact with you, and I believed—I believe still—she has a part to play in the design."

"Ahrd!" Bracht grumbled. "We hear more sorcerer's riddles."

"Think you so?" asked Ochen. "Listen, warrior—

have you not told me of your first encounter with Katya? How you believed her an enemy? Did your feelings not change, later?"

"The spaewife in Kharasul found her true," said Bracht, "and she proved herself, in Gessyth."

"But was there not also something else?" Ochen asked, his tawny eyes probing the Kern's face. "Something in you, beyond doubting?"

"What mean you?" Bracht demanded.

"That you loved her," said Ochen. "That in your heart, from the first, you saw her true."

Bracht's eyes hooded then, and he shrugged, hesitating before he admitted, "Aye, I love her. But what's that to do with this creature? Katya's a woman of flesh and blood, not . . ." He gestured dismissively.

"Think you that's not flesh covers her bones?" The wazir indicated Cennaire. "Blood runs in her veins, red as Katya's."

The Kern frowned. "She names herself revenant, wizard. Do you tell me she lies?"

"No, only that she is made something other than human, but can yet retain those emotions humanity feels," Ochen replied, a hand raised to quell the outburst Bracht's face threatened. "And that Calandryll, in his own way, is more than just a man. You know there's a power in him, and you accept that. Might you perhaps accept that that power imbues him with a vision beyond the normal? That he might, through that power, perceive the truth in Cennaire?"

"He saw her not for what she *is*," Bracht returned, "but for what she seems."

"Perhaps." Ochen turned then to Cennaire and asked her bluntly: "Do you love Calandryll?"

Like the Kern before her, she hesitated, caught off balance by the question, unsure. Love was not an emotion with which she was familiar. What did it mean? That she was prepared to risk her existence that he should live? That she would have his approval; could scarcely bear the pain she felt radiating from him? That she would—had!—turned from Anomius's service for fear he be slain, uncaring of her own fate? That she could not properly understand what she felt for him, but knew his touch, his smile, excited her in ways she had never before known? If that was love, then aye: she ducked her head, silent, gaze still locked on the fire.

"The uwagi might well have destroyed her," Ochen continued. "She's great strength, but even so those creatures could have rent her limb from limb—Horul, you've witnessed their power!—but still she chose to face them. For Calandryll's sake."

"Or Anomius's," said Bracht, obstinate.

"Think you she's no feelings?" Ochen asked. "Think you she does not fear death?"

"How can she?" the Kern demanded. "When she's no life to lose."

"And is that better?" the wazir countered. "Aye, she might not have died, but still been sundered. Think on it—to be rent apart and live still? Anomius holds her beating heart within the aegis of his cantrips, and so she would not have died. Only been torn apart, to live on, suffering."

"What do you say?" asked Katya.

"That she was prepared to face a fate perhaps worse than honest death," said Ochen. "For Calandryll's sake."

Katya nodded thoughtfully; Bracht frowned. Calandryll sat bemused, their words, their arguments, beating against ears numbed by revelation, an assault on the bewildered thoughts that filled his mind, racing, confused as the tumult of dreams.

Cennaire was revenant? Anomius's creation, sent to snatch the Arcanum? But he had held her, tasted her lips on his, and those lips had felt entirely human. Yet those same lips had voiced the truth of her making—and he could no more doubt that than he could doubt the now frightening realization that he loved her. It washed over him with a terrifying force, awful for all he heard, could not deny or doubt: he loved her. Not knowing he did it, he moaned, head lowered, lost in absolute confusion.

Ochen's voice came unwelcomed through the miasma of his thoughts: "Calandryll, did she not save you?"

"Aye," he said numbly. "She held me off from striking Rhythamun, when he stood in the uwagi's place. She carried me to safety, and she fought the beasts to save me."

Because she is a revenant; because she has that strength. The strength of the undead.

"And did she not bring you back to safety?"

"Aye, she did."

Because she survived where living beings could not. Because magic affects the living, not the dead.

"And yet, she could have fled, no? She might have gone into the forest. Followed us to Pamur-teng, to Anwar-teng, hidden from us, concealing what she is. But she did not—she chose to return, to bring you back."

"Aye."

Because she obeys her creator's commands? Because she is Anomius's creature? How can I love her, then?

"And do you love her?"

In his turn he hesitated. He wanted to deny it, wished that he might, and could not. Low-voiced, tonelessly, he said, "Aye."

He raised his eyes then, helpless, hopeless, wondering what it made him, that he confessed his love of a woman dead, undead, creation of magic, and that the magic of a sorcerer sworn his enemy. He saw Bracht's face, unbelieving; Katya's, enigmatic, troubled; Ochen's calm, approving, he thought. Most of all he saw Cennaire's eyes shine hopeful. He nodded and said again, "Aye."

"This is madness," Bracht snarled. "You're entranced."

"Perhaps he sees to the heart of it," said Ochen.

"The heart?" Bracht's clenched fist carved air, angry. "Her heart lies with Anomius."

"No!" Cennaire was encouraged by the helpless light she saw in Calandryll's eyes. The unmasked hostility she saw in Bracht firmed her somewhat: if they were to have the truth, then it should be all the truth. "My heart lies in that box he made, in Nhur-jabal. He travels with the Tyrant's sorcerers, warring against Sathoman ek'Hennem. He is confined by their cantrips, to the Tyrant's cause, and may not quit the host."

"Then why do you serve him?"

Katya's voice was deliberately calm, though she radiated a controlled tension, and Cennaire could sense the loathing the warrior woman sought to conceal, the suspicion. She sighed and said, "Perhaps I no longer do. Revealed, I can be of little use to him. I think that does he learn you know me for what I am, then he will destroy me."

Calandryll moaned, "No," head lowered, rocking where he sat.

Katya nodded and demanded, "But until now— before we knew—you obeyed his commands. Yet you say your heart lies safe in Nhur-jabal, and I ask again: why?"

Cennaire raised her eyes to meet the impassive grey stare. Judgment lay there, and threat, but reason, too, a willingness to hear out the tale in full measure before verdict was reached. "I live by courtesy of his magic," she answered. "He's only to lay hands on the box to destroy me. And he boasts that soon he shall be freed of the gramaryes that bind him. That so, he might return to Nhur-jabal; or when the war ends."

"He boasts?" Bracht interrupted, harsh. "You commune with him?"

"He gave me a mirror," Cennaire advised him, "ensorcelled. Through it I am able to speak with him."

"Ahrd!" The Kern was on his feet in the instant, striding to where the horses stood, rummaging through her saddlebags until he found the cloth-wrapped glass. He returned to the fire clutching the package as though he held a serpent. "This?"

"Aye." Cennaire ducked her head as she sensed the disgust emanating from the man, mixed with a measure of fear. "But worry not—save I voice the cantrips he taught me it remains but a mirror. It can do you no harm, neither can he see us, or hear what we say."

"It is as she says," Ochen murmured. "No more than a glass until magic wakes it."

Bracht set the mirror down, his expression become speculative. He glanced from it to Ochen, to Cennaire. "And do I shatter it? What then?"

"Then likely Anomius will realize he's found out," said Ochen.

"And have no further way to know what we do, or where we go," said Bracht. A wolfish smile curved his mouth as he drew his dirk, reversing the long knife, the pommel poised to strike.

"Wait!" Ochen's hand rose, stilling the blow. His painted nails glittered golden in the fire's light, his eyes burned into the Kern's, and Bracht hesitated, frowning.

"Why? You name yourself our ally, yet you'd leave her the means to commune with her master?"

"Think on it," urged Ochen. "Does Anomius believe his emissary discovered, he's no further use for her. What then?"

He turned to Cennaire, a question framed in the wrinkles of his face. She shrugged and said, "I think he'd likely destroy me for such failure. He's an unforgiving master."

Bracht chuckled wickedly and raised the dirk anew.

Calandryll cried desperately, "No!"

"No?" Bracht stared, amazed. "You say 'no'? You'd give Anomius eyes?"

"Strike and he'll likely destroy Cennaire."

Calandryll closed his eyes, head flung back. *Oh, Dera, what path do I tread? This is surely madness.*

"Aye," said Bracht. "So?"

Calandryll opened his eyes to face the Kern. It seemed a void opened inside him, a great, dark pit of pain and confusion, from which only one awful certainty emerged clear, all else chaos. He voiced it: "I love her."

Bracht's voice grew soft now, filled with horror, with disbelief. "How can you say you love her?"

"She saved my life," Calandryll muttered.

"For her own reasons!" Bracht bellowed, so loud the horses started behind them, whickering and stamping.

"I . . ." Calandryll shook his head, rubbed sweat-damp palms over a chilled face. "I do not think it so. I do not *believe* it so . . . She might have died herself. She might have fled . . . left me . . . but she did not. She risked herself for me!"

He fell silent, aware of Bracht's disbelieving gaze, Katya's pitying stare. He could scarce bring himself to look at Cennaire.

"There are other reasons," Ochen said into the silence, placatory. "Do we set aside Calandryll's feelings, then still there seems to me sound cause to leave that glass intact. First, do you shatter it, Anomius will likely send some other minion, and we cannot know its face."

"It would need find us," Bracht said, the dirk still poised.

"Aye, and we've a head start," Ochen agreed calmly, "but magic's a way of eating the leagues, and we might well find ourselves pursued by some creature we cannot recognize. We've a saying in this land—better the known demon than the stranger. While if we leave the glass, and allow Cennaire communication with Anomius . . ."

"Madness!" Bracht snapped.

". . . Then we may deceive him," Ochen continued. "Mislead him and trick him."

"With his creature in tow?" grunted the Kern. "Free to commune with him, and advise him of all we do?"

"Hardly." The wazir shook his head, his tone become exasperated, as if the Kern's belligerent obstinacy tried his patience afresh. "Think you she can use the mirror without we know it? I'd sense such use, even if you failed to see it. No, what messages she might send Anomius shall be of our devising."

"Better we smash the mirror now," said Bracht, "and end this thing's miserable existence."

Ochen shrugged, as if the Kern's suggestion was taken under consideration. He turned to Katya: "Two opinions are voiced clear. Bracht would see

Cennaire slain; Calandryll would have her live—
how say you?"

For long moments the Vanu woman met the wazir's stare with silence, as if she sought answers in
his narrow eyes, the lines that furrowed his face.
Finally she said slowly, "I believe you our friend,
old man, and yet you tell us you've known Cennaire for a revenant since the first. Therefore, I suspect you've some other reason. Do you tell it, and
then I'll answer."

"Women were ever more sensible than men,"
Ochen murmured, smiling approval. "Aye, I'll tell
it—I recognized her when I looked into all your
pneumas, back there atop the Daggan Vhe. I saw
the purpose in you three like honest fire burning in
a dark night. In Cennaire I saw a murkier flame,
confused, torn between those strictures laid on her
by Anomius and that part of her, that anima, entirely her own. I saw a creature lost, affected even
then by your company. It was as though the fire
that burns in each of you scoured the darkness in
her, cleansing. Also, I sensed she had a place in the
design that governs us all. What, I cannot say—
only that she becomes a member of your quest, and
that I believe it must fail without her."

Katya nodded. Bracht said, "Three and three and
three, wizard. Twice now spaewives have prophesied three. How so, if we become four?"

"That power the spaewives, the gijans, own is
not mine," said Ochen. "Theirs is a different talent, but do I hazard a guess, I'd tell you that those
scryers you consulted in Lysse and Kandahar spoke
of what was then, when this woman had no part
because she did not then exist."

"You weave a web of words and half-seen
thoughts," the Kern retorted irritably.

"Surely the future *is* a riddle," Ochen replied.

"Did the spaewife in Secca warn Calandryll of Anomius? Did the spaewife in Kharasul tell you of Jehenne ni Larrhyn? Did you"—a hint of accusation, or mischief, entered his voice—"deem fit to warn your comrades of that woman's interest in you?"

Bracht had the grace then to look embarrassed, and Ochen continued: "Cennaire was not then what she is now. The future is a many-branching road, each turning taken leading to another, all of it complex beyond ready understanding, easy discernment. And even when you spoke with spaewives, Tharn's dreaming clouded the occult plane, likely dimming their vision. I believe they could not see Cennaire's role then."

Katya, grave, asked, "So you tell us Cennaire's some part in our quest?"

"Have I not said it?" Ochen nodded. "I believe it so, but as we speak honestly now, I tell you I cannot be sure."

"How shall you—we—be sure?"

"She is now what she is," the wazir answered, "and fixed in that state while her heart lies ensorcelled in Nhur-jabal. Therefore a scrying may be had—I suggest we continue on to Pamur-teng and consult a gijan there."

"Save you influence her prophecy," said Bracht, doubtful.

"That, even the wazir-narimasu cannot do." Ochen laughed, shaking his head. "Oh, warrior, had I the time I'd explain it to you; though I wonder if you could understand."

"Therefore I must trust you?"

"What other choice have you?" asked Ochen, sharp again. "Think you truly that I league with those madmen who'd own the Arcanum, see the Mad God raised?"

"I do not," said Katya, and turned toward the Kern. "Put up your dirk, Bracht—what Ochen says makes sense."

For a while the Kern met her gaze, then he grunted, and sheathed the dagger. "And this?" He gestured at the wrapped mirror. "What do we do with it?"

Cennaire spoke then, hope rising inside her: "Why do you not hold it?"

Bracht shook his head. "Not I. I'd have nothing to do with Anomius's creations."

"Give it to me, then," Katya suggested, and smiled. "Save you no longer trust me."

"Take it." Bracht tossed her the small bundle. "You I trust. But . . ."

His eyes encompassed Cennaire and Ochen. Katya tucked the mirror beneath her hauberk and turned toward the revenant. "Do you prove our enemy," she said, "I shall break this thing. And be it in my power, I shall slay you."

Cennaire ducked her head in acknowledgment. It seemed a weight was lifted from her, for all Calandryll still refused to meet her eyes, though when she spoke, her words were directed at him.

"I'll not betray you," she said. "I've learned from you, and be it in my power I'll aid you all I can, even does Anomius destroy me for it. I'd own my heart again,-be that possible. You need not trust me, but I tell you that I'll not betray you. You've my word on that."

"Your word?"

Bracht's voice cut bitter into her burgeoning hope and she looked to Calandryll for some measure of support, but he was sunk in gloom, staring at the ground between his feet, and that cut deeper still.

11

OCHEN left them then, called to the funeral
pyres by Chazali, that he might perform the
rituals for the dead. The wazir's absense afforded
the questers a chance to talk among themselves
that was entirely unwelcome to Calandryll, who
felt his mind, his soul, benumbed by what he had
learned. He had sooner be left alone, or talk more
with the sorcerer, seeking resolution of the bewilderment, the confusion, raging inside him. That he
loved Cennaire, he could not deny: it was a fact
that burned through all the chaos of surrounding
knowledge. What repercussions it might have, he
dared not contemplate, nor knew what that love
made of him. A monster? A necrophile? Surely
Ochen had said she wore flesh, that red blood
coursed her veins, that she was capable of human
feelings; and yet that blood was pulsed by
Anomius's magic, the bones and muscles beneath
that flesh imbued with a terrible strength. Her lips
had tasted soft when he kissed her; but was that
softness the product of sorcery? She had promised

her aid, even at risk of her creator's wrath, at risk
of her own destruction; but could that promise be
trusted? Bracht had suggested he was entranced—
could that be true? Was he deceived by the woman?
Did magic beguile his heart, just as it did hers? He
felt despondency settle on him, bleak and grey as
the spell Rhythamun had left behind in the keep,
robbing him of purpose, leeching resolution. Into
his mind came memories of tracts read in Secca,
dissertations found in the palace libraries, of vam-
pires, the ungodly allure they exercised on the living.

Was he thus seduced? Was there some weakness,
some darkness, in him that was drawn to Cennaire? Reluctantly, he looked toward her—and
found he saw only a beautiful woman, the great
brown eyes that met his grave, perhaps even afraid.
But of what? Certainly not of his blade, for she had
touched that and the power in it had left her unharmed. Of Ochen's magic, then, should he call
upon the wazir to destroy her? But he had already
spoken against that, in her defense. Yet still she
was subdued, almost timid, he thought, and in that
moment she seemed to him only a woman, born
down, afraid, and he wished that he could smile
and reassure her.

He could not, then; only turn his face away, helpless, starting as Bracht said, "Do we speak?
Alone?"

Unthinking, he gestured around, at the kotu-zen
grouped about the pyres, chanting their responses
to Ochen's prayers, and said, "We are alone."

"Aye?"

Bracht's eyes hung cold and blue on Cennaire,
and she ducked her head, rose, and said quietly,
"I'll not intrude."

She smoothed her dirtied leathers and walked a

distance off, solitary, head hung. Bracht watched
her go, then rose himself, beckoning Calandryll and
Katya to follow him, walking to where the horses
cropped grass, the stallion snickering a greeting,
tossing its head as the Kern stroked the glossy
neck.

Soft, glancing to where Cennaire stood, he asked,
"Think you she can hear us?"

"She's eyes that cut the night," said Katya.
"Likely she's ears to match."

"What matter?" asked Calandryll dully. "Katya
holds the mirror, Ochen stands close—what if she
does overhear?"

"She'll know our every move," the Kern replied.
"Nor I am yet convinced we can trust the sorcerer."

"Dera!" Calandryll sighed, weary. "As he said—
what other choice have we?"

"That's what I'd discuss," said Bracht. "I like this
situation not at all."

Nor I, Calandryll thought. *I'd far sooner Cennaire were just a woman, not magic's creation.
Dera, but I wonder if I'd rather we'd never found
her. Or I not love her. But I do, and I think I cannot change that, be it for worse or better.* Aloud, he
asked, "What would you do about it?"

"We might quit their company," Bracht said.

"And lose ourselves in this unknown land?"
Katya shook her head. "Ochen's yet my trust, and
I believe he told it true when he spoke of war raging here. How should we gain entrance to Anwar-
teng, save in his company?"

"And there's the gijan," said Calandryll. "Do we
consult her when we reach Pamur-teng, then perhaps our doubts may be resolved."

"If we can trust her," Bracht countered. "Cennaire's Anomius's creature. Made what she is by

him, and he's surely our enemy. And Ochen knew that, and concealed his knowledge."

Calandryll nodded, struggling to rise above the despondency that gripped him. "How should we have reacted," he demanded, "had Ochen told us what he knew?"

Bracht frowned, a hand fastened on the falchion's hilt. Katya said, "We'd surely have left her behind. Or looked to slay her."

"Better we had," the Kern muttered.

"Ochen believes she's a role in this quest." Calandryll shrugged. "And whatever her reasons, she did save me."

"Ahrd!" Bracht's hand left the falchion to shape an angry fist. At his back, the stallion snorted, nostrils flaring. "We've talked that through—she obeyed her master. No more than that!"

Calandryll felt a pressure on his shoulder and turned to find the chestnut gelding nuzzling at his hair. The animal's placid affection was somehow comforting, and he rubbed absently at the velvet muzzle, saying, "Perhaps; perhaps not. I know only I was mightily glad of what she did. Perhaps she did act out of"—he paused—"love."

"How can a thing without a heart feel love?" Bracht grunted.

"Ochen said she yet has feelings," said Katya. "And even did she act on Anomius's orders when she went to Calandryll's aid she might have fled, after. Think on it, Bracht—whichever course she took, she must have known she should be revealed."

"You say you trust her?" asked the Kern.

"I say I am not sure," returned the Vanu woman. "Ochen, aye. Him I trust, and he believes she's a part to play—so I cannot but wonder if he be right, and Cennaire becomes a player in this design."

Bracht shook his head in helpless frustration. "I say we can trust none of them," he declared.

"And you'd ride out alone?" Katya asked. "We three, across all these Jesseryte lands? With warring armies in our path? I think we'd not last long."

"And be my doubts sound?" Bracht fixed her with an angry stare. "How long shall we last then?"

Katya offered no immediate answer. Instead, she turned to Calandryll. "How say you?" she wondered.

He shrugged, wishing himself elsewhere, in some safe place, away from dubiety, from decisions and choices; knowing even as the thought formed that such refuge was denied him.

"I think," he said slowly, painfully assembling thoughts that raced and fluttered like light-bewildered moths, "that we cannot succeed without Ochen, without the kotu-zen. I know that Ochen's magic joined Cennaire to save me from the uwagi—from Rhythamun—and that otherwise I should be dead. I see no choice save to go on in their company."

"Do you trust Ochen?" Bracht asked.

Calandryll thought a moment longer, then nodded: "Aye. And listen—even be your doubts true, surely he'll look to see us safe along the way. Save you doubt everything we've done, we are the three scried. Save the spaewives and the Younger Gods themselves deceived us, we are the three. Therefore, even does Ochen work some subtle betrayal beyond my comprehension—beyond my belief!—he must still seek to deliver us safe to our destination."

Doubt lingered in the Kern's eyes: Katya said, "This is logic, Bracht; irrefutable. Like Calandryll, I've faith in Ochen, but even were he trcacherous, he must aid us. Just as Anomius would have us deliver the Arcanum, so should Ochen."

Bracht studied them both awhile, a hand tangling absently in the stallion's mane, then ducked his head. "So be it," he allowed. "There's sense in what you say, and so I'll trust him for the nonce."

"And Cennaire?" asked Calandryll.

"Her not at all," answered the Kern. "And I tell you—does she turn against us, I'll take that sword from you and trust in Dera's blessing to destroy her."

Calandryll looked into the cold hardness of the Kern's eyes and lowered his head; brief, a sad acknowledgment. "You'll find no need," he said hoarsely. "Be she traitor, I'll look to slay her myself."

Doubt flickered in the steel of Bracht's gaze, but Katya motioned him to silence and set a hand, comforting, on Calandryll's arm. "The gods willing, there'll be no need."

Her voice was soft and he looked into her grey eyes and smiled wan thanks for the commiseration he saw there, aware the while that behind that sympathy lay a determination firm as Bracht's. Should the time come, his would be the last hand turned against Cennaire: his comrades, unhindered by gentle emotions, would not hesitate. He nodded in mute understanding.

"This shall not be a pleasant ride, I think," he murmured.

Bracht grunted tacit agreement. Katya said, "Let us hope it may be swift. Perhaps, in Pamur-teng, our doubts shall be resolved."

Aye, perhaps yours shall, Calandryll thought. *But mine! Does the gijan assure you of Cennaire's integrity, then you may rest easier in her company.*

*But me? How can I rest easy knowing I love a
woman undead?*

He turned away before Katya's obvious compas-
sion grew hurtful, going back to the fire, where he
filled a cup with tea, listless, wanting some occupation of his hands; wishing his mind might be similarly occupied. Dera, but the journey would be
unendurable while these doubts circled, like vul-
tures awaiting the final weakening of a stricken
beast.

He gasped as sudden pain exploded in his hand,
looking down to see the cup shattered, droplets of
blood oozing from between his tight-clenched fingers. He opened his fist, shards falling, and began to
pick the china splinters from his palm.

"Here, let me."

He turned to find Cennaire at his side, taking his
injured hand as she spoke, her fingers delicate, precise, as they plucked the jagged fragments loose.
For an instant he was prompted to snatch his hand
away, but she glanced up then, and in her eyes he
saw a plea for understanding and stilled the impulse. She smiled briefly and bent to her task, so
that the rising sun struck sparks of raven brilliance
from her hair and he smelled the scent of it, pine
and woodsmoke mingled, and felt himself dizzied
with confusion.

He sat immobile, benumbed, leaving her to perform her surgery, seeing Bracht and Katya come up
and halt, staring. The Kern's eyes were filled with
disgust, as if he watched a victim go willing to a
vampire's caress. Katya's were clouded, enigmatic.
She spoke softly to Bracht, her mouth close to his
ear, and they moved past, to stand closer to the
kotu-zen. Calandryll felt a soft pressure, a warmth
against his palm, and looked down to find Cennaire
sucking at his wounds.

That, for all his reaction ashamed him, was too much: he snatched his hand away, as if from a flame.

Cennaire wiped blood from her lips, her expression apologetic. "It's clean," she said hesitantly, and smiled sadly, "and I'll not contaminate you."

"I did not think . . ." His voice faltered, he shook his head, helpless. "Forgive me."

"How should I forgive you?" she murmured. "Should it not be I who ask that?"

"I do not know." He sighed and shook his head again, meeting her gaze. Dera, but those were eyes to drown in! "I am not sure what I know any longer."

Only that I love you.

He took refuge in formality, retreating behind the punctilios learned in his father's court. Carefully, rigidly, he said, "Lady, I take you at your word. I owe you my life, and you've my thanks for that, but until we reach Pamur-teng and consult the gijan there . . . I trust you understand."

Cennaire's gaze fell away as she answered, "Aye. It were foolish of me to expect else."

Save how can you not know? Burash, but I have never felt like this before. Can you not feel that?

She rose, pausing as she heard his voice, soft: "Cennaire? I pray it be as you say."

She found his eyes on her face, hopeful, frightened, and answered solemnly: "As do I, Calandryll."

He nodded, and for all his expression was forlorn, she felt hope rise, like a kindled fire.

THE morning was advanced as they rode out, the sun topping the surrounding forest to shine bright from a sky all cloud-streamered blue, the breeze that gusted from the north hinting at the year's aging. It skirled the smoke rising from the funeral pyres, drawing out the black in long pennants of mourning that drifted away over the trees like waning hope.

Calandryll rode deep in thought, and it seemed the omnipresent sense of dread he had felt before grew stronger, as if the drumming of the hooves became a threnody, the freshened breeze assumed a charnel taint, whispering of loss, of defeat and futility. He looked up, and it seemed the sky was livid with threat of storm, the clouds lamenting, the blue fouled with blood. The trees beside the road stood ominous, looming dark; bird song died, lost under the rattle of the breeze; the air became filled with the stench of dung and death. He groaned, his soul weighed down, and into his bedeviled mind came, subtle as a serpent, the thought that Tharn must surely win resurrection, that Rhythamun must doubtless ride too far ahead to halt, and cross into the Mad God's limbo, to use the Arcanum to raise his master.

He felt himself sinking into despair, megrims tugging at him, loosening soul from the confines of his body.

Does love do this? he wondered. *Does what I feel for Cennaire bring me so low?*

Almost, as the wind rustled an affirmative, he answered himself *yes* and gave up, let go to the awful despondency; almost, he felt his pneuma drawn out again, trawled by the despondent breeze. But somewhere deep a flame yet burned, hopeful, and he shook his head and told himself *no, not until she be proven false. Until then she's the right to my trust.* He remembered the cantrips of protection Ochen had taught him then, and mouthed them, and felt the shield of honest magic rise

around him, denying the horrid suction of despair.
He recognized then, as the sky became again blue
and clear and the breeze clean, that he was assaulted on the occult plane, that Rhythamun, or
Tharn, once more sought to suck out his pneuma,
to lure him into the realm of the aethyr and trap
him there. He smiled as the pressure eased and was
gone, feeling freed, and suddenly triumphant: a
small victory won.

He loved Cennaire. Aye, he loved her! That he
could not deny. But that love he would not allow
to endanger the quest. Paramount was the securing of the Arcanum, its delivery to Vanu that the
holy men might destroy the book. Did Cennaire
have a hand to play in that, then good; if not ...
He pushed the thought aside, praying that in
Pamur-teng she be proven true and all doubts resolved. Bracht would learn to trust her, and they—
all of them—go on to thwart Rhythamun's fell
design. Until that was done he would set his feelings aside, that they not endanger the higher purpose.

Aye! He laughed, throwing back his head, drinking
in the now-clean air, wrapping himself round with
the defensive gramarye, challenging Rhythamun,
challenging the Mad God himself, to defy that purpose.

It seemed that the wind snarled a moment then,
disappointed, but when he cocked his head, listening, it was once more only a rustling among the
pines. The birds sang again, squirrels chattered, and
from the undergrowth ahead a wild sow burst, followed by three plump yearling hogs as she scam-
pered, snorting irritably, across the road.

The warriors to either side turned toward him
and he smiled at them, confident in his newfound
resolution.

✤   ✤   ✤

IT was easier found than held as they journeyed on, for when they halted, at noonday and at dusk, he was forced into company with his comrades and Cennaire, and the divisions imposed by knowledge of her revenancy came to the fore.

It was easy enough to promise himself that he would set aside his feelings, defer judgments and decisions until they reached Pamur-teng; far harder to attain that objectivity as twilight shaded the road and he saw Cennaire dismount and hesitate, clearly unsure of her reception. Bracht ignored her with a painful ostentation, busying himself with the stallion and then gathering wood for their fire. Katya, while less obviously hostile, remained aloof, and the kotu-zen, alerted to her condition, withdrew to their own groupings. Calandryll found himself facing a quandary: should he risk Bracht's displeasure by inviting the woman to join them? Or should he go to her, which would doubtless anger the Kern the more? He paused, torn between loyalty and pity.

And smiled thanks for Ochen's diplomatic intervention.

The wazir sprang down from his horse with an agility that belied his years, smoothed out his opulent robe, ran fingers through his mustache, and bowed in a courtly manner to Cennaire as she stood indecisive.

"Do you join me, Lady? I should welcome your company."

He offered his arm, escorting her to a place a little way apart from Bracht and Katya, but yet clearly within their aegis, the signal clearer when he beckoned Calandryll to fill the gap.

"Doubts exist," he said as the fire kindled, "and

it would be foolish to pretend else. But I tell you this—that we ride together and should at the very least allow a truce."

Bracht carved meat and said, "Those arguments we've heard, wizard. I ride with you, but I need not like the company."

"Horul!" Ochen shook his head. "I've often thought my own people an unforgiving lot, but it seems we meet our match in you Kernish folk."

Bracht shrugged, spitting the meat on sharpened twigs, not bothering to articulate a reply.

"Mistrust breeds disaster," Ochen went on. "Did you not feel the touch of Rhythamun's magic to-day?"

Bracht shook his head. Katya, silent and thoughtful, passed out hard journey bread, smoked cheese.

"Aye." Calandryll nodded. "It seemed he sought once more to seduce me into the aethyr. But I spoke those cantrips you've taught me, and the feeling was gone."

"It will come again," the wazir declared. "He waxes ever stronger, and he's a new key to your unlocking now. You must be ever vigilant against his attacks."

Calandryll frowned, his eyes shaping a question.

"What did you think about," asked Ochen, "when the world grew grey and the wind smelled of blood?"

Calandryll paused a moment, then said, "Of doubts. I thought of Bracht's mistrust of Cennaire. Of . . . what I feel for her . . . and what she is . . ." From the corner of his eye he caught her glance then, hurt, and past her pained face, he saw Bracht's, angry and scornful. "I feared we should be sundered, fall to quarreling, be divided, and Rhythamun win the day."

"Which he looks for," Ochen said, nodding

grimly. "Like some poison seeking out the wounds into which it may flow, he looks to divide us, to prey on doubt and distrust."

"I felt nothing," Bracht said obstinately. "It was a fine morning."

"You've not that power Calandryll owns," Ochen returned. "I felt his attack; Calandryll felt it. He knows of Cennaire now, and likely guesses she's his enemy; what she feels, what Calandryll feels. No less, that mistrust comes between us."

"How?" Bracht demanded, suspicious. "How can he know what I feel? What Katya feels? Or any of us?"

Ochen sighed. "Have I not told you?" he asked. "There are two levels of existence—the one mundane, the other on the plane of the aethyr. Those with the occult power are able to cross betwixt the two, and their spirits—their pneuma—are strong on the occult plane. Calandryll is one such, though he's not yet the precise knowledge of it—that's a lifetime's study—but still he's strong there, and so Rhythamun is able to discern him. To learn somewhat of what he feels, and through that knowledge what those about him feel."

"What do you say?" Katya asked. "That Rhythamun can see us through Calandryll's eyes?"

"Not see us," Ochen answered patiently. "For that he would need send out a spy, what you name a *quyvhal*, but that he . . . senses . . . what Calandryll's pneuma feels, learns of our dissension and mistrust. He knows now that a bond exists between Calandryll and Cennaire, and that it drives a wedge between those who oppose him. Between you three. He looks to drive that difference wider, until none trusts the other and all fall down into confusion. The which must surely benefit him."

"So you say we should trust you?" Bracht said,

and stabbed a thumb toward Cennaire, "and this revenant?"

"I say that the wider you let the gap grow," Ochen returned, "the easier you make it for Rhythamun to attack Calandryll on the occult plane. Do you doubt him—because of his . . . sympathy . . . for Cennaire—then you build a barrier between you. You isolate him, and thus weaken the shield your comradeship builds, and Rhythamun may find a way through those chinks."

"I thought him protected by your magicks," the Kern snapped. "Have you not taught him cantrips? Has he not said already that he used them this day, to defend himself?"

"Aye," said Ochen, "but Rhythamun's strength—Tharn's!—grows more powerful by the day, and these assaults shall increase. And do you doubt one another, then you make his task easier."

"You ask for trust where that commodity is hard won," Bracht said. "It seems to me it were far easier if we were three again and riding alone."

"Aye, but you are not," said Ochen, "and that's the way the design runs."

Calandryll sighed as the argument turned back on itself, Bracht's obstinacy like a dog intent on pursuing its own tail. He looked at the Kern's hard-set face; at Katya's—enigmatic, as if she pursued the course of her own thoughts—and then at Cennaire.

She sat silent, her eyes downcast, her face partially hidden behind the sleek spill of her raven hair, her shoulders slumped. She seemed to him resigned, as if accepting whatever judgment might be delivered on her, as though she forsook hope and cast her destiny to the winds of fate. She seemed terribly alone, and he felt an impulse to reach out,

take her hand; and at the same time a dreadful revulsion.

This, he thought as Bracht and Ochen flung
words like bouncing shuttlecocks at one another,
might well continue throughout the journey to
Pamur-teng. Even beyond, should the gijan there
fail to persuade the Kern, and all the while
Rhythamun would doubtless prowl the aethyr,
seeking the chance to strike, strengthened by
Tharn and doubt. He thought then of that day's assault, and for all he had defeated the attack, knew
that he would not welcome another; wondered how
long he might resist, did mistrust continue to grow.

Ochen had suggested the power within him invested him with a sight capable of penetrating to
the soul, to the truths within: abruptly, he chose to
trust the wazir's observance, to put it to the test.

"I'd speak with Cennaire," he said, rising, beckoning her to her feet. "Alone."

She looked up then, startled, hesitating as Bracht
frowned, Katya's brows shaped a question, Ochen
smiled in seeming approval. Calandryll nodded, encouraging, and she rose, instinctively, nervously,
smoothing her tunic. He took her arm, courtly, and
she allowed him to lead her away from the fire, toward the trees, docile.

The moon was risen now, a slender crescent
again, wan against a hyacinthine sky pricked
through with silver stars. The wind sung cold
among the trees, its melody echoed by the lament
of wolves, the soft hooting of hunting owls. He
walked away from the fires, past the picketed
horses, the guards Chazali had set, aware of all
their eyes on his back, aware of their expectations
and their fears, their doubts. He continued on, his
hand formal on Cennaire's elbow, back down the
road until they were beyond earshot.

Then, a few short steps distant from the road, where tall pines swayed, rustling in the wind as if they gossiped, circling a narrow patch of coarse grass, he let go Cennaire's arm and turned to face her.

For a moment he stood silent, voicing a prayer to Dera that the goddess guide him to the truth. Then, aloud, he said, "Lady, we needs must talk."

"Of what?" Cennaire brushed back hair streaked silvery with stars' light, her eyes luminous on his face, her voice subdued. "What may I say that I've not already?"

It was as difficult to fight the urge to take her in his arms as it was to forget all she had done, who had made her what she was. He set a hand about his swordhilt, saw her eyes register that movement and shifted his grip, thumbs hooking his belt.

"Bracht believes . . ." He paused, contradictory emotions a turmoil in his mind. A deep breath then, a rush of words, best spoken swift lest his tongue should falter: "Bracht believes that what I feel . . . that because I love you . . . I am blinded. He believes you a traitor."

It was hard to face her as she smiled, wistfully he thought, and said, "He's made that clear enough."

"And yet Ochen claims you've a part to play in this quest of ours. I must decide ere this mistrust tears us apart."

Cennaire nodded then, her starlit features solemn, her eyes grave, and said, "And do you decide, shall Bracht accept it? He's an unforgiving man, I think."

"Aye." Calandryll smiled, brief and without humor. "There's that, but even so—do you convince me, then perhaps I may persuade him."

"How shall I convince you?" she asked, turning a moment away, head thrown back, eyes studying

the velvet sky, closing an instant as if in resigna-
tion, then open again, returning to his face. "Shall
I tell you that I made a choice when I saw the
uwagi take you? That I thought then only that you
might die, and I could not bear that thought? You
say you love me? I tell you, Calandryll den
Karynth, that I love you. No!" She gestured him silent as he was about to speak. "Hear me now; now
that we may speak alone, without interference or
interruption—I'd have you know what I am, exactly. After, when you know it all, judge me."

Her voice was edged hard as Bracht's face, steeled
to decision: Calandryll ducked his head, accepting.
He suspected, looking into her intense eyes, that he
should not welcome this confession, that he should
learn of things he might better prefer remained unsaid. It seemed the wind grew colder, the susurration of the trees more ominous. *Dera be with me
now*, he thought. *Be with me and guide me.*

Cennaire, for all the chill breath of the night
wind meant nothing to her, shivered, folding her
arms across her breast. She locked her gaze, unblinking, on his face, determined now that he
should learn it all. Did he turn from her after, then
so be it: for now she felt a need the truth be told in
its entirety, that there no longer be secrets between
them. She did not properly understand her motives,
only knew that along the way from Kandahar to
this forest clearing she had changed, become something other than the revenant Anomius had sent
out, something other than the woman she had
been, and that she must unburden herself to this
man.

"I was a courtesan," she said, only determination
preventing her voice from faltering, praying even as
she spoke that he might understand—should
believe—she was no longer the person she de-

scribed. "I was condemned to death for stabbing a lover. He refused me payment, and when I took his purse he threatened to denounce me—I put a knife in his belly, and I was condemned to death.

"Anomius found me in the dungeons of Nhur-jabal and ordered me freed. I knew not why, save ..." She shrugged, the meaning explicit. "He worked his magicks on me and I was his creature. His gramaryes lent me such powers ... Oh, I had known hunger before, but invested with his magicks food was pleasure, only; nothing more. I was strong; I need not sleep. I can see, hear ... Burash, but you know that. How else did I find you, when the uwagi took you? It was intoxicating. And he owned my heart—save I did his bidding, he would destroy me! He sent me out like a hunting dog, to find you, and Bracht. He knew nothing then of Katya. That he learned after I went to Vishat'yi."

She hesitated, lips pursed. An owl hooted, but otherwise the forest was grown still. Even the wind, it seemed, waited on her confession, the tall trees leaning closer, anticipatory.

"I learned of Katya, and where you went, from Menelian. That knowledge he gave me because he was confident of destroying me. He looked to slay me with his cantrips, but magic works better against the living, not against ... what I am. I slew him." This in a dull, dead tone. "And then I spoke the cantrip Anomius had taught me and was back in Nhur-jabal ..."

"How?" Calandryll asked, hoarse-voiced. "By magic?"

"Aye, how else?" Cennaire nodded. "He taught me that spell that I might return to him the easier."

"Then might you not have gone back," Calandryll said slowly, "even go back now? And take back your heart?"

"Wound round with Anomius's gramaryes?" Cennaire shook her head, starlight playing over the darkness of her hair. "Think you he's not set protections? I think that did I attempt that, I should die. That he should know of my coming and destroy me."

"Aye." Calandryll remembered the ugly little sorcerer and could only agree. "Go on."

"I went to Aldarin," she continued, "where I learned that Varent den Tarl was dead. I learned that from a man named Darth, who served den Tarl."

"I knew him," Calandryll said, his voice hollow as he added: "And did you slay him, too?"

Cennaire nodded. "He looked to take his pleasure of me. I'd have let him live, else. But he gave me scant choice."

"Dera!" Calandryll said, aghast. "You leave few alive behind you, Lady."

She ducked her head again. He stared at her, wondering that he could still love her: that he did, he could not doubt, even were it insanity.

"I learned from Gart and Kythan what it is you seek," she said as he motioned her to continue. "Those two I did not slay—you've my word on that. Though likely you'll not take it."

She laughed a hollow laugh and studied him with eyes that seemed haunted. He was not sure why he believed her, but he did—she had confessed to other murders. Why not, then, to those? "I take it," he said.

And she smiled: a glimmer of hope, and said, "From them I learned the rest, which you mostly know. I used the mirror to speak with Anomius, and he commanded me to find you and join you.

The rest you know—I came to the Kess Imbrun, to the Daggan Vhe, and there I saw Rhythamun for the first time."

She broke off, shuddering at the memory. She seemed then, for all Calandryll knew her undead, a woman imbued with preternatural powers, one who had slain men in obedience to her creator, entirely vulnerable. He steeled himself and demanded, "Aye? Continue."

"What I told you of him was true," she said. "*Is* true. I felt . . . Burash! It was horrible, what he did. To eat human flesh? To steal another's form?"

"And yet you still obeyed your master." It was an effort to hold his voice calm, to hide the revulsion he could not help but feel. "Anomius bade you join us, to take the Arcanum from us."

She looked at him then, her fate in his eyes, and nodded. "Aye, then." She swallowed air, cold, hope fading. "I joined you to take the Arcanum from you, for Anomius."

"So is Bracht right?" he demanded, the question chill as the wind. "Do you look to seduce me to that end? Is that why you saved me from the uwagi? In service of your master?"

"No!" Her voice rose loud, helpless, hopeless. "Burash, but I cannot ask you to believe me, even though all I've said is true! I know not what has changed me, but I tell you—I love you! I cannot bear the thought of your dying. What can I say? I have traveled with you—with you and Bracht, and Katya—and something in me has changed in your company. I'd have back my heart and be mistress of my own destiny again. I'd not see Rhythamun, or Anomius, own the Arcanum. I'd not see Tharn raised. Calandryll, I've not the right to ask or expect belief from you, but I tell you this—that I shall do all I may to see your quest succeed.

Burash! Does it cost me my heart, still I'll see you
succeed! Believe me or not, that is the truth."

The night hung still about them, the wind died
down, wolves and owls, all the predators of the
dark hours, fallen silent. The moon was a curved
blade against the sky, the stars cold and distant, an
impassive jury. Calandryll felt the weight of
decision—of indecision—heavy on his shoulders as
he studied her face. Her eyes were wide and shining, though whether in hope or defiance, he could
not be sure. He felt certain she had told him the
truth about her life—about what she had been, and
what she had done in service to Anomius. But the
rest? Could he believe she had changed so much?
That a creature made by magic, her heart no living
organ but some product of thaumaturgy, might so
dramatically shift her allegiance?

What if she lied, hiding her real intentions?

What if all she said was truth?

He wiped a hand over lips gone dry, sighing,
aware of a pressure building behind his eyes,
thoughts racing madly about his mind. He wanted
to believe her. But was that a wanting born of emotion, of what he felt for her? He coughed a bitter
laugh, thinking a moment of his father, thinking
what Bylath might have said, were he present. He
could imagine his father's scorn, his brother's contempt. And yet . . . and yet what he felt for this
woman surpassed all he had felt for Nadama den
Ecvin.

That, in the midst of all his confusion, remained
a fact hard as stone, as steel; and like a steel blade,
it cut him deep.

Did she lie, then he might likely need to slay her.
And would: of that he had no doubt. The notion of
the Arcanum in Anomius's grubby hands was as

abominable as the thought of Rhythamun's success.

Dera, he asked into the silence, *do you show me
the way of it? Show me the truth, I beg you.*

Not Dera, for this is not her domain but mine.

Calandryll gasped as the words struck his ears.
For a moment it seemed the night, the world, spun
whirling around him. He saw Cennaire start back,
eyes wider, turning to seek the speaker, even as he
recognized the sound came not from among the
trees, was not shaped by any human throat, but
rather echoed inside both their minds. She looked
then afraid as that realization dawned, and he
touched her, saying, "Wait," softly, and she looked
at him, and drew closer, as if seeking his protection
as shadow coalesced among the pines, taking solid
form.

He heard her give a small, frightened cry as the
shape emerged, and, unthinking, lay an arm about
her shoulders, holding her against him as he began
to smile, head bowed in obeisance.

Your land of Lysse, that is my sister's domain.

From between the trees came a horse, huge,
larger again than Bracht's great stallion stood above
the Jesseryte ponies. The stars were reflected in its
coat, or shone therein, for it seemed a thing of
shadow and light, not entirely distinct, but rather
shimmering, as if the force of life itself played and
danced within its form. Brilliance sharded where
hooves struck grass, it seemed the eyes shone
moonlight.

Calandryll said, "Horul!"

Aye, the god returned, *for this is my domain,
and I heard your call.*

The shape changed then, flickering in the instant
of an eye's blinking, faster, becoming no longer
equine, but a man-shape, naked and muscular, sur-

mounted with a horse's head, the mane flowing proud over massive shoulders, the eyes bright with intelligence.

Calandryll felt Cennaire press closer, trembling, and said, "There's nothing to fear. Save you lied."

She shook her head, but it was the god who answered.

She did not. All she told you was truth.

The weight of doubt oppressing Calandryll lifted somewhat at that. "Then she's one with us?" he asked. "She's a part to play in this quest?"

Aye, said the god. *Though it may cost her, or you, dear.*

"Do you explain?"

I cannot. A hint of laughter, rueful, light like falling stars shed from between the equine lips. *I am bound—did my sister, my brothers, not say as much? What aid is ours, we give you; but what aid we may give you is limited by designs beyond our making, by powers greater than us.*

Calandryll looked up—the man-horse form of the god overtopped him by a head or more—and said, "But I should trust her?"

Do you not love her?

"I do."

Without trust, what value has love?

"But . . ."

She was a courtesan? A mage stole out her heart, made her revenant? She has slain men you named friend?

"Aye! All that."

But still you love her?

"Aye. But . . ."

Think you change is impossible? Forgiveness? Look into your soul, and trust what you find there.

"You say Menelian's death, the others, count for nothing?"

I say you look for answers, and that I offer you those within my power to give. To take them, or not, that is for you to decide; but that te fleshly organ you name the heart is not the repository of the soul, but only a mechanism. The pneuma rests elsewhere, in every fiber of the being. In the flow of blood and the tissue of the muscle; in the bones and the skin. It is all of you mortal folk, the totality of you; not some single, isolated part. This upstart wizard may hold her heart, and so control her physical existence, but he cannot govern what she is. That shifts and changes, is altered by time and the influence of others, by folk such as you and your comrades.

Again, then, that spectral laughter, like the distant dance of stars in the night sky, far off, like the hint of sunlight rising through the mists of dawn.

It is your choice, Calandryll den Karynth—to trust her, or not. But if you love her, I tell you that you had best trust her. Put aside all she was, and trust in what she is now. Those deaths you spoke of? No, they are not nothing—they cannot be, for each life taken leaves a debt that must, in some fashion, be settled. But this woman may atone for her sins. Has she not already risked much on your behalf, on behalf of your quest?

"Aye, she has." He drew Cennaire tighter against him, suddenly aware of her arm about his waist, the pressure welcome. "But what further part has she?"

That I cannot say. Forces move within the realm you name the aethyr . . . Horul paused then, the great, black-maned head craning back, moving from side to side, nostrils flaring as though scenting the night. . . . *Forces far greater than mine, than any commanded by we Younger Gods. Tharn stirs, and would see us gone, and even now his strength is growing apace. Men feed it; men may defeat it.*

"You speak," Calandryll said, aware that he echoed Bracht, "in riddles. If men feed Tharn's power, and may defeat the god, why do you not show us the way?"

More laughter then, self-mocking, light dribbling from between the widespread lips to tumble down onto the grass, great arms spread wide as burning eyes locked on his face.

Is life not a riddle? Why did Yl and Kyta quit your world? Why give it over to Tharn and Balatur? Why not take it back, when the godwars came? I cannot answer you, Calandryll; not with simple words. You are bonded to what you are, and I—and all my kindred gods—bonded to what we are. There are chains about us all, and we none can break them; only seek to slip them, or learn to live with them. You must do what you must do, as must I; and more than that I cannot tell you.

It was on Calandryll's lips to retort: "More riddles," but he bit back the words and said instead, "But did you Younger Gods only lend us your aid, then surely we might defeat Rhythamun. Only bring us to him, and let us take the Arcanum from him, and we none of us need fear Tharn's resurrection."

Could we, Horul answered, *do you not think we would? We cannot! Men look to raise Tharn, and men must prevent that resurrection.*

"That's much to ask of men," Calandryll said.

Perhaps. But is it more than men ask of us?

"Then a lesser boon—do you lend your voice to convincing Bracht, Katya, be that needful?"

Were they here now, then I think they should believe.

"But they are not! Let me bring them; or come to where they are."

We've not the time.

Again the great head swept round, about the confines of the trees, up toward the twinkling stars. Were they a little dimmed? Calandryll felt the unpleasant prickling of trepidation, as if the air grew sullen with impending storm.

Tharn would deny even this much, were he able. But he's not yet so strong. Even so . . .

The god broke off, head again flung back, the equine nostrils flaring. Calandryll followed his gaze and it seemed a curtain was drawn across the heavens. The stars, the moon, were lost, not behind cloud or the pale misting of dawn, but gone, as if they existed no longer.

He stirs, he waxes angry. Horul's eyes returned to Calandryll, to Cennaire. *I've no more time. I must depart, lest his wrath descend on you. Go on your way in knowledge that your heart speaks true, and that atonement may be won. Now— farewell.*

He turned, moving across the clearing, becoming again a horse, stars' light and moon's shine, trailing brilliance as he reared and galloped skyward, toward the heart of the oppressive absence that lay across the firmament. Calandryll stared, awed, as the god rose, a shooting star now, a comet, that raced headlong into the vacancy.

Then light exploded, blinding, and the pines were shaken, bent, by a silent wind. So fierce was the blast, Calandryll felt himself totter, Cennaire's grip firm about his waist, her eyes wide and frightened as she trembled, pressing against him as if, even in her terror, even as she held him upright, she looked to him for strength, for support.

The searing flash died, leaving only afterimage,

the trees sighed upright, and all was still a moment. Then shouts disturbed the night, and the whickering of unnerved horses, torches flared, and the shapes of kotu-zen, of Bracht and Katya, approached.

"Come," Calandryll urged gently. "We must tell them what Horul said."

"Shall they believe?" Cennaire asked.

"Perhaps. I do."

This time, as they walked back toward the road, he took her hand.

12

T HE others met them on the road, swords drawn, alarmed, only Ochen seeming calm, as if he sensed what had transpired. Calandryll assured them all was well, returning to the fires to answer the questions that came in aural bombardment. He had hoped that Horul's divine intervention would convince his comrades of Cennaire's integrity, but he was disappointed. They had not witnessed the appearance of the god, and it seemed impossible to dissuade Bracht from hostility, his hawkish features planing into lines of hard skepticism as Calandryll recounted all the god had said, his audience silent, reserving judgment until he was done, the Jesserytes looking then to Ochen for confirmation, though it was Bracht who broke the silence.

"A trick," he declared with sour finality. "Some gramarye of Anomius's making, designed to beguile, that his creature become trusted. None others saw the god, only you. Can you surely say it was not some conjuration?"

"Had you been there," Calandryll told him, "you'd not doubt."

"But I was not," the Kern replied. "Only you and she. And you are clearly entranced."

Calandryll flushed at that, in part embarrassed, in part angry. He looked toward Cennaire, who smiled helplessly and shrugged; he turned to Ochen, asking, "Can you not convince him? Or do you, too, believe I am beguiled?"

"I believe you speak the truth. But . . ." The wazir, like Cennaire, shrugged, as if he doubted his ability to persuade the obdurate Kern, looking then to Bracht, his voice solemn. "A magic greater than man's walked this night. Power immeasurable strode the aethyr, and I felt it. That was no making of sorcery, neither Anomius's nor Rhythamun's, but of godly proportions. Did you not see the sky cloud, Bracht? Could you not feel it?"

"I saw cloud hide the stars," Bracht answered. "A storm built, and there was lightning. I saw that, and no more."

"Horul!" Ochen sighed. "You see with your eyes, not your soul. Had your god only gifted you with that other sense when he drove those nails from your hands . . ."

He shook his head, resigned into silence. Bracht frowned and demanded gruffly, "Do you insult my god, wazir?"

"No," Ochen replied, "I say only that your vision is limited by prejudice."

Bracht barked a dismissive laugh. "Is it prejudice that I mistrust a thing created by a sorcerer sworn to slay me? I hear her condemned out of her own mouth. Ahrd! Do you wonder I find it hard to accept this tale?"

Cennaire listened to their debating less with her ears than with those other senses granted by her revenancy. Bracht was firm in his doubt, his refusal to trust her sharp and hard as tempered steel. In him, dubiety was like the falchion he carried: edged and rigid, unbending. Calandryll emanated a confusion of emotions. Love bled from him, but like fever sweat—tainted with the poisons of squeamishness at all she had done, all she had been, the fear that he might lose Bracht's friendship. She turned her preternatural attention to Katya, and found a confusion similar to Calandryll's: belief was there, that Calandryll spoke only truth, that had he been deceived, Ochen should know it, therefore that Horul *had* appeared and declared her true. Katya wanted to believe, to accept, but mingled inextricably with that acceptance was a doubt born of Bracht's disbelief, a desire to take the side of the man the warrior woman loved, the result confusion.

Is this what love is then? she wondered. *Certainty and doubt all tumbled together? The opinions of friends balanced against heart-felt emotions? Trust where common sense declares none can exist? To believe when belief is impossible?*

She turned her attention to Ochen, and found him protected by his magic, unreadable. A natural, instinctive defense? Or something else?

Chazali was far easier: his emotions gusted out, fierce, hidden only from natural senses by the discipline of his caste, which hid his feelings from men, but not—never—from her. He believed Calandryll, believed that Horul had appeared, and consequently believed all he had heard. That she had been a courtesan meant nothing to him, only that his god had declared her true. That she was created by Anomius troubled him—distaste there—but not distrust. He was angered by Bracht's rejection—of

his god, as he saw it—and tempted to take the
Kern's argument from Ochen's hands and answer it
with his sword.

Burash! she thought suddenly, *does this go on,
we play into Rhythamun's hands. We fall on ourselves in doubt.*

Then, beyond hesitation, firmed now by forces
beyond her understanding she knew with utter
surety that she was committed to the quest. She
chose not from sudden emotion, but from an inner
deliberation, a certainty past questioning, as if
Horul had somehow washed away her doubts, the
uncertainties and self-interests disjected by the
god. And yet it seemed her presence drove a wedge
between the questers, that mistrust set them at
loggerheads.

"Listen!" Her voice forced silence on their arguing and their faces turned, startled, toward her. She
looked to Bracht, allowing her gaze to encompass
Katya. "You do not trust me. I cannot blame you
for that, and no matter what I tell you, you'll likely
not believe. But, do you hear yourselves? You argue
round and around in pointless circles—Calandryll
tells you Horul vouched me true; Bracht claims it
was a conjuration. Trust flees, and its going aids
only Rhythamun. Your disbelief breeds doubt like a
festering sore."

Her voice was fierce and for long moments the
Kern faced her with narrowed eyes, a hand upon
his swordhilt, as if he anticipated she might attack
him. She faced his stare unflinching, willing him to
believe even as she sensed his refusal, thick on the
night air. Then he shrugged without giving answer.

"Do we face facts?" Ochen asked into the silence
that fell then. "Trust or no, we go on together, and
in Pamur-teng consult a gijan. Perhaps the spaewife
shall persuade our obdurate friend. If not"—he

shrugged, sighing—"mayhap Horul will appear
again. Whatever, we've little enough choice save to
continue. So—do we set this arguing aside for now
and find our beds? Or do you prefer we debate the
night away?"

"And be I right?" asked Bracht, not at all mollified.

"I tell you that you are wrong," said Ochen wearily, "but even be you right, Cennaire offers you no
harm. Even does she serve Anomius, she needs you
alive, no? Save all the prophecies be wrong, it is
you three, and none others, can wrest the Arcanum
from Rhythamun, and save you succeed in that, the
book is useless to her creator. That, my doubting
friend, is simple logic."

"Aye," the Kern allowed with a reluctant grimace.

"Then do we sleep?" the wazir suggested, answered by Bracht with a sullen nod.

They settled in their blankets then, Bracht and
Katya across the fire from Cennaire, Calandryll and
Ochen like guardians to either side, the night
heavy with distrust.

THE days that followed were little better. Bracht
spoke to her only at need, and then but curtly, in
monosyllables. Katya was more generous, but cautiously, aware of the Kern's hostility and unwilling
to fuel his animosity. Calandryll, for entirely different reasons, grew distant, troubled by the divisions
and his own confused emotions. Chazali and his
warriors were meticulously polite, their attitudes
shaped by the knowledge that their god accepted
her, but only Ochen seemed untroubled by her condition, as if he saw her now as a victim, certainly

as a potential ally, and consequently she found herself much in the wazir's company.

He was still greatly occupied with Calandryll's
instruction in the occult, and while no further sorcerous attacks manifested, he devoted time each
night to warding their camp with protective
magicks, but when not so busied, he sought out
Cennaire and spoke with her as a friend. He was,
she recognized, looking to set an example, to break
down the barriers risen among the party, and at the
same time intent on learning all he could of
Anomius. It mattered little enough to her, far more
that the wrinkled mage offered her a friendship
otherwise denied, and she told him all she could remember of her creator and his plans.

"I believe," he remarked one night as they sat
about the fire, "that the time fast approaches you
should use that mirror."

"What say you?" Bracht glowered from across
the flames. "That she should advise her master of
our intentions?"

"To an extent, aye." Ochen's face was fissured,
simian as he beamed at the suspicious Kern.
"Think you Anomius does not wonder where we
go, what we do? Likely he grows impatient for
news."

Bracht readied an angry response that was curtailed by Katya's hand upon his arm, her voice soft
in his ear, bidding him be patient and hear out the
wazir. Calandryll, intrigued, motioned for Ochen to
continue.

"From all Cennaire has told me of this sorcerer,"
Ochen declared, ignoring Bracht's low-voiced cor-
rection of that title to "her master," "there are limits to his patience. So—let us give him such news
as will placate him awhile."

"Why?" came Bracht's blunt question.

"For several reasons," Ochen returned patiently, "foremost that we learn where he is."

"What matters that?" the Kern grunted.

Ochen drew in a slow breath, as though forcing himself to patience. Softly, soothingly, Katya murmured, "Do we hear out the reasons, Bracht?"

The wazir smiled his gratitude for that intervention and answered, "Does he escape those gramaryes binding him to the Tyrant's cause, think you he'll not come seeking the Arcanum himself? I'd know him still fettered, lest we find a powerful enemy at our back."

"Could he find us, even freed?" Calandryll asked.

"It might be." Ochen's face composed in lines of gravity. "I've the feeling this Anomius commands great power, and so I'd know precisely where he is. Does he grow impatient, I say we should placate him with such news as we choose to impart— enough he's satisfied Cennaire goes loyal about his business."

"And you'd trust her in this?" Bracht's voice was weighted heavy with sarcasm.

"My god has vouchsafed her integrity," Ochen returned, ignoring the Kern's dismissive grunt, "so, aye. But for your sake, I say she shall use the mirror only while observed."

"And reveal ourselves to him?" Bracht barked. "Ahrd, man, you know he can see out through that cursed glass."

"He shall see only so much as we'd have him see." Ochen chuckled, grinning as if delighted at catching out the Kern. "We shall all of us be present, to hear what Cennaire tells him." He paused, his grin widening as Bracht frowned, clearly reveling in the Kern's incomprehension. "You seem to forget"—he chuckled—"that I, too, am a sorcerer, and not without some small talent."

"For riddling," Bracht muttered, his expression sullen, aware that Ochen toyed with him.

"We shall be invisible," said the wazir. "All of us, save Cennaire."

He paused again, smiling mischievous glee.

"And he'll not know it?" Calandryll asked cautiously. "Not sense our presence?"

"No." Ochen shook his head, his smile still wide, as if he delighted in the notion of tricking another wizard. "The mirror is a device of communications only. It shows what any window would show, and no more. He shall see nothing save Cennaire and the room she uses."

Calandryll nodded, accepting. Bracht offered no comment, save the thinning of his lips, the dismissive flash of his eyes. Again diplomatic, Katya said, "This seems a sound enough plan."

Beside her, the Kern voiced an inarticulate sound, shrugging, and settled to the honing of his sword, deliberately distancing himself from further discussion.

"We are agreed, then," said Ochen. "In Ahgra-te, Cennaire shall become *our* spy."

"When shall that be?" she asked.

"Another day should see us there," Ochen told her cheerfully. "So, by dusk on the morrow."

She nodded, saying nothing more, for all she felt horribly afraid. That Ochen might work a gramarye of unseeing, she had no doubt, nor that it should delude Anomius. But she? Should she be able to conceal that knowledge from the warlock? And did he sense betrayal, surely he would destroy her. She looked then to Calandryll and knew she had no wish to die, for different reasons now, and simultaneously that she was resolved to give whatever aid was in her power. She would, she recognized, follow Ochen's instructions, even at cost of her existence: it was a strange realization, unfamiliar for its altruism.

She felt a hand touch hers then, and turned to find Calandryll smiling grave encouragement, knowing from his expression that her emotions had shown upon her face. *Burash!* she thought wonderingly, *do I change so much? Did Horul change me, or does love?* She met his smile as he squeezed her hand, albeit briefly, and murmured, "No harm shall come to you."

She nodded, aware of Bracht's disapproving glance across the fire, and replied, "I trust not."

"Trust Ochen," he encouraged, "and the Younger Gods."

She answered him, "Aye," but even as she said it she thought on Horul's words—that the Younger Gods were limited by strictures beyond man's comprehension, and that Tharn waxed stronger, and her trepidation grew. Doubt tumbled over doubt then, for did Anomius, in his own malign way, not serve Tharn? And was she become a true member of this quest, should her demise not serve the Mad God's purpose? Therefore might Tharn not in some fashion alert Anomius to her shifted allegiance, and her maker know her for turncoat?

She felt Calandryll's hand withdraw, wishing that he would hold her, comfort her. She yearned then for such reassurance, and had Bracht not squatted disapproving across the fire, Katya enigmatic at his side, she would have turned to Calandryll and put her own arms about him, to feel him close. *And what then?* she wondered. *Would he hold me, or would he turn away?* She stifled the sigh that threatened to escape her lips, fixing her eyes on the flames as she endeavored to quell her fears, and the disappointment that rose as Calan-

dryll busied himself with the small repairs of tack
and harness necessitated by their journeying.

Overhead the sky stood dark, cloud blown up on
a freshening wind to obscure the stars, the moon
flirting among the rack. The omnipresent sensation
of dread hung like an aftertaste in the night, held
off by the cantrips taught him, but growing stronger with each passing day, with every league that
brought them closer to the battle waiting ahead.
Beside that confrontation his tumbled feelings
seemed small, but still he wished they might be resolved. And knew that likely such resolution
should be denied, save that, somehow, in some
manner he could not imagine, Cennaire regain her
heart and become once more a natural woman.
Could that be accomplished, he thought, then all
should be well.

He tied a final stitch and set his work aside,
yawning. The camp was silent, save for the night
sounds of the animals and the crackling of the fire.
Bracht and Katya were already wrapped in their
blankets, and those of the kotu-zen not warding the
perimeter were dark and silent shapes, slumbering.
Ochen lay a little distance off, his feet toward the
flames. Cennaire lay still but not, he thought,
sleeping. He looked toward her and smiled wanly.
If she saw, she gave no sign, and he stretched out
himself, unpleasantly aware of the distances between them all.

AHGRA-TE lay on the northernmost limit of the
forested country, a boundary marker between
woodland and plain. The road rose up for half a day,
climbing to a final wide terrace that ran timbered
to a line of solid darkness stretching as far as the
eye could see to east and west. That, the questers

were advised, was the edge of the true Jesseryn Plain, the Ahgra Danji, which in the Jesseryte tongue meant "Great Wall." It loomed above the town, towering vast over the wooded country, as if storm clouds solidified and lay upon the land. It was visible even as they traversed the final stretch of roadway, daunting as the trees gave up their hold to fields and farmland, a barrier near as impressive as the Kess Imbrun itself, lit by the rays of the descending sun.

The town was built at the foot, where falls cascaded down the rockface, mill wheels turning furiously in the torrent, the river that subsequently gouged a path across the flat terrain diverted by dams and barrages to form a semicircular moat that warded Ahgra-te to the west, south, and east. To the north, the Ahgra Danji was an ample buttress, and from its foot, within the confines of the moat, the town was further defended by high walls of wood set at intervals with watchtowers. It was a place, Calandryll thought, that should be mightily difficult to take, did the war raging on the Plain spread to the south of the Jesseryte lands.

As they drew closer he realized the place was more akin to the city-states of Lysse than those few other centers of habitation he had seen in this mysterious land, for proximity impressed its sheer magnitude on the approaching riders. The wall that faced them spread for close on half a league, and he calculated the eastern and western walls no less, turning in his saddle to see his comrades staring awed at the ramparts, albeit they were dwarfed by the rockface behind.

Two bowshots from the walls, Chazali barked a command that sent two men at a gallop toward the guardpost set on the southern edge of the moat. They paused a moment there, then thundered

across a drawbridge to disappear behind the walls.
The kiriwashen reined his mount to a slower pace,
his men forming into a column behind. Ochen
brought his animal alongside Chazali's, and the
questers fell naturally into pairs. Calandryll
flanked Cennaire, glancing down from his taller
horse to see the Kand woman studying the place
with wondering eyes.

"If they name this a town," he called, "what
must their great holds be like?"

"Vast, like Nhur-jabal," she answered, with a
smile he thought was nervous, assuming she anticipated her contact with Anomius.

"You've naught to fear," he said by way of reassurance. "Only do as Ochen advises, and Anomius
shall be none the wiser."

She nodded, unspeaking, and he fell silent, staring at Ahgra-te as the walls began to fill with folk,
like an audience lining the upper levels of an am-
phitheater, and Chazali's two forerunners came
thundering back. Faces peered from the ramparts,
and from the gates came a double column of half-
armored pikemen who formed an avenue between
guardhouse and gate.

"I thought all kotu gone to the war," he called
ahead.

Ochen turned briefly, swaying awkwardly in his
saddle, and answered, "Kotu-anj are left here as
rearguard."

It was all the explanation the wazir had time to
give, else he should have lost his precarious seat as
they crossed the bridge and the drumming of
hooves on wood gave way to the clatter of shoes on
stone. There was a moment of darkness as they entered the gates, and then light and confusion as
they emerged into a shadowed square filled all
around with the figures of kembi and other digni-

taries. Chazali and Ochen reined in, though neither
made any move to dismount as a deputation—of
notables, Calandryll assumed from the magnificence of their robes—stepped forward, bowed low,
and offered profuse welcome to the honorable
kiriwashen of Pamur-teng, the revered wazir, and
their most honored guests.

Calandryll guessed that Chazali's forerunners
had warned the leaders of Ahgra-te that outlanders
rode with the column, but even so he was aware of
sidelong stares, filled with curiosity, as the
kiriwashen gave formal answer and the notables
shouted for the crowd to part, the pikemen trotting
ahead, leading the way into the town.

It was, to eyes better accustomed to the avenues
of Lyssian cities or the open spaces of the world, a
claustrophobic place. The streets were barely wide
enough a cart might pass between the buildings
that stood to either side, four stories high, so that
they reached almost to the inner walkways of the
walls against which they were built, as if the entire
town were a single huge fortress cut through with
narrow passageways. Dusk was falling now, and
though lanterns were lit and windows bled light,
still the path was gloomy, oppressive despite the
welcome of the inhabitants. The air, after the clean
scent of the woodlands, was heavy with the myriad, near-forgotten odors of any city, but here the
stranger for the mingling of unknown spices, the
scented sticks that burned in doorways, the smell
of exotic food. Faces peered from every opening,
and now that he was more familiar with the
Jesseryte physiognomy Calandryll could see the curiosity writ there, the wonder that kiriwashen and
wazir should ride in company with foreigners.

It was a relief to emerge into an open square for
all the bulk of the Ahgra Danji loomed overhead: at

least the sky was visible here, dark blue and already sprinkled with stars, the risen moon a promise to the east.

Like Ghan-te before it, this square was faced with a temple, stables, and inns. The kotu-anj disappeared into the most splendid of the latter, while the kembi and their fellow notables offered their backs for footstools, precipitating the same confusion as had arisen in Ghan-te. When Calandryll finally succeeded in dismounting unaided, he saw the kotu-anj herding folk from the inn, guessing the hostelry was cleared for occupation by the visitors.

He stared about, intrigued by this odd city—"town," Chazali and Ochen had named it, but it seemed too large for such diminutive appelation, prompting him to wonder again about the size of the northern tengs—and through the milling crowd saw a priest emerge from the entrance of the temple. This was a vast structure, occupying most of the square's north flank, the horsehead symbol of Horul magnificent with gold leaf and jet above the wide doors. The priest was equally splendid, his robe iridescent silver, sparkling in the lanterns' light, but, Calandryll saw, much younger than Ochen. He was attended by six acolytes in robes of green and gold, each bearing a thurible, all swinging in perfect unison, trailing faint streamers of perfumed smoke. He halted a few steps from the doors, the acolytes moving into precise line at his back, and raised his hands, chanting a prayer that was also a greeting.

Formality reined now, Ochen explaining that he and the kotu-zen must pay due respect to their god.

Calandryll answered with a bow. "We'll see our animals stabled and await you in the tavern."

Ochen murmured his thanks and walked toward

the waiting priest. Chazali followed, his men coming after, leaving their horses in care of the kotuanj. None seemed overly eager to take charge of the larger horses, and the outlanders led their mounts toward the stable, finding stalls readied. They unsaddled and set to currying the animals, seeing them comfortable before making their way to the inn.

The place was empty, save for the owner and his serving people, a large, low-ceilinged room set round with long tables and the faldstools that were the usual seating of the Jesserytes. What windows existed were cut into the frontage of the building, small and square and already shuttered. Lanterns were lit at intervals along the walls, but they afforded no more light than those of the keep, so that the chamber was dim, shadow pooling beyond the scant radiance. Instinct sent Calandryll's eyes roving the shadows, aware that Bracht and Katya followed suit. He smiled and called a greeting. And saw the Jesserytes flinch, gasping, stark surprise showing on their faces as they heard their own language issue from the mouth of an outlander.

"Are we so strange?" he heard Bracht mutter, and nodded, murmuring, "Aye, to them we are." Then to the innkeeper and his folk, "Greetings. We ride in company of the kiriwashen, Chazali Nakoti Makusen, and the wazir, Ochen Tajen Makusen, of Pamur-teng. They bade us await them here."

The innkeeper took a wary step forward, folding his ample belly in a bow. Calandryll saw his head was bald, though he wore both mustache and beard. He ran a pink tongue nervously over fleshy lips and said in a faltering voice, "Greetings to you, honored guests. We were appraised of your coming, and bid you welcome. I am Kiatu Garu, owner of this humble establishment. How may I serve you?"

"Ale, do you have it," Bracht declared, cheerfully ignoring the man's obvious discomfort. "Wine, else."

"I'd take a bath," said Katya.

"All is available," Kiatu assured them, bowing afresh.

"Then, Katya, do you and Cennaire use the bathhouse," Calandryll suggested, "while Bracht and I await you here?"

The Vanu woman nodded, Cennaire an instant later: this would be the first time she was alone with Katya since confessing her revenancy, and she wondered what might be said. No matter, she decided, for she was committed now, and did Katya scorn her, or decry her, still words should not harm her. She followed the taller woman across the ill-lit chamber, to the door Kiatu indicated, where a nervous serving woman waited.

Calandryll, for his part, wondered what might pass between him and Bracht in this moment of privacy, thinking that it might well be an opportunity to speak openly of their differences. He felt abruptly nervous: they had spoken hardly at all since the night of Horul's manifestation, and he was afraid that free discussion might drive wider the rift between them. He followed the Kern to a table set along one wall, taking a seat beneath a lantern as Kiatu brought them ale.

Bracht took a healthy swig and grunted his approval. Calandryll drank slower, unsure whether he should broach the subject of Cennaire or remain silent. It was, as it happened, the Kern who spoke first.

"We've not said much, you and I," he declared, glancing first at Calandryll and then at his mug.

To his surprise, Calandryll realized Bracht was embarrassed. He said, "No. Not since . . ."

He shrugged, letting the sentence die. Bracht took another swallow and finished for him: "Horul appeared to you."

Calandryll turned on the faldstool to face the Kern. "You believe he did? It was not some conjuration?"

"I've spoken long with Katya on this," Bracht answered slowly, frowning at his ale, "and she's persuaded me it *was* likely Horul. Ochen is convinced, and you've no doubts. So . . ."

He broke off, shrugging. Calandryll said, "It was the god, Bracht. Of that I've no doubt at all, nor of what he said."

"That Cennaire becomes our ally?" Again Bracht shrugged, his frown deepening. "Perhaps. But I cannot forget what she is, nor who made her that. Neither that you love her—even knowing all she's done."

Calandryll was silent awhile. Then: "Aye. But think you that does not trouble me?" His voice trailed away and he shook his head helplessly. "Dera, I know not whether I should love her or loathe her! Horul said I should forget her past, follow my heart—that she's reborn, and should be forgiven what she's done. But think you I can forget that? No, I cannot!"

"This is no easy thing." Bracht tilted his mug and called for more. "And these past days I've thought only of my own feelings, not at all of yours."

Calandryll recognized the apology and smiled briefly. "Save that I love her, I'm no more certain what they are," he said softly. "The killings—aye, those I can forgive. At least, I think I can, for she acted then on pain of Anomius's wrath, in fear of her . . . life . . . and I've shed blood enough along this road."

"None innocent," Bracht interjected.

"Perhaps," Calandryll sighed. "Perhaps that's a thing for the gods to decide."

Confidently, Bracht said, "The Younger Gods can find no fault in you, my friend. Ahrd! Those you've slain, you've slain for this quest's sake."

"And now Cennaire becomes a part of that," returned Calandryll. "Horul said as much, and Ochen believes it so. Yet what am I become, that I love a woman without a heart?"

"Unlucky," said Bracht, his mouth shaping a tight and humorless grin.

"Would that she might regain her heart and become no more than mortal," Calandryll murmured. "It should be easier then."

"Perhaps Ochen might find a way," Bracht suggested.

Calandryll glanced sharply at the Kern. "How so? Save we reach Anwar-teng and defeat Rhythamun, my concerns are of no importance."

"Perhaps after, then," Bracht said, and chuckled. "Do we succeed. Do we not, I think all our concerns shall be ended."

Calandryll nodded, himself chuckling at that grim humor. "Aye. But meanwhile? Shall we go on as before, or do you name Cennaire ally now?"

Bracht paused before replying, toying with his mug. "Katya is largely convinced," he said slowly, "and she persuades me that Ochen is a true friend. I think perhaps my doubts were born of anger. Ahrd, but I thought these Jesserytes our enemy before I came to know them better. I was mistaken then—perhaps I was wrong, too, about Cennaire."

Calandryll stared, wondering if the Kern was truly won over, or if he merely looked to patch their friendship.

Bracht shrugged, drank ale, and went on: "I'll not

say I like what she's done, nor that I trust her yet. But there have been divisions come between us, and those can only threaten this quest—I'd not see them grow wider. I tell you now—can I trust this gijan we're to consult, and she pronounces Cennaire one with our cause, then I'll name her ally."

It was, Calandryll knew, as close as the Kern would come to confessing a wrong, an elaborate apology offered by a proud, hard man. He accepted it gratefully, thankful that the gap sprung up between them was closed.

"But does she prove false," Bracht added grimly, "then I'll slay her if I can."

"Aye." Calandryll ducked his head, accepting that. "And betwixt here and Pamur-teng? Shall you treat her as a friend?"

Bracht, in turn, nodded. "I'll not promise I can forget what she is," he said, "but you've my word I'll endeavor to be more courteous."

"My thanks," said Calandryll.

"Ahrd, shall comrades such as we fall out over a woman?" The Kern chuckled, some measure of good humor returned. "Even be she heartless. Now—do we drink more of this Jesseryte ale?"

"Surely." Calandryll shouted for fresh mugs, his spirits lifted, as if a weight were taken from his soul.

Katya and Cennaire joined them in a while, and from the expression on the Kand woman's face, and the way they spoke together, Calandryll saw that a similar conversation had taken place in the bathhouse. It cheered him that their differences were mended, for all he must still wrestle with his own conscience: that Bracht and Katya chose to accept Cennaire resolved but one problem—there remained the disquieting fact that he loved a woman animated by sorcery.

It was difficult to think of her as such when she smiled and he felt his heart lurch, marveling at the perfection of her face, the glossy spill of her raven hair, and he once more took refuge behind a screen of formality. It was easier when Ochen, accompanied by Chazali and the kotu-zen, entered the tavern. Easier, too, for Kiatu and his staff, though Calandryll could still read amazement on their faces, that wazir and kiriwashen should so casually accept the presence of foreigners, indeed, should converse with them as if with old friends.

That discipline that seemed a natural part of the Jesseryte character stood the landlord in good stead then, as he oversaw the serving of the meal, for all his eyes wandered frequently to the outlanders' faces and he started each time he heard them speak his language.

The fare was excellent, a luxury after the long days on the road, fish served in spicy sauces, and cuts of pork and venison roasted with strange herbs, a gravy fragrant with wine. They ate well, listening to what news of the civil war had come south. The siege of Anwar-teng continued, they learned, though the sorcerers standing with the rebel forces worked hard to prevent the transfer of news by occult means, what messages had broached their barriers sporadic. The priest had advised Ochen that the armies of Pamur-teng and Ozali-teng moved north, while the rebellious kotu-zen of Bachan-teng remained within their hold, ready to block the line of march. As best he knew, no major battle was yet fought, the main forces of the rebels still en route to Lake Galil, where Anwar-teng yet stood inviolate.

"And Rhythamun?" asked Calandryll. "Is there news of him?"

Ochen and Chazali exchanged a look at that, and the wazir nodded somberly, the kiriwashen's face dour.

"Ten days past a kotu-anj came here," Ochen replied. "He declared himself a messenger sent from the keep, riding for Pamur-teng. He took a fresh mount and continued northward without delay."

"Did the priest not recognize him for what he is?" gasped Calandryll.

"No." Ochen shook his head regretfully. "He'd no cause to suspect the man, and only wished him godspeed on his way."

At his side, Calandryll heard Bracht mutter a curse. For his own part, he sighed and murmured, "Ten days? Dera, but he gains on us."

"We've one small advantage," said Ochen. "He gave his name as Jabu Orati Makusen."

"A very small advantage," Calandryll observed.

Ochen smiled faintly, nodding agreement, and said, "But still a gain, for we know his clan now."

"What use is that?" asked Bracht.

Chazali answered, his voice grim: "Does he look to join the army out of Pamur-teng, he must first explain his presence—why he did not remain at the keep. Does he succeed, then he must continue his charade, and find himself assigned to the column of the Orati clan."

"Ahrd! Think you if we call out his name, he shall spring forward?" Bracht grunted, shaking his head slowly. "Or shall the clan stand in line while Cennaire studies each face?"

Chazali took no offense at the Kern's bitter humor, only shrugged, opening his hands in a gesture of helplessness. "We can overtake the columns," he declared. "That, at least. Then, do I speak with the kiriwashen of the Orati, he can check through his men."

"Save Rhythamun possess some other," Calandryll said. "Or avoids the army altogether."

"He must still enter Anwar-teng to reach that gate," Ochen said quietly. "Or go on to the Borrhun-maj."

"And Anwar-teng stands yet," Chazali added. "And the Borrhun-maj is a long ride off."

"And Rhythamun ten days ahead," said Bracht, "with more delays likely left in our way. And he able to shift his shape again."

A ruminative silence settled then, the enormity of their task daunting. It seemed impossible they should overtake the sorcerer, but rather trail forever after him, until he reached his goal and Tharn was raised. They each became lost awhile in private thoughts, none happy, until Ochen broke the spell.

"But still we go on, no?" he asked. "Do we but gain Anwar-teng, we've the aid of the wazir-narimasu."

They each then looked at him, surprise in some eyes, solemnity in others, and Bracht said, "Aye, of course we go on. What else?"

The Kern's tone suggested the wizard's question was redundant, a foolishness. Calandryll chuckled, his spirit rising. "Dera, but we've seen only a little bit of the world yet," he announced. "Think you we'd leave the Jesseryn Plain unexplored?"

"Or the Borrhun-maj," Bracht added.

"Or whatever lies beyond," said Katya.

"Nor forget Vanu," the Kern continued, grinning now. "Remember there's a matter I'd discuss with your father."

Katya's smile grew broad, laughter sparking in the grey of her eyes, though her voice was deliberately grave as she said, "But only after the Arcanum is delivered safe to destruction."

"Oh, aye," Bracht replied, matching her tone. "Only after that small matter is settled."

Calandryll saw Chazali watching their exchange with narrowed eyes, as if he wondered at their sanity, and found himself laughing. Across the table, Cennaire looked from one to the other, herself bemused that they found such humor in a situation so fraught with peril, and realized her own lips stretched in a smile: such optimism, such laughter, was infectious.

"We depart at dawn," Chazali declared, his tawny eyes solemn, wondering if he would ever properly understand these strangers.

"And there's some small business to conduct this night," said Ochen, turning toward Cennaire, "be you ready."

Her laughter died; her expression grew somber. She ducked her head: "As you wish."

THEIR rooms were located on the topmost floor of the inn—the height commensurate with status, Ochen explained—with narrow windows affording a view over the rooftops of Ahgra-te, the beds wide, the floors richly carpeted. They were spacious quarters, but still Cennaire's grew crowded as they gathered there, listening to Ochen advise the woman what she should tell Anomius, and what hold back.

She nodded solemnly at his instructions and Katya drew the mirror from beneath her shirt, passing it to Cennaire. The Kand woman took the glass from its pouch, warily, as if she mistrusted the device. Calandryll saw her lick her lips, a hint of fear in her dark eyes, and gently touched her shoulder.

Ochen said, "Now do I work my own gramarye, and then you shall use the glass."

She nodded again, watching as the sorcerer motioned the others to stand together, raising his hands as he began to intone the arcane syllables of the spell. The scent of almonds flooded the chamber, the forms of the questers and the wazir shimmering, disappearing.

Ochen's voice came out of nowhere: "Do we keep silent now. Cennaire, do you summon him?"

She ducked her head and mouthed the cantrip taught her. The mirror swirled, colors vying in its surface, the almond scent again sweet on the air, fading as the kaleidoscope resolved into the unpleasant features of Anomius.

"You take your time, woman."

The voice was faint, but still distinct: Calandryll heard it and grimaced as he peered over Cennaire's shoulder. Anomius grew no lovelier; nor, it seemed, better humored.

"I've not had opportunity ere now," she answered.

A snarl of disapproval, then: "So tell me how you fare about my business."

"Well enough I think. We are in a place named Ahgra-te, riding north after Rhythamun."

"You're close?"

"He's yet some distance ahead, but we hope to overtake him."

"When?"

"I cannot say for sure. We ride for the Borrhun-maj still, where they believe he must go. Also, we've learned his name."

"That's little enough."

"Aye, but something, surely. And what more might I do?"

"Um. They trust you still? They do not suspect?"

"No. They trust me—I am accounted one with them now."

"Good. And Calandryll, Bracht? Do you find favor with one or the other?"

Almost, Cennaire blushed then. Certainly, she feared she should give herself away: it was an effort to hold her expression confident as she replied, "Aye. I believe Calandryll favors me."

"Excellent. What of the Jesserytes?"

"They help us on our way. As I told you before— they count Calandryll a hero for the slaying of Rhythamun's creatures back on the Kess Imbrun. They still believe we travel to Vanu."

"I suppose I must be satisfied."

"I can do no more, save I quit their company and roam ahead of them. Would you have me do that?"

"No! That you remain with them is paramount. It's still my belief that only they may wrest the Arcanum from Rhythamun, and you shall be present then, the mirror ready."

"And you? Shall you come then?"

"I shall. Oh, most definitely I shall."

"Are you freed then? Have you vanquished the Tyrant's sorcerers?"

"The time is not yet ripe. But fear not, my creature. It shall be as I promise."

"You'll come when they've the Arcanum?"

"Have I not told you so? Aye, so long as you've the mirror, I've the means to join you. But not yet; for now it's far better they know not my hand in this."

"And the war? How goes that?"

"It draws to a conclusion. Xenomenus holds all the coast now, with only Fayne Keep to take. Sathoman lairs there, like a beaten animal. Were it not for the cursed Lyssians, I should have taken that hold."

"What part do the Lyssians take?"

"The god-cursed Domm of Secca raises an invasion force. Our spies advise us he's a fleet at his command, and the support of the western cities. They raise their army, thinking to strike while we fight with Sathoman. Ha! Tobias den Karynth shall learn the error of his pride, does he come against me."

"You?"

"Aye, me. Were it not for his ambition, I'd have delivered Sathoman to the Tyrant ere now. But Xenomenus would have all his sorcerers strengthen the defenses along the coast against the Lyssian threat. In consequence, we delay the final conquest. E'en now I'm in Ghombalar, warding against Lyssian attack."

"Alone, or do you work still with the Tyrant's sorcerers?"

"I am forced to work with them. But enough now recognize my powers that I am counted the mightiest among them."

"And shall they therefore free you?"

"Once Ghombalar and Vishat'yi are secured against the Lyssians, we turn north again, to finish Sathoman. That done, I'll have my freedom. By their will, or my own."

"You are truly the mightiest of sorcerers, that you can break the gramaryers binding you."

"Indeed, I am. And even now some speak to free me. Only mewling fools argue against that."

"But what if their voices are heard?"

"Of that, I've thought, woman. Xenomenus would have me deliver him Sathoman's head, and for that I must broach the magicks defending Fayne Keep. Only I may do that, and once I have—think you I'd not pondered the future? I left such occult devices in Faye Keep as shall cut these fetters like melted butter. And then I shall be paramount. I need only delay until you've found me the Arcanum. Now, enough. They approach, and I'd not have them suspect what I do. Use the mirror again when you may. Until then, go about my business."

"Aye, master. Farewell."

A swirl of color, the scent of almonds, the mirror once more only a glass, a simple vanity. Cennaire let go a long, slow breath, staring at her reflection a moment, suddenly aware how very afraid she had been of facing Anomius, of lying to him. She felt a wash of relief as she replaced the glass in its pouch and returned the package to Katya. Only then did she turn, and Calandryll saw her shudder, her smooth forehead moist. He moved toward her even as Ochen mouthed the cantrip that restored him to sight, the chamber once more perfumed with almonds, taking her hands as he saw them tremble. He felt her fingers tighten on his and smiled, looking to comfort her, for he saw that she was anxious and more than a little afraid.

"Was that done well?" she asked nervously.

"Excellently," Ochen declared. "I learned much from that. Anomius is far stronger than I'd thought. We must play him carefully."

"You name that excellent?" Bracht's voice regained a measure of suspicion. "Did I hear aright, Anomius has the means to break his bonds and go where the mirror is. Is that excellent?"

"To know that much of our enemy?" Ochen countered. "Aye, I'd say it so."

"Do you explain?" Katya suggested.

"We've some measure of his strength now," Ochen replied. "We know his whereabouts, and that he'll not attempt to interfere until he knows

Cennaire has the Arcanum in sight. Thus, we may forget him for the while, save I think we might send him another message when we reach Pamurteng. But we need not fear his presence yet."

"Riddles," Bracht grunted.

The wazir chuckled, his ancient visage creasing in myriad wrinkles. "Anomius suspects nothing," he said confidently. "Do you not see? By means of that glass, thanks to Cennaire, we may control Anomius. Now, the hour grows late, and we depart at dawn—do we therefore find our beds?"

The Kern and Kakya nodded, voicing agreement. Calandryll moved to follow them, but Cennaire clutched his hands, a plea in her eyes as she studied his face.

"Do you remain awhile?" she asked softly. "I'd have your company a little while, save you cannot bear to be alone with me."

For an instant he hesitated, embarrassed. Katya was already gone into the corridor, but Bracht paused, his expression equivocal, then shrugged, going after her. Ochen smiled mischievously, and before Calandryll had entirely made up his own mind, went out, quietly closing the door.

"Do you ask it, Lady," Calandryll replied.

Cennaire said, "I do."

13

A single lantern, encased in amber glass, lit the chamber; starlight came faint through the narrow window, affording the room a crepuscular intimacy that was augmented by the absence of furniture. There was the bed, on which Cennaire sat, and a faldstool. Calandryll would have gone to that, but the woman still held his hand and he was loath to break that contact: he took a place beside her, on the bed. It was, he noticed, easily wide enough for two. He caught the scent of her fresh-washed hair, the musky perfume of her skin, and was suddenly aware of the proximity of her body. He felt a dryness in his mouth and swallowed, ran a tongue over his lips, looking down at her hand in his. It was a small hand, and delicate, the skin smooth, warm: he could scarce believe the strength he had witnessed there. He was simultaneously afraid to turn his head, to look at her, and impelled to do so.

Her skin was very tan in the dim light. Sparks of red and silver glinted in her hair. Her eyes were huge, liquid pools. Her mouth seemed red as blood. He swallowed again, those senses that were male and basic, unthinking, urged him to draw closer, to put his arms around her and press her to the bed. He did not think she would object; rather, he felt, as she returned his gaze, she would welcome it. But still there remained, in that other part of his mind that was objective, distanced and logical, the knowledge of what she was. He saw the tiny tic of pulsing blood beneath the soft skin of her throat, and thought how good, how sweet, to put his lips there, to taste her flesh beneath his tongue. And then, a mental hand tugging at the sleeve of his desire, that no mortal heart propelled that blood along its course. He closed his eyes a moment, anguished, and cleared his throat.

"Lady?" His voice came gruff and awkward to his ears and hers. "You'd speak with me?"

Cennaire ducked her head, studying him from beneath long lashes, disappointment in her eyes, rapidly hidden, lest he should believe she looked to seduce him, as Anomius had commanded. Might he not believe that was her intent, even with a god as her guarantor? Burash, but she wished he would hold her; indeed, could scarce resist the impulse to touch his face, draw his mouth toward hers, bring him down beside her on the bed. And was horribly afraid he should pull back, that she would see loathing in his eyes.

"I feared Anomius should know what I did," she murmured, unable to repress the shudder that thought brought. "I feared he should see through me, and destroy me. I'd not be alone for a little while."

"Nor shall you be," he promised. "Though you've naught to fear—he suspected nothing. You played your part well."

She smiled, wan, and said, "But still he has that power over me." She was reluctant to say out loud "my heart" for the reminder it should give.

Calandryll said it for her: "That he holds your heart in his ensorcelled pyxis? Aye, that's a terrible power. But . . ."

He paused, frowning, those thoughts that had wandered the avenues of his mind since first she had told him of her creation, of the power Anomius commanded, of the mirror, of all she'd done, taking distinct shape, forming a potential resolution.

Cennaire waited, studying him with a longing she could barely conceal. This was, beyond all doubt, love, that she could take such pleasure from the simple observance of his features, of the play of lantern's light in his sun-bleached hair. Desire, too, but of a kind she had not known before, gentle as it was fierce, needing his approval, his reciprocation, in equal measure with the simpler lust. She made no move, only waited, content for the moment that he should still hold her hand and not spurn her.

Slowly, a note of caution in his voice, he said, "I've thought on that. Perhaps the mirror holds the answer."

"How so?" she asked tentatively when he fell silent again.

His eyes narrowed as he pondered, looking not at her now, but into some future possibility. Then: "It's clear what Anomius would have you do—ride with us until the Arcanum is secured, then have you use the glass to bring him where we are. Doubtless he counts on surprise and his own occult strength—likely your aid, too—to wrest the book from us."

"Aye." Now Cennaire frowned, wondering where his musing led. "That much seems clear."

"And," he continued, "his power appears limited by distance, no less than those fetters he wears. Why else send you about his business?"

"I do not understand," she whispered, as hope arose.

"Were we to deceive him," he murmured, "to persuade him to come to some place far from Nhur-jabal, where Ochen—the wazir-narimasu—might entrap him with their magic, then perhaps he could not harm your heart. But you, knowing that gramarye of transportation, might return to the citadel . . . Aye! Ochen with you, perhaps, if that be possible. Or I. Then, it might be you could secure the pyxis unharmed, and bring it to Anwar-teng, where the wazir-narimasu might return your heart, and you become again . . ."

He broke off, face flushed with embarrassment, the fear that he should insult her, hurt her.

Now it was Cennaire who completed the unfinished sentence: "Mortal? Think you that possible? That the wazir-narimasu might give me back my heart?"

"Be they great as Ochen claims," he said, nodding. "Then aye, I do. Though I'd speak of this with Ochen ere such attempt be made."

"But you?" Excitement was in her voice, hope. "Think you it might be done? Truly?"

He faced her then, solemn, and said, "'Twas sorcery took your heart; surely then, sorcery might restore it to you."

"The gods grant it may be so," she said fervently, hands tightening on his. Then lowered her eyes, herself embarrassed now, and that an unfamiliar feeling. "And then should you truly love me?"

"Lady," he answered, "I love you now."

"But this"—she loosed one hand to touch her breast, Calandryll's eyes following the movement,

his breath a sudden intake—"this ... absence ...
stands between us."

He was abruptly flustered, cheeks reddened, his
gaze shifting, from where her hand pressed tight
the material of her shirt, to her face. Awkwardly,
honestly, he answered, "Cennaire, I cannot tell you
it be otherwise. Dera, but could I only forget that!
Could I, then I should; but I cannot. I love you, but
I cannot forget that."

She wondered then what clouded her vision, surprised to realize it was the moisture of tears: it was
an unfamiliar sensation. She let them flow, unable
to stem that flood, uncaring, staring blindly at his
face as she wept in mournful silence.

Calandryll reacted without thought, simple emotion controlling him as he loosed her grip upon his
hand and reached to touch her cheek, his fingers
gentle, moving as though of their own accord to her
shoulders, to her hair. He drew her close, his arms
around her, his face buried in the raven hair, feeling
her embrace, the trembling of her body against his
chest. Helplessly, he whispered, "Cennaire, I love
you. I pray we may regain your heart. I love you."

"And I you," he heard her mumble, her lips soft
against his throat, where his shirt hung open. "But
still this stands between us."

It was pain to them both as he answered, "I cannot deny it. Forgive me, but I cannot."

"You've nothing to forgive." A shock ran through
him as her mouth moved against his flesh. "It is I
should ask that. For all I've done, and all I've
been."

"No!" He pushed her back, a hand upon her
shoulder, a hand against her cheek. "What you've
done and been, that lies in the past. It means nothing! Has Horul himself not absolved you? Should I

deny a god? Dera, but even Bracht admits error in
this, agrees you become one with our quest."

He forbore to mention the Kern was not yet entirely resolved. That would come to pass, he was
certain—for now he wished only to reassure her, to
comfort her. The tears that glistened on her cheeks
struck pain into him, each droplet a needle prick-
ing his soul.

"Katya said the same," she murmured, endeavoring without success to stifle her sobs. "I hoped,
therefore . . ."

Her voice tailed off and she sat, her shoulders,
her breast, shaking as she wept, her eyes luminous, shedding tears that ran unhindered down her
cheeks. Calandryll was barely conscious what he
did then, compelled by a need that transcended
logic, dismissed memory, banished hesitation. He
saw before him only a weeping woman: the woman
he loved; not sorcery's creation, but a woman,
beautiful, sobbing. He knew not how the distance
between them closed, only that he kissed her, that
she responded, that her lips were soft, salted with
her tears. It seemed that gravity laid them across
the bed, that a force beyond his understanding
commanded his hands, his fingers. He was not sure
how it came about that his clothing was gone, and
hers, only that now he knew no reservations, that
what she was no longer had meaning, save that she
was a woman and he loved her. He was little
enough experienced, and she, for all she was well
versed in such matters, felt herself virginal, even as
she held him and guided him, her tears drying, replaced with joy as he came to her.

She felt reborn as they lay together, the past—as
he had told her—dismissed, she with her first true
lover. He had not known it should be like this, so
urgent and so fond, such pleasure found in her plea-

sure, his a wakening fire answered by hers, desire augmented by love.

THEY lay together, entwined, as the night fell down into still darkness and then the pearly announcement of dawn. A cock crowed, a dog barked, Ahgra-te began to wake. Calandryll stirred, at first unsure where he lay, wondering at the soft warmth that pressed against him, the musky scent that filled his nostrils. He opened his eyes, the sun not yet above the horizon, and in the gloom saw Cennaire's sleeping face, her hair a blue-black spread across the pillows, her body outlined beneath the tumbled sheets. He felt desire move anew, and then, as if she sensed his eyes upon her, hers opened and he wondered—a fleeting, guilty thought—if her preternatural senses told her she was watched.

An instant of remorse then, a pang of guilt, banished as she opened her arms and murmured, "I love you."

"And I you," he answered, going to her again.

When both were spent, stretched languid with their arms about each other, he wondered what Bracht, what Katya, should think of this, and then day and all its concerns impinged. Gently, he disengaged her arms and pushed aside the sheets, once more awkward, embarrassed as he wondered what his comrades might say did they learn that he and Cennaire were now lovers.

"We depart at dawn," he said. "I had best find my chamber."

"Do you tire of me already?"

There was coquetry in her question that he, in his lack of experience, failed to recognize, answering earnestly, "Never! But . . ."

She rose to her elbows, careless of the sheet that fell from her breasts, aware of the excitement in his eyes as he turned and again saw her nudity. Aware, too, of the hesitation in his voice, realizing its source as he fumbled with his discarded clothing.

"You'd not have the others know of this night, that we are lovers now?"

"I think . . ." He broke off, awkward, not wishing to offend. "Did they . . ."

Cennaire laughed, rising to her knees, moving close to him, that she might hold him, her lips against his neck, smoothing the tangle of his golden hair.

"They should disapprove? I'd shout it. I'd publish it abroad."

"That would not . . . They might not . . . I doubt . . ."

She silenced him with her lips, briefly, pushing him gently away then, smiling as she said, "But I'll not, do you deem that the wiser course. Though it be hard not to declare my love, still I'll be silent if that's what you wish."

Calandryll touched her cheek, returning to the lacing of his shirt. "They might not"—he shrugged, uncertain—"understand. I'd not see fresh differences arise."

"Nor I." Cennaire grew solemn, slipping lithe from the bed, seeking her own clothing. "For both our sakes. That you understand, that you love me, is enough."

Calandryll found his boots and tugged them on, buckled his swordbelt in place. "It shall be mightily difficult," he declared, musing.

"Do we spend nights along the trail, aye," Cennaire returned, chuckling. "For I shall find it hard to sleep alone now."

"And I," he replied. "Dera, Lady, but I love you."

She looked up from her dressing, not going to him, only smiling, seeking in her turn to ease his doubts, wondering the while that she should feel like this.

"Shall it then be our secret?" she suggested. "We've declared our love, but none save we need know . . ." She gestured at the crumpled bed. "And along the road to Pamur-teng, beyond, we shall each sleep solitary."

"That shall," he answered gravely, "be hard. But, aye, I think that likely the wiser course. Until, perhaps, Pamur-teng."

"How shall that change matters?" she asked.

"The gijan—the spaewife—there shall confirm your role," he answered, utter conviction in his voice, "and then all must recognize the part you play. None shall object then, that we be lovers."

"Save . . ." She once more touched her breast, and was suddenly afraid that such reminder should again set a distance between them.

"That you are revenant?" Calandryll wondered how he could find it so easy to pronounce that ugly word. Had it not been that alone had held him back from coming to her earlier? Now it seemed that had no meaning: she was what she was, and did mortal heart or conjuration propel the blood along her veins, the courses of her arteries, still that blood flushed her cheeks, warmed her lips. That she was revenant no longer mattered, was no longer a barrier between them. He had seen her weep, and those tears had tasted salt, had been entirely natural. They had, he realized, washed away his doubts, his fears. He could no more think of her as an undead creature than he could believe himself a necrophile. She had become, weeping, only Cennaire, only his love. "Shall you be different then, do we recover your heart? Shall that render you worse, or better? I love you now, and I shall love you then. Do any find fault with that, then the fault is in me, and they must direct their objections at me."

Her smile was radiant in the faint light of the early morning, and she went to where he sat, putting her hands upon his cheeks, cupping his face as she bent to kiss him, soft and swift, holding him a moment after, gently, his head against her breast.

"You are gallant," she murmured fondly. "Once, in the keep, when Ochen advised me I should speak with Anomius, I told him—Anomius—that you were a gentle man. I meant it then, and now I know it true. But still . . ."

She let him go, stepping back, studying his upturned face with affectionate eyes, those growing serious as she continued, "But still—as you have said—think you Bracht, Katya, shall approve?"

"I know not," he answered. "I care not. They must accept the scrying of the gijan."

"But you must care!" she told him, urgent now, their arguments reversing. "Is Rhythamun to be defeated, there can be no dissension."

He shrugged defiantly: he loved this woman—how should his comrades object once the gijan had scried her true?

Cennaire saw that in this she was the wiser, far more experienced than he in such matters. Fleetingly—a memory from a past she would sooner now forget—she thought of other young men, innocent like him, who had come to love her. They, too, had been careless of opinion, guided by their lust, their love, and had learned to their cost that not all their friends saw the world through their passion-clouded eyes. That, she could not let happen now, neither for his sake or her own, not for the quest's sake.

"I'd not come betwixt you and your comrades," she declared, touching a hand to his lips as his mouth began to form a protest. "No, hear me out. I love you, and were it possible I'd spend each night 'tween now and the world's ending in your arms. But that should be foolishness, did it sunder you from your comrades. That Bracht no longer names me enemy is a great step forward—let us not jeopardize that."

"But we speak of times after Pamur-teng," he protested. "Once the gijan scries your future, surely Bracht can find no fault."

"Save I've not yet my heart," she returned, "and so he might well object."

"No!" he cried fiercely. "I do not, so how should he?"

"But you did," she said. "Before."

Calandryll felt a warmth suffuse his cheeks at that, and sighed, shrugging. "I'd ask forgiveness for that," he muttered. "I was a fool."

"No, you were not," she told him gently. "You were a natural man, and felt a natural revulsion."

Her tone, her smile, removed the sting of reproach from her words, but still Calandryll sat shamefaced, so that she could not but move toward him, stroke his hair, his cheek.

"There's no blame," she murmured. "Ask not for forgiveness, for there's no need."

He took her hands, holding them, and repeated back her words, precisely, so that they both smiled again.

"But still," she pressed, "Bracht remains a natural man, and he does not love me, and so might well find fault that we be lovers. At least, were we to express ourselves openly."

"I am not ashamed of it," he argued.

"Nor I," she replied, "but we speak now not of

us, but of those who ride with us, who are our allies and our comrades, whose confidence we must surely retain. Do you not see it?"

For a while Calandryll sat staring at her, frowning as he clutched her hands, then, reluctantly, nodded. "Aye," he allowed at last, "I do."

She said, "Let us agree that this night be our secret, at least until we reach Pamur-teng and consult with the gijan. Do I then win Bracht's—Katya's—wholehearted confidence, then shall we declare it."

"And do they, as you fear, object still?" he asked. "What then?"

"Then," she said, herself reluctant now, finding a strength she had not known she possessed, finding it in him and what she felt for him, "we shall behave as do they. Are they not bound by their vow?"

"That—their vow—" he answered slowly, "is different. Katya is of Vanu, and the customs of Vanu demand such obligation. You are of Kandahar, I of Lysse, and it is not the same."

"But still perhaps the wiser course," she returned.

"Perhaps," he allowed, and grinned. "But I am neither of Vanu nor Cuan na'For, and I am not at all sure I should find it possible to observe such a vow."

"Think you it should be easy for me?" she asked, answering his grin with her own smile. "It shall be very hard indeed."

His expression then reminded her of a child denied some coveted pleasure, and she could not help but laugh, and take his face again in her hands, and kiss him briefly, drawing back before he had chance to clutch her, for fear they should fall again onto the bed and reveal to their companions all she looked to hide.

"Listen," she urged, holding him at arm's length, "do we agree on this to Pamur-teng, at least, and after speak again?"

He studied her awhile, then sighed, and ducked his head in slow agreement. "Until Pamur-teng. But we must surely halt awhile there. A day or two—a night or two . . ."

His eyes asked a question, and she nodded, and said, "Can we hold it a secret between us, then aye—come to me there, and you shall find a welcome."

"And does the gijan convince Bracht?" he asked.

"Then all is well," she told him.

"And if even that scrying fails?" he demanded. "What then?"

"Then we go on as if vowed," she said, "to Anwar-teng."

For a moment Calandryll's brow creased, his expression become dark, then he smiled again and said, "Where we shall find the wazir-narimasu, and, the gods willing, they shall restore you your heart, and none can object."

Cennaire's smile grew wistful at that, her answer soft: "The gods willing. I pray it be so."

"As do I," he declared, his voice fervent. He reached then for her hands, seizing them before she had a chance to step back, holding them as he rose to stand before her, his expression grave now. "And, Lady, do we survive this quest, and deliver the Arcanum safe to destruction, I ask—be your heart returned you, or no—that we be wed, and remain always together."

Cennaire had not thought to blush—had not since taking up her former profession—but now she did, looking up into his solemn eyes, wondering.

"Sir," she asked, "would you truly wed me? Knowing all about me that you know?"

"I would," he answered, sincerity writ clear on his face, loud in his voice. "So—how do you reply?"

"That you honor me," she said.

And he returned her: "No. Rather, you would honor me."

"Then, sir, I answer you aye, with all my heart."

Almost, they laughed at that, for now they could, those reservations that had stood between them dispelled and forgotten. Instead, they kissed, tenderly at first, and then with mounting passion, until Cennaire pulled back and set firm hands against his chest, holding him off.

"No, not yet, not now," she gasped. "Remember we are vowed until Pamur-teng. Better that you go now, ere we are discovered."

"This shall be mightily difficult," he remarked, and she answered him, "Aye, it shall," and propelled him gently to the door.

He paused there, studying her face as if to commit her features to memory. He touched her cheek, and she held his hand an instant there, glorying in the warmth of his callused palm, then again drew back, motioning that he should leave.

He sighed and ducked his head, listened awhile, then opened the door and stepped out into the passageway beyond.

It was dim, lit by a single window at its farther end and that illumination faint, for the sun was not yet fully risen, but only a handspan as yet over the eastern horizon. Sounds came from the rooms below, but the corridor was silent, empty, as he paced toward his own chamber. He was almost to the door when another across the way opened to reveal Ochen.

The wazir was dressed for the road, his expression difficult to interpret in the crepuscular light, but Calandryll thought he smiled. Knew it as the ancient mage came close, his features creasing in striated wrinkles as he raised a hand in greeting, or perhaps in blessing.

"I trust," he murmured, a hint of mischief in his voice, "that you passed an agreeable night."

"Aye." Calandryll nodded, not knowing what else to say, confused and a little fearful that Ochen might disapprove, did he learn the truth.

"And Cennaire is well?"

"Aye."

Ochen's smile announced a knowledge of what had transpired, confirmed by his next words: "What passes between you is your concern and hers, none others. You've my blessing, do you ask it; and my advice, too."

"I'd have them both," Calandryll returned.

"The one is yours," Ochen said, "sincere and whole of heart. The other—perhaps it were better to keep this from your comrades."

"We'd agreed on that," Calandryll explained. "To Pamur-teng, at least. After shall depend on the gijan and Bracht, Katya."

"A wise decision," the sorcerer remarked.

Calandryll nodded his thanks, paused an instant, and said, "We spoke of regaining Cennaire's heart. Of taking it back from Nhur-jabal, that it be her own again. Shall that be possible?"

"She'd have it so?" asked Ochen.

"She would," said Calandryll. "Do you but ask her, and she'll say the same."

"Excellent." The wazir's smile grew a moment wider, then faded as gravity overcame his face and he said, "It may be done, though only with powerful magic. And no little danger. I cannot, alone, but the wazir-narimasu . . . Aye, they could, perhaps."

"Then do we reach Anwar-teng, and ask they do it," Calandryll declared.

Ochen paused a moment before replying, and when he did his voice was solemn, a note of caution there. "Ask, certainly," he said.

Calandryll frowned at the delay, at the tone. "You doubt they'll agree? Why should they refuse?"

"I do not say they shall," the mage answered. "I say only that I cannot speak for them, and that what you ask is a difficult thing, and perilous."

Fear drove a sudden dagger into Calandryll's soul: Ochen's responses seemed to him equivocal. "I like this not," he said. "Do you speak plain?"

The sorcerer's answer gave him no more comfort. "I cannot scry the future as does a gijan," Ochen told him, somewhat evasively, he thought. "Nor do I say it shall not be—only that I do not know."

"But do you doubt it?"

The ancient spread his hands wide, succeeding in expressing both regret and a lack of knowledge, of certainty. "I would suggest," he said, "that you put that matter aside until we reach Anwar-teng."

Calandryll would have questioned the old man further, for the absence of immediate confirmation, the hint of doubt he discerned in Ochen's voice, worried him, but the inn began to stir now, and Ochen denied him the opportunity with the observation that he had best enter his room, lest he be found already dressed in the corridor and his secret be guessed. He could only agree, albeit with reluctance, halting by the open door to ask that they speak again along the road.

"Do you wish it," Ochen agreed, and Calandryll must be content with that.

He went into the chamber, closing the door behind him, and readied what little gear he carried for departure. It was an afterthought to disarrange his bed, rumpling the sheets and indenting the pillows, as if he had passed the night here, not with Cennaire. The memory stretched a reminiscent smile across his mouth, and then he sighed at thought of his imposed celibacy. *Dera*, he murmured, *do you grant that Bracht and Katya, both, shall understand and I am forever in your debt.*

Then a fist pounded and he heard the Kern's voice: "Do you sleep still?"

"No," he answered, composing himself, "enter."

Bracht came through the door, saddlebags across his shoulder. He studied Calandryll's face and grinned. "Ahrd, but did you sleep at all? You've a night bird's look about you."

"Not much," Calandryll returned truthfully.

The Kern's grin faded, replaced with a speculative expression, and he said, "I left you with Cennaire . . ."

A question hung between them, and almost, Calandryll blushed, turning away as if busying himself with saddlebags. Casually as he was able, he said, "We talked—she was afraid." It was not entirely a lie.

"Afraid?" Bracht's response confirmed the wisdom of secrecy. "What's a revenant to be afraid of?"

"Anomius," Calandryll returned, defensive now. "Dera! Bracht, think you she knows no fear? Anomius yet holds her heart ensorcelled, and might well destroy her, did he but learn she takes our side."

"Aye," the Kern allowed without overmuch enthusiasm, "that's true, I suppose."

"Suppose?" Calandryll felt anger rise. "He's but to return to Nhur-jabal, to that pyxis. Think you she's without feelings? I tell you, no! She was terrified he should discern she betrays him—she sought my company awhile."

"Hold, hold." Bracht raised both hands in mock defenses. "I asked only a simple question."

"With subtler meaning," Calandryll snapped.

Bracht frowned then, studying him with quizzical eyes, and he feared he had let too much slip, cursing himself, reminding himself that he must set tight rein on his temper.

"I know you love her," the Kern said, softer, "and I thought perhaps . . . But no, surely you'd not bed her, knowing what she is."

It was hard to hold back the truth, hard to hold back his anger. *Dera,* he thought, shocked, *do we already fall to arguing? I must be careful.* As mildly as he was able, he asked, "And if I had?"

"I'd count you"—Bracht shrugged—"strange. Ahrd, what mortal man would bed a dead woman?"

"Cennaire is hardly dead," Calandryll replied curtly.

"Nor yet alive." Bracht fidgeted with the bags slung on his shoulder, clearly ill at ease with the path their conversation took. "Hear me, my friend, for I know you love her, and that cannot be easy for you. I've yet to come to terms with what she is—perhaps I shall not—but I'd not see that come between us."

"Nor I," Calandryll declared.

"Then do we make compact?" asked the Kern. "Agree we'll not discuss her condition further, or what you feel for her?"

"Aye," said Calandryll eagerly. "Save one last question—were she to regain her heart, how should you think then?"

"You think it possible?" asked Bracht, curious now.

"Ochen believes the wazir-narimasu might accomplish it," Calandryll explained, setting aside his doubts.

"And you'd see it done."

It was not a question and Calandryll nodded: "As would she."

"She'd lose much," Bracht murmured.

"But regain her mortality," Calandryll said. "Be once more only a woman."

"For your sake? Does she love you so much? Truly?"

"I believe it so," Calandryll replied, "in equal measure with my belief that she becomes one with our quest."

Bracht shrugged, eyes narrowed as he pondered this. Then: "For me, the gijan's yet to confirm her part in our quest, but be that done, and the Jesseryte wizards make her again mortal, you've my word I'll name her friend. And for the nonce our compact shall stand."

"So be it," Calandryll agreed, anger dissipated. "Now, do we find our breakfast and depart?"

The tension that had arisen was gone as they quit the chamber, meeting Katya and Cennaire emerging from the latter's room. Calandryll greeted them formally, and Cennaire replied in kind, though their eyes locked, bright with their hidden knowledge. Katya responded more casually, her grey gaze lingering awhile on Calandryll's face, as if she saw some change in him. She said nothing, however, and they found their way down through the levels of the hostelry to the main room, where Chazali and his kotu-zen, and Ochen, were already seated, eating.

It was difficult for Calandryll to maintain the camouflage of formality. Cennaire, by chance or design, was seated to his left, and he found it hard to resist the urge to turn toward her, to speak fondly, to touch her. Proximity brought a flood of remembrance, filled with images of that night, and he found himself regretting the necessity of pretense. More than once he caught Katya's eyes upon him, speculative, and while she gave no overt sign of awareness, he began to wonder if she guessed that he and Cennaire had become lovers in more than name. Perhaps, he thought, she saw such signs as Bracht and the other men along the table missed; perhaps some female intuition allowed her to read the truth upon his face and Cennaire's. He was relieved when the meal ended, and they departed.

Ochen spoke briefly with the priest as Chazali saw his men formed in a column, a squad of pike-bearing kotu-anj waiting to escort them to the gates. The foot soldiers trotted ahead, clearing a way, their warning shouts loud in the early stillness. The sun was only a little way above the horizon as yet, invisible between the towering buildings and the high walls, and Ahgra-te seemed scarcely better lit than at twilight, a close-packed, claustrophobic place that Calandryll was not sorry to leave.

Beyond the walls the open space and morning offered welcome freedom, the great bulk of the Ahgra Danji looming vast over the town, its dark stone brightening as the rising sun sent lances of brilliance flashing over the rockface. Their path swung north at the crossroads outside the walls, running alongside the fast-flowing river, past mills and scattered smallholdings, where gettu paused from their labors to bow in obeisance to the higher caste kotu-zen. Within half a league they had reached the foot of the cliff, where two black stelae, twice the height of a mounted man, marked the commencement of the road.

Beyond the great pillars the way rose gently at first, wide enough several riders might go abreast without danger of falling, then, still wide, angled steeper up the cliff. It proceeded in a series of traverses, winding east and then west, and back again. In places it was built out from the rock, that wagons and the like might pass more easily, or halt awhile, those terraces walled, and supported by huge buttresses. It seemed to Calandryll they climbed with the sun, pacing the orb as it rose steadily higher into the blue sky, lighting their way as if in welcome, striking colors from the rock as choughs and ravens wheeled level with the column, screeching, turning curious yellow eyes on the riders. The scarp deflected the breeze that had previously blown from the north and the morning grew warm, the azure above streamered with pennants of cirrus like the windblown tails of great white horses. At the head of the column, Chazali set a swift pace, climbing remorselessly upward, as though, the hindrances of the forested country left behind, he would reach Pamur-teng as soon he might.

That suited Calandryll well enough, for besides the urgency of the quest, he now had a more personal reason to wish an early arrival in the hold of the Makusen clan. He turned in his saddle, looking toward Cennaire, smiling, and she looked back, her teeth white between the luscious red of her lips. She had left her hair unfastened this day, and it fluttered about her face in the thermals rising up the cliff, sleek and black as the wings of the avian escort. He thought she had never looked lovelier, and then melancholy that they must keep up their pretense: it would be hard this night to sleep alone.

The sun continued its ascent until it stood directly above them, and then moved on toward the west, but Chazali called no halt, holding a steady pace until early afternoon, when they breasted the last heights of the Ahgra Danji.

As at the foot, the summit of the road was marked with stelae, set like great sentinels on the very edge of the cliff. Chazali rode on a little way and raised a hand, calling for a halt beside a stone-walled basin fed from the river that splashed nearby before tumbling in a rainbow spray over the rimrock. The kotu-zen began to dismount, but Calandryll sat his gelding awhile, staring at the terrain ahead.

It was unlike any he had encountered in all his traveling: a panorama of flat grey-green that swept away as far as the eye could see, unbroken save for stumpy turrets of grey in the distance that seemed scoured smooth by the wind. That blew stronger here, and far colder than across the lowlands, setting the surface of the odd landscape to rippling, like the water of a scummy pond. He sprang down, aware now that the coloration was that of scrubby grass covering arid, stony soil. The wind struck sharp on his skin, a reminder that autumn advanced, bringing with it the threat of winter. He brought the chestnut to the drinking trough, still staring northward, thinking how this Jesseryn Plain must be under snow: it was a disturbing thought, knowing Rhythamun ten days ahead.

"You are pensive."

He turned at the sound of Cennaire's voice, seeing her hair streamered on the wind, a sable contrast to the clouds above, and smiled, resisting the urge to draw her close, at least take her hand and hold it awhile. Instead, he nodded, running fingers through the gelding's mane, and answered, "I thought of how this Plain must be in winter."

She, better used to the warm clime of Kandahar,

shivered, and said, "Aye. I think it must be an inhospitable place."

Chazali, overhearing their words, said, "It is cold, aye. But not so bad. Our winters are mostly spent within the holds, protected and warm."

"But this season," asked Calandryll, "with the war raging? Or shall it halt for winter?"

The kiriwashen shook his head. "I think this war shall continue. I think Tharn fuels the hearts of those mad enough to warm their hands at his fire."

"Save we overtake Rhythamun," Calandryll replied, "and take the Arcanum from him."

"Horul grant it be so," Chazali returned gravely, and favored them both with an impassive stare. "At least we shall make better time here. Save the warlock has left another rearguard."

His remark prompted Calandryll to savor the air, easing a fraction the occult protections he now set up by habit. Immediately, he drew them close again: the land stank of evil, of malign chaos. It was, in physical terms, as if a thousand carcasses rotted, their stench carried on the wind. It insulted his nostrils, assailed his senses, leaving a filthy taste on his tongue. Now he shivered, and Cennaire asked, "Does this cold afflict you?"

He shook his head, palming water from the well, that he might swill out his mouth and rid it of the aethyric sapor. "Not that," he answered, "but the malignity that rides the wind. Do you not sense it?"

She frowned, shaping a negative gesture. "I've not that power you command."

"Almost, I'd sooner not possess such ability." He shuddered, looking to the north, toward the wind's source. "It's a charnel thing."

"Tharn's dreaming breath." Ochen joined them as the kotu-zen brought food from saddlebags replenished in Ahgra-te. "Do you hold close those protections I've taught you, Calandryll."

"I shall," he replied decisively. "Dera, but to know that reek could leech out the senses."

"Aye." Ochen nodded, agreeing, his seamed face grave. "That and worse. Overmuch of that awareness can overturn the mind, bring the pneuma more readily within the aegis of the Mad God."

"Then I'm glad I've no such talent," Cennaire observed, "for it seems as much curse as blessing."

"Is not all power?" asked the wazir, his voice mild. "The occult talent, swordskill, wealth, they all may work for good or ill. Their use is dependent on the owner."

"There are philosophers in Lysse claim power corrupts," Calandryll remarked, "that the greater a man owns power, the greater becomes his corruption."

"It is likely so," Ochen returned, "for men are generally far weaker than they think, and shorter of sight. Certainly, the wazir-narimasu are of similar opinion—hence do they forswear the belligerent usage of the magicks they command."

"They must be very wise," Cennaire opined.

"And I'd speak of them," said Calandryll. "What they might accomplish."

"Aye, do you wish it." Did Ochen's face cloud then? "But not now. Tonight, perhaps, have we time."

And Calandryll must be content with that, for the kotu-zen already ate, and Bracht called for him to follow suit, lest he ride hungry through the afternoon. He had sooner done that, and talked with Ochen, but the wazir answered the Kern's shout with his own, and they went to where Bracht and Katya lounged on the impoverished grass.

It was a meal taken swiftly, Chazali soon enough

calling for them to mount and be gone, and they climbed once more astride their horses, commencing their northward journey at a steady canter.

AFTERNOON advanced toward dusk. The turrets Calandryll had seen from the rim of the Ahgra Danji came closer, resolving into squat, smooth buttes of yellowish-grey. They stood like stubby fingers, pointing in reprimand of the wind that scoured their flanks, and as the sun closed on the skyline and a moon now waned to a sliver clambered up the sky, and stars pricked through the burgeoning twilight, it seemed almost that they supported the heavens, like pillars.

The sun fell below the far horizon, painting the sky there red for a while, then giving up its hold, leaving the welkin to the moon and its attendant stars. The grass shone silvery in that light, and it seemed they rode the surface of a vast, shimmering lake. The buttes stood black and starlit in the night, suddenly mysterious as the piles of some inconceivably gigantic temple, fallen down into ruins. The wind increased, chilling the air, whistling eerily over the surfaces of the stone columns.

Chazali brought them to the shelter of a butte, a spring at its foot feeding a well carved with the insignia of the Makusen clan. Grass grew denser there, sufficient that the horses might graze on their picket lines, and wind-tortured trees provided fuel for fires. A guard was mounted, and Ochen worked his magic to establish further defenses; soon meat roasted and kettles bubbled as they settled for the night. Calandryll was delighted, although little surprised, to find Bracht true to his word: Cennaire was included in their conversation, as if the censorious silences of their approach to

Ahgra-te had never been. He spread his blanket next to hers, across the fire from the Kern and Katya, feeling a small, traitorous regret that they were not alone.

He had, however, little enough time for that, as, immediately they had done eating, Ochen called him away, that he might continue his occult tuition.

The wazir led him away from the fires, past the watching sentries, to where starlight painted the wall of the butte pale silver, easing himself gingerly to the ground. Calandryll recognized the source of his discomfort and asked why he did not employ his magic to ease his riding, or at least his soreness.

"Too easy," Ochen returned, wincing as he sought a softer spot, "and perhaps hazardous."

"How so, hazardous?" Calandryll wondered.

Ochen bunched his robe beneath his buttocks before replying. "Each gramarye registers within the occult fundus," he explained. "Think of the aethyr as a pool, and every cantrip as a stone—the greater the spell, the more noticeable the ripples. Rhythamun knows by now you've a grasp of that talent he saw from the first; he knows a mage rides with you. Perhaps he watches the aethyr, and I'd not yet tell him where we are. Also, each gramarye requires an expenditure of strength, and albeit such a spelling as you suggest would be but a tiny effort, still I'd hold all my power close."

Calandryll nodded his understanding, then frowned as he saw a contradiction. "But if Rhythamun might sense your spelling," he asked, "how shall he miss the defenses you erect each night?"

"A good point," Ochen commended. "It hangs, however, on a subtle difference—the gramaryes I employ to defend our camps are general things:

warding spells attuned to no particular person." He chuckled ruefully. "On the other hand, do I use my talent to ease my poor, aching buttocks, then the gramarye must be of an individual nature, attuned to me alone. That might, were our enemy observant, reveal me to him."

Calandryll murmured understanding, then asked: "But in Ahgra-te, when you rendered us invisible, was that not a personal spell?"

"It was," Ochen agreed, "but there I'd spoken first with the priest, who is also, of course, himself a wazir, and together we established a protection."

Again Calandryll nodded, and again found a question. "And now? When you tutor me, does that not reveal us?"

"We work within the aegis of the gramarye warding this whole camp," Ochen answered, "and for now you do little more than memorize the cantrips, master the invocations and the mental concepts. Such should be protection enough for the nonce. Later, perhaps, there may be danger."

"As we come closer to Tharn's limbo?" asked Calandryll.

"Aye. You felt him on the wind today," the wazir said, "and you felt his reek come stronger. The farther north we travel, the worse that will become, the greater the Mad God's influence."

"What of the wazir-narimasu?" Calandryll frowned, assembling his thoughts. "Shall their influence not wax greater as we close on Anwar-teng?"

"That's true," said Ochen, "but remember they strive to defend the hold against the rebels' siege. And likely strive the harder to hold closed the gate they guard."

Each explanation seemed to raise a fresh question: "Save Tharn wakes, how can that be?" Calandryll demanded.

The wazir's robe rustled as he shrugged, starlight glinting a moment off his painted nails. "I thought you understood that the slumber of a god is not like that of men," he said. "Tharn rests in limbo, sleeping, aye; but he dreams, too, and feels the blood that flows on this mortal plane, the wars men fight, the dreams they entertain of conquest. Such feed him and strengthen him, and even dreaming he affects our affairs. Likely he probes the gate in Anwar-teng, or alerts Rhythamun of its existence, and so, likely, the wazir-narimasu exert their powers to hold that portal secure.

"Now, be that explanation enough, do we continue your tutoring? Or have you further questions for a saddle-weary sorcerer?"

"None more than what I've asked before," Calandryll said, "concerning Cennaire."

Ochen sighed: Calandryll felt suddenly uneasy.

"Your lessons first," the wazir declared. "After, be we not both too weary, we shall speak of Cennaire, and of her heart."

Something in his tone sent a shiver of apprehension down Calandryll's spine.

14

"Necromancy such as Anomius has employed," Ochen said when the lesson was done and Calandryll pressed him further on the matter of Cennaire's heart, "is not practiced here—nor by any civilized folk, for that matter—and consequently is not a thing with which I am overly familiar. Nor would I be, save I'd aid Cennaire."

"You told me her heart might be restored her," Calandryll protested, alarm edging his voice.

"It may be done." Ochen raised defensive hands. "But . . ."

He paused, and Calandryll waited, breath baited, his own, living, heart pounding nervously, for he heard in the sorcerer's voice a hesitation that set his nerves to tingling, apprehension growing. "But?" he prompted.

Ochen sighed, hands folding, lost in the wide sleeves of his green robe. For a moment his gaze encompassed the night, the stars, the sickle of the moon, then his eyes turned to Calandryll's face, somber. "You deserve the truth, unalloyed," he

said at last, "and that I'll give you. But first, a
warning: the truth may not be what you want to
hear. No, wait," as Calandryll's mouth opened, his
eyes narrowed. "Hear me out, knowing that I speak
holding insufficient knowledge, that I speak of the
worst that may be, and that—Horul and his kindred gods willing—the worst may not come to pass.
It may be that you and she gain your hearts' de-
sires."

Calandryll ducked his head, indicating acceptance even as his lips pressed tight together. It
seemed an icy hand ran down his spine.

"So," Ochen went on, low-voiced, "let us consider the situation. To restore Cennaire to mortality requires that her heart be freed from Anomius's
clutches. To achieve that end, the pyxis must be
brought from Nhur-jabal—and I'd wager Anomius
has set it round with powerful gramaryes. That
alone should be hazardous, none here knowing the
citadel. But—does Cennaire describe that place in
minute detail—it might be accomplished."

He broke off, nodding as if approving, or confirming, the statement: Calandryll felt his spirits soar.
Then fall again as Ochen continued, "But that may
not be the way of it, may not be a pattern in this
design. I've told you before that it is not my talent
to scry the future, and also that it is my belief a design exists in all of this. Perhaps Balatur, like his
brother, dreams and sends you help; perhaps those
powers that govern even the Younger Gods take a
hand. I cannot say, only that it seems to me it was
fated Cennaire should join you, and that she should
become your ally."

"Then," blurted Calandryll, unable to hold silent
any longer, "surely Balatur—the Younger Gods—
whatever power exists beyond them, must aid us in
this?"

"Perhaps," said Ochen slowly, "but think on this—were it fated that Cennaire become one with your quest, then perhaps her revenancy is needful. Perhaps she must remain revenant, is she to aid you."

"No!" Calandryll's voice rose in denial, in frustration. "That cannot be!"

"What may and may not be is for the gods, for destiny, to decide," the wazir replied, "not mortal men. But heed me—I do not say it must be so, only that it may be. Perhaps you shall have your wish."

"And perhaps not," muttered Calandryll, his voice grown bitter.

"And perhaps not," echoed the sorcerer. "Be that so, would you turn from your purpose?"

Calandryll stared at him, disbelief in his eyes, and shook his head. "No," he answered. "In Tezindar I—we three—vowed to pursue this quest to its end. I'd not renege on that undertaking, no matter what. But still I'd see Cennaire regain her heart."

"And if that's not to be?" asked Ochen.

Calandryll turned his face from the wazir to the sky, aware that tears threatened to course his cheeks, that he ground his teeth in frustration, that his hands bunched in angry fists. Dera, but it was hard! And, as Bracht was wont to remark, it seemed all dealings with the occult resulted in the piling of riddle upon riddle. There seemed no clear answers, only a shifting webwork of possibilities. He swallowed, forcing himself to calm, his hands unclenching to wipe absently at his eyes, and strove to hold his voice even as he replied, "Then it shall not be, and I must accept that. It shall not alter my course."

"Were she mortal, you should be dead ere now," Ochen remarked, seeking to offer what comfort was his to give.

"A part of this design you perceive," Calandryll muttered.

"Likely," said the wazir, "for it seems to me one thing piles upon another in ordered sequence—Anomius sends Cennaire out ahunting, she his creature then. She encounters you and finds her—forgive me?—heart is changed. Your company, your influence, shifts her allegiance to such extent she is willing to sacrifice herself. She becomes, sincerely, your ally. None of this should have come about were she not revenant, and so it may be that she is destined to remain so."

"Surely only while this quest lasts," Calandryll returned. "Do we succeed, then surely she's played her part and the wazir-narimasu cannot refuse to return her heart."

He waited on Ochen's reply, but when it came the sorcerer's voice was held carefully calm: "I've little doubt but that they should make the attempt."

It was equivocal, and Calandryll felt his mouth dry, presentiment mounting. Ochen's hesitation was unnerving and he motioned for the old man to elaborate.

"You ask no easy thing," Ochen said slowly, thoughtfully. "To undo such magic, reverse those gramaryes . . . If any can, then the wazir-narimasu, in concert . . . Aye, they might."

"Only *might*?" Harsh, that question, tinged with fear.

"I can promise no more." Ochen sighed, ducked his head as if unwilling to meet Calandryll's fervent eyes. "Such sortilege is dangerous—it might well leave Cennaire without life of any kind, a heartless shell."

Calandryll said, "Dera!" in a voice soft with dread.

"This need not be. I cannot answer for the wazir-narimasu. Perhaps it can be done successfully; but I know it cannot be done without great risk." The wazir met his gaze now, a hand emerging from the folds of his sleeve to gesture helplessly. "I warned you I should speak plain."

"Aye." Calandryll laughed: a single, bitter sound. "That you did."

"Better you should know it now," said Ochen, "than when we reach Anwar-teng. I believe you'll need all your senses alert then."

Calandryll ducked his head, silent awhile, shoulders slumped, staring at the dark ground. Then he looked up, at Ochen, and forced a smile, sad. "Aye," he admitted, the word a sigh. "Best I be prepared for the worst."

"Should the worst not be that Rhythamun succeeds?" the sorcerer asked mildly. "That Tharn be raised and all these concerns count for nothing?"

"Aye." Calandryll's voice was resolute, and very weary. "Now do we find our beds? Or would you tutor me more?"

"We've done enough for one night," Ochen returned him, "and Chazali will ride out come first light. So . . ."

He rose, groaning, a hand pressed to his back, muttering vivid obscenities concerning horses and saddles and the frailty of his aging flesh, so that Calandryll felt a reluctant smile stretch his lips, which was likely Ochen's intent.

Save for the sentries, the camp slept. Bracht and Katya lay a little way apart by the banked fire, Cennaire across the smoldering timber. Calandryll stretched beside her, wondering if she slept; wondering, too, if he should advise her of Ochen's dour warning. Did she ask, he decided, thinking it were better they held no secrets from each other.

He saw her eyes, then, the fire's glow reflected there, and her hand extended from beneath the blanket that covered her. He took it, the touch of her skin, the pressure of her fingers, a shock of excitement, desire. Low, she whispered, "What did he say?"

Soft enough he should not disturb their slumbering companions he told her, seeing her face grow grave, her grip upon his hand tightening. "So be it," she murmured when he was done. "I'd ask the gods grant the doing of it, but if that's not to be . . ."

"What I feel for you shall not change," he told her.

"Nor shall my feelings. But still I'd have back my heart," she returned, and laughed softly, her smile bemused as she added, "I'd not thought to want that so. Not until I knew you."

He brought her hand to his lips then, kissing her fingers. Pulling back as the temptation to draw her close, to fold his arms about her, became almost irresistible. *Dera*, he thought, *is this what Bracht and Katya have felt each night? I'd not believed it could be so hard.*

Aloud, he whispered, "Lady, this is not easy."

"No," she answered, "but still we made a vow."

"Aye," he groaned, the sound loud enough Bracht stirred, eyes opening an instant, hand tightening on the falchion's hilt, where it lay upon the Kern's chest. He rose on one elbow, saw Calandryll, and grunted, closing his eyes.

"Sleep," urged Cennaire, and Calandryll answered her, "Aye," softly now, and let her retrieve her hand.

He composed himself with difficulty, his mind filled with thoughts of Cennaire and all Ochen had said, the one tumbling over the other so that he

slipped unknowing into dreams of passion and despair, restless under his blanket.

FIRST light found him bleary-eyed and dry of
mouth, grunting as he rose, the blanket tangled
from his oneiric musings. He kicked it away, yawning as he surveyed the desolate landscape. The sun
was not yet over the horizon, the sky there opalescent, pale herald of the new day. Birds sang as he
splashed his face and set to drawing his dirk over
the stubble that decorated his cheeks and jaw. The
kotu-zen moved with their customary silent efficiency, setting kettles to boiling, preparing their
horses for departure. Katya tended the questers'
fire, and Cennaire went to aid her, while Bracht
gave his stallion its usual morning attention.
Calandryll smiled wearily at the two women and
wandered away, finding privacy along the lee of the
butte. That need satisfied, he returned to the fire,
drinking the tea Cennaire offered him, accepting
the smoked meat and journey bread Katya had
warmed over the flames.

The night's fast broken, they saddled their
mounts and kicked the fires dead, then rode out
from the shelter of the butte. Beyond the stubby
prominence the wind blew hard from the north,
beating cold against faces, setting the horses'
manes to tossing. Calandryll sniffed the air, wondering if he caught the scent of impending snow.
Certainly, it seemed the farther north they traveled, the closer they came to winter: the sky was
now become a hard, cold blue, what clouds it carried long mares' tails of pennanted cirrus, white
against the cerulean heavens. The sun that climbed
above the eastern edge of the world shone fulgent,
more silver than gold, offering little warmth.

That came as the morning aged, Chazali setting
the same swift pace as the previous day, holding it
until the sun stood directly overhead, then halting
where another butte marked another spring. They
drank the crystal water and chewed hurriedly on
cold meat, a little bread, and then recommenced
their journey.

As dusk approached, the buttes that had dotted
the plain thinned, finally disappearing behind
them, the way ahead devoid of landmarks other
than the ravines and occasional stands of stumpy,
twisted trees that grew in defiance of the arid soil
and the seemingly eternal wind. They halted in the
poor shelter of one such stand as twilight gave way
to full night, their fires small for want of timber,
the wind, unchecked by bastions of stone, a fierce
presence, howling over the flatlands to rattle
branches and streamer the flames, scattering sparks
into the night.

"You spoke aright," Bracht remarked as they ate,
and when Calandryll frowned his incomprehension: "That this is a glum place."

"There are worse," Ochen, sitting with them,
remarked. "The Borrhun-maj is a harder land than
this."

"But, at least, mountains," Katya observed wistfully.

"Likely we'll see them soon enough," Bracht
said, grinning. "Shall you be happy then?"

Katya smiled back. "I'd sooner my own mountains of Vanu; with the Arcanum safe in our
hands."

THE days passed, the leagues eaten up as a hungry
man wolfs food. The terrain broke up into ridges of
low hills and shallow valleys, streams more numer-

ous, and little hursts of stunted trees. Once great banks of dark cloud blew southward on an icy wind, and once snow fell, no more than a brief flurry, but clear warning of winter's advance. They saw no sign of habitation in the empty landscape, neither villages nor farms, nor much indication that any form of animal life existed on the Jesseryn Plain. It was, to Calandryll's way of thinking, a depressing place, and on those few occasions he opened his senses to the occult, he found the horrid reek of mounting evil ever stronger, as if he came steadily closer to the gates of a charnel house new-filled with rotting corpses. Ochen continued to tutor him in the lore and usage of thaumaturgy, and those lessons, lasting long into the ever colder nights, were a kind of boon, for he found his blanket chilled and weary, his head abuzz with all he learned, and that made it a little easier to resist the temptation Cennaire's presence afforded. When they found time to speak they said no more of her heart and its restoration, tacit agreement between them, though neither could forget the possibility that she not become again mortal, or perhaps die in the attempt.

Then, on a day when cloud hung low in the sky, stretching a forbidding grey curtain across the heavens, they came in sight of Pamur-teng.

The hold stood at the center of a wide strath, banded to north and south by ridges of gentle hills. It looked, in the distance, akin to the keep on the Daggan Vhe: a square, squat block of yellowish stone, rendered dull by the overcast, but as they thundered closer Calandryll saw the resemblance to the keep was one of design alone. This hold was infinitely larger, far greater than Secca even. It grew before him, vast and cubic, utterly unlike any city he had seen. There were no external walls such as

surrounded the cities of Lysse, nor a moat, or barbi-
cans. Like Ahgra-te before it, Pamur-teng was fortress and city in one, its outer defenses intrinsic
with its internal buildings, all melded together in a
single homogenous entirety. It was constructed so
that each enormous wall faced a compass point,
the southern facade, toward which they came,
marked at its center by a huge double gate, the
outer surfaces covered with sheets of hammered
metal inlaid with the sigils of the Makusen clan.
Closer still, he saw embrasures like watching eyes
set in the stone, commencing high on the wall and
running in regular lines out to either side, upward
almost to the ramparts that soon loomed above.
From those, suspended from long beams, hung
metal cages that a further examination showed
held prisoners. Some, he saw, held only bones: he
wondered at the nature of Jesseryte justice.

Then Chazali shouted a command and two men
brought their horses out of line, galloping ahead to
halt at the gates and pound upon the metal. The
gates swung ponderously open, revealing a tunnel,
black as night, from which kotu-anj came running,
forming in two pike-bearing lines. As Chazali and
Ochen drew level with the foremost pikemen the
kotu-anj raised their weapons, bringing the butts
thudding down as they roared a greeting. More
lined the tunnel beyond, and within that confined
space the sound was deafening.

The tunnel spanned the width of two buildings
before emerging on a crepuscular plaza, the buildings that contained the square six stories and more
high, with stone stairways and windows from
which expectant faces gazed, narrow passageways
running between. The sheer weight of stone, the
smooth, high faces of the buildings, was daunting,
oppressive: Calandryll was reminded of an anthill.

The more so as they progressed farther into the teng, following a smooth-paved road flanked on either side by pavements, those packed with cheering folk, more staring from windows, or from small stone balconies that added to the obliteration of the sky. His first impression, he saw, had been correct—this was as much a fortress as a city, a place easily defended, and horribly difficult to take. It seemed they passed between night and day as they went on, traversing avenues where shadow pooled, into squares—always squares, geometric and precise—that allowed a little of the day's dull light to enter. On and on, the shouting of the onlookers echoing off the high walls, until they rode down a passageway that ended at a metal gate, the wall above set with slender windows at which dark faces showed. Chazali reined in, halting the column, and Ochen turned awkwardly in his saddle to explain that they entered the kiriwashen's home.

The gate was opened by two elderly kotu-anj and the outlanders found themselves riding down a second tunnel, this devolving on a courtyard different to any they had seen before.

A marble fountain played at the center of an atrium large as a Lyssian city square, paved with flagstones set in a pattern of black and white rectangles, a colonnaded portico surrounding the enormous plaza. Above, balconies extended in serried ranks, climbing up to the topmost level, men and women in outfits of varying degrees of magnificence standing there, watching eagerly. Calandryll gasped as it dawned on him that this was, in fact, the home of the entire Nakoti clan, a virtual town within the city. He stared about, identifying stables, smithies, workshops, armories, as the yard filled with smiling, excited Jesserytes.

Servants came running to assist the kotu-zen

from their horses, four halted by a gruff command
from Chazali that held them back from the foreigners. Calandryll watched as a woman came forward,
three children at her side. She was short, and delicate as a porcelain doll, her dark hair gathered in a
long tail, her slanted eyes accentuated with cosmetics, her lips small and painted a bright red, the
same vivid color evident on her long nails. She
wore a robe of pale blue, chased with golden
threading about the hem and cuffs, and as she approached, its swaying revealed golden slippers, the
toes pointed. Two of the children were girls,
dressed in miniature facsimiles of the woman's
robe, the other a boy, wearing a scarlet tunic over
loose pantaloons of shiny black silk, a child-size
dagger sheathed on his belt, his feet encased in low
boots of black leather. The woman bowed low; the
children followed suit. Chazali bowed. Then removed his helmet to expose a huge smile as he
opened his arms, sweeping up the woman, who
laughed and draped her arms about his neck.

"The Lady Nyka Nakoti Makusen," Ochen murmured by way of explanation. "The girls are Taja
and Venda; the boy is Rawi."

It appeared that Chazali's greeting of his wife
marked an end of formalities: folk came from all
four sides of the great courtyard to fall upon the
kotu-zen in noisy welcome as servants led their
horses away to stables that Calandryll realized
occupied one entire side of the atrium. Several hovered close to the outlanders' mounts, clearly unsure what protocol governed here, that settled by
Bracht's suggestion that they see their own animals
stabled.

They waited, however, until Chazali had released
his wife and taken up each child in turn, his expression no longer impassive, but alight with plea-

sure as he held them. When he was done, he turned, ushering his family forward to meet his guests.

The Lady Nyka bowed deep, murmuring that they were welcome in the home of the Nakoti, while the three children eyed the strangers with curious looks, the two girls giggling nervously as they were beckoned forward to offer carefully practiced bows before edging back to the shelter of their mother's skirts. Rawi, although clearly disconcerted by the presence of these tall, oddly dressed outlanders, marched up to them with a stiff back, bent almost double, and declared in a loud voice that they were, indeed, welcome if they were friends of his father.

"They are," said Chazali, favoring his son with a proud look, and raised his voice that all should hear him: "These are my guests, and friends to the Makusen. Indeed, friends to our land and our god. Count them as blood kin, and serve them well while they sojourn in our teng."

"And shall that be for long?" asked his wife, to which Chazali shook his head and answered, "I fear not. The war calls, and we ride out on the morrow."

Nyka nodded as if she had expected no other answer, her expression unaltered, but in her eyes Calandryll read sadness that their reunion should be so brief. She gave no other sign, but turned to Ochen, bowing, and said, "I bid you welcome, as always, wazir."

"And I you, Lady," the old man returned, answering her bow with his own. "And ask your forgiveness that this visit be so hurried, and we with much to attend while we are here."

"Better a short visit and a long peace," she murmured, and turned her tawny eyes on the questers.

"Baths are prepared, and chambers. I trust you will find the attire selected pleasing."

Calandryll said, "We are in your debt, Lady Nyka."

"No." She shook her head. "Rather say that we stand in your debt, for what you attempt. Do you leave your animals here, they shall be well attended."

"I've no doubt of that," returned Calandryll with a smile, "but I suspect your servants had rather we executed that duty. And it is our custom to attend our own mounts."

"Aye." When she smiled she seemed scarce old enough to have borne three children. "They are somewhat in awe of your great beasts, especially the stallion. Be it your custom then, I'll have a man await you, and when you are done, he shall bring you to the baths and your quarters."

"Our thanks," he replied, and bowed again.

She clapped her hands and a servant, dressed in a tunic of russet silk and yellow pantaloons, came forward. She spoke briefly, the man bowed and turned toward the guests, his face held carefully composed, as if the arrival of foreigners fluent in his tongue was an everyday occurrence.

"Do you follow me, honored gentlefolk?"

Calandryll paused, looking to Ochen, and the wazir nodded, saying that he would find his own quarters and meet them later, with the gijan.

They saw their mounts bedded down and followed the servant out, across the atrium again, and through a low doorway into a hall, up dim-lit stairs that climbed steadily higher to the topmost level of the building. The servant—Kore, Calandryll learned was his name—bowed them each into adjoining chambers, waiting patiently as they stowed their gear in cabinets of inlaid rosewood, their

weapons on racks, before bringing them to separate
bathhouses, whose ceilings were great panes of
glass that offered a view of the sky as they luxuri-
ated in near-boiling water, soaps scented with san-
dalwood removing the grime accrued on their
journey. More servants, these in short white robes,
gathered to douse them with cold water when they
emerged, offering afterward huge towels of soft cotton that they would have applied themselves, had
Calandryll and Bracht not chosen to perform that
task unaided.

They found their own clothes gone when they returned to the outer chamber where Kore waited,
explaining their leathers were taken to be cleaned
and should be delivered to their quarters ere night
fell. As temporary replacement he offered loose-
fitting robes of dark blue, and soft slippers, that
they donned for the walk back to their chambers.

"Do you find the clothing the Lady Nyka has selected unsuitable," Kore murmured at the door,
"then I shall bring you more. Do you require aught
else, you need but ask—I shall await you here."

He bowed, watching as they each went into their
room.

Calandryll explored his quarters, marveling that
the interiors of these Jesseryte buildings should be
so different to their dull exteriors. The floor was
constructed of some highly polished wood, warm
underfoot and scattered with thick rugs of brilliant
colors, a wide bed covered with a blue and scarlet
spread occupied the center, at its foot a padded
stool. There was a washstand, and a small table of
rosewood, inlaid like the cabinet, held a decanter
and four goblets of delicate ruby crystal. The walls
were hung with sheets of soft green silk that lent
the chamber the feeling of an airy tent, save that it
was dim, the only sources of illumination the sin-

gle lantern suspended from the white plaster ceiling and the tall, glass-paneled doors that opened onto the balcony running the length of the outside wall. He crossed to that, noticing with a thrill of excitement that the balcony gave access to Cennaire's room, and with surprise that the roof he could see across the width of the atrium was a garden, filled with small, exotic trees, shrubbery, and vines that wound about little pergolas. He returned inside to dress, thinking that the nature of Jesseryte architecture reflected the personality of these mysterious folk.

Clad in the borrowed outfit, he inspected himself in the mirrored panels mounted in the cabinet. As in the keep, a shirt, a tunic, pantaloons, and boots had been provided, though here, in Chazali's home, the outfit was far grander. The shirt was silk, of a white so brilliant it seemed to sparkle even in the poor illumination of the chamber; the pantaloons were dark blue, faintly iridescent; the boots of soft, black hide, sewn with silver, the toes curling upward to points; the tunic was of a green akin to the drapery of the walls, bulked out at the shoulders and fastened around his waist with a golden sash. A jet horse pranced within a circle of crimson on chest and back, the perimeter of the disk embroidered with the emblems of the Nakoti Makusen. It felt strange to wear such finery: he had grown accustomed to his leathers.

He turned from his examination as a fist pounded the door, opening it to greet Bracht, the Kern dressed in similar fashion and no more comfortable than before.

"I'd feel happier had I my own plain gear," Bracht grumbled, crossing to the table to fill a glass. "Still, their wine is palatable."

Calandryll followed him, taking a goblet for himself. "We sojourn here but the single night," he said. "And after, I doubt we'll enjoy such hospitality again."

Bracht grunted a noncommittal reply and wandered to the balcony. The day waned fast, the sky still heavy with louring cloud, the square below almost lost in the burgeoning shadows. The chambers situated about the surrounding walls showed as dim rectangles, emitting a low babble of sound. The Kern returned inside, filling his glass afresh as he shook his head in puzzlement.

"These are curious folk, these Jesserytes," he remarked. "Ahrd, but to see these places from the outside . . . Yet behind their walls, they live in palaces. But so dim."

"It's their way." Calandryll chuckled as Bracht set down his goblet to fidget with sash and tunic. "And tomorrow you shall have your own plain gear back, and ride the open country again."

"Praise Ahrd for that," the Kern muttered.

A discreet tapping brought them both to the door. Kore stood there. "Forgive me," he murmured blandly, "but the wazir Ochen Tajen Makusen requests your presence."

"A moment."

Calandryll went to the table, setting down his goblet. Bracht's was already there and they quit the chamber, each going to a woman's room, knocking.

Cennaire's voice answered Calandryll: "Enter."

He opened the door and halted on the threshold, gape-mouthed. In leather riding gear she was lovely; in the robe provided in the keep she had been splendid. Now—he could only stare, wide-eyed, lost for words. Her hair was piled up and fastened with jeweled pins that sparkled against the black, emphasizing the slender column of her neck. Her eyes were outlined in the Jesseryte fashion with kohl, her lips and nails with bright crimson. She wore a high-collared robe of pale pink silk that seemed to flow over the contours of her body, fastened with tiny amethyst buttons, the hem and sleeves embroidered with a red that matched her cosmetics, slippers of pink visible beneath. She would, he thought, grace any palace; and then thought to tell her so.

"Thank you, my lord," she said with mock formality, performing an adroit curtsy.

Calandryll was about to reply in kind when Bracht's loud cry of "Ahrd!" brought his head around. He saw the Kern gaping at Katya. The Vanu woman was coiffured as was Cennaire, her piled flaxen hair all set with pins of jet. Her robe was a pale blue, her lips and nails a roseate pink. Bracht stood shaking his head and muttering "Ahrd!" as if he could think of no other word.

"The Lady Nyka sent a hairdresser to us," Cennaire explained. "And a woman skillful with cosmetics."

"They did you justice," declared Calandryll, regaining a measure of composure, "though their task was surely easy for what they had to work with."

Katya heard the compliment and studied Bracht with a mock haughty expression. "Do you perhaps take lessons from Calandryll?" she suggested.

The Kern could only nod, wide-eyed, his jaw dropped. "I . . ." he spluttered. "Ahrd! I . . . You . . . Never . . ."

His embarrassment was alleviated by Kore, who coughed diplomatically, reminding them that Ochen awaited their presence. Calandryll offered his arm to Cennaire as if at court, and Bracht, after a moment's hesitation, did the same to Katya. The Vanu woman chuckled as they proceeded down the twilight corridor, calling over her shoulder to Calandryll, "Do we have time along the way, perhaps you'll attempt to school this barbarian in his manners."

"A difficult task," he answered, "but I'll do my best."

At his side, Cennaire leaned closer and whispered, "You've noticed the balcony?"

Calandryll felt his cheeks grow warm, unsure whether embarrassment or excitement caused the flush. "I have," he said.

"It's not so chill a night my windows need be closed," she murmured, and he returned her, "Lady, I shall be there."

"Good." She pressed a moment against him, smiling, then drew apart as Kore halted and tapped on a door, calling through it that they were arrived.

They entered a chamber set with a food-laden table, the wazir seated at the farther end. Calandryll saw that candelabra had been placed about the room, as if in deference to the guests, and that the table was set with six places. Ochen motioned them to the stools set either side and dismissed the waiting Kore.

When the door was closed he said, "I thought perhaps it better we should eat here, alone. Chazali and Nyka have little enough time together, and I'd introduce you to the gijan."

As if that cue had been rehearsed a figure came in from the balcony. Calandryll assumed it a female figure because she wore a robe of black, high-throated and sewn with silver horseheads, the argent a match with her hair, that piled up like Katya's and Cennaire's, fixed in place with sable pins. Her face gave little indication of her sex, being both devoid of cosmetic and webbed with even more wrinkles than Ochen's. She seemed so old as to have somehow passed beyond the definitions of gender, though beneath snow-white brows her eyes glinted with intelligent light. When she spoke, her voice was a rustling whisper that seemed too soft to be heard so well.

"I am the gijan Kyama," she announced. "Ochen tells me you'd have a scrying of me."

Calandryll said, "Aye, do you agree."

"Readily." She laughed, and the sound was a twinkling as of silver bells. "But first, do we eat? And you shall tell me all you've done to bring you here."

She took the empty place, at the table's farther end, facing Ochen, who filled a glass with wine and passed the decanter to Calandryll. It rounded the table, back to the wazir, before the gijan spoke again.

"So, you come together from the world's four corners," she rustled. "The first outlanders to visit Pamur-teng, or any other hold. Do you tell me this tale from its beginning?"

Calandryll nodded, and glanced toward Bracht, to Katya, both of them indicating he should speak on their behalf.

When he was done, the food was almost gone, and none there wished for more. He drank a glass, his mouth somewhat dry from the recital, and awaited Kyama's response.

She studied him awhile in silence, her face so mapped with lines he could read nothing there, then turned her attention slowly to the others. He thought perhaps she weighed them, each in turn, and that this was a very different manner of scrying than was practiced by the spaewives of Lysse or Kandahar. The silence stretched out: none spoke, only waited on her.

Finally she said, "Ochen, do you call a man to clear this table?"

Calandryll had anticipated some weightier pronouncement, not so prosaic a request, and he found he must struggle not to frown and ask her what she had discerned from her lengthy examination. Ochen, however, appeared to find nothing odd, and rose, going to the door, two servants on his heels as he retook his place.

All waited in silence as the debris of their meal was removed, only a single decanter and their glasses left behind. Then, when the last plate was taken away and the door closed on the departing servants, the gijan said, "So, now I've knowledge of your past—do we look toward your future?"

Beneath the level of the table's edge, the movement hidden, Cennaire took Calandryll's hand, finding courage in the contact. It felt, for all she knew she bore no heart, but only what Anomius had put there in its place, that the organ pounded a fierce drumbeat against her ribs. She felt her mouth go dry and with her free hand raised her glass to her lips. It was a conscious effort to stay the trembling that threatened to spill the ruby vintage over her robe, for she believed she fast approached a crossroads in her destiny, and that what this ancient woman scried in her, and all of them there present, should likely decide her future. Carefully, she set the goblet down, grateful for the pressure of Calandryll's fingers and the confident smile he turned toward her.

It was a confidence he did not, entirely, feel, but rather an attempt to reassure the woman he loved. No less himself: as did Cennaire, he felt the future hung now in balance, and he voiced a silent prayer to Dera—to all the Younger Gods—that this scrying give him what he wanted to hear.

"What must we do?" he asked, pleased that his voice came clear, unsullied by the trepidation that knotted in his throat.

"Do you each take one another's hand," Kyama said. "Ochen's no part in this, but only you four."

They did as she bade, Calandryll lifting the hand he still clutched from under the table, reaching across to take Katya's, she taking Bracht's, the Kern and Cennaire each reaching toward the ancient spaewife.

"I know not how this is done in those lands you come from," she said, "but here I'd ask you remain silent while I trance. What questions you may have I'll answer later, as best I may. Now . . ."

She closed her eyes, head tilting back, the dry, creased skin of her throat stretching taut. For a while she was still, then she began to rock gently, and to chant, little more than a murmur, too low the words might be discerned. With Ochen's lessons to aid him, Calandryll understood this was not sorcery but rather communication with the inosculation of fate's skeins, the gijan imbued with that particular talent that granted her knowledge of the intertwining network of her clients' destinies. Such vision of the future was limited, both by the ability of the spaewife and the complexity of the web she sought to observe. He waited, nervous.

Kyama's droning chant ended abruptly. Her head fell forward, chin to chest, then snapped back, upright, her eyes still closed as she spoke, her voice no longer a rustle, but deeper, louder.

"You four take a hazardous road. Do you follow that path to its end you shall face dangers unimaginable . . . Dangers worse than plain death, even for that one of you who owns no heart. Powers move against you, to thwart you and destroy you. They'd have their revenge of you, those powers. And they are mighty . . . Greater than any one of you, though together, four, you are perhaps strong enough.

"I cannot see so far. Those you'd defeat, those you oppose—who oppose you—cloud my vision. The strands run out into darkness, but for a little way your purpose sheds light. You may succeed—it is within your power. Or you may not—victory is within the power of your enemies.

"They are several, your enemies. One is close, the others distant. One may, unwitting, aid you, and be that so, his wrath shall be great. Keep your wits about you, do you go where likely you must. Strength, sword skill, shall not alone be enough, you shall need also that power one of you commands, and that another holds. Trust—let trust be the keystone of your union. Without trust you become nothing and shall be defeated.

"No more do I see. It is too dark, too complex. The strands entwine, a maze. I . . . No! Too late. There is no more."

Kyama's head fell forward again, her body limp. A thin streamer of spittle hung from between lips gone slack. Her hands loosed their hold and she would have pitched facedown against the table had Bracht not moved to halt her. She moaned softly, stirring, and Cennaire brought a goblet to her mouth.

The gijan sipped, then swallowed stronger, and murmured her thanks, straightening on the faldstool. She looked from one to the next, her eyes again bright.

"Did you hear that which you wished to hear?"

"That we are four," Calandryll said, looking at Cennaire, "aye."

He turned his gaze on Bracht, who shrugged and found sufficient grace to smile shamefaced and say,

"You're owed an apology, Cennaire, and that I offer."

"And I accept," she answered. "Gratefully."

"But," the Kern added, turning toward Kyama, "there's much I fail to comprehend. You spoke of several enemies, and those I think we know—Rhythamun, Tharn himself, Anomius—but which may unwitting aid us?"

The gijan shaped a gesture of helplessness: "I cannot say. Only that do you use your wits you may deceive one to your advantage."

"And the powers we command?" asked Calandryll. "You spoke of two with power."

"There is power in you all," she answered. "The power vested in you burned bright, and that shall be both beacon and blade in your battle. But the other . . . that was darker and I could not clearly see in which of your companions it lies."

Across the table Bracht exhaled slowly and murmured under his breath, "Riddles."

Kyama laughed at that and said, "This talent of mine is no precise thing, warrior. It is not like your sword, to be drawn and used as you command, to strike where you'd put your cut. I look into a shifting, tangled future, and what I see I tell you. But those skeins I'd follow turn and twist and are not always easy to track. Were you four simple folk looking to forecast your destinies, then I could give you plain answers. But you are not; you go against a god, and you've such enemies as can turn fate on its head. That makes my task the harder."

"But we are now four?" Calandryll said. "And should trust one another."

"Do you forgo trust," Kyama replied firmly, "then you are not four, and only be you four may you hope to achieve victory. That much I read clear."

Calandryll smiled and took Cennaire's hand, openly now.

She offered him a smile in answer and looked to the gijan. "You know me for a revenant, no?" It was easier, now, to say it, though still she felt a pang of trepidation, fearing the response should not be that she wished. "Shall I get back my heart? Shall I become again what I was?"

The ancient spaewife paused a moment, then reached out to pat Cennaire's left hand where it rested, clenched, on the table, the gesture reminiscent of a grandmother comforting a nervous daughter. "Already you are not what once you were, but something better," she said. "I think perhaps the Younger Gods have touched you, and taken from you your sins. But more than that I cannot tell you, for of all the skeins I saw, yours was the most tangled. I am sorry, child, but whether you shall win back your heart, or no, I cannot say."

She paused then, and Calandryll, intent on all she said, thought perhaps she frowned—so furrowed was her face he could not tell for sure. Then: "You've a part to play, though, and that of great importance. Of that much I am certain, but I cannot tell you, precisely, what or how."

"Do you tell us shall we be together at the end?" he asked.

"The end?" Kyama spread wide her hands. "There are too many ends, each one dependent on the steps taken before." She glanced an instant at Ochen: "I thought you'd schooled him better, old friend." Then to Calandryll again: "Do you not understand? What we gijans scry is nothing fixed, but a changing pattern. Had this warrior of Cuan na'For not elected to welcome this woman as a comrade, your quest might well have failed, for she's vital to it. Did she elect to remain safe here, as you once suggested, you'd have little hope of victory. Should some rebel slay this warrior woman of Vanu, the future shifts.

"I do not tell you what must be, but what may be. That is the nature of my art. And you four oppose such enemies as make my task the harder— you go against a god, and gods, even dreaming, own such power as can change the future. All well, then aye—you shall be together at the end. And Cennaire shall have back her heart, and you shall deliver the Arcanum to Vanu's holy men, who shall destroy it, and Vanu shall be wed to Cuan na'For, Kandahar with Lysse, and all shall, as those who spin tales for our children have it, live happy after.

"But I'd not deceive you and tell you it shall be so, for I do not know. You've the chance, and I pray Horul you succeed; but shall you win or lose, I cannot say with any certainty."

It was as Reba, in far off Secca, had told him, and he ducked his head in acknowledgment, knowing he asked too much, dared hope too high: the future was no straight road, but a branching thing. But still he could not help but feel a measure of disappointment. He squeezed Cennaire's hand, seeking to comfort her for what he thought must be a blighting of her hopes, and was surprised to hear her say, "We can ask no more. That we be truly now four is enough."

"Said well," Kyama complimented. "And now I'd ask you excuse me, for I am wearied by this scrying."

"Aye." Ochen stood. "We've a long road ahead, and I suggest we all of us find our beds."

Did his eyes linger a moment, amusement twinkling there, on Calandryll and Cennaire? Calandryll knew not, only that the suggestion was greatly welcome: he sprang enthusiastically to his feet. "Our thanks for what you've done." He bowed to Kyama, to Ochen, offering Cennaire his hand as she rose.

IN his chamber he shed his borrowed finery for the robe Kore had provided, waiting as long as his racing heart allowed for Bracht and Katya to find their beds, then slipped silent on bare feet from his room to the balcony. The glassed doors of Cennaire's chamber stood ajar beneath closed drapes. He eased through.

She lay beneath the sheets, her hair loosed now, spread raven over the pillows. The cosmetics were gone from her face, and she was smiling. He shed the robe and went toward her, thinking that did his heart beat faster it must surely explode. She said, soft, "Do we not speak of the future, and what may be, but only of now."

Calandryll answered, "Aye," and went to her.

15

S NOW met them a day out of Pamur-teng; not a
full-blown storm, but clear enough warning
they rode headlong into winter. It came in flurries,
gusted on the fierce wind coming down from the
north, from the Borrhun-maj, a wind strong enough
it should have driven off the cloud that hung low
and grey across all the sky, but did not. The overcast remained, sullen, foreshortening the horizons,
denying the pale sun passage through its drab barrier, the land below gloomy for want of light. Between dawn and dusk the day remained somber,
depressing, as if the elements themselves contrived
to Rhythamun's purpose.

Chazali set an urgent pace, eager to join the army
sent ahead from his home hold, marching now a
little east of north, on a line that would bring the
warriors of the Makusen directly to Anwar-teng.
Bachan-teng lay due north, the bulk of its warriors,
as best the kiriwashen was informed, still within
their hold, poised to march against either the
Makusen forces or those advancing out of Ozali-

teng. He hoped, he had told the questers as they made swift war council on the morning of their departure, that the engagement of forces should occupy Bachan-teng sufficiently they might slip by unopposed. How they should pass through the siege lines to enter Anwar-teng, they chose to leave for later decision, when they might better view the obstacles in their way.

That decision had come swift enough: the alternative was to delay while the kotu-anj of the Makusen were examined in hope of identifying Rhythamun in his Jesseryte form—did he remain in that stolen body. It seemed as likely he should have taken another's shape, or gone on alone; and that must mean granting him further advantage by the search. Better, they had decided, to alert the sorcerers traveling with the army that one among the kotu-anj was perhaps a warlock, and trust that were it so, the wazirs should uncover him and halt him there. Better they should reach Anwar-teng, consult with the wazir-narimasu, that the most powerful of all the Jesseryte mages be able to lend what help was in their power.

"Can you not alert them to the danger?" Bracht had asked. "Speak with them from here?"

And Ochen had shaken his head, his wizened visage troubled, and said, "Were I able, I should have done that ere now, my friend. But I cannot— Tharn waxes daily stronger, and those misguided wazirs who lend their support to the rebels find their powers increased. Between the Mad God and them, communication through the aethyr is made impossible now. Anwar-teng stands alone in terms both physical and occult."

"But not for long," Chazali had declared, his voice flat with barely suppressed anger, "for the loyal tengs march, and soon enough shall fall on the insurgents, and the Khan and the Mahzlen be freed."

Ochen had nodded at that, but said nothing, and on his face Calandryll had thought to see doubt, as if the sorcerer found it impossible to share the certitude of the kiriwashen. He had found, however, no opportunity to discuss that doubt, for Chazali had shortly announced their departure, impatient, albeit he was clearly loath to quit his family so soon after arriving, to join the Makusen army, the sooner to restore his homeland to order and balance.

They had found their horses then, and ridden out of the kiriwashen's palatial home, an image blazened on Calandryll's senses. The Lady Nyka stood with her children at the center of the atrium, beside the fountain. The sun was not yet high, and the surrounding walls cast gloomy shadow over the little group, for all their robes were brilliant. Chazali had taken up his daughters, Taja and Venda hugging him, near to tears. Rawi had stood manfully holding back his disappointment, bowing formally, then hurling himself into his father's arms, declaring that should Chazali fall in battle he would be avenged.

"Aye, of that I've no doubt," Chazali had said, pride in his voice. "But for now you've a duty here, and that important."

Then he had embraced his wife, and stroked her cheek with a tenderness Calandryll had not before seen in him, and donned his helm, swiftly locking the veil in place, as if he would hide tears.

He had mounted, barked a command, and led his men out through the gates at a brisk trot. Calandryll had looked back a moment, and seen Nyka and her children standing forlorn, watching: four innocents caught up, like all the world it seemed, in the crazed machinations of the Mad God and his insane acolyte. Calandryll had looked to Cennaire then, seeing her lovely face set purposeful, and wondered if they should survive; and pushed the thought away, seeking to fix his mind on thoughts of victory.

They had quit Pamur-teng to a dinning chorus from the folk who lined the narrow streets, the shouting echoing from the great gates until those closed behind them, ponderous, sealing off the vast citadel. Chazali had driven hard heels against his horse's flanks then, lifting the animal to a gallop that carried them swift across the valley to the northern hills, not speaking or looking back, riding like a man who seeks to leave memories behind him.

On the third day out of the hold the snow began to fall unceasing. The sky assumed a livid hue, like diseased flesh, the wind easing a little, as if its task were done, sufficient cloud piled across the heavens that it might rest awhile. The flakes came drifting down careless at first, sizzling on the fires as they broke their fast, then thicker as they rode out, blowing directly into faces that stung with the cold, melting on the heated bodies of the horses, limiting vision so that they progressed blindly into the pale opacity. Chazali called no halt, neither slowed their pace, but continued on at a steady canter even as the masking veils of the kotu-zen were painted with the flakes, and the folds and edges of their jet armor, so that they resembled strange creatures, all black and white.

At least the Jesseryn Plain was firm enough to withstand the onslaught, Calandryll thinking that had they ridden the gentler terrains of Lysse or

Cuan na'For, the ground should soon be mired, the snow transforming the land to a marshy consistency that would surely have slowed their progress. As it was he began to wonder how long the storm should last, how deep the snow might layer on the unyielding soil.

That night, as they built fires from what little timber was available from the hurst that did its poor best to fend off the wind, he asked Chazali how they should fare, did the snowfall continue unabated.

"Poorly," was the kiriwashen's curt answer. "For a few more days we may go on unhindered, but does this Horul-damned snow keep up, it will begin to bank and slow us."

"Shall it?" Calandryll asked. "Keep up?"

Chazali had raised his veil, and paused a moment to wipe his face, looking up at a sky gone too early black, then grunted. "Likely," he said. "It's the look of a long fall. And the feel of thaumaturgy—such a storm should not come so early in the season."

He had excused himself then, pacing off, soon hidden behind a curtain of white, to inspect the guards he set, and Calandryll had gone to the warmth of the fire.

Bracht and Katya sat there, and Cennaire, all huddled in cloaks, preparing tea and warm food. The tent found them in Pamur-teng throbbed in the night wind. Calandryll took a place beside the Kand woman, sharing the oiled canvas she had spread. He told them what Chazali had said, and Bracht shrugged.

"Does it slow our progress, then surely it must slow Rhythamun," he suggested.

"Save Rhythamun likely employs sorcery to aid his progress," Calandryll returned.

"Is Rhythamun able to employ magic to speed his progress," Cennaire suggested, "then might not Ochen?"

Their faces turned to Calandryll, acknowledging his larger understanding of such occult matters. He frowned, uncertain, and said, "I am not sure. He tells me that the employment of such gramaryes as benefit individual folk are like beacons in the aethyr, and so might alert Rhythamun to our location."

"And enable him to attack you on that plane?" Cennaire shuddered, snow falling from her cloak's hood as she shook her head, alarm widening her eyes. "I'd not see that. Even must we go slow."

Calandryll smiled at her concern, for all he knew frustration at the prospect of delay. "I am but a novice in such matters," he said. "Best we ask Ochen himself."

"Ask me what?"

The wazir came out of the snow, wrapped in a fur-lined cloak his face like some small animal peering from the burrow of the hood. He settled on a corner of the spread canvas, extending his hands toward the fire, turning inquisitive eyes from one to the other. Calandryll outlined the gist of their conversation.

"Calandryll speaks aright," he said. "Do I speed our passage with cantrips, I risk sending Rhythamun notice of our position. Save it becomes unavoidable, I'd not chance that."

"And does it become needful?" Calandryll asked. "Do we find our way blocked?"

Beneath the voluminous folds of his cloak Ochen shrugged. "Then perhaps I must risk it," he said quietly. "I'd sooner not, but should it prove the only way . . ."

Cennaire voiced a small, inarticulate sound of

helpless negation. Calandryll smiled at her, turned to Ochen. "Surely we must reach Anwar-teng as soon we may," he said. "Is that not of paramount importance?"

Ochen nodded. "Aye—so long as we may reach the hold intact." He laughed, the sound empty of humor. "The choice would seem to be betwixt skillet and fire: we must reach Anwar-teng swiftly, but without alerting Rhythamun, and perhaps it shall prove impossible to do the one without the other. He's an advantage in that."

"Ahrd!" Bracht exclaimed. "Does everything favor him?"

"Here, now," Ochen said, "Tharn favors him. The god would be freed, he senses his minion drawing ever closer—he does all he can to aid Rhythamun."

"Did Chazali speak aright, then?" asked Calandryll. "Is this storm of occult origin?"

"It's the dimensions of wizardry," Ochen returned. "Cold winds, rain, those are the natural characteristics of the season. This snow comes too early and too hard, as if between one day's ending and the next's dawning we plunge into winter."

"And little we may do about it," murmured Bracht sourly.

"Save press on," said Calandryll.

"Aye." The Kern gave him a brief, grim smile. "Save press on as we have always done."

They ate then, electing by common, unspoken consent to leave the subject of Rhythamun, and talked instead of the war, the battle plans of the loyal tengs.

It remained a conversation that offered scant reassurance, for no matter how sound the strategy its execution must surely lead to a great letting of blood—which should strengthen Tharn. And did the god wax strong enough, and Rhythamun gain entry to his limbo, then all was for naught. It came full circle back to Rhythamun: whatever the outcome of the war, its prosecution must inevitably aid the Mad God.

It was a notion dismal as the sullen sky, and it weighed heavy on Calandryll's mind even as Ochen tutored him further, his responses abstracted enough the wazir called an early end to the lesson, sending him thoughtful to his bed.

He woke to a world become pristine under a blanket of snow. It lay thick over the ground, to his knees as he went shivering out, the tents white hummocks, the black armor of the kotu-zen a stark contrast; and the fall continued. The wind had died in the night and now the flakes came vertical from a sky all forbidding grey, silent and thick, promising to drift, to block the road. He cursed as he saw it, knowing they must be slowed, that Rhythamun thereby win further advantage.

They blew their fire to fresh life and took a hurried breakfast, tending horses irritable at such discomfort, likely thinking, did they think at all, that the stables of Pamur-teng offered warmth and better food than the grain doled out. And then Ochen surprised them.

They were mounting as the wazir came up. "I've spoken with Chazali," he announced, "and we're agreed we must make all speed to join the army. Therefore, I shall employ my magic to clear us a path."

Cennaire spoke before any other had chance: "What of Calandryll?" There was urgency in her voice, fear. "Shall you not endanger him?"

"I think not," Ochen answered her. "Not while we ride with the kotu-zen. Does our enemy investigate the occult plane, he'll find a party coming from Pamur-teng, aided by such sorcery as all the wazirs must now surely employ. Horul willing, he'll look no deeper, but assume us only latecomers. All well, the size of this group shall camouflage us. Even so." He paused, looking to where Calandryll sat the chestnut gelding. "Do you employ those protections I've taught you."

Calandryll nodded.

"Then we proceed," said Ochen.

He heeled his mount to where Chazali waited, moving a little way ahead as the kiriwashen formed his men in column of twos. Then he extended a hand, his painted nails glittering even in that dull morning, shaping sigils on the air, that redolent of almonds as he murmured his cantrip. It was a powerful gramarye. The air shimmered, pale light forming an aura about the slumped shape of the wazir, growing, the nimbus an ethereal, golden mist that swept abruptly forward as his voice rose to a shout and he pointed, as might a man send out a questing hound. It seemed then a silent wind, hot, rushed before them. Snow swirled in whirling white clouds, dissolving, a path clearing, a tunnel shaping, invisible save as the falling flakes defined it, denied entrance by the spell. Ochen lowered his hand, urging his horse forward.

They followed the glow, a friendly will-o'-the-wisp, riding the path it plowed, the exposed ground hard, frozen grass crackling under the hooves. Calandryll voiced the protective cantrips, his senses alert to warning of occult attack even as he smiled reassurance at Cennaire, where she rode beside him, concern writ clear on her lovely face.

Within the aegis of the gramarye it seemed they rode through a spring day, almond-scented, the light that preceded them leaving warm air behind, even though the snow still fell all about, the landscape to either side carpeted deep in whiteness, the trail behind rapidly filling. Chazali brought his mount alongside Ochen's and their pace quickened, a hard canter once more. Calandryll, closer attuned to the occult by the spell he wove, again caught the charnel reek that came from the north. He voiced a second cantrip and the air was cleansed, but still he rode wary, knowing Ochen gambled, that his soul was the stake, did the gamble fail.

By noon he felt more comfortable. No attack materialized, and their speed seemed such that they must soon catch up with the army. *But then,* he thought, *after—what then? We five ride on alone, and does the snow continue this gramarye becomes as much hazard as help.* He pushed the thought away: let tomorrow take care of itself. Only let us halt Rhythamun. Only let us wrest the Arcanum from him.

For two more days they followed the light of Ochen's magic without attack or hindrance, and then, as if conceding the struggle, the snowfall abated. The sky cleared, the miserable grey replaced with a hard, steely blue. The sun shone silvery gold, offering no warmth, and the wind got up again, a wolf wind that howled out of the north, knife sharp, raising drifting clouds of icy particles from the deep-drifted snow. It was a relief to all their spirits, to see the sun, to see clear again, but still the wazir must maintain his gramarye, for the land was laden heavy from the storm, and save he clear their way, they must flounder through chest-deep banks.

THEY found the army where the land lay flat, a ridge line of low hills far off to the west, beyond them, Ochen said, Bachan-teng. Ahead, the ground was trampled in a vast swath, a great roadway chopped through the white blanket by magic and men, more men than Calandryll had ever seen gathered in one place. They spread across the flat in a line of darkness that reminded him of his first sight of the Cuan na'Dru, stretching out to east and west almost farther than his eyes could see. Before them went a sweeping cloud of golden light that shimmered brilliant in the afternoon sun, snow shifted from the horde's passage as if by some inconceivable shovel. The icy air was sweet with the perfume of almonds, so strong it almost overcame the odors of horse droppings and metal, oil and wood, canvas and men's sweat; all the myriad, mingled smells of an army on the march.

Cavalry—at least a thousand men, he thought—formed the rearguard, more flanking the baggage train and the plodding infantry. The vanguard stretched beyond sight, led, he assumed, by the assembled wazirs, whose magic cleared the way. The sheer enormity of the Makusen forces was imposing; the thought that this was but one army, from a single teng, that it joined with another of similar size, that the rebels must field equal numbers, was more than his mind could hold. It seemed as if half the world must march to this war.

As if his thoughts were read, he heard Ochen say, "Tharn must delight in the prospect of so much bloodshed."

He answered softly, awed by the incredible prospect spread before him, "Aye."

There was no need now for the wazir to maintain his own gramarye: the massed sorcerers heading the army had cleared the way well enough, and Chazali heeled his mount to a gallop over the churned ground, hailing the riders who spun to meet him, they answering with shouts of welcome.

His men, Ochen, and the questers galloped after the kiriwashen, an escort forming about them, speeding them past the long line of marching soldiers to where the commanders rode behind the van of wazirs. Calandryll wondered if Rhythamun watched them go past, looking out from the eyes of Jabu Orati Makusen.

There were fifteen kiriwashen, Chazali the sixteenth, each representing a family lieged to the Makusen. Each commanded a thousand kotu-zen— more kotu-anj and kotu-ji—all the clan warriors, save those few left behind on the march. The din was tremendous, a cacophony of hooves and thudding feet, creaking wagons, snickering horses, the braying of mules, the clatter of weapons and armor, the voices of the men. Chazali must raise his voice to a near shout to be heard as he introduced the questers and advised his fellow kiriwashen of all that had transpired. He offered a succinct report, the details left for later, when the army should make camp, and as he spoke Calandryll was aware of the eyes that studied him and his comrades, speculative, from behind the concealing veils.

In turn the commanders told of their progress, unopposed as yet, while of the armies advancing from Zaq-teng and Fechin-teng there was little news: those insurgents already stationed outside the walls of Anwar-teng maintained the siege, awaiting the arrival of the main forces, content until then to hold the citadel isolated. And that condition extending beyond the physical, they said, for there was such a clouding of the aethyr now that contact with the wazir-narimasu, or occult observation of the rebels, was become impossible.

It seemed to Calandryll that to locate Rhythamun's stolen form in so vast a horde was no less impossible. Had the warlock elected to join the

army he likely knew by now the questers had
caught up, and would therefore take measures to
conceal himself, either by once more shifting his
shape, or by slipping away. Both seemed possible,
even easy, among so many men. More likely, Calandryll thought, he had gone by the army, eschewing
its slow progress to ride solitary to . . . Anwar-teng?
Or farther, to the Borrhun-maj? Did he attempt the
former, then the questers must make all haste to
the citadel, hoping to overtake their enemy. Did he
choose the latter, then it still appeared their most
favorable course remained the ride to Anwar-teng.
There, did they succeed in overtaking Rhythamun,
they might find the powers of the wazir-narimasu at
their beck, and prepare a fitting welcome. Did he attempt the Borrhun-maj, then they could go through
the gate and set an ambush in the world beyond.
That they should come upon him along the way,
and defeat him there, Calandryll could not believe:
they had dogged Rhythamun's footsteps for too long
that he might hope for so simple a solution.

He waxed impatient as the Makusen horde continued its inexorable march, the kiriwashen unwilling to halt while the day still granted sufficient
light they might draw closer to their destination.

He must wait, however, until the wan sun descended behind the western ridge and shadows
lengthened across the snowfields. And then wait
longer as the great mass of men and animals bivouacked for the night. Only then, when tents and
pavilions had been set up, guards posted, fodder
doled out, and fires been lit, did the commanders
and the sorcerers agree to hear in full council what
Chazali and Ochen, the questers, had to tell them.

They gathered in a pavilion that might have
housed a family, the wind setting the Makusen
standards to crackling overhead, the symbols of the

clan emblazoned on walls and awning. Inside, braziers were the sole source of light, the wood they burned aromatic. The canvas of the floor was spread with carpets, and kotu-ji erected a long table flanked by faldstools. Food and wine were served and the kotu-ji departed. Aijan Makusen, supreme commander of Pamur-teng, sat erect at the table's head. He was old, for all he sat stiff-backed, stern, and soldierly, his ringleted hair white, his beard the same. He it was led the premier clan, to which all others swore fealty, and it seemed to Calandryll he radiated a palpable sense of authority. Chazali and Ochen sat with the questers at the table's foot, not speaking until Aijan Makusen gestured his permission.

Kiriwashen and wazir introduced the outlanders then, fleshing Chazali's earlier brief report with detail. Calandryll, elected to speak on behalf of his comrades, was invited to describe their quest to the crossing of the Kess Imbrun. When he was done and sipping wine to assuage a mouth gone dry with the telling, tawny eyes studied him in silence, that finally broken by a wazir he dimly recalled was named Chendi.

"This is a frightening tale you bring us," Chendi declared, "and did Ochen Tajen and Chazali Nakoti not speak on your behalf I'd find it hard of believing. But . . ."

He paused, slanted eyes pensive, a hand stroking at the oiled beard he wore. Another—Dakkan, Calandryll thought was his name—spoke into the gap: "But do we not all feel what stirs now, fouling the aethyr? Is our aim not the securing of Anwarteng against the Mad God, in equal measure to the rescue of Khan and Mahzlen?"

"Aye, so it is," said one named Tazen. "And what Ochen saw we all have seen, in greater or lesser measure, and this war, the clouding of the aethyr, all the signs indicate they speak the truth."

"You'd have us examine every kotu-anj of the Orati?" asked a wazir whose name Calandryll had forgotten. "That should take two days or more."

"As long—or longer—to allow this woman," a kiriwashen named Tajur grunted, eyes skeptical as they rested on Cennaire, "to study their faces."

"And that with no surety of success," said a wazir, "for be this Rhythamun what these outlanders claim, he might well assume another's body while we search."

"Which should mean we must examine every warrior in our companies," said another.

"Horul!" declared a kiriwashen Calandryll thought was named Machani. "How long should that take? With Anwar-teng in jeopardy each day!"

"This warlock shape-shifter is not among the Orati." This defiantly from the wazir of that clan. "I'd know it, were it so."

"He's a sorcerer of great cunning," Ochen said, his tone diplomatically mild, "and great power. That waxing greater the closer he comes to Tharn."

A kiriwashen nodded, eyes moving from Ochen to Chazali. "You're persuaded to their cause, Chazali Nakoti?" he asked.

"I am," Chazali replied. "I believe all they say. I believe we renege our duty to Khan and Mahzlen—to Horul himself!—do we not aid them."

Aijan Makusen spoke then for the first time, and all fell silent.

"Shall Ochen Tajen not soon be named wazir-narimasu? Can any here doubt the loyalty of Chazali Nakoti? Can we then doubt their belief, that these outlanders war with Tharn himself? That some among them have spoken with our god? I say we must aid them as best we may."

Protests erupted then: that the giving of such aid must halt the army's advance too long, work to the advantage of the rebels; that there could be no certainty of finding Rhythamun among the massed humanity of the Makusen forces; that perhaps these outlanders were employed by the rebels to slow the army; that perhaps they ensorcelled both Ochen and Chazali.

The tumult died as Aijan Makusen raised a hand. "For my own part I cannot believe a wazir of Ochen Tajen's undoubted power might be so seduced," he declared, "and so, that Chazali Nakoti is not enspelled, for Ochen should know it. Therefore, I cast my vote for belief and aid."

Dark faces turned toward the old man, tawny eyes studying him, some with acceptance, Calandryll thought, but others with disbelief. Chafing, he wondered how long this debate should continue, how it should be settled. He turned a grateful gaze on Ochen as the wazir offered a solution, looking first to Aijan Makusen, speaking when the supreme commander nodded his assent.

"I am not ensorcelled," he said, "neither Chazali. But that none here present entertain doubt I suggest you examine us. Look into our minds, and then into those of our outlander allies, and you shall know the truth of what we tell you."

"That would seem a satisfactory resolution," Aijan Makusen said. "Do you others agree?"

There was a murmur of consent and the assembled wazirs rose, beckoning Ochen forward.

The ancient sorcerer faced them almost defiantly as they locked their eyes on his wrinkled face. They began to speak, in unison, and the great tent filled with the scent of almonds. It took no more than a few heartbeats, not so long as Ochen himself had taken to enter the minds of the questers, back in the keep atop the Daggan Vhe. "So, do you see clearer now?" he demanded when it was done, and the wazirs nodded, murmuring their agreement.

Chazali rose then, accepting the examination for all Calandryll read resentment on his face, and then, in turn, each of the questers. Calandryll felt the thirty eyes fasten on his, and it was as though he pitched headlong into darkness, falling. He staggered, shaking his head, as he felt their hold released, the insubstantial tendrils that had wandered the pathways of his brain withdrawing. For an instant his ears rang, and then he heard the wazir named Tazen say, "There can be no doubt. All we have heard is true."

"Horul!" said another. "Shall we see Tharn raised then?"

"It shall not be through any want of our aid," Aijan Makusen said, his slanted eyes narrowing as they turned to Ochen. "What would you have done, wazir?"

"I'd go on to Anwar-teng," Ochen answered, "in company with these four—I deem it the wiser course that we apprise the wazir-narimasu of all we know, as soon we may. For the rest, I'm in agreement with these others that Rhythamun may evade discovery—may perhaps not be among the Orati even—but still I'd have a search mounted."

"To search the army—to thus delay—can only aid the rebels," a kiriwashen murmured. "Shall that not favor the Mad God?"

"'Does Rhythamun gain that limbo where Tharn rests the rebels shall need no further aid," Ochen said.

"No less shall the bloodshed of this war aid the god," a wazir whose name was Kenchun offered.

"Save these outlanders succeed, it would seem the Mad God gains whichever way we turn."

"I cannot stand idle by and see Anwar-teng despoiled," Aijan Makusen warned. "Mad God or no, we've a duty to Khan and Mahzlen, and that we cannot forswear."

"Aye," said Ochen, "that I know. I'd find a compromise."

It seemed to Calandryll as he listened to them that the Jesserytes were not a people much given to compromise of any kind. On the faces of the kiriwashen he could see alarm at the prospect of granting the insurgents such time to strengthen their position as the searching of the army must take; on the faces of the wazirs he saw the contradicting pull of clan duty and fear of Tharn's resurrection.

"A compromise?" he heard Aijan Makusen say. "How may we achieve that, without betrayal to our duty or our god?"

Ochen thought a moment. Then, a wry smile curving his lips: "Only with difficulty; only with a little patience I fear some shall find hard come by."

"Does it not conflict with those duties we owe the Mahzlen," Aijan Makusen said, his eyes scanning the assembly, issuing an unspoken command, "then we shall find such patience."

Ochen nodded and said, "Then this night I'd ask the kiriwashen and the kutushen—all the officers—to pass word among their followers. Is any man aware of strangeness—a friend who seems not himself, sickness, anything untoward—let him report it. I'd ask that the ranks of the Orati be searched for Jabu Orati Makusen. Does he come forward"—a doubting smile curved the wazir's lips—"then let the wazirs bind him with gramaryes and slay him. Does he look to flee, the same. Does Rhythamun yet hold that luckless form, he may well seek to take another. Be that the case, Jabu Orati will be dead, but likely the occupation of Rhythamun's next victim will be noticed. Remember always that you deal with a sorcerer of terrible strength!

"All this, I know, must delay the march, but Horul willing, not for too long."

He paused for breath and the wazir of the Orati—Kellu, Calandryll remembered was his name—said, "Must we examine every kotu-anj among our warriors, that shall delay us longer."

Aijan Makusen spoke again: "We shall allow two days for such investigation, occult and physical, as you require. Does that commence this night it may be done in such time, I think."

"Do we all bend to the task," said Kellu, "then, aye."

"Shall you not join in this, Ochen Tajen?" asked another.

Ochen sighed, shaking his head. "I fear that all this may prove fruitless," he murmured, ignoring the gasps, the grunts of outrage that met the announcement. His voice grew stronger as he continued, "But nonetheless needful! Does Rhythamun seek to conceal his foul self amid the men of Pamur-teng would you have it said we failed in our duty? That we, lax, allowed him such refuge?"

He waited as the kiriwashen and the wazirs voiced denial.

"The search shall be made," said Aijan Makusen. "Even be it time wasted, I'd not have such accusation made. But swift! We've another call on our loyalties."

"Aye, that I know," Ochen said, "and would not ask for more. As for me—I ride on, to Anwar-teng."

"You'd have an escort?" Aijan Makusen asked.

"No, though I thank you," Ochen returned, and

encompassed the questers with a gesture, "we five shall go alone. The insurgents are less likely to find so small a party, while a larger group must surely be noticed. Horul willing, we shall gain the teng unharmed."

"And do you not?" asked Kellu, to which Ochen shrugged and smiled a silent answer.

"Should we find Rhythamun," asked Dakkan, "what are we to do with the Arcanum? How shall we recognize the book?"

Ochen looked to Calandryll, motioning that he should speak. He said, "It is a small book, bound in black, the title inscribed in red. It seems an insignificant thing, save for the malign aura it bears. We are sworn to deliver it to Vanu, as I have told you, that the holy men of that land might destroy it."

"Then do we find it, and you be slain," said Aijan Makusen with blunt pragmatism, "we shall deliver the book there. My word on that."

"Then you've our thanks," Calandryll said.

A grim smile divided the old man's stern features for a moment. "I'd no more see the Mad God raised than concede the rebels Anwar-teng. I pray Horul you succeed." The smile disappeared as his eyes swept the table. "So, we've much to do and long leagues yet to march. Do you kiriwashen go to your duties, then; and you wazirs to yours."

The commanders and the sorcerers rose, quitting the tent. Chazali paused, studying the questers. "I've another duty now," he said, "and must go to my Nakoti. Should we not meet again ere you depart, know that my prayers go with you, and you shall be ever welcome in my home." He turned to Ochen. "Horul be with you, old friend. I pray we meet again ere long."

"And I," the wazir murmured.

They clasped hands, and then Chazali bowed

deep to the questers, again to Aijan Makusen, and
spun round, marching briskly from the pavilion.

"I, too, have duties I must attend," said Aijan
Makusen, "do you excuse me."

It was a tactful dismissal: Ochen bowed and the
questers followed suit, going after the wazir out of
the tent.

The night was loud now with more than the
natural clamor of a bivouacked army as the
kiriwashen and the wazirs went about their tasks.
Orders rang out, riders cantered by, soldiers came
from tents and cookfires; all was disciplined confusion, the unprecedented presence of foreigners in
the midst of a Jesseryte army ignored. They found
their horses where the standards of the Nakoti fluttered over the ranked tents and saw the animals
bedded as comfortably as was possible, bringing
their gear to the pavilion Ochen indicated.

It was smaller than the great tent of Aijan
Makusen, but still luxurious, divided into compart-
ments, with rugs scattered about the floor and braziers filling the interior with warmth. Ochen
showed them where they might sleep, Calandryll
and Bracht separated from the two women by a
wall of heavy silk. The forward area was set with a
table and faldstools, open to afford a view of the encampment, and the wazir stood there, looking out
at the bustle.

"Think you he's here?" Calandryll asked, coming
to stand beside the smaller man.

"No." Ochen shook his head, his next words
confirming the doubts Calandryll had earlier felt.
"Was he ever here, he saw us arrive and took his
cue to depart. He draws too close to his goal that
he'd risk discovery."

"Then why suggest this search?" Bracht gestured

at the camp, buzzing now like a disturbed hornets' nest.

"For fear I'm wrong." Ochen sighed wearily, his voice dropping close to a whisper as he added, "And to slow the army's advance, Horul forgive me."

"What?" Confusion set a frown on the Kern's face. "Why?"

Ochen moved from his observation, crossing the vestibule to a brazier. He stretched out his hands, palms forward, to the flames. "I believe," he murmured, almost too low they might hear him, "that Rhythamun likely avoided the line of march. Did he join the Nakoti legions, he must travel at the army's pace, and he's likely impatient now; eager to reach his goal. I believe he goes on, to An'war-teng or the Borrhun-maj.

"And the closer he comes to Tharn, the stronger he becomes, the greater the *likelihood* of his reaching the Mad God. You know that shed blood is meat and drink to Tharn, that war augments his power. Think then what the arrival of this army at Anwar-teng must mean, think what blood must spill when these loyal forces encounter the rebels."

He turned from the brazier, and in its dim light his face was grave, hollowed with a dreadful doubt. Calandryll nodded, understanding. Bracht continued to frown, and Ochen explained, "Do all these thousands and all the thousands of Ozali-teng fall on the thousands of the rebels, then the land must stink of blood. There's the irony of it—the loyal forces would defend the gate; but to defend that gate can only strengthen Tharn." He shook his head, sighing again, and it seemed to Calandryll the weight of all his years sat heavy on him, his vitality suddenly drained. "I'd not give the Mad God that feasting sooner than is inevitable. The longer that battle is delayed, the better your chance of defeating Rhythamun, for does full war commence I believe our enemy shall find such power granted him as to render him unvanquishable.

"I cannot halt the war. Horul, but I'm by no means sure I should! It's a conundrum to defeat the wisest mage—does battle commence, then likely Rhythamun becomes insuperable; does Anwar-teng fall . . ."

His voice trailed off, exhausted. Callandryl said, hoarse, "Then likely Rhythamun wins."

Bracht said softly, "Ahrd!"

Ochen said, "And so I gamble. I hope that we may enter Anwar-teng before full battle is joined. I hope the wazir-narimasu shall lend you such aid that you defeat Rhythamun before he grows too strong. I pray Horul that I do the right thing."

There was anguish in his voice, doubt writ clear on his face. Calandryll said, "You do what you can; what you must," seeking to reassure him, and Ochen laughed, once, a harsh, bitter sound, and said, "Aye, and in the doing, do I betray my clan? Do I grant the insurgents entry to Anwar-teng?"

"What if you be wrong?" asked Bracht, offering support. "What if Rhythamun docs still own the body of this Jabu Orati, and rides with this horde?"

Ochen looked up at the Kern, a rictal smile stretching his lips. "Then we had best hope he be soon found," he answered, "and sleep wary this night. But I doubt I'm wrong."

Katya spoke then, for the first time. "I believe you right," she said gently. "In all you do."

Ochen nodded his thanks, but Calandryll saw he took little enough comfort from their reassurances. He struggled for some formula that would resolve the wazir's dilemma, but could find none, save: "Surely the defeating of Rhythamun, of the Mad

God, is a duty higher than that owed your clan. Surely it's a duty owed Horul, owed all the Younger Gods. Dera, should Tharn be woke the Makusen shall likely exist no more! Do we defeat Rhythamun, then all the world stands in your debt."

"But still," Ochen said softly, "my blood is Jesseryte blood, and all my life I've served the Makusen. To deceive my fellows so sits hard with me."

"There's no deceit," said Katya. "As Bracht says—it may be that Rhythamun remains within these ranks, and therefore such investigation as you've suggested is needful."

"But I perceive it as deceit," Ochen returned, "for I remain convinced he's gone on."

"Two days is scarce time enough to swing the balance of this war," Bracht said. "You take over-much blame upon yourself."

"Perhaps." Ochen shrugged. "But then again, perhaps I had done better to speak honestly with my peers."

"No." The Kern began to protest, but the wazir raised a hand, effecting a wan smile, and said, "No more, my friends, I beg you. I know you look to convince me, but this is a matter for my own conscience and none other. I must wrestle with it alone, and I am mightily wearied. Do we find our beds?"

Bracht would have argued further, but Katya took his hand, drawing him away. Calandryll said, "Until the morrow, then," and turned toward Cennaire, offering his arm, courtly, bringing her to the partitioned sleeping quarters. He would have kissed her, but both entrances stood open and so he bowed, smiling for all he was concerned at Ochen's discomfort, bidding her good night. She answered in kind and stepped into the chamber, dropping the entry curtain behind her. He stood a moment, frowning, then went to join Bracht.

There was no brazier and the chamber was shadowy, the canvas wall vibrating softly under the wind's caress. The sounds of the vast encampment came through. Calandryll yawned as he shed his swordbelt, resting the scabbard against the frame of the low bed. He tugged off his boots and padded to the washstand. As he splashed chill water on his face he heard Bracht say, low, "Ahrd, but it pains me to see the old man so torn. I've grown fond of him."

"Aye." Calandryll stretched on the bed. The pillow was hard, but after so many nights with only his saddle it seemed a great luxury: his eyes grew heavy. "He's proven a true friend."

Bracht said something else, but he failed to discern the words, nor could he summon the energy to question his comrade. Sleep beckoned and he could barely murmur the protective cantrips taught him before he gave in and allowed slumber sway.

Dawn came bright, the sun a white-gold disk at the horizon's rim, the sky poised undecided between blue and grey, the wind died away, the air sharp-edged. Smoke rose in myriad columns over the camp, and the odors of cooking food mingled with the scent of almonds as the wazirs went about their searching. Of Chazali there was no sign, and the questers ate their breakfast with Ochen, brought them in the pavilion by two kotu-ji.

Immediately they were done they found the Nakoti commissary and secured such supplies as they should need for the remainder of the journey to Anwar-teng. None made reference to Ochen's doubts of the previous night, and the ancient mage seemed to have set his misgivings behind him. He was, however, somewhat subdued, and when Calandryll solicitously inquired the reason, he replied that such constant use of magic as he had employed to clear their path to the army had wearied him.

"Horul willing," he declared as he heaved himself awkwardly astride his mount, "the snow shall be frozen hard enough I may rest a little as we ride." Then he chuckled, a measure of his customary good humor returning. "As much as my ancient bones can rest upon so unyielding a creature as a horse."

"Do I break trail?" Bracht suggested, and Ochen waved his agreement, looking about a moment as though he bade kinsmen and friends farewell. The Kern tapped heels to the black stallion's flanks and trotted out, the others behind, past the ranks of tents and men, the mules and horses, the wagons, all spread in orderly formation, as if some nomadic people wintered on the desolate flatlands.

It took the better part of a hour to clear the camp, and then they traveled virgin snow, crusted hard and scoured by the wind. Their pace varied, swift where snow was frozen, supporting the weight of animals and men, slower where the horses must plunge through drifts banked up and soft.

By noon, when the pale sun hung overhead like an impassive, watchful eye, the great encampment was lost behind them, ahead the glittering sweep of the unbroken snowfield. It shone bright in the sun's harsh light, threatening the fresh hazard of snowblindness, and Bracht called a halt, fetching kindling from his saddlebags to start a small fire. They brewed tea and ate sparingly of the provisions, and when they were done the Kern took sticks from the flames, allowing the blackened tips

to cool and then daubing the charcoal around his
eyes. He applied the same rough protection to each
of their faces, and they stared at one another,
laughing at the clownish effect.

"Dera, but we resemble a flock of owls,"
Calandryll declared, chuckling. "Do we also possess their legendary wisdom?"

"In Kandahar the owl is a symbol of death,"
Cennaire observed, instantly regretting it.

"Here, it may save our lives." Bracht flung the
last stick away. "We'll have little chance of success
do we go blind."

That night, and for fifteen more, they camped on
the snowfield, in tents secured from the commissary, Katya and Cennaire in one, the three men in
the other. Their fire was, of necessity, small, and
even wrapped in the heavy cloaks Chazali had
given them—their blankets draped protective over
the horses—they were chilled. At least the wind remained quiescent, as if they had traveled in a matter of days from autumn's ending to dead of winter.
Darkness came early and dawn late, and the air lay
still, keen as a knife's edge in nostrils and mouths,
numbing on exposed skin. By day the sky was a
blue so pale it seemed almost white, blending im-
mutable with the land. By night it was a black so
dense the new-filled moon and the stars seemed
not to pierce the obfuscation, but to struggle
against a darkening that was wholly unnatural. Despite the protective gramaryes he employed,
Calandryll could no longer entirely fend off the ol-
factory manifestation of Tharn's sending. The charnel stench intruded on his senses as if the reek
became so strong it found chinks in his occult ar-
moring, and he found he must once more struggle
against the horrid feeling of desolation, of despair,
that threatened to leech out his will. Almost, it

seemed the land lay already under the dominion of the Mad God.

On the morning of the sixteenth day they struggled up a snow-encrusted ridge that ran like the backbone of some buried monster across their path. Stone showed, dull grey and shocking after so long traversing the blank whiteness of the snowfields, along the crest. There, as if the stone marked a boundary, the snow ended; beyond, the ridge sloped gently down, rock giving way to winter-dulled grass that spread over a shallow river valley. The river ran, grey-blue and broad, from a great expanse of water. On the north bank, diminished by distance, stood a hold. On the grass before the citadel, along both banks of the river and partway along the shore of the lake, stood an array of tents, horse herds like shifting shadows on the land, men too far away to see.

"Anwar-teng," Ochen said.

"And none too easy to reach," murmured Bracht.

"Save these approaching riders," said Cennaire, whose eyes were the keenest there, "be a welcoming party."

16

THEY had come down off the ridge's crest to put the stone concealing at their backs: it seemed impossible any should have sighted them.

"Can you be sure?" Bracht asked.

Cennaire said, "There are twenty horsemen. Kotu-zen by their armor, and riding hard toward us."

The Kern mouthed a curse. Ochen said, "Magic! The turncoat wazirs use their powers to espy intruders, Horul damn them."

Calandryll said, "Do we follow this ridge along, might we avoid them? Might we reach Anwar-teng before they reach us?"

"Thaumaturgy guides them," Ochen replied. "Likely they'll follow wherever we go."

Bracht was already unshipping his bow from its protective wrappings, adjusting the quiver against his saddle. "Then we must fight," he declared.

Ochen nodded absently, turning to Cennaire. "Are there more?" he asked.

She shook her head. "No, only these twenty."

The wazir nodded, thinking a moment. Then: "Do we follow the ridge toward Lake Galil, and fight only when we must."

Bracht glanced up at the sky and said, "It's a while before the light goes, and until then they've the advantage of us."

Calandryll and Katya brought bows from their packs; strung them. Ochen said, "Let us gain what time we may. Do we close on Anwar-teng, perhaps we'll find help from that quarter."

"Do we stand here debating?" asked Bracht. "Or do we ride?"

They rode. Pell-mell across the downslope of the ridge, grateful for the sounder footing of the grass, thankful they need not flee across the snow. Bracht led the way, the black stallion stretching into a furious gallop, Katya urging on her grey behind, then Ochen, bouncing and cursing in the saddle, followed by Cennaire, Calandryll alongside.

Cennaire turned, peering northward, and shouted, "They change direction to head us off."

Calandryll returned her, "How far?" and she answered, "A league, perhaps."

And they on fresher horses than our poor tired beasts, he thought. *How long before they intercept us?* Ahead, the ridge curved a little, turning north before petering out onto the grass that swept gentle down to the lakeshore. There were tents there: the rebel forces. It seemed they ran from one danger into another. It seemed impossible they should reach Anwar-teng unscathed; nor any more likely they could fight a way through the armies sieging the citadel. *Dera, Horul,* he thought, *do you aid us now? Have we come so far, only to fall here?*

There was no answer, only the furious drumming of the hooves, the gusty breath of near-blown horses. The sun looked down, indifferent, from the

bleak sky and it seemed the fetid reek grew stronger, anticipatory. The kotu-zen drew closer, enough
that now he could just make them out, twenty
black shapes galloping hard at an angle toward the
questers' path, guessing—or told by sortilege—their
intention.

They reached the ridge's ending and Bracht
snatched on the reins, the stallion wickering irritably as it halted. Katya was taken by surprise, almost colliding as she steered her grey around the
curvetting black, turning to come back alongside
the Kern.

"What do you do?"

Bracht flung out his bow, indicating the terrain
ahead, the shadow line of tents along the lake. "Do
we go on, we're caught. Better we face them here."
A savage smile stretched his lips. "They're only a
score, and we've the advantage of height here."

"And do we defeat them?" Calandryll dragged
the chestnut to a stiff-legged halt. "What then?
There shall surely be more sent out."

"Can we stand them off until dusk we've darkness for our ally." Bracht sprang down, bringing his
quiver from the saddle. "And perhaps Ochen's sorcerers. Or his magic."

Calandryll looked to the wazir, undecided.
Ochen studied the land ahead and nodded. "Bracht
understands these matters better than I," he called.
"And have the rebels seen us, then likely the
wazir-narimasu, also."

"And your magic?" Katya asked. "Can you use
that now?"

"That should be hazardous still," Ochen said. "It
may be they take us for scouts, and so better if you
can defeat them without my aid."

"Then do we see our mounts safe among these

stones." Battle joy flashed in Bracht's blue eyes. "For it's a long walk to Anwar-teng."

Without awaiting a response he led the stallion in among the lithic detritus that marked the ridge's end, tethering the snorting beast. The others followed suit, leaving the animals protected by the rocks.

Swift, Bracht barked orders, sending Katya and Calandryll out on a line where the stones looked down onto the grass. Cennaire and Ochen crouched at the center, a little way back. Calandryll glanced at the Kand woman and smiled, she answered him with a wave, her dark eyes worried as she watched him take his position.

It was a place easily defended. The slope, for all it was gentle, must slow the riders somewhat, and if they chose to match the questers with arrows, they must fight without cover. Did they attempt to charge, bringing the fight to close quarters, they must climb the gradient under fire. Calandryll set his quiver close at hand, upright against a boulder, and nocked a shaft, waiting.

It was not long before the twenty kotu-zen showed distinct on the plain: it seemed an eternity. They came on at a gallop, slowing as they saw their quarry had not broken cover, reining in to study the cuesta. Their armor was dark crimson, marked on chest and back with the sigils of their clan. Longbows stood in scabbards behind their saddles; all wore swords; two held long-hafted war axes. They conferred, out of bowshot, heads turning to survey the ridgetop, faces hidden behind their helmet veils. One motioned with the ax he carried, sending the rest into line on either side. For a heartbeat that seemed to Calandryll to stretch out for long moments there was a silence broken only by the stamping of impatient hooves. He drew his bowstring taut, sighting down the shaft. There was a shout, soon followed by a medley of war cries, and the riders charged.

They came within bowshot: Calandryll loosed his shaft. Saw it imbed in crimson armor even as he snatched another from the quiver, nocking and sighting in a single fluid motion, wondering in the instant that action took how strong was Jesseryte armor. The man he hit seemed unaffected, even when the second arrow sprouted from his breast-plate.

"Their faces!" Bracht roared. "Aim for their faces!"

Calandryll adjusted his aim, and saw a veil pierced. Likely the hit man screamed: battle shouts and hoofbeats hid all other sound. He saw the Jesseryte sway in his saddle, sword dropping from his hand. He nocked and swung leftward, bow-string throbbing as the shaft was flighted. His tar-get rose in the stirrups, rigid as his head flung back, tumbling over his horse's hindquarters. The first warrior still sat his mount, urging the animal on, his fallen sword replaced with a wide-bladed dag-ger. Calandryll fired again, the range far shorter now, the arrow driving deep into armor, the Jesseryte shuddering as it hit, then slipping side-ways from the saddle, dragging his horse's head round before his gauntleted fingers let go their hold. The horse screamed angrily, bucking, almost on the rocks, then cantered away, downslope. Its rider lay awhile on his side, then staggered to his feet, retrieving his dagger. The broken lengths of three arrows protruded from his breastplate, an-other from his face. Calandryll thought he saw blood running from under the veil as the kotu-zen began to weave an erratic course toward the boul-ders.

Seven men lay dead, twelve were still mounted, their armor decorated with shafts. They seemed less deterred by the slaughter of their comrades than enraged. They spun their mounts, thundering partway back down the slope to turn and charge again. The wounded man continued his solitary advance, halted by the arrow Katya sent with dreadful accuracy into the right eye hole of his veil. Calandryll heard his scream then, shrill as he fell to his knees, a hand beginning to reach up, then halting, suddenly, his head dropping forward. He pitched onto his face and lay still.

Three more died in the charge, flung from their horses as feathered shafts sprouted lethal from their veils, driving hard through the vulnerable links into the softer flesh beneath, finding targets in eyes and mouths and brains. The rest turned back, regrouping out of bowshot.

Bracht shouted, "Cennaire, do you see them reinforced?"

She came from where she waited with Ochen, running to Calandryll's side, looking out toward the distant huddle of tents, and answered, "No. There's none others approach."

"Good, for I run short of shafts." Bracht laughed, a wild cry of battle lust, and glanced at the sky. "Dusk draws closer. Do we stand off these few left and then, save we've slain them all, slip away."

Calandryll felt Cennaire's hand resting on his shoulder and turned his head a little, to rub his cheek against her grip. She smiled grimly and stroked a hand over his long hair as he called to Ochen, "Shall they not know us gone, with magic to aid them?"

"Likely," replied the wazir. "But we've little other choice, save to go back."

"And have them find us out on that snow?"

Bracht shook his head. "No, my friends. We stand or fall here."

Further debate was curtailed by the enemy. They charged with drawn bows now, sending long, crimson-painted shafts winging before them. Calandryll ducked, pushing Cennaire back, as three arrows rattled off the boulders to either side. He heard Bracht shout, "Hah! They replenish our quivers," and brought his own bow to bear.

The defenders still enjoyed the advantage of height, the attacking kotu-zen forced to expose themselves as they rose in their stirrups to use their longer bows. Two more were slain, the charge turned back again.

"Here!"

Calandryll found Cennaire beside him, her outthrust hand clutching gathered Jesseryte shafts. He took them with a grunt of thanks and waved her back to cover, forgetting in the heat of the moment that arrows offered her no harm.

The riders charged a fourth time. The waning afternoon filled with the susurration of exchanged fire. Calandryll found his quiver emptied and nocked a crimson shaft. He noticed the head was viciously barbed. Then saw it lift a man from his saddle, spilling him down among the bodies already littering the slope. Horses went riderless now, milling on the gradient, some turning to canter away from the fight, others running wild alongside the remaining attackers, halting only at the rocks, to rear and flail their forehooves, shrilling madly, as if they joined the surviving kotu-zen in outrage at the slaughter.

The questers resisted the impulse to shoot the animals, less from any altruistic motives than the need to conserve ammunition: for all they sent the

Jesserytes' own shafts back, still they stood perilously close to finding themselves without arrows.

A final headlong rush saw three more crimson-armored bodies dispatched to Zajan-ma—and the four surviving warriors into the rocks.

They dropped their bows as they came close, springing limber from their plunging animals for all the weight of their armor. The riderless beasts afforded them cover, a living, surging barricade of flesh and muscle they drove before them, in among the stones, swords in hand.

Calandryll tossed his bow away, the straight-sword flashing from its scabbard to parry a blow that would otherwise have divided his skull. His riposte glanced off a red breastplate and he flung himself to the side as the heavy Jesseryte sword endeavored to carve his ribs. He struck again, the blow slowing his attacker even though it failed to sunder the man's helmet. He was driven back, seeking some chink in the crimson armor; finding none. The Jesseryte advanced, fulvous eyes glaring from behind the masking veil. Through the rocks, Calandryll saw a second come running to take position beside the first, the two moving apart, that they should attack from both sides. He heard the clamor of steel on steel, on armor; heard Bracht's bellowed curse. From the corner of his eye he caught fleeting glimpses of the Kern and Katya retreating back through the jumbled stones, forced like himself onto the defensive by the seemingly impregnable armor of the kotu-zen.

He stepped past a boulder and damned his ill luck as he realized he now stood in a cleared spot, wide enough the two Jesserytes might easily flank him. Then something clattered off a helmet and one man staggered, loose kneed, his sword arm dropping. There was a second impact and his veil

drove inward. Red gouted from the eye holes and
the kotu-zen fell down. Calandryll parried an attack. Saw his attacker halt as a stone bounced from
the sweeping cheek-piece of his helmet, then totter
as another struck his breastplate. A third whistled
past Calandryll's head to strike the helmet where it
protected the warrior's brow. For an instant the
head was snapped back by the force of the blow:
Calandryll lunged, driving the straightsword up,
the point piercing the Jesseryte's jaw, his brain. The
man grunted and collapsed, his weight threatening
to wrest the sword from Calandryll's hand.

He snatched it loose and saw Cennaire standing
with a rock in each hand, poised to throw, her expression fierce. "Lady," he cried, "you save me
once again."

She smiled, fleetingly, and darted away, to where
Katya faced an opponent, driven back against a
semicircle of boulders, unable to retreat farther, or
to find a weakness in the man's armor. Calandryll
followed her, in time to see her hurl the stone with
terrible force, sending the kotu-zen staggering side-
ways. She flung another missile, that crashing
against the crimson helmet, the man groaning and
dropping to his knees. Katya sprang toward him
then, her saber darting, searching out the vulnerable places in his armor, severing his throat.

Cennaire scooped up new stones and ran to
where Bracht dueled, the falchion a blur in the
dimming light, fending off the attack of the
Jesseryte's heavier blade. One stone smashed with
deadly accuracy against the kotu-zen's helm, the
second against his knee. He toppled, one leg
twisted at an unnatural angle, and Bracht leapt
astride him, a hand tugging back the helmet as the
other slashed the falchion across the windpipe.

"My thanks." The Kern raised his bloodied

sword in salute. "Now do we quit this place ere they send more."

They hurried to the horses, Ochen there before them, reins gathered in his hands, muttering oaths as he manhandled the recalcitrant beasts toward them. Overhead, the sky darkened swifter than it should, as if a storm gathered. To the west the sun painted a band of sanguine light across the horizon; to the east the moon was hidden behind the strange obfuscation. To the north fires pricked the plain with myriad distant glows. They mounted, studying the way ahead, all with the same thought: that it should be mightily difficult to pass unscathed through the massed ranks of the enemy.

"I think," said Ochen, "that the time has come to take a chance."

Bracht laughed hugely at that and said, "We've not already?"

"I'll chance the use of magic." Ochen's answering smile was fleeting. "I'll attempt to contact the wazir-narimasu."

"Do we wait," asked Calandryll, "or do we ride?"

"Ride," said the mage. "Ride and pray."

They heeled their horses down the slope, Bracht in the lead, holding the stallion to a fast canter, reserving the animal's strength for a final gallop. The sky assumed a midnight hue, unlit by moon or stars, though sullen light played, balefire that flickered a morbid red. The reek of Tharn's malignity grew, with it the sense of horrid, hopeless oppression. Riding hard on Ochen's heels, Calandryll caught the brief waft of almonds. He turned, reassuring himself that Cennaire remained alongside, and voiced a half-spoken prayer.

Do you Younger Gods hear me now. Do you aid us, be it in your power, that we enter Anwar-teng unharmed.

The fires ahead came closer; brighter, threatening. The sounds of men and animals drifted over the grass. The pounding of their horses' hooves counted out the minutes, the steady diminishment of the distance between them and the hostile ranks before. Calandryll rode with straightsword in hand, thinking that did the Younger Gods, the wazir-narimasu, not come to their aid, they must surely die outside the walls of Anwar-teng. Overhead, the balefire seethed, the air sullied with its stench, as if flesh corrupted, burned. They drew closer to the encircling fires . . .

. . . Closer still, enough now that they heard the alarums ringing strident from the enemy camp. Bracht shouted, "Gallop! Ride for your lives!" and gave the black stallion its head.

. . . And a riderless horse joined their charge, a great horse, taller than the stallion, its hide a jet in which starlight danced, as if it were composed not of flesh but elemental matter. Its eyes flashed fiery, and where its hooves struck the ground, brightness like splintered shards of sun erupted, silent despite the tremendous speed of its passage. It overtook them, and it seemed they were caught up in the vortex of its passing, their mortal mounts dragged onward, hooves seeming no longer to touch the earth, but to run above it, on the air itself, unhindered by the limits of physical existence. Calandryll said, "Horul! Praise be!"

And in his mind—in all their minds—there came a silent voice:

What aid is mine to give you shall have. Was that not promised? Did you doubt then? Think that I and all my kin should forsake you? Nay, we stand with you as best we may. Remember that where you go.

Ahead, riders came out to meet them, lancers and mounted bowmen.

Misguided fools, came Horul's thoughts, contempt and pity mingled. *They know not what they do.*

Arrows lofted and disappeared in sparkling coruscations as they neared the god. The lancers charged and the leading horsemen were bowled over, flung back against their fellows as if by an unimaginable wind. Several yelled in terror and turned from the god's headlong rush. Behind him the questers thundered through the perimeter of the camp, fires flung wild beneath their hooves to ignite pavilions, stacked bales of hay. The insurgents' horses shrilled their fear, plunging on the picket lines, tethers snapping as they bucked and reared, freeing them to run wild through the confusion that gripped the bivouac.

The walls of Anwar-teng loomed above, beacons bright with promise of refuge along the ramparts. A blue radiance, pale, but strengthening steadily, rose from the citadel to confront the balefire that gathered concentrated overhead. The charnel reek of Tharn's manifestation was opposed by the sweet scent of almonds. From the embrasures along the walls shafts flew, and faint through the tumult of pandemonium that rose from the besiegers came shouts of encouragement.

The teng's gates creaked open, blue light bright there, and armored men, archers, running a little way clear to form an avenue into which the god brought the questers.

Horul halted, rearing, within the aegis of the gates. Vast hooves pawed air, and from the flared equine nostrils fumed brilliance, like tumbling starlight.

I leave you now. Where you soon go I cannot fol-

*low, nor any of my kindred, save in spirit. Know
that you go with our blessings, with our gratitude,
and our hope that you succeed, that you return
safe.*

The warriors of Anwar-teng—their armor a blue
to match the radiance overhanging the hold,
Calandryll dimly noticed—drew back. Horul's great
haunches bunched and the god sprang skyward,
light trailing behind, the hooves striking silent on
the air. The balefire gathered before him, as if malign power massed in opposition within the aethyr.
The gates swung to even as Calandryll followed the
god's progress, the thud of their closing overwhelmed an instant later by a tremendous thunder-
clap, a fireglow that leapt across the heavens,
momentarily bathing Anwar-teng and all the surrounding plain, Lake Galil, in fierce red light.

Then darkness as eyes near blinded adjusted to
the ensuing gloom. Calandryll felt the chestnut
move under him, blinking as he struggled to regain
sight, finding a kotu-zen leading him into the bowels of the citadel. He rubbed at his eyes and called,
"Cennaire?" hearing her answer him, her voice
hushed, awed, from close behind. Ahead, as sight
returned, he saw Katya, Bracht at her side, Ochen
before them, deep in conversation with the three
brilliantly robed men who strode briskly alongside
the wazir's horse.

None spoke further as they proceeded into the
hold, down avenues and roadways crepuscular for
all the lanterns hung from the high, surrounding
buildings, toward the center.

A square there, entered by four roads extending
toward the cardinal points of the compass, the
buildings that formed its walls each marked with
the horsehead emblem of the Jesserytes' god. They
dismounted—none came to aid them, but rather

stood back respectful—and on Bracht's insistence saw their animals safely stabled. Then haste, Ochen and the three robed men bringing them swift down corridors and across dim-lit halls, up winding stairways, to a great chamber set high, its ceiling pierced like that chamber in the keep with a roundel of clear glass. Through it, Calandryll saw the sky was once more dark and baleful, layered with ominous light, though here there was no sense of oppression, no redolence of Tharn's fell emanation. He looked about.

As if in deference to stranger custom, the chamber was lit with lanterns and candelabras, their glow reflecting off bare stone walls, the plain wood floor. It was a simple chamber, unadorned, at its center a round table, that ringed with faldstools, more standing empty than were occupied by the men who waited there, studying the incomers with wondering, narrow eyes. The three who had met the questers at the gate moved away, taking places among their fellows, and Ochen stepped forward, bowed, and named the questers one by one.

Calandryll studied the men seated around the table. All were old, their faces wrinkled, to greater or lesser extent like Ochen's, most white-haired, though a few yet boasted grey, and some even departing vestiges of the Jesserytes' characteristic black locks. All wore robes of splendid color, the spectrum displayed in magnificent combinations.

The introduction done, a man at the table's farthest limit motioned the newcomers to seat themselves. He, it seemed, was elected spokesman, for when they took their places the rest remained silent as he said, "We bid you welcome to Anwarteng, friends. We are the wazir-narimasu, and I am named Zedu. We owe you thanks for what you have attempted . . ."

"*Have* attempted?" Calandryll caught the ominous meaning of that past tense and interrupted, courtesy dismissed as sudden fear arose. "How mean you, *have* attempted?"

Zedu studied him a moment, and in the slanted, fulvous eyes, Calandryll thought he saw despair. None others spoke, the silence filling up with menace. Zedu sighed, summoning his next words with obvious effort, each one a hammer blow, driving another nail into the coffin of hope.

"A day agone a rider came to Anwar-teng. A messenger from the loyal holds, he claimed; slipped through the rebel lines by dint of cunning. Jabu Orati Makusen, he named himself."

"Ahrd!" Bracht's cry was loud; his fist thudded on the table. "Rhythamun! He came here."

Calandryll heard Cennaire's sharp intake of breath; was aware of her hand, tight upon his arm. He heard Katya, her voice harsh with urgency, demand, "And you hold him? In the names of all the gods, tell me you hold him."

Zedu's face, the faces of his fellow sorcerers, gave mute answer: Calandryll felt a hand clench within his belly, tight and hard on his entrails. His mouth was abruptly dry, and as he saw Zedu's head move in negative gesture, an inarticulate cry burst from his lips.

"We do not hold him. Horul forgive us, but . . ."

The mage's answer was drowned by Bracht's shout: "You let him go? Ahrd's holy blood! How? Did you not know him for what he is?"

The faldstool clattered to the floor as the Kern rose, fists bunched in helpless anger, his eyes blazing cold and blue at the wazir-narimasu who sat shamefaced before his wrath. Katya reached out, touching his arm, urging him to calm even though her own grey orbs flashed stormy.

"Tharn waxes powerful," Zedu went on, apology in his tone, a recrimination directed inward. "Even dreaming, he sends what fell aid he may to those who'd see him risen. He contaminates the minds of men . . ."

"And fuddles yours?" Bracht snatched the stool upright, set it down with angry force. He turned to Ochen. "Help, you promised, from these hedge-wizards. They'll know Rhythamun for what he is, you said."

Ochen gave no answer, his ancient face ashen now, his eyes wide with horror, his head slowly shaking, as if he would deny all that he heard. Bracht retook his seat, glaring furiously at the assembled mages. They offered no response to his insult; could only sit, eyes downcast, withered by the Kern's scorn, his outrage.

Had this news come outside the walls of Anwar-teng Calandryll thought he should likely have succumbed to desolation. Here, though, he could think clearer, as if the magicks of these shamefaced sorcerers created an atmosphere of calm, in which he was able to overcome despair, to think beyond disappointment and rage. To Bracht he said, "Do we hold in our tempers and hear Zedu out?"

"To what end?" Bracht snarled. "He tells us Rhythamun is come here unrecognized, and roams free. To where think you he roams?"

Calandryll motioned the furious Kern to silence, turning back to Zedu. "Do you continue?" Even as he spoke, he knew the answer to Bracht's rhetorical question.

The wazir-narimasu smiled wan thanks. "We were duped," he said. "Perhaps, were we less concerned with this accursed war, we should have known Jabu Orati Makusen for what he was." He snorted, a bitter sound, filled with self-condemnation. "We grew prideful, I think, believing none should pass our scrutiny, even when our attentions were focused on those forces gathered beyond our walls. So it was this man was granted entry, Tharn's fell power like a concealing shroud about him. Horul, but he wasted no time! That communion he holds with the Mad God was his guide, and he found the gate . . .

"Aye, he found the gate and went through it!"

His voice faltered into silence. Calandryll drew deep, rasping breath. It seemed the tissues of his throat congealed, that his heart hammered on his ribs, driving blood in hot and heavy pulses through his skull. Hoarse, he asked, "When?"

"Today," came the low-voiced response. "At sunset, when Tharn's power waxes strongest."

"As we fought," he heard Bracht gasp. "Ahrd, but that attack was intended to delay us, were we not slain. Even as Horul came to our aid, Rhythamun moved ahead of us."

We stand with you as best we can. Remember that where you go.

Rhythamun gone through the gate, the Arcanum with him. Had that been Horul's meaning? Had the god known, even as he delivered them safe to Anwar-teng, that the citadel was but a waystation along their road? He struggled to order his thoughts, to achieve a balance, a coherency of purpose, that they not concede the struggle. Had they not talked of crossing the Borrhum-maj? Of pursuing Rhythamun wherever the warlock ventured? Of entering the gate themselves, should it be needful?

Aye, they had. But that had been before, when hope —albeit faint—existed of overtaking their foe. Of confronting him on mortal terms. Now that hope was gone and two poor choices waited stark for the taking: to give up, to concede Rhythamun the victory; or to pursue him into that limbo where the Mad God lay, where the power of both master and servant must surely wax overwhelming. The thought, no longer some far-off notion but forbidding reality now, was frightening. Ochen had spoken of the wazir-narimasu lending their powers to the quest, of schooling him further in those skills the wazir deemed he needed, were he to confront Rhythamun on the occult plane. There should be no time for that now—were they to clutch what slender strands of hope remained, they must go unprepared into limbo.

He turned to his companions, needing to speak before dread clogged his mouth, before the enormity of what he knew they must do became too daunting.

"Then do we sit here debating, or do we go on?"

Katya's eyes met his, lit stormy grey: "Through the gate?"

"After Rhythamun."

"We took a vow in Tezin-dar," said Bracht. "I'd not renege my given word."

"Aye, we did," Katya said, and smiled a cold smile. "And so we go on."

Calandryll turned to Cennaire, and she said, "I go where you go."

"Then"—he encompassed the wazir-narimasu in his gaze—"do you bring us to this gate? Swift, ere Rhythamun has chance to employ the Arcanum's gramaryes."

The sorcerers glanced one to the other, hesitant, their expressions ranging from disbelief to naked wonder. Zedu drew a nervous hand down the silver length of his beard and said, "No mortal man has ever returned from that place beyond the gate. Do you venture there, it may well be you go to your deaths."

"And if we do not go through?" Calandryll fixed the mage with angry, urgent eyes. "Shall we wait here to bid Tharn welcome? Does Rhythamun succeed and the Mad God be raised, I think our lives shall not be very long. Save, perhaps, in count of suffering, for Rhythamun has sworn to take his revenge of us."

His voice was flat, filled with a deadly calm: Zedu and all his fellows flinched at its lash. Zedu asked, "Be you set on this course?" Another said, "Dare we risk the opening of the gate? Is Tharn raised, it were better that portal be held shut." And then another: "Be Tharn raised, think you we can hold the gate closed?" And another: "This is a decision for all, in council."

"Shall you sit debating while Rhythamun goes to his master?" The table shuddered under the impact of Bracht's fist. Blue eyes flung a challenge at the sorcerers. "Shall you talk out the hours to the Mad God's raising?"

Katya made no physical gesture, but her voice was a goad, like a storm wind blowing: "From Vanu I came, to deliver the Arcanum to destruction. The world I've traveled on that quest. It does not end here!"

Calandryll turned to Ochen. "In Dera's name, in Horul's name, do you persuade them? We've no time now to lose!"

The ancient wazir seemed borne down by what he had heard, sunk beneath an awful weight of despondency, sitting slumped, his eyes closed as if he fought back tears. For a moment Calandryll thought his words had gone unheard, but then Ochen's eyes opened and he shuddered, as if waking from a bad dream. He raised his head, staring down the length of the table, and nodded.

"You are the wisest, the greatest, of us all," he

said, and though his voice was soft, still it carried, clear in all their ears, "and I only a wazir, not one of you. But this I tell you—that these four have walked with gods, and go about the business of the Younger Gods; foreordained are they to this purpose. They alone may defeat Rhythamun; they alone may prevent Tharn's resurrection. Do you stand in their way, you stand condemned by Horul and all his kindred gods. Do you delay them, do you not give what aid you may, then in Horul's name I tell you that you league with Tharn!"

There came a murmuring from the wazir-narimasu at that, a susurration of affront and outrage, support and dissent. Calandryll stared about, wild-eyed in his impatience, thinking that did he but know the location of the gate he would go there, fight his way there if need be. It seemed the minutes ticked out in long ages, each one taking Rhythamun a step closer to his fell goal: he ground his teeth in frustration, roundly damning the sorcerers' vacillation. Bracht sat raw-featured in his anger, Katya tense beside him, lightning in her grey eyes; Cennaire sat still and solemn, a hand unnoticed on Calandryll's arm.

Then Zedu motioned for silence, raising his voice to be heard over the hubbub. "Does Ochen speak the truth, he's every right to address us so, and we do, indeed, stand condemned." Argument died, the wazir-narimasu turning toward their elected spokesman. Zedu paused, the chamber falling silent, "And I believe him. Ere long—do we survive—he shall be counted among our numbers, and I've no doubt but that he speaks aright. I cast my vote in favor—I say we bring these folk to the gate, and swift."

"And what of those others who've say in this?"

demanded one dissident. "Shall their voices not be heard?"

"They man our defenses," said Zedu. "We've not the time, I think."

"We've not the right to make such decisions save in full convocation," the other argued. "Let runners be sent to them."

It looked to Calandryll that argument should erupt afresh, that proposal and counter should tick and tock the minutes out until the dialogue be ended by Tharn's coming. In his ear he heard Bracht hiss, "Ahrd! Be these the wisest of all Jesserytes? They babble like children, squabbling out the world's ending." He nodded, grunting helpless agreement, and turned to Ochen.

"Might you not bring us to the gate alone?"

Ochen shook his head wearily, and said, "To the gate, were we not halted. But not through it—I've not the cantrips of opening, and seven are needed for that task."

Calandryll groaned, returning his attention to the debate in time to hear Zedu declare, "Do we send runners then time wastes. And do we summon all here, who shall maintain the gramaryes of protection? I tell you we must forgo convention and agree this thing among ourselves, now."

A supporter said, "Aye! And my vote is cast with Zedu, with Ochen."

"Ochen's not a vote in this," returned the quibbler.

Ochen seemed then to summon an inner strength. He rose to his feet, straight-backed, his voice a tocsin, commanding. "Nay, I've not a vote, save that which every being in this sad world of ours has—to choose betwixt the Younger Gods and Tharn—and that I cast for Horul and his kin. Nay, I'm not among your number—and be this the manner of your governance, the way of your counsels, I'd not deem it any great honor, for I perceive you little different to ordinary folk. This brave Kern has said it—'They babble like children, squabbling out the world's ending.' Horul, already you've admitted yourselves duped by the Mad God's servant, let him pass through the gate! And now you sit quarreling like fishwives as he draws ever closer to his master." He paused, the eyes that ranged the wazirnarimasu glinting tawny, furious, subduing them so that none voiced objection or interrupted, as if they sat transfixed by his wrath. "I say again—your vacillation serves only Tharn's purpose! I tell you—bring these brave folk to the gate and send them through! They'd chance their lives, and more, to save this sorry world of ours, while you ... You'd quibble and debate matters of protocol as the world falls down about your ears. You'd argue pro and con until the Mad God walks our world. Send them through, I tell you! Put an end to this fainthearted caution and send them through!"

His oration ended on a shout, after it a long silence, broken at last by Zedu.

"I say we heed Ochen's words. We stand censured, and I say we send them through the gate."

From around the table came sundry eager *Ayes*, then slower agreement from the more hesitant, until only a handful remained objecting, and they finally swayed by their fellows, so that concord was at last reached.

"You'd go now?" asked Zedu, looking from one to the next.

The questers looked in turn at one another, and it seemed to Calandryll they stood at the brink of a precipice, an aethyric chasm far greater, far deeper, than even the Kess Imbrun. To leap into that rift was to suffer only physical wreckage; the step he knew they would take now promised far worse. He saw Bracht's fierce, grim smile; Katya's resolution writ firm on her lovely face. He found Cennaire's hand and met her eyes, saw her nod. "Aye," he said, speaking for them all. "We'd go now."

"Then may Horul and all his kin walk with you," said Zedu, rising. "Do you follow and we'll bring you there."

BACK then, descending stairways, traversing corridors, until they came once more to ground level and passed out into the plaza, the wazir-narimasu a bustling throng of color about them, Ochen beckoning them close, speaking urgently as they went.

"I'd have had more time to verse you the better in matters occult. But . . . Remember those lessons you've had, Calandryll. That knowledge should stand you firm, do you but call on that power within you. Remember, all of you, that you are as one, a gestalt where you go. And you've that blade that Dera blessed . . . there's power in that. Horul, but I'd have had more time . . . No matter; fate decides. Katya, you've the mirror? Aye? Excellent."

The roiling mutter of thunder drowned out his words, and through one narrow window cut into the wall of the corridor they hurried down, Calandryll saw malign crimson lightning engulf the sky, momentarily dimming the blue radiance that domed the teng. A dreadful wind, noisome, gusted, sending the beacon fires along the ramparts to streaming lines of turbulent flame. A second embrasure revealed scintillating tendrils of blue that wavered under the wash of red, trembling, assailed, but then interweaving to reestablish the protective vault.

They passed along a loggia where the colonnades and the roof trembled, quivering under the sonic impact of thunder. Across the sky passed bolts of man-made lightning, fireballs hurled from the besiegers' catapults, some consumed by the blue radiance, a few landing in showers of sparks and gouts of flame on rooftops or streets. And all the time, through the rattle of the thunder and the eerie howling of unnatural wind, Ochen spoke, as if he would, urgently, impress upon them what knowledge was his to impart, remind them of all he had given, and all they had learned.

"Remember what the gijan, what Kyama, scried: 'You may succeed—it is within your power.' "

Calandryll held silent his memory of her subsequent words: "Or you may not—victory is within the power of your enemies."

"Remember," Ochen continued as they crossed the plaza, "that 'one may, unwitting, aid you, and be that so, his wrath shall be great. You shall need also that power one of you commands, and that another holds. Trust—let trust be the keystone of your union. Without trust you become nothing and shall be defeated.' "

Bracht said, "Trust we have now—the rest remains a riddle still."

"Aye, perhaps," said Ochen as a door was opened and they plunged into a lightless corridor, "I'd hoped the wazir-narimasu should enlarge on that. Oh, Horul, had we only more time!"

"We've not," said Calandryll bluntly, seeing a torch flare ahead, shedding scant radiance along the gloomy passage. "Do you give us your interpretation?"

"I've wondered what it should be," Ochen returned, and fell silent awhile as they descended a narrow stairwell, the walls cold and smooth, pressing close.

The stairs ended in a low-ceilinged chamber that smelled of ancient stone, unused, a metal door black at the farther side. Zedu went to it and pressed his palms against the surface, murmuring, the words filling the chamber with the scent of almonds. Six of the wazir-narimasu followed him in turn, and then he grasped a ring and swung the door open, speaking again so that pale, achromatic light, sourceless, illumined a farther descent.

"You've two enemies, I think," Ochen said. "Rhythamun and Anomius."

"This is not," Bracht remarked over his shoulder, wryly, "unknown to us."

"But perhaps the one might be turned against the other." Ochen's voice faded as the stairway angled, returning as it straightened, falling ever deeper beneath Anwar-teng: " 'One may, unwitting, aid you.' "

"How?" asked Calandryll.

"I know not." Ochen sighed. "Only that I've sensed some design in Cennaire's presence since first I met her. What else did Kyama say? Aye, that's it—'You shall need also that power one of you commands, and that another holds.' "

"I've my sword," Calandryll said, "and whatever power you say rests in me."

"And Bracht's Ahrd's sap in his veins," said Katya. "Might that be it?"

"I cannot say for sure." Ochen shook his head ruefully. "Perhaps. And there's power in Cennaire, too; both that Anomius gave her, and some knowledge of magic."

Another door then, ensorcelled, again opened by seven of the wazir-narimasu. As they voiced their cantrips, Cennaire said, "I've those enhancements revenancy gives me, but what use shall they be where we go? And magic? I know that gramarye of transportation Anomius taught me, and that which works the mirror, none others."

"Time, time," Ochen muttered. "Had I only pondered more on this . . ."

"And none now," said Calandryll as Zedu led the way down yet another steep stairs, his magic once more conjuring wan radiance to light their passage. "Save we descend into the very belly of the world."

"Perhaps it's enough," Ochen murmured. "The power in you, the sword; Ahrd's sap in Bracht's veins; those gramaryes Cennaire commands. You've the mirror still, Katya?"

"Aye," answered the Vanu woman, tension leeching her voice of amusement. "I've not lost it betwixt your last asking and now."

"Forgive me." Ochen shook his head, speaking absentmindedly.

The stairs ended in a final chamber, carved from the bedrock on which Anwar-teng stood, doorless save for the entryway, lit only by that glow Zedu's magicks produced. Doorless, but—to eyes become familiar with such portals—gated. It was a small chamber, cubic, crowded with the press of bodies, the farther wall decorated around all its edges with sigils, those seeming to vibrate and pulse with insensate life, as if they fought unseen pressure from an unseen place. Between them stood plain stone, and it seemed that from the stone, oozing from its lithic pores, came a miasma that struggled with the surrounding cantrips, seeking release, seeking to penetrate the mortal world, as if occult powers pressed hard against the barrier.

Zedu said, "This is the gate. This is the reason Anwar-teng was built—to hold it closed."

Bracht said, "A pity you failed to guard it better."

Calandryll said, "Do you work your magicks then? And send us through?"

Zedu nodded. Calandryll took Cennaire's hand and said, "But first I'd ask a boon of you."

The wazir-narimasu ducked his head: "Be it in our power, it is yours."

"I'd ask," Calandryll said, "that do we return safe, you bend all your occult skills to restoring Cennaire her heart. Likely you know her for a revenant—if not, Ochen shall recount the story— and I'd have you make her again mortal."

As had Ochen before him, so Zedu hesitated, looking to Cennaire. "You'd have this?" he asked.

"I would," she said. "Do we return; be it in your power."

"What you ask is not done easily," he warned, "if it can be done at all. There's danger in it—the pos- sibility of failure. Better, perhaps, that you remain as you are."

"No!" Cennaire's voice was firm. Her grip tight- ened on Calandryll's hand. "I'd have back my heart and be once more mortal, no matter the danger."

"As you wish." Zedu ducked his head. "Do you return safe, then you've my word we'll attempt it."

The answer was not so confident as Calandryll would have wished, and he feared he saw doubt on Zedu's face, but there was no time left for further questioning. "Then we've a battle to fight; do you send us to it," he said, and unsheathed the straightsword.

He drew Cennaire to his side. Bracht and Katya moved close, blades naked, ready.

Ochen said, "Horul go with you, my brave friends. I await your safe return."

Calandryll smiled grim thanks as Zedu and his fellow mages commenced their cantrip.

The chant mounted in volume and the sigils

blazed bright as the perfume of almonds filled the
chamber. It seemed the primordial stone of the
wall blurred then, melting into an absence, beyond
which lay nothing save a terrible darkness. The
blade of Calandryll's sword seemed to flicker as if
possessed of independent life as foulness gusted
from the vacuum before him, a corpse-breath vent-
ing. He glanced sidelong at his comrades, seeing
their faces set grim, resolute, and knew his own
held a matching expression. He paced a step forward, toward the limbo beyond the stone, beyond
mortal ken. It seemed to beckon. It seemed a maw
waiting to devour them. The chamber faded from
his sight, Ochen, the wazir-narimasu, with it. He
heard Bracht say, "So, do we stand here watching?
Or do we bring the fight to Rhythamun?"

And he laughed, wild, and walked into the darkness of the void.

17

*U*NLIKE the gates that had brought them to and from Tezin-dar, this. Those transitions through the interstices of the worlds, mundane and occult, had been mercifully brief. Not so this passage: this was a descent into a vortex of turbulent color, incandescent, blood that was fire, fire that was blood, crimson and scarlet, vermilion, carmine, a sanguine spectrum, as if they were swallowed by some inconceivably vast beast, a creature of nonsubstance down whose gullet they were sucked, microbes in its immensity. There was heat: a roaring, pulsing holocaust, fervid, sucking air from straining lungs, forcing tongues of leeching flame down seared throats, melting, it seemed—it felt—the pulpy matter of eyeballs, devouring the organs the probing flames searched out. And stench: a fetor of moldering flesh, putrid and corrupt, mephitic, unendurable in nostrils that surely must be roasted, watering eyes that must surely be liquescent tears on unfleshed bone. Hope was redundant here: an abstraction, meaningless, impotent in this transition of agony. Neither did time any longer exist: there was only the eternal *now* of the gate's imposed suffering.

Then recognizable pain, as when burned flesh encounters ice, solidity cold beneath them, startling in its immediacy, freezing air upon their faces, fire and flame replaced with utter cold, with black and white that whirled around them, stinging with myriad pinprick blows.

Calandryll groaned, levering himself upright, the straightsword a crutch as his head spun and tormented muscles threatened to forgo their duty, to pitch him down, loose-limbed and helpless as a babe. Willpower alone held him up, his head turning slowly, sight returning slower. The very air hung white about him, freckling darkness. He sucked in great lungfuls, gasping as his lips and tongue and throat burned afresh, seared now by cold's fire. He squinted, surveying this shadow world, and saw nothing save the whiteness, the darkness. He turned from it, finding Cennaire rising tottery to her feet, her raven hair all dusted white. He offered her his hand, but she it was supported him, lending him her revenant strength, so that for a while they clung together, then went to where Bracht and Katya clambered, looking to one another for aid, to their feet. For a little while their memories of that dreadful passage warmed them, then the cruel immediacy of the present intruded and they shivered, chilled numb, each breath painful.

"Ahrd," husked Bracht, "but I thought us destroyed then."

"We live," Katya said, and added, a wary afterthought, "or so I think."

Calandryll raised his face skyward, if sky it was that hung above them. "Aye," he said, "we live, and this is likely the roof of the world, likely the Borrhun-maj."

"Ochen spoke of guardians," Bracht warned through teeth that began a castanet chattering. "If this is, indeed, the Borrhun-maj."

"If the Borrhun-maj it be," said Katya somberly, "we've little to fear from those creatures Ochen described, for we shall not live long in this."

She gestured with her saber at their surroundings, at the candid wilderness, and the peril of it struck Calandryll with a terrible urgency. They had neither food nor fire, not the kindling or the sparking of it; the air was thin, barely filling their lungs, threatening to collapse those organs, slowing blood's flow, minds dazing as limbs numbed. They should, he realized, freeze before they starved.

"This cannot be the ending of it," he said, hearing his voice come harsh, straining for the air he needed to shape the words, those punctuated by the chattering of his teeth. "There must be a second gate."

"Be it like that last," Bracht croaked grim laughter, "I wonder if I prefer this."

Calandryll lacked the energy to answer the Kern's brave sally. It seemed his lips grew too numbed to shape a smile even, and he only shook his head, eyes straining to pierce the night, the snowfall, finding nothing, neither landmarks nor hope.

Cennaire it was who saw, her vision once more surpassing their mortal eyesight. She turned slowly around, unaware, it seemed, of the crystals that frosted her lashes, the flakes that caught and froze in her hair. She pointed and cried triumphantly, "There! Something stands there!"

They began to trudge, the snow deep, to their knees and higher, clinging as if it would delay them

long enough the cold might take them in its forlorn
embrace. To struggle onward was an extortionate
task: far easier to rest, to halt, to lie down; to die.
Cennaire went in front, crushing down a path of
sorts, returning to help where help was needed.
They sheathed their swords, lest hands freeze to
hilts, stumbling drunkenly, heads swimming as
the poor, thin air robbed them of sense, of direction, none objecting to the strong arms she lent
them, holding them up when they should have
fallen, bringing them on when they might have
succumbed.

They traversed a level place for a while, and then
the way rose, sloping upward, a hard climb for all it
was but gradual and not at all steep. They could see
nothing, save the snow; felt little save pain as the
dreadful cold penetrated their bodies, numbing
blood in its course, dulling the beat of tortured
hearts. It seemed to Calandryll he roved an eternity
of blank cold, no longer a living man but an autom-
aton, empowered by purpose alone, enabled only by
Cennaire's strength.

None spoke as they made that climb, which
seemed to them forever, as if they clambered step
by awkward step over the roof of the world, a life-
time of ascent, up to the unforgiving sky, where
stars shone distant, disinterested in the waning of
the lives below. They pricked out night's sable canopy, visible now, for the snowfall was ended here,
as if they climbed too high for that chill precipita-
tion. The stars and a moon waxed full, a vast blue-
white orb hung like cyclop's eye above. Calandryll
thought he might reach out and take it in his hand,
had he only that much strength left.

"There." Cennaire stretched out an arm. "Do
you see?"

They turned, slowly, three ice-beings, pale shapes

that blended with the whiteness all around, life bleeding from them surely as if from wounds. Calandryll thought it little wonder no human creature, sorcerer or no, had returned from this place; and then how Rhythamun should have survived. That the warlock lived yet, he was certain. He knew not how, only that his enemy lay ahead—if direction yet held meaning in this place between the gates, in this place that existed, he sensed, in both the real world and the realm of the aethyr. He knew not how—only that within him some sensate compass turned its pointer to Rhythamun's pneuma.

Before them, a shadow thing marked out by its obfuscation of the stars, stood a gate to nowhere, two great megaliths upright against the night, sarsen stones crossed by a lintel, within their aegis nothing, an absence that swallowed sky and stars. Calandryll gaped, wondering how it could be he had not seen so stark a monument. Then gaped again as he perceived shapes, shifting on the snow, moving toward them and the gate.

"What are they?" Cennaire cried, horror in her voice as her enhanced sight outlined them clearer than Calandryll could discern.

"The guardians, likely," was all he could force out in answer.

"Then best we hasten," she said.

Stumbling, benumbed, they moved toward the gate. The guardians moved swifter, spatulate feet propelling them at a shambling run across the snow. They stood hunchbacked, and even then taller than a man, great bulky shapes of shaggy silvery fur, broad-shouldered, with dangling arms that ended in hooked talons. As the questers staggered toward the gate, Calandryll saw white eyes, empty of pupils, glowering from beneath craggy brows, nostrils invisible beneath the fur that draped the wide faces, parting where jaws all filled with serrated fangs gaped wide in anticipation. They ululated, the sound eerie in the silence, thin and high, like the howling of distant wind, full of menace, of blood-promise. They came fast, how many impossible to tell, for they blended with the landscape, and shifted, prancing, challenging with their yammering cries and flailing paws.

Unthinking, Calandryll pushed forward, staggering to the fore, the straightsword drawn now, instinctive. He thought his fingers frozen to the hilt, and wondered how in this awful cold he should find the strength to fight such creatures.

We stand with you as best we may.

Horul's promise; Dera's blessing on his blade: it seemed his blood coursed stronger then, his cold-fused joints suddenly more limber, as if the sword itself, or the promise, infused him with warmth. The guardians wailed in rage, advancing: he went to meet them.

One, larger than the rest, outpaced its fellows, greeting his challenge with a viciously taloned paw that slashed at his face. He brought the sword down, cleaving the limb, reversing his stroke to carve the furred belly. The creature screamed, in pain now, its blood a dark shadow on the silver fur, the snow. It staggered and was shoved carelessly aside as its companions thronged closer, vying with one another to confront these intruders. Calandryll swung the blade wide as they closed upon him. They were vast so close, their sheer size, their numbers, blocking sight of gate and sky, his companions. He cut again, desperate, fighting for his life, intent solely on driving through this barricade of living flesh to the waiting portal, on surviving this attack.

He ducked beneath a questing paw that should have taken off his head had it found that target, and drove his sword deep between ribs that grated on the blade as he turned the steel, gouging a livid wound there. He had thought perhaps the sword should dispatch these monsters as it had dealt with occult creations before, but these seemed physical, and were only wounded by his blows—the guardian swayed a moment, standing when weaker flesh should have fallen dead, and then was thrown aside by another that looked to overwhelm him with its bulk, its jaws agape, the fangs daggers. He thrust the sword into the maw, gagging on the foulness of the beast's breath, the sullen odor of its body, and flung himself clear as it toppled, skull pierced.

They might be slain, then. But what good that, when there were so many? How long before sheer weight of numbers overwhelmed? He cut and thrust and hacked, his comrades hidden in the press. He wondered, fearfully, how they fared, they without Dera's blessing on their steel, Cennaire without a weapon.

A lull then, a gap between the shuffling bodies revealing them locked in desperate combat, Bracht's falchion darting swift, Katya's saber slashing, Cennaire grappling barehanded. Speed and sword skill alone kept them alive—but for how long? Calandryll dodged between two grim creatures, his blade a shimmering blur that trailed blood in its wake as he hurled himself toward the Kand woman, the guardian that threatened to bear her down. He swung the straightsword with all his strength against the beast's spine, bone cut and breaking, Cennaire's face glimpsed brief, fierce, as she turned to face another.

He fought for his own life then, aware even as he paced out the steps of that deadly dance that

Cennaire avoided the paw that reached for her and clutched a wrist so thick her hands failed to encircle the limb. She was lifted up, helplessly kicking at the beast, its free paw questing for her throat, she, for all her strength, barely able to fend off the slashing talons. Calandryll dispatched his own attacker and went again to her aid, slashing the creature's legs, severing hamstrings, Cennaire springing clear as it bellowed and fell. He drove the sword down into the neck, severing vertebrae, Cennaire moving closer, as if she sought the protection of his presence, his blade. Over the high-pitched shrilling of the guardians he shouted, "We must find the gate before they overcome us!"

Cennaire nodded, and together they fought their way to where Bracht and Katya stood, barely able to hold the furious beasts at bay.

The very numbers of the creatures, and their sheer ferocity, afforded some slight advantage, for they made no effort to attack in concert, but sought individually to confront the questers, jostling one another, even lashing at their fellows in their eagerness to reach their prey. Numerous shaggy bodies littered the snow, but it seemed that for each one that fell, the darkness birthed more to augment those already contesting entry to the gate.

It seemed a hopeless battle. That the quest must end here, atop the Borrhun-maj, and Rhythamun escape to raise his fell master. The guardians were too many; they were too strong. They might be slain, but ere long they must overcome the questers by sheer weight of numbers alone: Calandryll roared, "Together! Back to back, and find the gate!"

He acted on his own words, spurred by fear of Rhythamun's victory, hacking with a terrible vigor at the howling creatures that yet stood betwixt him and the portal. Limbs fell sundered; all around the

snow grew dark with spilled blood. He knew
Cennaire fought at his side, trusted that Bracht and
Katya stood behind as he sought to carve a way
through. The guardians shrieked furiously, more
and more emerged from the night. *Oh, Dera,* he
thought, *shall we die here? Does it all end here?*

And then, as bloodied steel clove a skull, he saw
the gate, clear, the path a moment open. He yelled,
"Now! Swift! I'll hold them off."

He swung the straightsword in a wide arc as the
guardians ran to block the way, moving aside that
the others might go by him into the gate. He heard
Bracht shout, "Together, or not at all!" and then
gasp. He turned his head, fearing the Kern slain,
and saw Cennaire move past him, dragging Bracht
and Katya bodily with her.

She halted a bare handspan before the portal,
screaming, "Calandryll, now!"

He answered, "Aye!" and hacked at an angry,
bestial face, cut a thrusting paw, felt another scrape
his chest, and flung himself back, against them,
propelling them all into the gate.

Now they were leaves blown down the avenues of
time; flotsam on the winds of eternity. They
floated weightless, noumenal in the vacancy between tellurian and aethyric hyles. There was only
quiddity, as if flesh were stripped painless from
bone and bone dissolved in the instant of entrance.
They were pure motes of ego, no longer carnal but
become atmans, incorporeal: they existed now only
as pneuma.

As sparks rising from a god-built fire they drifted
in absence. Sensation no longer existed, nor senses:
there was only *being.* And in Calandryll a sudden
realization that it was toward this end Ochen had

tutored him so fervently. The cantrips and the
gramaryes the wazir had taught him had been but
exercises—useful enough in that substantial world
they had quit, but meaningless in this everlasting
now—designed to prepare his atman, his pneuma,
for this exigency, to shift the pattern of his thinking, the very fabric of his mind, toward that level
that should allow him control, the hope of survival,
in this nullity.

He had not the least idea how he did it: thought
was pure here, a thing of itself, less the outcome of
ratiocination than the fact of whatever existence he
now inhabited. Perhaps it was that power sorcerers
and spaewives discerned in him; perhaps it was
some gift of the Younger Gods. The source mattered no more than the cause—only the affect held
meaning. He willed it, and it was: they emerged in
the realm of the aethyr.

They stood upon a greensward, beneath a sky of
gentle azure, cumulus drifting majestic on a soft
breeze, the sun benign on their faces. A hurst of
splendid oaks rustled softly at their backs and before them ran a river painted all blue and darting
silver by the sun. Little flowers, cerulean and saf-
fron, sprinkled the grass; birds sang. Across the
river, hazy in the distance, stood an edifice of white
and gold, splendid. Calandryll looked toward it, and
knew Rhythamun was there, and dreaming Tharn.
And that save he held this plenum extant, it should
dissolve and become another thing, a thing of
Rhythamun's creation, or Tharn's, or perhaps of the
First Gods. He turned to his companions.

They stood befuddled, staring about as if un-
trusting of their eyes, their senses, as if they anticipated the dissolution of the solidity beneath their
feet, a return to that state of unbeing, or to the ice
wastes of the Borrhun-maj.

"Where are we?" Bracht asked. "What place is this? Another Tezin-dar?"

Cennaire drew close as he answered: "This is the aethyr—limbo. Tharn rests there." He pointed across the river, to the mausoleum. "And Rhytha-mun."

"This seems"—Katya stooped, plucked a flower, and held it to her nose—"entirely substantial. I had thought limbo should be . . . different."

"Limbo is . . ." Calandryll struggled for the words that might rationally explain concepts he did not rationally understand, then shrugged. "Limbo is nothing, nonmaterial . . . A concept, and so may be shaped to what you will. Ochen should explain it better than I."

The Vanu woman studied him awhile, frowning. Then: "Do you say this world is your mind's mak-ing?"

"*This* world, what we see"—he gestured around—"aye. I know not how, only that I was able."

"That power in you," she said softly, awed.

Bracht, blunter, said, "You create all this?"

And Calandryll answered as best he could. "Not create it, I think, but impose my will upon the matter of creation."

"Ahrd," the Kern said softly, almost reverential-ly. "Are you become a god then?"

"No." Calandryll shook his head, smiling. "Were I that, I'd find it simpler to deny our enemy. I've that power in me, I suppose—what Ochen saw, and the spaewives—and that combines with Ochen's teaching, that I can better comprehend the stuff of limbo, of the aethyr, and so shape it to my wishes. To Rhythamun this is likely a very different place."

"To Rhythamun . . . aye," Bracht murmured. "I wonder what he sees."

"Likely his sight is shaped by his pneuma," Calandryll said.

"Then to him, this likely a poisonous place," Bracht returned. "You say he's there?" His gaze moved past Calandryll to the marbled splendor in the distance.

"Aye." Calandryll nodded, certainty in his voice. "The Mad God lies there, dreaming of resurrection."

"Then do we go there?" Bracht demanded. "And halt his dreaming?"

Calandryll thought it should likely not be so easy. Whatever power lay in him he thought must be equaled or outweighed by that knowledge Rhythamun possessed. The warlock had lived long ages, accumulated the ill wisdom of centuries, and now—so close to his fell goal—he should not readily concede the battle. But he said, "Aye," confidently, and began to walk toward the river, aware of Cennaire's eyes on him, admiring, almost worshipping.

Bracht stepped out as if devoid of doubt; as if, at last come close to their quarry, he foresaw only victory. It was Katya who echoed Calandryll's uncertainty. "How came he here?" she wondered. "Seven wazir-narimasu it took, to open the first gate, yet Rhythamun went through solitary. And alone, he survived the Borrhun-maj to reach this place."

"He's powerful," Calandryll said. "He commands great magicks."

Katya nodded, falling silent, a cloud passing over her face. Her grey eyes flashed stormy, but she said no more.

"Shall honest steel prove sound here?" demanded Bracht.

Calandryll frowned, unsure of the answer. At length he said, "I think it likely. We're fleshed, no?

We feel the breeze, the ground beneath our feet—
so likely solidity becomes imposed on the insubstantial, and our blades own the same reality as we."

"Ahrd! A simple aye or nay would have suf-
ficed." Bracht chuckled, as if he reveled in the prospect of the final confrontation. "I've no head for
these metaphysics. Be all this of your making, then
only hold my blade secure and sharp-edged, and I'll
give you Rhythamun's head."

Calandryll smiled and took Cennaire's hand, reassuring himself that she and he were, indeed, substantial. He felt less confident of success than
Bracht, and wondered if that was the Kern's func-
tion in the gestalt Ochen had spoken of, Bracht's
foreordained part in the quest: to furnish them
with optimism, to bring them on when fainter
souls might falter, careless of danger. *And were
that so,* he mused as they hurried toward the river,
*what role does Katya play? What Cennaire? What
is my part?*

That question he could not readily answer, and
cursed himself for it: they came ever closer to their
goal, and that evasive knowledge should likely
prove vital to their success—or their failure. He
gnawed at the problem, dredging conversations
with Ochen, the pronouncements of Kyama and
the other spaewives, from his memory. Those last,
hurried words of the wazir's came clearest, but still
fragmented . . .

One may, unwitting, aid you . . .

*That power one of you commands, and that an-
other holds . . .*

*Perhaps the one might be turned against the
other . . .*

A notion, nebulous as yet, began to form. He
turned to Cennaire.

"When Anomius ensorcelled the horse you rode

across Cuan na'For ... Did you not tell me he looked out from the mirror? Worked his gramarye even from Kandahar?"

"Aye," she answered, confused. "He had me hold up the mirror, that he might see the horse. Why?"

"Perhaps ..." He shook his head. "No, it's nothing. A thought only."

It was akin to the remembrance of a dream, or its telling to another, as difficult to pin down, to voice.

He set it aside as Bracht spoke. "Do you give some thought to the fording of this river?"

He stared at the burn. Burn? From across the sward it had seemed little more than a brook, likely shallow, easily crossed. Now he saw it wider, turbulent, the water raging angry over threatening stones, too deep to wade, too fierce to swim.

"It changes!"

Katya's voice was warning, alarmed. He stared about, seeing the gentle pasture across the barrier had become a wasteland, desolate, all bleak and rocky, scattered with sad, twisted trees. The sky changed hue, the placid azure replaced with ominous lividity, the softly billowing clouds shaping black anvils now, on which lightning was struck by the hammer of grumbling thunder, the wrack driven by a whistling wind.

"Rhythamun!" he gasped. "He shapes this."

"And bleak as his cursed soul," Bracht said. "What do we do? Shall the Ahrd-damned gharan-evur halt us now?"

The Kern's voice was angry, his blue eyes cold as they stared at the torrent, beyond to the mausoleum, that yet grand, the marble shining under the louring sky. He fingered his falchion's hilt as if he would draw the sword and contest with the elements. There was only wrath and frustration in his stance. Calandryll thought that did no other course present itself, then likely Bracht would plunge into the torrent, rejecting the obstacle: he drew strength from that.

"No!" He stared at the water, at the miserable vista beyond, and inside himself, instinctively, he found the power of creation, triggered by Bracht's anger, fueled by his own determination. "No, he shall not."

A bridge imposed itself across the flood, solid stone that rose in a sweeping, elegant arch, wide enough they might all four go side by side. Katya gasped; Cennaire started in amazement. Bracht said, "Well spelled," approvingly, as if he took for granted occult powers he had once viewed with consummate suspicion. Calandryll stared, wondering at his own abilities.

They started across, and it seemed the river raged louder in defeat, rising against its banks to hurl itself at the pilings of the arch, fuming, as if it would bring down the structure. It failed, at least until they trod the farther bank and had no further need of the bridge, which sighed and tumbled down, the blocks dissolving as the black torrent washed over them.

Bracht said, grinning, "Now do you only restore the sun and conjure us horses?"

He jested, but Calandryll chose to take him at his word, directing the force of his will at the tumultuous sky, commanding the storm clouds begone, the lightning cease.

He failed: the storm ran closer, fulgurant brilliance striding the sorry landscape like the stilted legs of some vast insect, the wind strengthening, carrying the odor of corruption, the thunder growling as if in anticipation. He said, injecting more humor than he felt into his voice, "I fear we must bear this, and afoot."

"Well enough." Bracht clapped his shoulder. "Likely you need to practice."

Calandryll grinned and answered the Kern, "Aye," but as he surveyed the cheerless vista he knew they walked a domain of Rhythamun's making now. It was a forbidding place, as if the oppressive, doom-laden atmosphere that had invested the Jesseryn Plain assumed solid form. They trod scoria, the myriad cavities pocking the slag emitting a vile, sulfurous odor. The wind, that should have been cold, was humid and cloying. The thunderheads built with impossible rapidity, rising, merging, re-forming, to fill all the sky with a darkness pierced by the blasts of lightning. The trees shook, bare branches clattering, the sound like the rattling of bones. Rain should have fallen, but none came, only the supernal storm, like an inchoate beast challenging them with its rage.

In all that horrid panorama only the mausoleum stood bright, grandiose; and that, Calandryll thought, fit, for Rhythamun or Tharn—whichever's will created this landscape—would surely deem it proper that the resting place of the Mad God stand out ostentatious and resplendent.

They moved on; and the storm moved to meet them.

Calandryll bound his will tight, focusing desire, establishing around them a protective aegis that fended off the lightning, the shafts sparking as they struck the immaterial shield, coruscating as had the mundane missiles over Anwar-teng, failing to penetrate. The storm raged in its impotence, thunder buffeting their ears, setting their heads to ringing, speech impossible in that turmoil: they pressed forward.

In time—though time was an imposed concept in this place, which stood beyond time—they came in

clearer sight of the mausoleum and halted, surveying the great edifice.

The storm ringed it, a fulgid diadem, ominous
calm at the center. It reached toward the sky, vast
as the tengs of the Jesserytes, appearing as a single,
solid block of purest marble, struck through with
veins of glittering gold. From those corners they
could see slender towers, each topped with a
gleaming cupola, rose. There were no windows, nor
any doors. At their feet was a moat fashioned, like
the necropolis, of marble, smooth, steep walls descending to turgid liquid, red and sluggish as blood.

"Another bridge?" Bracht suggested. "Perhaps a
portal?"

Calandryll summoned his will, assembling as
best he could that power he still did not properly
understand, and felt it somehow opposed, as if another mind contested the creation. He heard malign laughter, and then a horribly familiar voice,
fulsome, sardonic:

"My congratulations—I'd not thought you
should advance so far. I'd thought to have my revenge of you within that other world, which soon
the Lord Tharn shall rule. But no matter. You are
here, and so my victory grows the sweeter for
knowing you stand so close, yet entirely unable to
prevent my Lord's resurrection." More laughter
then, horridly contemplative. "Aye, poor fools, you
shall be blessed ere you go into eternal suffering—
you shall see Lord Tharn in all his risen glory, and
I in mine! Think on that, fools, while you wait
powerless. Contemplate your fate while I employ
that book you delivered to me to raise my Lord.
When that task's done, your fates shall be dispensed."

The voice faded, applauded by roiling thunder,
the riotous dance of lightning. Calandryll ground

his teeth, willing a bridge to shape, a gate to form: without success. He heard Katya ask, "Can you not span this filthy pond?" and shook his head, chagrined.

Bracht said, "Ahrd, must we stand waiting here, like beasts for the slaughterer?"

Cennaire asked, "Can you do nothing?" and he shook his head, groaning in terrible frustration, and told them, "I've not the power. So close to Tharn, Rhythamun's will vanquishes mine. Dera, were Ochen only here to lend me his knowledge!"

"Might not the mirror summon him?" Cennaire wondered. "Might your magic not shift its focus?"

Like a beacon shining dim through darkest night that nebulous thought he had earlier gnawed on took firmer shape ... *One may, unwitting, aid you. Perhaps the one might be turned against the other* ... He seized Cennaire's hands, surprising her with his sudden enthusiasm, his cry of "Aye! My thanks for that," and beckoned them all back from the bloody moat.

"This shall be mightily dangerous," he began, and heard Bracht snort disbelieving laughter and demand, "More perilous than awaiting Tharn's resurrection?"

He smiled grimly and shrugged, and said, "I know not even if it shall be possible. But ..." He paused, assembling his thoughts, weighing doubt against the certainty of Rhythamun's success. The others waited, curbing impatience. "I doubt I might shift those gramaryes Anomius invested in the mirror. I know not even if those gramaryes shall have power here. But ..."

He hesitated: this plan bore the delineaments of desperation. Bracht said fiercely, "Go on!"

"Can it be used from this realm," he said, "and Anomius is able to transport himself here ..."

"Anomius?" Skepticism rang stark in Bracht's voice. "You'd double our enemies?"

Katya said, "Hold, Bracht. Hear him out."

Cennaire, her eyes wide, fixed on his face, said, "The scrying! You interpret Kyama's words!"

Calandryll said, "Aye! Anomius owns greater knowledge of the occult than I. Perhaps he might win us entry—use his power against Rhythamun."

"On our behalf?" Bracht shook his head, the words sharp-edged with doubt. "Even can the mirror bring him here, think you he'd aid us? And should he defeat Rhythamun—what then? Should he not do what Rhythamun does, and the outcome be the same?"

"Perhaps," Calandryll admitted. "But I can think of no other course."

He felt Cennaire's hand clutch tight on his arm. She said urgently, "It's his belief only you three may take the Arcanum."

"This seems to me a thing of skillets and fires," said Bracht. Then shrugged and grinned, "But what other weapon have we?"

"It should be apt justice," said Calandryll, "to bend Anomius to our usage."

"I say we attempt it," Katya said.

She turned her gaze on Bracht, who nodded, and fetched the mirror from beneath her hauberk, passing it to Cennaire.

The dark woman took the glass, her eyes troubled as they fixed on Calandryll. "What do I tell him?" she asked.

He pondered only an instant. Then: "That we stand before Tharn's sepulcher, but cannot enter. That we three inspect the place, leaving you alone. That you deemed it timely to advise him. The rest"—he stretched his lips in dour smile—"is up to him."

She nodded and unwrapped the mirror; began to
voice the cantrip. Calandryll beckoned the others
away. It seemed the acrid reek emanating from the
grey scoria strengthened; that the gold veining the
marble of the sepulcher writhed, enlivened by
Rhythamun's wild magic; that the very substance
of the mausoleum pulsed, anticipatory.

They stood too far away they might hear
Anomius's responses, but from such words of
Cennaire's as they caught, pitched deliberately loud
enough they should hear, they gleaned a little information . . .

"Aye, we passed through . . . The war is won?
Sathoman ek'Hennem defeated . . . In Nhur-jabal?
The bracelets are gone? Then you are no longer
bound . . . Aye, before it. See?"

They watched as she raised the mirror, turning it
along the facade of the sepulcher, moving it slowly
from side to side. The air before the glass shimmered. Calandryll thought that were the stink of
sulfur not so strong, he should have smelled almonds. He drew the straightsword, hearing Bracht's
falchion hiss from the scabbard, Katya's saber from
its sheath.

The shimmering coalesced. A form took shape:
Anomius stood there. A predatory smile distorted
his fleshy mouth, and his bulbous nose quivered,
scenting triumph. Hands brushed the soiled frontage of his black robe. He stared at Cennaire, a mottled tongue extending to lick at pallid lips. "This
was well done," he declared, nodding his approval.
He eyed the mausoleum, then turned to survey the
landscape.

And shrieked in fury as he saw the three questers, moving swift toward him, swords extended.

He raised his hands, patulous mouth beginning a
cantrip that was halted unspoken by the straight-

sword Calandryll inserted between his teeth.
Bracht's falchion pricked his wattled throat; Katya's
saber touched his ribs, above his heart. Calandryll
said, "One syllable said wrong and you die."

The wizard's sallow features contorted in frustrated rage. His watery eyes squinted angry and
malign at Cennaire. Around the straightsword's
steel, the words distorted by the blade and his impotent wrath, Anomius muttered, "For this you
shall suffer. I've still your heart, remember."

"But we, your body," Calandryll declared, turning his blade so that Anomius must perforce fall silent, or lose his tongue. "And a use for it. Do you
then hear me out? Or shall you die, now?"

Unmasked fury burned in the sorcerer's pale
eyes, but—as best he could with sharp steel between his teeth—he nodded. Calandryll held the
sword in place, a gag on interruption, as he explained.

"You stand before Tharn's tomb, and Rhythamun
stands within. He's the Arcanum, and he employs
those gramaryes that shall raise the Mad God.
Doubtless you sense that working e'en now—save
it be halted, Rhythamun shall emerge triumphant.
We've not the way to bridge this moat or shape an
entry to the sepulcher, but I believe you might.
So—do you lend us that aid? Or perish now?"

He eased his blade from the angry mouth, waiting for Anomius to speak. When the ugly little
man did, it was in a voice laden with mockery:
"Why should I aid you?" His eyes flickered, furious, to Cennaire. "Doubtless this turncoat has told
you I'd have the book for my own, and so I ask
again—why should I aid you?"

"Because"—Calandryll forced more confidence
than he felt into his voice—"you cannot take the
book without us. And because if you refuse, then

you shall die with us. Think you Rhythamun shall let you go free?"

Blubbery lips parted in ungenuine smile. Anomius said, "Aye, there's that, but also another thing—I suspect you forget those occult strictures I placed upon you and this Kern, that you may neither do me harm."

"I think," Calandryll returned, certain now, "that those cantrips are become devalued. Shall we put them to the test? Bracht, do you prick him?"

Bracht's grin was pitiless as he turned the falchion's point against the wizard's throat. Anomius jerked back, a hand rising to the little wound, his eyes fixing angry on the blood he found coloring his fingertips.

"So that safeguard is denied you," said Calandryll, aware even as he spoke that the aethyric stuff of the mausoleum pulsated stronger, that the sanguine moat began to bubble, to stir. "And do you employ some other gramarye, then you've no chance left of taking the book; neither of surviving this place. Do you refuse your aid, you die with us."

Anomius stared at Calandryll. "You've grown in cunning since last we met," he blustered, "but still I think you've not the stomach to slay a man in cold blood."

"Calandryll, perhaps," Bracht said, his voice cold, promising no clemency, "but not I. Do you refuse, I'll put my blade in your belly and have the pleasure of seeing you die before me."

The watery eyes swung toward the Kern, finding no hope of mercy there, only the certainty of painful death: the bald head ducked in acknowledgment.

"Say then I aid you—bridge this moat and grant you entrance to the tomb—what then? I'll not suppose you believe I shall watch you take the Arcanum without I seek to wrest it from you."

"No." Calandryll smiled, the expression humorless. "I'd not suppose that. But we'll take that chance."

"Then it would seem we reach impasse." Anomius turned, studying the mausoleum a moment. "Great magicks are at work in there. Ere long Tharn shall rise and, risen, doubtless slay you. You cannot enter without my aid. What do you offer in return?"

"Your life," Bracht said.

Anomius chuckled, a liquid, bubbling sound, akin to the moat's horrid stirring. "You seek my aid and threaten my death? Do I refuse, you'll slay me. Does Rhythamun succeed, I am slain." He shook his head. "I'd have a better bargain of you."

Calandryll thought a moment, aware that each passing instant brought Rhythamun closer to his goal, the Mad God closer to resurrection. "Do we succeed," he said, "then you shall go free. We'll do you no harm."

Again, Anomius laughed, scornful, and said, "You know I'll have the book for my own, am I able. Why, then, should I believe this bloodthirsty Kern shall not slay me once my usefulness is done?"

"You've my word," said Calandryll.

"And his?" Anomius stabbed a dirty thumb in Bracht's direction; turned a nail-bitten finger toward Katya and Cennaire. "And theirs?"

Calandryll looked to his companions, his eyes urgent in their demand for promise. Bracht said, unwilling, "Do we succeed, I'll not slay you. My word on it."

"And a Kern's word is his bond," Anomius sneered. "And yours, miladies?"

"You've mine," Katya said; and Cennaire: "I'll not raise hand against you."

"Then the bargain's struck." Anomius shook black sleeves from pale wrists. "A strange alliance, eh?"

Dera, Calandryll asked silently, *grant this fell arrangement succeed.* "Do you look to deceive us," he heard Bracht say, "you shall taste my blade."

"As your wiser friend remarks," Anomius returned, his voice contemptuous, "I've need of you, just as you've need of me. Now do you close your mouth and leave me to my work?"

The Kern's eyes flashed anger. Calandryll motioned him back a pace, Anomius yet within sword's reach as he raised his hands and began to chant, the almond scent wafting strong as he mouthed the arcane syllables.

Calandryll felt occult power mounting in Anomius; felt, too, the opposition, but that abstracted, as if the larger part of it was concentrated on the rituals of resurrection, hastening toward that end, menacingly confident of victory. Strong, even so, that defensive magic, so that he lent Anomius what power was his to give to driving it back, the struggle invisible, a thing of wills and sorcery that he did not properly understand, but gave his aid instinctively.

Thunder roared as if in protest; lightning flashed wrathful. Anomius's chanting rose to a crescendo— and a bridge of black light spanned the moat, at its farther end a narrow portal from which the odor of corruption gusted.

"Swift now!"

Veins stood engorged at Anomius's temples, and from his eyes dribbled tears of blood, the steps he took toward the bridge unsteady for all his urgency. Calandryll pushed past him, Cennaire at his side.

Bracht and Katya herded the sorcerer onward,
swords ready at his back.

The bridge was unfirm beneath their feet, viscid
as the red tendrils that rose from the moat,
questing sensate as they sped across. Ahead the
door stood black and formless as those gates that
had carried them into this occult realm, stark contrast to the golden veining of the marble, that flowing now, trembling and vibrating, the marble itself
pulsating, all stimulated by the magic worked
within.

They hurled themselves into the portal, fetor
nauseous about that dread threshold, slowing,
awed, as they entered the resting place of the Mad
God.

Space held no more meaning here than time or
substance. Likely each one of them perceived a different place, informed by individual senses, by
Rhythamun's conception, which overlay their
sight. To Calandryll it was a hall of inconceivable
vastness, a single impossible chamber, extending
beyond eye's range in dazzling magnificence. Gold
burned with the intensity of suns from walls and
floor and roof. Great pillars of vibrant marble rose
to heights invisible, lost in the blazing glory above.
At the same time, the one image overlayed upon
the other, coexistant, it was a foul and miserable
crypt, dank and fetid, noisome with the scent of
putrefaction, that mingling with the cloying perfume of almonds, red light, as if flame shone
through bloodied glass, flickering, sending shadows
menacing across the scabrous floor.

The latter image was brief, overwhelmed by the
other as Rhythamun's will asserted itself, donating
his malign god the grandeur his crazed mind
deemed fitting. It was an unintended boon: the

light in which he bathed his master afforded the intruders clear sight.

At the center of the hall, too distant they might see as clearly as they did, stood a catafalque of solemn jet, a stepped construction that rose three times a tall man's height, upon it a golden sarcophagus, brilliant, bier and coffin both contained within a red nimbus. The body the coffin held was not visible; the man who stood beyond it was.

Rhythamun no longer wore the shape of his Jesseryte victim, but stood naked, himself, his pneuma given form. Once, in Cuan na'For, Calandryll had briefly seen that face. Now he saw it clear, fleshed. It was a visage superficially handsome, but imbued with such innate evil that the clean planes, the aquiline features, seemed distorted by their inherent wickedness, the mask of flesh no more than a brief imposition over the iniquity beneath. The warlock wore a robe of gold, dark hair flowing loose over broad shoulders. His arms were extended above the sarcophagus, his hands reverentially holding a small, dark-bound book: the Arcanum. His violet eyes were glazed, his lips moving as they spoke the incantations.

Calandryll shouted, "Rhythamun!" and the eyes focused, turning toward him.

In the instant of his shout, even as the proud head turned, Calandryll and his companions stood at the foot of the catafalque. Rhythamun looked down upon them. A frown sped across his face and was gone, replaced with a leer of outrage. He lowered the Arcanum, head bending to survey them over the coffin's massive bulk.

"You dare interrupt me?" He gestured at their surroundings. "Here? You dare enter my master's temple? You dare set foot within Lord Tharn's holy sepulcher?"

"Aye!" Calandryll roared, and charged the bier unthinking, straightsword raised, possessed with a terrible wrath, righteous, intent on halting the unholy ceremony.

He flung against the nimbus and it was as though he contested with the sea, or struggled against quicksand. A foot touched the lowest step and he was slowed; a weight, imponderable, pressed down. He fought the pressure: gained a second step. He thought his lungs must burst; that fire consumed his innards. He thought his brain must melt and flow out through liquid eyes, his straining mouth. He was returned to the golden floor. He saw Bracht make the same attempt, and also slow, straining against the aura surrounding the coffin as if unseen ropes bound and restrained him. Rhythamun laughed, the sound echoing from the pillars. Bracht groaned and collapsed upon the lowest step. Katya sprang forward, dragging the Kern back.

"I think," said Rhythamun, "that I shall delay your fate awhile. I shall allow you the honor of witnessing Lord Tharn's resurrection with your own eyes. After all, are you not to thank in some small way?" He flourished the Arcanum, mocking them. "Had I not this tome, I'd not have owned the cantrips to bring me solitary to this place, nor those last gramaryes of raising. So, stand you there and await your fate."

"And I?" Anomius stepped from where he had sheltered, behind them, hidden from Rhythamun. "Shall I await my fate like these? I think not. I'll have that book of you, and soon."

His hands extended, flinging magic that filled the mausoleum with sound, as if the storm that ringed the place was brought inside. The glitter of gold was lost under a flash of brilliance that transcended light, an achromatic assault felt in the raw material

of nerves, visceral. Rhythamun gasped, tottering a
step backward, encompassed in wildfire blaze, his
cold eyes widening, surprised. He righted himself,
one hand upon the sarcophagus's rim, and hurled a
magical response that enveloped Anomius in
flame. The smaller man stood engulfed, wreathed
with ardent coruscation, from which emerged luminous shafts, darting like lambent arrows at
Rhythamun, who struck them aside, deflected off
an occult shield, as he voiced the words of his
spell, the fire enfolding Anomius growing fiercer
with each complex utterance.

Calandryll and the others stood forgotten for the
moment, mere observers of the thaumaturgical
duel. Both sorcerers appeared imbued with equal
strength, neither gaining the upper hand, but only
holding one another to stalemate. It came to
Calandryll—a gift of Ochen's teaching—that they
both drew their power from Tharn, the god indifferent which should prevail. It mattered nothing to
him which should be victorious, for they were both
bent on the same end, which should only benefit
his foul cause. For now the Mad God was a foun-
tainhead of impartial potency, urgent only for
awakening, careless which acolyte should rouse
him from his dreaming.

The sepulcher reverberated to the tumult of their
battle, pungent with the scent of their magicks.
Overhead, the golden light was bedimmed, shadow
and flame mingling in equal measure. The impossible pillars shuddered, dust like the detritus of rotted cerements drifting down. Cracks raced across
the golden floor, dark blemishes exuding the stench
of sulfur and putrescent matter.

Calandryll saw Rhythamun raise both his hands,
and realized they no longer held the Arcanum.
Through the fulgurations of warring sortilege he

spied the book: it rested on the coffin's edge. He
clutched Bracht's arm, pointing with the straightsword, shouting into the Kern's ear, through the be-
numbing blasts.

"Think you we've our chance?"

"Do we find out?"

Bracht's features were grim. Calandryll nodded
and they darted forward, intent on gaining the bier
unnoticed. The nimbus threw them back again, ungently, as if it, too, gained strength.

"Ahrd!" Bracht grunted as they clambered to
their feet. "Must we stand helpless by and watch
this? Can we do nothing?"

Katya shouted over the dinning: "Save we inter-
vene, the victor shall surely destroy us!"

And into Calandryll's mind, as if whispered,
clear, mouth to his ear, came memory of Ochen's
words, in Anwar-teng: "Remember, all of you, that
you are as one, a gestalt where you go."

He beckoned the others close and said, "Have I
the proper understanding of it, we must attempt
this together. Not as four separate folk, but as
one."

"We've naught to lose," Bracht said. "Save our
souls."

And Katya: "They stand already in jeopardy."

Cennaire said nothing, only took Calandryll's
hand.

"I think blades shall not avail us in this," he
said, sheathing the straightsword. "Trust is our
strength now. And belief in our cause."

Katya thrust her saber home into the scabbard.
After a moment's hesitation, Bracht put up his falchion.

It took trust to approach the bier unarmed. Calandryll felt it as a palpable thing, real as the forms
they wore in this aethyric place, solid as the blade

that weighted his belt. It was a dependence on one another, a trust born of comradeship and acceptance, devoid now of doubts, cemented with their shared purpose, mistrust banished. It was their shield as hostile magic blasted all about them, the sword that sundered the defensive aura, allowing them to mount the catafalque, climb steps that trembled under their determined feet, as if even in his dreaming, Tharn sensed their coming and stirred, nervous.

Briefly the nimbus sought to halt them, to drive them back. Calandryll felt the opposition, and denied it, aware of their four pneumas linked as one, a single entity possessed now of a single intent, that empowering the magic that resided in him, flooding him with strength, just as, malign, Rhythamun and Anomius drew strength from the dreaming god: they climbed resolute, joined in their ambition.

And reached the platform atop the bier, the sarcophagus at its center, poor enough concealment as they crouched and crept toward the book. Unholy light sparked about them, the scents of rot and almonds combining miasmic, suffusing air that crackled with the unleashing of sorcerous power. Rhythamun stood close now, but diverted by Anomius, so intent on the battle he failed to see the hand that crept stealthy toward the Arcanum . . .

. . . Seized the book and was gone.

From hand to hand it went, Calandryll's the one that snatched it, passing it into Cennaire's keeping, she to Katya, the Vanu woman on to Bracht, who held it close as they descended back down the jet steps, those throbbing now, pulsating visibly, as if in rage. Bracht gave the book to Katya, and she, an expression of distaste creasing her tanned features, as though she must embrace a serpent, placed it secure beneath the mail of her hauberk. They moved,

still as one, a little way from the bier, not yet confident of success, swords coming instinctive from
scabbards.

Anomius became aware of them then, and of the
absence. His fleshy lips stretched in brief, triumphant smile, and the cantrip he chanted faltered an
instant.

Rhythamun saw the expression, followed the
sideways flicker of the watery eyes, and prodigious
anger overwhelmed his face. Calandryll saw death,
and worse, in the furious violet gaze and then the
terrible light that struck Anomius.

The warlock was hurled from the bier, sent
crashing down the steps, perverted flame wrapping
him in obscene embrace. Tongues of black fire
lapped at his robe, his flesh. He screamed, struggling to his feet, the soiled black robe disintegrat-
ing so that he stood naked, skin blackening,
crisping charred under the dreadful attack. His
mouth opened and flame gouted from his throat.
His eyes burst and more fire spouted from the emptied sockets. His flesh was consumed and he stood
a burning skeleton, internal organs roasting, bursting. Then the bones, blackened, collapsed, falling
in a clattering pile that was soon dissolved by the
awful sable fire. Of Anomius nothing remained
save a drifting cloud of inky smoke.

"My thanks for that diversion, but now I'll have
the book."

The questers turned to where Rhythamun stood,
a grimace of horrid triumph curling his lips. Veins
throbbed in his neck, his golden robe smoldered,
down cheeks scorched by Anomius's magic ran
tears of blood, but confidence was an aura about
him, and threatening might. He came down from
the catafalque, hands raised, weaving an intricate

pattern, beginning a cantrip. Calandryll cried,
"No!" the straightsword lifting.

Light flashed anew from Rhythamun, and
Calandryll felt himself lifted, flung clear, subjective
time stretched out in the instant, so that he saw
Bracht and Katya hurled aside, to safety, as
Cennaire interposed herself between them and the
blast the warlock sent to destroy them. It washed
over her, raven hair streaming. But she lived.
Calandryll heard Rhythamun curse; Cennaire
shout wild laughter and cry, "That magic shaped to
harm the living cannot affect me!"

Calandryll came to his feet even as the mage
commenced a fresh incantation, one that surely
must consume Cennaire. He was unsure whether
his feet or his will alone sped him forward, only
that he stood before Rhythamun, and that he must
strike before the spell was shaped.

The straightsword descended in a terrible arc. It
seemed slow to Calandryll. It seemed the gramarye
must end before steel struck, that Cennaire must
be destroyed, the wizard take back the Arcanum,
raise Tharn. He saw Rhythamun's lips moving, the
eyes that shifted to focus on his face, anger and
contempt mingled there. And the blade halted in a
numbing blast of thunder, lightning exploding
where blessed steel and fell magic collided.

He felt an awful shock run fiery down the roadways of his nerves, the straightsword almost flung
from agonized fingers that trembled about the hilt.
It seemed he clutched a rod of molten metal that
consumed his flesh, that he must let go the sword
before it destroyed him. And knew he could not—
must not!—for from within himself, from Ochen's
teachings and his own poor understanding of the
occult, a warning voice cried loud that here, in this
battle, Dera's touch imbued the steel with that

power that alone could oppose the dreadful might
Tharn invested in his minion.

He willed himself to ignore the pain. Told his
eyes they lied, that his hands did not blacken, the
skin not crisp and curl from scorching bone. He
strained against Rhythamun's spell, seeking to
drive the sword down against the wizard's skull.

He could not; but neither could Rhythamun
force back the blade, turn his magic on Cennaire,
on Bracht and Katya, where they huddled, wary, ex-
cluded from this cataclysmic struggle.

This, Calandryll knew with awful certainty, was
his battle alone, his the power that might—*Oh,
Dera, only might?*—defeat the mage. He stared into
the violet eyes, his own blazing furious, and saw
doubt flicker there. He forced a laugh then, and it
seemed the blade descended a fraction, that the agony eased a little. Rhythamun retreated a step. A
single pace only, but one that seemed to Calandryll
a confirmation, perhaps not of victory, but of its
possibility. That was sufficient: he strained anew
against the power encompassing the warlock, and
saw beads of bloody sweat burst from his enemy's
forehead. He knew not how he drew on that power
he commanded, only that it was a source within
him, strengthening, salving, imbuing him with a
vigor, a surety of purpose that transcended pain. It
was occult power and his own determination, the
joined wills of Bracht and Katya and Cennaire, of
all who would contest Tharn's resurrection, even at
cost of their own lives: it filled him, firmed him,
their strengths his. He knew not how he used it,
only that he did.

And the straightsword was no longer a molten
thing, no longer a rod of agony, scourging, but the
means to victory, to Rhythamun's defeat. It fell a
little farther, and then, of a sudden, crashed down

to splinter blackened marble as Rhythamun sprang back.

Calandryll snatched it up defensive as he saw the doubt in the mage's eyes replaced by horrid fury. Hands sullied by Anomius's sortilege lifted to shape patterns in the air, to send a bolt of black light swifter than a serpent's darting tongue against him. He cried, "Dera!" and it was a battle cry as he swung the sword against his enemy's magic.

Thunder bellowed anew. The fabric of the sepulcher shuddered. Black light became transfigured, sharded with gold, with sparkling silver, blinding. The perfume of almonds hung a moment stronger than the stench of corruption. Calandryll thought surely he was slain, felt surprise that he yet stood living.

Rhythamun's eyes sprang wide, as if he could scarce believe the evidence they gave him of Calandryll's survival. For his part, Calandryll stared narrow-lidded, near dazzled by that explosion of brilliance, anger fueling him, inflaming, lending its own righteous strength to occult power. Before him he saw the madman who would deliver the world to Tharn, to chaos. The man who had duped him, used him, confident of mastery, contemptuous of all those mortal, ordinary folk he believed his puppets, inferior. This was the man who would see all brought down under the foul heel of the Mad God, helpless sacrifices to his insanity, to his lust for power. And then, beyond the anger, there was a kinder emotion: pity, that mingled with contempt, and sorrow. Rhythamun was evil—he could entertain no doubt of that—but the sorcerer was, too, utterly insane, so consumed by his ambition that he scarce knew what he did, and for that, for all he must be slain, Calandryll was able to pity him.

In that moment Calandryll became something
more than a man. He was the instrument of the
Younger Gods, the embodiment of order in opposition to chaos, of humanity confronting wanton destruction.

He knew then that he might win this struggle.
He should likely die in the execution, but did he
only prevent Tharn's raising then still he won.
That alone was of import now—no longer his life,
or his love of Cennaire, not Bracht or Katya; only
victory, the defeat of Rhythamun, the denial of
Tharn's mad dreaming.

He roared and launched himself forward, the
straightsword raised like the very wrath of the
Younger Gods.

And Rhythamun's hands came up again, sending
fresh magicks at him, magicks that were struck
aside by the whirling blade, dismissed to burst uselessly about the mausoleum, that vibrating to a different rhythm now, trembling as if in fear,
shuddering, cracks running like opened veins
across the floor, rents gaping in the walls. Somewhere a pillar crashed, shattering, dust blowing in
a filthy cloud. Behind him, unseen as he advanced,
a pale hand clutched upward at the rim of the sarcophagus, nails scrabbled a moment and fell back.
He went on, intent only on victory.

Disbelief replaced the anger in Rhythamun's eyes
now, and then fear took its place. The warlock retreated. Calandryll advanced. Sable flame lashed at
him; hammer blows pounded at his chest; his hair
burned; leather scorched. Such magicks as should
have slain a mortal man were flung against him
and ignored: he advanced. The straightsword was a
shield before him, glaive of wrath, a beacon of
hope. He felt the power in it, the power of the goddess; and more, as if all Dera's kin set benign might

in the steel. And beyond even that, the power of men, of Bracht's fierce courage and Katya's determination, Cennaire's faith, and Ochen's belief. He advanced remorseless.

And Rhythamun fell back, desperation on his handsome, evil face as his sortilege clashed against the blade. He stumbled, a hand reaching toward a cracking pillar, steadying himself, the cantrip he shaped faltering. With a terrible shout Calandryll ran forward, the straightsword raised high.

The warlock gasped, "No!" as the blade descended, no longer slowed by his sortilege, no longer halted.

It fell against his face, the skull divided, and Rhythamun screamed, a dreadful lingering howl of banished hope, defeated ambition.

Calandryll felt his wrists, his arms, jarred by the blow, a moment of pain, of wrenching nausea, as if he touched quintessential horror, an evil beyond comprehension. Then relief, triumph, like a clarion in the midst of battle. Something went out of him, as if, its work done, a power quit him: he was only himself again. He felt a moment empty as he watched Rhythamun's slain body shimmer, dissolving. There was no gradual dissolution, no aging of flesh or collapse of bones into dust. Rhythamun was simply gone, as if, defeated, those magicks that had so long bound him to corporeal existence gave up their hold. The echo of his dying scream faded and there was only a bloodied golden robe, empty. Here, in the realm of the occult, within the aethyr, Calandryll sensed that the sorcerer's pneuma was destroyed, his threat forever ended. Rhythamun was at last truly dead.

He reached down, using the hem of the golden robe to cleanse his sword, sheathed the steel, and turned to his companions.

Cennaire came into his arms, holding him tight, so that he thought a moment that his ribs should break.

"I feared you should be slain," she said against his mouth, and he answered, "I feared you should die, and that I could not bear."

For long heartbeats nothing else existed, only they two, embracing, and then Bracht's voice intruded.

"We've the Arcanum now, and our enemies slain. Do we flee this fell place, then, ere it fall down and trap us here?"

Calandryll moved back from the circle of Cennaire's arms, seeing the chamber no longer glorious, but dismal, the sorry crypt of his earlier, brief vision, the resplendent sarcophagus only a poor stone cist now. The cavern shuddered, dust and fragments of rock falling from the gloomy roof, the cracks that striated the jagged floor widening by the moment. He said, "Aye," and they ran toward the egress.

Outside, the bloody moat was become a narrow stream that sprang from an outcrop of blue-grey granite. Clean water ran there, and the brook was easily jumped, beyond it pristine grass, verdant under a benign sun. They moved away, looking back as stone groaned, seeing the cave's mouth collapse, sealed under an impassable weight of rock. Calandryll thought he heard a shriek of rage, of disappointment, then, but it might only have been the sound of falling stone. He turned his back to the tomb and took Cennaire's hand, seeing Bracht and Katya walking arm in arm, the Kern reaching out to take Cennaire's elbow, all of them smiling as they strode across the lush grass.

"I trust," Bracht called, "that you've a way to return us to Anwar-teng. Or perhaps direct to Vanu."

"To Anwar-teng, I hope," Calandryll replied, "for we've a boon to claim of the wazir-narimasu."

He felt Cennaire's grip tighten on his hand and elation was tainted with doubt. The battle was won, Rhythamun defeated and the world saved from the Mad God, but that should be a soured victory could Cennaire not gain back her heart. He thought on that incertitude he had heard in Zedu's voice, heard expressed clear in Ochen's words, and wondered if there was yet a price to pay, disappointment waiting drear to transform triumph to loss. He forced a smile: he could not allow the uncertainty he felt expression on his face or in his voice. It must be possible they return her heart! After all this, it must be possible!

"How shall you do it?" asked Katya. "Have you such magic?"

He frowned then, and shook his head, sudden alarm startling his heart. "I've not the least idea," he said, wondering if they must remain here, prisoners of the aethyr.

Cennaire said, "Is that not a gate?"

They looked to where she pointed: proud from the grass, where none had stood before, rose a framework of roseate stone, great upright megaliths surmounted by bulky lintel, within their aegis not darkness, but a spectrum of colors, welcoming.

Calandryll said, "Aye, I believe it is," and they walked toward the portal.

18

THERE was no interim on this journey between the worlds, no icy wastes or hostile guardians, nor any pain: it seemed as though, Tharn's threat ended, the aethyric passageways grew calm. They stepped together into the gate, there was a moment of nullity, a brief sensation of timeless descent, and then they stood inside the subterranean chamber, deep beneath Anwar-teng. The sigils decorating the grey stone blazed an instant as if in farewell, and then faded, leaving only bare rock behind, the scent of almonds dissipating as the gate closed forever. They tottered, disorientated, clutching at one another for support. The chamber was cool and lit with a soft golden glow from candles that burned with an even flame, unmelting. They lit the startled face of Ochen, rising from a faldstool, his slitted eyes opening wide, soon followed by a mouth that stretched in a smile of welcome, his wrinkles creasing in joy.

"Praise Horul! Praise all the Younger Gods! You return." He came toward them, arms flung wide as

if he would encompass them all in his embrace.
"We feared you slain, the battle lost. But then—
Horul, it was a wonder! A sign you triumphed! No,
wait, doubtless you're wearied. Do I bring you to
where you may tell your tale in comfort? You'd
take wine? Food? Horul, but I'd hear everything."

His words tumbled out, spilling one over the
other in his eagerness, his relief, even as his hands
went from one to the other, touching as if he would
reassure himself living creatures came back. Bracht
asked, his voice carefully inquiring, "Did you
doubt our return then?"

Ochen laughed, the sound like triumphant bells
tolling victory, and answered, "For a while, aye.
Horul, my friends, you've been a while gone."

"How long?" asked Calandryll as the wazir ushered them from the chamber, pausing only to lift
the warding spells. "Surely but a few days."

"Weeks, more like," said Ochen as they climbed
the narrow stairs. "We've taken turn and turn
about, waiting by the gate. Some gave you up—
thought you dead, or trapped."

"But you spoke of a sign," Calandryll said.

"Aye—that the *battle* was won." The silvered
head turned back, twinkling eyes regarding them
fondly. "That was clear enough, but not that you
survived it. Horul, the hours I've spent seeking sign
that you lived!"

"We do," Bracht called, his voice echoing cheerful off the walls, "but where we went there was no
wine. You spoke of wine?"

"That I did." Ochen's laughter rang loud in answer. "And those who'd hear your tale. So, do I
curb my tongue ere you grow bored with the telling?"

"Save first you tell of this sign," Calandryll
asked.

"Aye." Ochen nodded, solemn a moment. "Thus it was: the armies out of Pamur-teng and Ozali-teng converged, poised to attack. The lines were drawn—there should have been such bloodshed!—but then . . . Then it was as if the rebels woke from a dream, as if the blindfold of Tharn's deceit was lifted. Their leaders sued for peace. They pleaded for it! They threw themselves on our mercy, some fell on their swords; their wazirs declared themselves beguiled. Praise Horul—praise you!—there were but few lives lost in skirmishes. They struck their camp and e'en now march homeward. Then we knew you were victorious, that the Mad God was defeated."

He paused as they emerged into a courtyard. Overhead a pale sun hung in a steel-blue sky, not long risen. The air was crisp, devoid of magic's scent or the chill of unnatural winter; instead, autumn perfumed the clean air. Folk stared, leaving their tasks, converging on the group as they strode across the yard, cheering as they entered a building where more Jesserytes watched in awe.

"We knew that victory won," Ochen continued as they climbed stairs, "but when you were not then returned . . . Horul! Then I began to fear your victory pyrrhic. Weeks passed . . ."

"It seemed to us no more than a little while," Calandryll murmured. "A day or two."

"That place you went turns on a different clock, I think," the wazir replied. "Tell me . . . No! Wine first, and all present to hear."

He brought them to that chamber where they had first spoken with the wazir-narimasu, the central glass admitting clean light now, some sorcerers already waiting, others hurrying in as word spread through the citadel that the questers were come back safe. Calandryll looked for Chazali, only to learn the kiriwashen had returned to Pamur-teng, to which hold, Ochen assured him, word would be sent instantly. Wine was brought, and food; the room grew crowded, abuzz with questions, curiosity a palpable thing. Finally all were gathered and the doors closed. Zedu took a place at the table's head, Ochen seated on his left hand, the questers to his right.

Zedu said formally, "To Horul and your own gods we give praise for your safe return. To you we give praise for all you've done—the world stands in your debt."

Farther down the table someone murmured, "The Younger Gods themselves stand in their debt," which was answered with a murmur of agreement.

Zedu asked, "Do you then tell your tale?"

Silence fell. Bracht swallowed meat and motioned with a filled cup that Calandryll should act as spokesman. He looked to Katya and Cennaire, who both nodded. He began to speak.

The telling was punctuated with gasps, murmurs of approval, and awe. When he was done Zedu turned to Ochen: "The gate is closed?"

"Sealed." Gravely Ochen ducked his head. "None shall pass through that portal again. And once the Arcanum is delivered to Vanu, none shall again find a way to Tharn."

"This was bravely done," said Zedu, "and for that journey you'd now make you shall have such an escort as . . ."

Calandryll interrupted the sorcerer. "There's a boon owed ere we depart."

Zedu's gaze wavered at that. Beside him, Ochen's smile froze, his expression troubled. The chamber was abruptly still, as if the wazir-narimasu held their breath, unsure what might now transpire. Calandryll held his eyes firm on Zedu's face.

"The matter of Cennaire's heart."

It seemed to Calandryll the mage sighed. He felt Cennaire's hand take his. Turning, he saw her lovely face planed grim. He said, "Aye. The matter of its return."

Zedu nodded, motioning that Ochen should speak on his behalf, on behalf of all the wazir-narimasu. There was a pause that seemed to stretch out, timeless, and then Ochen faced them both with solemn mien.

"You are fixed on this course?"

Such doubt underpinned the question Calandryll almost shook his head, almost said, "No. Save you be certain she shall live, I'd not risk it." But it was not, he recognized, his choice to make. That decision belonged to Cennaire.

She said, "Aye," with a certainty absolute.

"It shall not be easy. It may not be possible. Anomius no longer offers any threat. Might you not reconsider?"

"I'd have back my heart and be once more mortal."

Calandryll saw her eyes blaze, determined, and in that moment, in that look, felt his love flare afresh, heightened by the danger he heard in Ochen's voice, the courage in Cennaire's. *Dera*, he thought, *I cannot lose her now. That I could not bear.*

"You've great powers as you are."

"I'd give them up. I'd have back my heart."

"It may not be within our power to regain the pyxis, unseal the gramaryes Anomius set thereon."

"If not within yours, then whose?"

"You've great faith in us."

"Aye." Said simply.

Answered with: "Think you the sorcerers of Nhur-jabal shall readily give up the box?"

"Think you they'll not? Think you they'll leave me be, Anomius's creation?"

"Aye." Ochen smiled wanly. "There's that to consider. But also your existence. We might obtain the pyxis, safe. Bring it here . . . keep it here."

"No!" She did not shout, but still her voice was thunder in the room. "What I am I'd be no longer. What I am taints me—marks me as Anomius's creation! I'd be myself, entire, owing nothing to any man, save what I choose to give."

This with a glance at Calandryll, a brief smile that he answered with his own, proud for all the fear he felt. Dera, but it was far easier to face Rhythamun than this subtle torture. This was the confrontation they had set aside along the road to Anwar-teng. He wondered—traitorous thought—if he should argue with her, and told himself again, *No,* that this could not be his decision, only hers.

He heard Ochen say, "We cannot promise you success."

And Cennaire return, "Still I'd ask you to attempt it."

"Even though it risk your death?"

"That was risked not long ago. And a boon was promised in return."

"Aye, it was, and we stand by that promise. But even so . . ."

"Even so, I'd have you do it."

"So be it. Would you rest, and we make the attempt on the morrow?"

She hesitated then, her eyes finding Calandryll's, and he saw fear in the great brown orbs. Then she turned again to Ochen and said, loud, "Best it be done now." And then, so soft none others there could hear, "Ere I weaken and gainsay myself."

He held her hand tight as Ochen ducked his head in solemn agreement, and whispered, "Would you not rest first? Shall tomorrow not be soon enough?"

He wondered if that were said selfishly. If he sought to spin out the sure time left them, to delay a little longer the possibility he should lose her.

She answered him, "No, my love. I'd do it now, for fear it be not done at all."

In that instant he thought her courage far outweighed his own. He raised her hand to his lips and said, "Then let's do it."

Neither noticed Ochen rise and come toward them until his voice intruded. "Do you then think on Nhur-jabal?" he asked. "Concentrate your mind on that chamber where Anomius took your heart, that we may see where we must go."

Calandryll let go her hand as the wazir came between them, his painted nails bright as they touched Cennaire's cheeks, tilting back her head as he stared into her eyes. The scent of almonds wafted pungent. Calandryll was dimly aware that all the wazir-narimasu concentrated their gaze on Ochen; that Katya touched his sleeve, reassuring; that Bracht sat grim-faced, a fist about the falchion's hilt. Then Ochen loosed his hold and stepped back, nodding to himself, turning to Zedu. "We've the image of it," he said.

Zedu paused a heartbeat before replying. Then: "Even so . . . to travel thus on another's memory alone."

Calandryll said, fierce now, "A boon was promised."

"Aye." Zedu looked a moment shamefaced. "It was, and it shall be granted. Be it in our power."

Calandryll had sooner the sorcerer not added that

last, but he ignored it, taking Cennaire's hand again.

Ochen said, "Cennaire must be our guide. I go . . . Who else?"

"I," said Calandryll, echoed by Bracht, by Katya.

"Seven there must be to hold this cantrip firm," said Ochen. "You've power sufficient, my friend. But, Bracht, Katya . . . I fear your presence should only endanger this undertaking."

"I go," said Zedu, and then three more. Cennaire said, "Do we go swift, then? Please?"

Ochen nodded and beckoned, and the seven moved a little way apart from the rest, forming a circle, shoulder to shoulder. Calandryll put an arm around Cennaire, pressing her close as the wizards began to chant, their arcane words setting the chamber to flickering like a candle seen through rain-washed glass. The scent of almonds waxed strong . . .

. . . and they stood within another chamber, this bright-lit by autumnal sunshine, opulent despite the dust that greyed the floor, the furniture, a hearth standing empty, the scent of desertion clear as magic's perfume faded.

"Anomius's quarters," Cennaire said, excitement and tension mingling in her voice. She clutched at Calandryll's arm. "He brought me here."

"And the pyxis must be here," said Ochen. Then, softer, "I hope."

"And soon those who'll wonder at our presence," said Zedu. "I doubt Anomius hid the box in any obvious place, but rather employed some gramarye of concealment. Do we bend our will to its finding before we're interrupted?"

Like questing hounds testing the air for sign of prey the wazir-narimasu began to examine the rooms. Calandryll stood helpless with Cennaire, one arm about her shoulders, a hand fingering the hilt of the straightsword, ready to draw should any oppose them. Such magic as was needed for the finding of the pyxis was not his to command, and he felt himself supernumerary, useless save that his presence was a support to Cennaire. She stayed by his side as the Jessertyes went about their search, coming with him to the door, where he set an ear to the paneled wood, listening for approaching footsteps, voices. Recognizing what he did, she drew him back, smiling nervously, and said, "Leave this to me. My ears are yet superior."

"Aye." He acknowledged the logic of it, even as he cursed his inaction: it allowed too much time, space, to fill up with fear. What if the wazir-narimasu failed to find the box? What if the surrounding gramaryes proved too strong? What if the Tyrant's sorcerers had already removed it? He looked from Cennaire to the busy thaumaturgists, willing the pyxis to appear, willing some bright-robed man to proclaim discovery.

Cennaire said, "Someone approaches."

Calandryll snatched the straightsword half its length from the scabbard before reason prevailed: better to plead, better to rely on the power of the wazir-narimasu. The sword slid back and he called a soft warning that was answered with a curse from Ochen.

"Can you not employ magic?" he asked. "Hide us? Seal the door?"

"I'd not contest with fellow mages," Ochen replied.

"And do they look to prevent our search? Shall you not oppose them then?"

"As best we may," the mage returned.

"This should be sufficient." Calandryll felt comforted. "I've seen your magicks at work."

Ochen snorted, not turning from his task. Over his shoulder he said, "I was a wazir then. I am wazir-narimasu now, and sworn to use no belligerent magic."

Now Calandryll cursed. Cennaire said, "They're at the door. They speak."

The wood was too thick he might hear what was said, but the sudden wafting of the familiar almond scent told him a cantrip was voiced. More mundane was the click of tumblers in the lock as a key was turned. Calandryll motioned Cennaire back, settling a hand firm on swordhilt.

The door opened, revealing a group of seven men, their robes black and silver, decorated with cabbalistic designs. Behind them, filling the corridor, clustered soldiers, too many leveling crossbows. Calandryll prepared to sell himself dear.

An old man, his features patrician, raised a hand, part warning to the intruders, part an order that those with him hold their fire. He said, "I am Rassuman, sorcerer to the Tyrant of Kandahar. What do you here?" His tone was commanding, but also curious.

It was a moment before Calandryll, his ears grown accustomed to the Jesseryte tongue, recognized the language. He ducked his head, briefly formal, diplomatic, not taking his eyes from the sorcerer's face, and answered, "We seek a box. A pyxis . . ."

"Anomius's creature!" Behind Rassuman a grossly fat man pointed an accusing finger. "Slay her!"

"No!" The straightsword was in Calandryll's hand, defensive. He shouted, "Ochen! Ward us, for Dera's sake!"

"Hold, hold," urged Rassuman. "And you, Lykander, do you still your tongue a moment?

We've a marvel here, and I'd know the making of it. They cannot elude us, and as yet offer us no harm."

He spoke with serene confidence and the obese sorcerer grunted, scratching irritably at a wine-stained beard.

Rassuman looked again at Calandryll, at Cennaire, and said, "The woman I recognize; and as Lykander remarks, she is, indeed, the revenant Anomius made. But you, my bellicose young friend, who are you?"

"Calandryll den Karynth. Anomius is dead."

Rassuman said, "Ah, I see it now. You've something of Lysse about you."

Lykander said, "The domm's brother! Therefore our enemy. Slay him! And the exotics, too."

"Given his name the relationship is unarguable." Rassuman's voice was mild. Calandryll thought perhaps his eyes twinkled, that he enjoyed baiting the fat man with the soiled beard. "But our enemy? That I doubt, as his brother proclaims him outlaw, and poor Menelian named him friend. And these others? I suspect it should be a harder task than most to slay them, for I perceive great magic in their presence. So, shall we talk awhile, ere we fling gramaryes at one another?" He smiled calmly, gesturing that Calandryll should continue. "You say Anomius is dead?"

"Aye." Calandryll nodded, relaxing a fraction. "He was slain by Rhythamun as they contested for the Arcanum."

To Rassuman's right a younger mage smiled, stroking a hand as if in satisfaction. On his left a man murmured, "This is one of whom Menelian spoke."

Rassuman grunted, ducked his head, and asked

more urgently, "And that fell book? Where is it now?"

"In Anwar-teng, on the Jesseryn Plain." Calandryll lowered the straightsword as he outlined the tale of Rhythamun's defeat, Anomius's demise, all that had gone before.

When he was done Rassuman nodded thoughtfully and said, "So you'd remove the pyxis and restore the revenant her heart. Be all you said the truth, then she deserves as much."

"You forget Menelian!" Lykander protested.

"I also choose to forget that you favored Anomius," said Rassuman, such steel in his tone that the fat man paled, falling silent. Then: "We sought that box without success. Our aim"—he glanced apologetically at Cennaire—"was to destroy this lady. When Anomius slipped his bonds and fled, we set these chambers round with gramaryes, lest he return. That you entered is a wondrous thing. These . . . wazir-narimasu, you name them? . . . must be sorcerers of great power to defeat our cantrips. Should we engage in battle, I suspect none should gain much and many suffer."

Calandryll saw no reason to explain the peaceful nature of the Jessertyes' magic. Instead he ducked his head, smiling, and said, "I see no need for battle. Do you leave us to our search, we'll be gone once the pyxis is found."

"We might do more," said Rassuman. "We might join you in the hunt. Perhaps, does Kandahar join with Jesseryn Plain, we might succeed."

The wazir-narimasu had left off their searching as the conversation went on, awaiting its outcome with defensive magic readied. Now Calandryll turned to them, explaining Rassuman's offer. Ochen it was who answered: "Such aid is welcome. Likely, do we join our magicks, we may find the box. But do we first gift ourselves with tongues, and thus save yours the task of translation."

A little more was needed as Calandryll explained the suggestion, and then the Tyrant's sorcerers dismissed the guards and came into the chambers. For a while the air crackled, rich with the almond scent as the wazir-narimasu enspelled the Kands.

"Burash!" Rassuman declared when it was done. "Such a cantrip's a mightily useful thing. Now, do you tell me how you managed to enter here?"

Calandryll waxed impatient as occult lore was exchanged. Cennaire clung to his arm, still nervous in the presence of men she had for so long believed must seek her destruction. Indeed, Calandryll thought, watching their faces, there were some would still. Lykander and the one named Lemomal yet wore hostile expressions: there was one, Caranthus, who seemed indecisive; but the rest were wholehearted in their offer and their efforts, and they held sway, carrying the others with them.

Impatient he was, but even so intrigued to learn of events in the wider world. Order was restored to Kandahar, Fayne Keep reduced to rubble and Sathoman ek'Hennem's head even now rotting on the battlements of Nhur-jabal. His brother's dream of conquest was ended with a storm—of Burash's making? he wondered—that left the great invasion fleet sunk at anchor, Tobias gone back in high dudgeon to Lysse, where Nadama had borne him a son already named heir to the High Throne. The great affairs of the world were settled. Save for that one that now was paramount in his mind. He began to fret as the westering sun shone fainter through the windows.

At last, however, the assembled wizards were done with talking and turned to the task in hand. The chambers grew heady with magic's perfume, droning with the chant of cantrips. And then Zedu, working in harmony with Rassuman, shouted triumphantly from the sleeping quarters.

Calandryll and Cennaire forwent etiquette as they thrust magicians aside, bursting into the room to see the Jesseryte, an expression of distaste on his swarthy features, holding the pyxis.

It was a very simple thing, of plain, black wood, undecorated. Zedu set it down as if it were poisonous, and all there gathered, staring.

"The gramaryes of binding are much weakened by Anomius's death," Rassuman murmured, "but even so, not easy of undoing. Do we attempt it, all of us? It should be safer thus, I think."

They looked one to the other, then to where Cennaire stood. A sorcerer Calandryll remembered was named Cenobar said gently, "The undoing shall be dangerous, Lady. And that but the first step."

"The second," she returned softly. "The first was the finding of it, and that's a step taken now. I'd complete this journey back."

"As you will," said Rassuman.

Calandryll felt Cennaire's fingers dig hard into his flesh as the sorcerers ringed the pyxis, their backs, black Kand robes alternating with brilliant Jesseryte, blocking view. His nostrils clogged with the almond scent, intoxicating; the air shivered, shimmering, sparking blue and silver. Outside, the sky crimsoned with the sun's descent beyond the Kharm-rhanna, shadow denied within the chamber by the coruscation of occult light. Then silence and a slumping of shoulders, the light dying, the almond scent fading. Someone said, hoarse-voiced, "By all the gods, Anomius owned power."

Then Ochen said, "It's done. Do we proceed to the next step?"

"Best you go swift," said Rassuman, and turned to face Cennaire. "Those gramaryes with which Anomius protected the box are lifted, but with their lifting so, too, are those spells that invest you with life weakened. You've little time left, Lady. I pray Burash you've sufficient."

Cennaire nodded silently, staring wide-eyed at the pyxis. Calandryll felt cold sweat bead his brow. To succeed so far only to fail for lack of time? Dera, should Anomius yet revenge himself? Dry-mouthed, his voice husky, he said, "Then do we go without delay?"

"We cannot aid you further," Rassuman murmured. "May the gods speed you."

"Aye." Already the wazir-narimasu came together, Ochen reaching out to take Cennaire's hand, to draw her within their aegis. Calandryll went with her, holding her close as the chant began and the darkening room shifted, flickering in and out of sight to become . . .

. . . the council chamber in Anwar-teng, Bracht and Katya starting up as the seven figures coalesced, their expressions urgent, questions forming that Calandryll met with an outthrust palm, turning to Ochen.

"How much time have we? What must you do?"

"How much time I cannot tell." Ochen peered about the chamber, his fellow sorcerers busying themselves as Zedu barked orders. "Not much, I think. Horul, but Anomius thought far ahead! This must be done swift, and without hesitation."

"Say you we can be defeated?" Calandryll hugged Cennaire close, she silent, as if, her path chosen, she consigned herself to fate. "That even now . . ." He bit back the words and asked instead, "Can you not replace those gramaryes of binding? Earn a little time?"

"No," said Ochen curtly. "Once undone, those spells may not be woven again. This is a thing from which there can be no turning back ... There is only success or failure now. And you've a part to play in this."

"I?" Calandryll shook his head, confused. "Name it, and I'll do it. But what *can* I do? I'm no mage. For all you've tutored me, I scarce understand this power I own."

"Love is seldom easily understood," said Ochen.

"Love?" Calandryll frowned at the enigmatic response. "What's love to do with this?"

He felt Cennaire moan then, shuddering within the compass of his arm. He turned his face toward her and saw her pale beneath her tan, her dusky skin become ash-hued. The eyes she raised were wide with pain, leaking tears. Her teeth began to chatter and she moaned again, bending, a hand pressed to her breast.

Low-voiced, she gasped, "The spell unwinds, I think."

"Dera, no!" Calandryll drew her close, calling on whatever magic he commanded to aid her, calling on the Younger Gods to ease her pain, grant her time.

That power remained dormant; nor did any god respond. He held her, feeling her shake as if ague wracked her, her body cooling as if its life drained out.

Ochen shouted, "Swift! We must act now, and here. Clear the table!"

Hands reached for the detritus of the meal, and wine jugs, cups. Swifter were the falchion and the saber Bracht and Katya swung, sending plates, cups, all of it tumbling to the floor. Delicate china broke, wine ran like blood. Wazir-narimasu began to chant, urgently, others to painting sigils on the wood, arcane symbols that glowed bright, loosing the almond scent.

"Disrobe," Ochen said.

Cennaire's hands fumbled, her fingers shaking, numbed, at her clothes' fastenings. Katya spun, snatching Bracht's dirk from the sheath, roughly shoving Calandryll away as she slashed the lacings of Cennaire's tunic, hacked off the shirt beneath. Calandryll tugged the ruined vestments clear, and caught Cennaire in his arms as she cried out and fell. Katya knelt, ungentle in her urgency as she yanked the boots from Cennaire's feet, the dirk slicing fast through leathern breeks, the undergarments.

"Set her down."

Ochen pushed Calandryll toward the table, indicating the pentagram marked there, and he lowered Cennaire to the wood, the light emanating from the sigils reflected in the sweat that glistened on her naked body. Her eyes fluttered open and her mouth moved: Calandryll leaned close to hear.

"I love you," she whispered. "I've no regrets, no matter . . ."

Her voice tailed off. Her eyes closed. Her mouth hung slack.

Calandryll cried, "No! You cannot die! You must not!"

"She's not yet gone." Ochen thrust him aside, stooping over the supine form, hands moving in intricate patterns that left trailers of light behind, touching her mouth, her breast, her forehead. The wazir-narimasu stood in a circle about the table, their chanting soft now, so that Calandryll heard very clear Ochen's next words.

"This part shall be the hardest. Hard for us and worse for you."

"Worse?" Calandryll shook his head, dismissing

the question: there was no time for redundant words. Instead he asked, "What must I do?"

Ochen glanced sidelong at Cennaire, as though to reassure himself the vestiges of life remained. Urgently, he said, "There's a power in you that transcends even such magic as we wazir-narimasu command. *And you love her!* That, above all, is the vital factor now."

Helplessly Calandryll muttered, "I fail to understand."

"You need not, only act," said Ochen. "Yours must be the hand that takes out what Anomius set within her. Yours the hand that puts back her living heart."

Calandryll gasped, gaping, as sudden sweat ran chill down ribs and spine, "I cannot! I've not the skill. I'm no chirurgeon. Dera, I'd kill her!"

"You must!" Ochen's hand fastened hard upon his wrist, the wrinkled face tilted up, narrow eyes burning with a dreadful intensity as he stared into Calandryll's. "Hate it was took out her heart and made her revenant—Anomius's hatred of you and your companions. Love it must be that restores the organ. Without love, we've no hope of success— and of all here, your love is the strongest. Do it! Or see her die!"

Calandryll moaned, a groan of heartfelt agony, of awful indecision. He gazed at Cennaire, her body slick with sweat now, the rise and fall of pumping lungs slowing, her lips gone pale, as if the coursing of blood faltered.

"Do it!" the sorcerer repeated, remorseless. "Or see her die! It's in your hands."

Calandryll's teeth gritted, lips stretched back in rictal grimace. He willed his hands to still their trembling: without effect. Then fingers clutched his shoulder, spinning him round to face Bracht.

"Do it." The Kern's voice was steady, steel-hard as the blue eyes that locked his gaze. "Quit your mewling and do it."

"Do you truly love her, you can." Beside the Kern Katya's grey eyes shone fierce. "The gods will guide you."

Dumb, he nodded, a silent prayer shaping in his mind: *Dera, be with me now. Do you love me, be with me. Have I served you, grant me the strength to do this.* He turned from those determined eyes, blue and grey, to find Ochen's tawny slits, and ducked his head in frightened acceptance.

"What must I do?"

Ochen's smile was fleeting. "Dera placed her blessing on that blade you wear. Use that."

Calandryll drew the straightsword unthinking. Then hesitated, staring at the blade. No chirurgeon's tool this, no delicate scalpel but a length of forged steel made for life's taking, not its renewal. It seemed a clumsy, cumbersome thing now.

"That shall serve better than any scalpel." It seemed Ochen read his mind; or the expression on his face. "Trust in your goddess."

Calandryll licked parched lips, passed a hand over tear-blurred eyes. *Dera, I place my trust in you.* Aloud, he said, "Tell me what I must do."

Ochen touched Cennaire's ribs, one long nail scratching a faint line, dark against the pallor of her dying skin. "Cut here."

Calandryll took a deep breath, closed his eyes a moment, then leaned against the table, both hands about the straightsword's hilt. Suddenly they were firm, steady, no longer shaking. His vision cleared. It seemed in that instant he felt the power of the goddess in the steel. His heart calmed, no longer racing, but pumping an even beat. He set the blade against the line Ochen had drawn and cut.

Flesh parted, peeling from the wound. A few drops of blood oozed. There should have been more, a flood did she still live. He forced the doubt away.

Ochen said, "Deeper," and he cut again, down through the underlying tissue until he saw exposed within the cage of ribs a lump of black clay.

The chanting of the wazir-narimasu grew louder, their words imbuing the darkening chamber with radiant blue light. It seemed to Calandryll to wind and flow about the blade, that pulsing of its own now, scintilla dancing within the metal.

At his shoulder, Ochen said, "Sever those ties that bind it."

The straightsword was light, weightless it seemed, sure as any scalpel, his hands resolute as he cut through the linkages of arteries and veins, severing those connections with Anomius's magic.

"Take out that abomination."

He set the sword aside, unaware whose hands took it from him, and reached into the cavity, lifting out the clay. It burned his palms, a sour odor of corruption and decay offending his nostrils, as if its final moments of existence were spent in spite, last lingering memories of Anomius's malice. He turned, and Ochen reached to take the fell burden from him. Zedu, still mouthing the incantation, leaned forward, passing him Cennaire's heart. That lay warm in his hands, and he thought, or hoped, he felt it pulse. He saw Ochen drop the clay into the pyxis a sorcerer extended, and the lid close.

Ochen wiped his hands and said, "Now give her back her heart."

Gently, delicately, he set the organ in place.

"What now?"

"For you, no more. This part belongs to us."

Ochen stretched out his arms, hands palms-

downward above the wound. His fellow sorcerers
came closer, their outthrust hands a benign canopy.
Their chanting deepened and the air crackled with
the power of their magic, blue fire dancing, envel-
oping them and Cennaire in its glow. Calandryll
watched, breath held, as flesh moved, tubes writh-
ing, extending to the still organ, touching it, joining, reconnecting the channels, the conduits of
mortal existence. The sundered flesh moved, the
lips of the wound closing until only a thin pink
line remained. Then that, too, was gone, and Cennaire lay again entire.

Ochen once more touched gentle fingers to her
breast, her lips, her forehead, and then, one by one,
all of the wazir-narimasu did the same. Their
chanting reached a crescendo and the blue radiance
enveloped Cennaire.

Then silence, a dying of the light.

Calandryll felt his held breath come out in a
ragged sigh.

Cennaire lay still.

No hint of life lifted her ribs; no breath came
warm from her cold lips; her eyes stared wide and
sightless.

Calandryll saw, as if time slowed, as if this final
disappointment must be drawn out, lingering, that
each final particle of dashed hope be savored,
Ochen turn toward him, desolation etched clear in
every wrinkle of his face. He saw the mage's lips
move, heard each word come ponderous, a threnody of despair.

"I fear we were too late. Oh, Horul! There's no
more we can do. Cennaire is truly dead."

"*No!*"

Calandryll flung the smaller man aside, hurling
himself at the table, at Cennaire's corpse.

"*No!*"

It was cry of absolute denial, blind refusal of his eyes' testimony, of Ochen's words. There was no grief in it, not yet; rather it was a scream of rage, of total rejection. He cupped Cennaire's ashen face, lifting her head. Her cheeks were cold. Her raven hair spread, dulled now that magic's illumination was gone, a dark and lifeless shroud. He shouted, "No," again, and, "You cannot die. Not now," and pressed his lips to hers.

What the others there present saw then he did not, for he held the woman he loved in his arms, seeking to infuse her with his own life, to breathe his vitality into her corpse, and he was blind to all else.

What the rest saw was a manifestation of starlight, of moon's glow, the coruscating essence of a god bound in sparkling shadow and dancing radiance, elemental matter shaped in form of a man, save for the great jet horsehead, the eyes alight with benevolent fire.

Horul reached out one hand to touch Calandryll's shoulder, unnoticed.

Life you gave us, that Tharn should have taken. A service well worthy of reward, that. And so a life in return, in gratitude, in my name and those of all my kin.

Gravely, the god nodded, mane of night and stars shifting, fluttering proud. The hand left Calandryll's shoulder, the smoldering eyes surveyed the chamber, and then Horul was gone on a silent wind.

Calandryll did not see the god, neither heard him speak, but he felt flow into him and through him a tremendous power. Not that strength that had invested him as he fought with Rhythamun, though it was akin to that, but something greater: the very power of life. He felt it blaze, fiery, down the roadways of his being, his heart become the engine that

drove lungs become a furnace that pushed the
power out, past his lips, into Cennaire. Into her
mouth, her throat, her veins, her heart, filling her.
He felt her lips grow warm and move against his,
her arms rise to encircle him, clutching him. He
felt her ribs rise, and fall again, breath sweetly stifled against his mouth. He pulled back, gazing into
eyes no longer lusterless, but shining, vital; alive.
He shouted laughter and pulled her to him anew.

In time they drew apart, and by then the assembly was recovered enough from the shock of
Horul's manifestation that Katya had thought to
ask a gown be brought. Cennaire drew it on, suddenly demure, her eyes ablaze with wonder.

"I thought," she said softly, weak as yet, resting
in the curve of Calandryll's arm, "that I was lost. I
felt . . . nothing. Dead."

"You live," Calandryll returned her, his mouth
against her glossy hair. "Praise all the gods, you
live."

"And I am entire? Myself again?"

"Aye," he answered her. "Your heart is once
more yours. Yours alone."

"I think not." A hint of coquetry entered her
voice. "For it's a new owner now."

"And mine," he said, "is yours. For so long as
you'd have it."

"That," she told him earnestly, smiling, "shall
be a very long time. Indeed, for all my life."

Across the chamber Bracht said, "Ahrd, but I
sicken at all this sweetling talk. Do we find wine
and celebrate in fitting manner?"

But he was laughing as he said it, and an arm lay
about Katya's shoulders, and she drove an elbow
against his ribs and said, herself laughing, "Better
you take heed, Kern, for I'd hear the same from you
ere long."

Bracht exaggerated a frown of dismay at that, then shrugged and sighed, and said, "Calandryll, do you tutor me then? Lest I offend this woman I intend to wed."

Calandryll answered him, "Willingly, though I suspect it shall be the hardest task we've yet faced."

"Likely it shall," said Bracht, but Calandryll barely heard him, because he was kissing Cennaire again, and so did not see the Kern turn Katya's face up and follow suit in practice of his first lesson.

THEY quit Anwar-teng under the indifferent gaze of a wintry sun. The ground was churned by the feet of the rebels, by the hooves of their horses, the wheels of their departing wagons, but the season froze it hard, and with spring's advent even those last memories of Tharn's madness should be forgotten. The wind blew clean and cold, devoid of the Mad God's charnel reek, fluttering the banners of their escort, a century of kotu-zen, Ochen riding with them as they went eastward, to Vanu. To the holy men of Katya's land, who should at last destroy the Arcanum, that none of Rhythamun's ilk, or Anomius's, again have chance to dream of dominion, to seek the resurrection of the Mad God. That the world be once more safe from chaos, and men go about their affairs under governance of the Younger Gods alone.

They turned a moment in their saddles, hands raised in salute and farewell to the wazir-narimasu, the young Khan, and the Shendii, who stood by the gate, their presence token of the respect accorded the questers, and then looked only forward, to the future.

"Shall you be wed in Vanu?" Calandryll asked Katya.

She looked to Bracht and her smile was glorious as she answered, "Does this Kern still want me, aye."

Bracht said, "I've wanted you since first I saw you. Ahrd, but I knew not I'd such patience."

Katya laughed long, reaching out to take his hand, and asked, "And you? Shall you two wed?"

"It's my wish," said Calandryll solemnly.

"And mine," said Cennaire, meeting his earnest gaze with a smile.

He was surprised as he realized he had never seen her blush before. He thought that tomorrow, and all their tomorrows, should be joyous.

About the Author

ANGUS WELLS was born in a small village in Kent, England. He has worked as a publicist and as a science fiction and fantasy editor. He now writes full-time and is the author of *The Books of the Kingdoms (The Wrath of Ashar, The Usurper, The Way Beneath)* and *The Godwars (Forbidden Magic, Dark Magic, Wild Magic)*. His next novel will be a single volume fantasy called *Lords of the Sky*. He lives with his two dogs, Elmore and Sam, in Nottinghamshire, where he is at work on a new novel for Bantam Spectra.

LORDS OF THE SKY

The upcoming fantasy novel
by Angus Wells

Lords of the Sky tells the story of a conflict that brings together two peoples in a clash of cultures and magics over the one land they both call their home. The tale begins, however, with a small boy in an obscure fishing village. From his perspective as an old man, worn by life and much wiser for the wear, Daviot begins his story: how his feet were set upon the path that would ultimately make him Mnemonikos—one who remembers the history of his people—and how that path was an integral part of the upheaval that would reshape the only world he knows.

I was a fisher child. I played on the sand, amongst the beached boats and the black pines. I hoarded shells and bird's eggs. When the brille swarmed, I waded in, knee-deep, to haul the nets. I swung a sling and pulled girls' hair; fought with other boys: I was a child like other children. On the cliff above the village I had a camp, a secret place: a fortress as great as Gahan's keep; a bastion from which I and Tellurin, and Corum defended Whitefish village against the Kho'rabi. Sometimes I *was* a Kho'rabi knight, and with my bark-peeled blade wrought slaughter on my friends, though I always liked it better when I had the part of noble Gahan's man—a commur, or a jennym, even a pyke—for then I felt, with all the intensity of childhood's fierce emotions, that I fought for Kellambek, to hold off those invaders the Sentinels could not prevent from crossing the Fend.

What did I know then of the Comings?

Little enough: to me, the Kho'rabi knights, the kingdom of Ahn-feshang, they were legends. When I was very young my mother used to tell me that should I disobey her, a Kho'rabi knight should come and take my head. I spent some small time cowering beneath my blanket at that, but as I grew older, sneered. Kho'rabi knights, what were they to me? Creatures of legend, of no more account than the fabled dragons of the Forgotten Country, who had gone away before even my grandfather was born.

But then, in my twelfth year, I saw the Sky Lords.

I did not clearly understand it at the time, save that all the village mantis had preached, and all that Thorus and my parents had told me, became amalgamated in one instant of inchoate terror, as though the nightmares of infancy took form from shadow and became real: the thing that dwells beneath your bed emerging, physical, fanged and horrible.

It was the end of summer. The sky was cobalt blue, the sun a sullen eye that challenged observation. There were no clouds, and the sea was still, unrippled. I was on the sand, passing my father the tools he needed to sew gashes in his nets. Battus and Thorus worked with him on the skein.

Thorus was the first to see it, dropping his needle as he sprang to his feet, shouting. My father and my uncle were no slower upright, the net forgotten on the warm sand. I followed them, staring to where they pointed, not sure what it was they pointed at, or what set such fear in their eyes. I knew only that my father, who was afraid of nothing—not tides or storms, I thought then—*was* afraid. Battus shouted and ran from the beach, and I felt their fear, like the waft of sour sweat, or a drunkard's breath.

I remember that Thorus said, "They come again," and my father answered, "It is not the time," and then told me to run homeward, to tell my mother that the Sky Lords came, and she would know what to do. I suppose, in reflection, that he assumed Battus would warn the mantis, and he send someone north to the Holding, that the aeldor be warned.

In any event, I was sent from the beach as all the men not at sea gathered, staring skyward, and I lingered a moment, wondering what held them so rigid, like old statues.

Against the knife-sharp brilliance of the sky I saw a shape. It seemed, in that moment, like a maggot, a bloated grub taken up by the hot late-summer wind, a speck against the eye-watering azure, that drifted steadily toward me.

I wondered why it promoted such consternation.

Then my father, knowing me, shouted, and I ran to our cottage and yelled at my mother that the Sky Lords were coming.

I think that then, for the first time, I truly knew what terror they induced.

Tonium and Delia fashioned castles from the dirt of our yard. My mother screamed at them, bringing them tearful to her arms, she so distraught she found only brief, hurried words to calm their wailing as she gathered them up. The bell hung above the cella began to sound, its clanging soon augmented by a great shouting from all the women, and the old men, and the howling of confused and frightened children. My mother snatched Delia's and Tonium's hands in hers, shouted at me to follow, and drew my siblings, trotting, away from the house towards the cella. The mantis stood atop the dome. I remember that the sinews in his fat arms stood out like cords from the effort of his bell-ringing, and that his plump face, usually set in a smile, was grim, his head craned round to peer at the shape approaching across the sky. All around me I heard the single word: Kho'rabi, said in tones of awe and terror. I wondered why, for the thing in the sky was as yet very small, no larger than the shapes of the sea gulls that were the only other things to break the blue. I watched as the mantis gathered up the skirts of his robe and slid ungainly down the sloping side of the dome. Robus, who owned the only horse in Whitefish village waited nervously. I saw that he had belted an ancient sword to his waist; and that all the men, and not a few of the women, carried weapons of one kind or another: fish knives, axes, mattocks. The mantis spoke urgently with Robus and though I could not hear what was said, I perceived it had a great effect on Robus, for he dragged himself astride his old horse and slapped the grey flanks with his blade, sending the animal into a startled, lumbering trot out of the village in the direction of the Cambar road. Then the mantis shouted that all should follow him, and led the way to the cliff path, up through the pines to the fields beyond, where a track wound by drystone walls to a wood where caves ran down into the earth.

In the confusion I became separated from my mother, and as I watched the worried faces of those who passed me, wondering why so many cheeks shone with tears, I succumbed to childhood's temptation.

I was afraid: how should I not be? I was but twelve years old, and all around me were folk I knew as calm neighbors and friends; and now all wore the same expression, masked with fear and desperation. I *was* afraid, but I was also intrigued, fascinated to know the *why* of it. As I ducked clear of the throng, I saw the last of the villagers go by, five grandfathers in rear guard, clutching old swords and flensing poles. They were so anxious they failed to spot me where I crouched beside a wall, and in moments a cloud of dust, raised by hurried feet, hung betwixt me and them. With the unthinking valiance of innocent youth, I turned back toward Whitefish village.

My father was there, and Thorus, and I wondered what they did, and why the shape in the sky produced such fear.

Oh, I had heard tales by then of the Kho'rabi knights, of the Sky Lords. I had listened to Thorus tell of how he had been a pyke, wielding his blade in the last Coming, when two airboats landed. But Thorus was old, and all we children knew that the Sky Lords came but when the shifting of the worldwinds and the waxing power of their mages allowed, and that was more time than I could then conceive of. It was a matter of lifetimes, I thought then. And so, quickly, my fear became laid over with curiosity, and I watched the dust cloud skirl away toward the wood, and turned back toward the village.

I knew my mother would be angry when she found me gone, but I dismissed that concern and ran back to the cliff path.

I halted among the pines, where they edged and then fell down over the slope, looking first at the village and then at the sky. The village was empty; the beach was lined with men. The sky was still that steel-hot blue; the shape of the Sky Lords' boat was larger.

I could discern its outline now: a cylinder of red, the color of blood; the carrier beneath was a shadow sparkling with glints of silver as the sun struck the blades of the warriors there. I wondered how it had come up so fast, unaware, then, of the occult powers that drove it across the sky. I watched it awhile, my eyes watering in the sun glare. I looked back and thought perhaps I should have done better to go after my mother and find the safety of the wood, where the ancient crypts ran down into the earth.

Instead, I ran down to the village, through the emptied houses to the beach, to my father.

He did not see me at first, for his face was locked on the sky, etched over with shadows of disbelief. He stood with a flensing pole held across his chest, high, the curved blade striking brilliance from the sun. It was not the manner in which a flensing pole was normally held and it was a moment before I recognized that this was how I had seen the poles clutched when men argued, and threatened to fight. Thorus stood beside him, and in his mottled hand was a sword, not rusted like Robus's old blade, but bright with oil, darker along the edges, where the whetstone had shaped cutting grooves. It was a blade such as soldiers carried, and for a moment I stared and lusted after such a weapon.

I suppose I must have made a sound. Perhaps that of foot on sand, or a cry of admiration, for my father turned and saw me, Thorus with him, though their faces bore very different expressions.

My father's was angry; Thorus's amused. I felt a fear greater than anything a Kho'rabi knight might induce at the one; pleasure at the other.

My father said, "What in the God's name are you doing here?"

Thorus said, "You breed warriors, Aditus."

I remember that very surely.

I would likely have run away then, back through the village and up the cliff path, across the fields to the wood, far more afraid of the look gouged over my father's face than of any Kho'rabi knight. But Thorus said, "Blood runs true, friend," to my father; and to me, "Best find yourself a blade if you stand with us, Daviot."

My father said, "God's name, man, he's only a boy," but I was swelled with pride and honor and found a discarded net hook that I picked up for want of better weapon, and strode with all the majesty of twelve years' growth—and all its ignorance—to stand between them, and Thorus laughed and clapped me on the shoulder hard enough I tottered, and said, "Blood to blood, Aditus."

My father's face remained dark, but then he grunted and nodded and said, "Likely they'll pass over. So, you can stay, boy. But on my word, you run for the caves. Yes!"

I nodded, without any intention whatsoever of keeping my word: if the enlarging shape of the Sky Lords' boat dropped fylie of the Kho'rabi knights upon us, I planned to stand shoulder-to-shoulder with my fellow warriors. I planned to die gloriously in defense of Whitefish village, in defense of Kellambek.

I was a man then: I am older now, and wiser.

I watched the ship grow larger, my hands tight on my hook. It came up faster than any natural wind might propel it. I saw that the blood-red cylinder was all painted with occult sigils, and that the long basket beneath was spread with more. I saw the glimmer of the magic that drove it, trailing back from the pointed tail like heat haze against the sky, like the shifting translucence of fire's glow. The sea gulls that were a constant punctuation of the sky fled before it, and I suddenly realized that the cats that prowled the shoreline were also gone; likewise the handful of dogs our village boasted. That seemed very strange to me—the absence of such familiar things—and I glanced around, my valor threatened. I saw that my father's knuckles bulged white from his tanned hands, and that Thorus's lips were spread back from clenched teeth in a kind of snarl. I realized then that a terrible silence had fallen, as if this unexpected Coming drove stillness before it, or the presence of the Sky Lords absorbed sound. No one moved. I stared in shared dread, feeling the shadow of the boat fall over me, which it should not have done, for the sun westered and that shadow should not—nor could—have reached us yet.

But it did, and I trembled, for all my youthful bravery, in its cold. My father did the same, though he sought to hide it from me, looking down at me and smiling. I thought his smile was like the grin I had seen on the faces of drowned men.

Then the great shape was directly above us. I stood, trembling, cold weight heavy on my head and shoulders, the sand no longer warm under my feet. I craned my head back, seeing that the airboat hung high above us, though it darkened all the village, and where it rode the sky, strange stars and prancing shapes showed through the blue, as if elementals sported there.

Some arrows fell, unflighted by the height, and fired, I think, in amusement; a fisherman named Vadim even caught one in his hand, that feat producing a shout of encouragement from all the rest.

And then the ship was gone, passed beyond the cliff and out of sight.

It was both disappointment and relief to me: I had anticipated glorious battle; I was also glad that horrible weight was passed. I enjoyed the way my father held my one shoulder, Thorus my other, and both told me I had played my part, even as men went running to the cliff, to follow the ship's passage.

I went running with them, still clutching my hook, for they all still held their weapons, and I was suddenly possessed of a dreadful fear that the ship had gone past the village to land in the fields—the wood—beyond, and disgorge the Kho'rabi knights to massacre my mother and my siblings, and all the others hiding in the caves. But Thorus hauled me back and shouted at my father that the wind was wrong and whatever magic the sorcerers of Ahn-feshang commanded, it was not enough to ground the boat to disembark the fylie.

Even so, I was not satisfied, nor my father, until we topped the path and saw the ship drifting on, over the wood, disappearing into the haze of the afternoon sun, like blood drying on a wound.

Robus, mounted on his old, slow horse, had reached the aeldor's Holding during the night. The watchmen had brought him before the lord, who had immediately ordered three squadrons to patrol the coast road, one to ride instanter for Whitefish village.

They arrived a few hours after sun's rise; dirty, tired, and irritable. To me, then, they looked splendid. There were twenty of them, their warrior's plaits decorated with little, bright feathers, and shells: tokens of their calling. They wore shirts of leather and mail, draped across with Cambar's plaid, cinched in with wide belts from which hung sheathed swords and long-hafted axes, and every one carried a lance from which the colors of Kellambek fluttered in the morning breeze, round shields hung from their saddles. There was a commur-magus with them, clad all in black sewn with the silver markings of her station, a short-sword on her hip. Her hair was swept back in a tail, but bound with a silver fillet, and decorated with two long eagle's feathers; and, unlike her men, she seemed untired. She raised a hand as the squadron reached the village square, halting the horsemen, waiting as the mantis approached and made obeisance, gesturing him up with a splendid, languid hand.

I, and all the children—and most of our parents, no less impressed—gathered about to watch.

The soldiers climbed down from their horses. The magus, too, dismounted, conferring with the mantis, and then followed our plump and friendly priest to the cella, calling back over her shoulder that the men with her might find breakfast where they could, and ale, if they so desired, for it seemed the danger was gone.

I felt a measure of disappointment at that: I had become, after all, a warrior, and was reluctant to find my new-won status so quickly lost. I compensated by taking the bridle of a horse and leading the animal to where Robus kept his fodder. I had never seen so large an animal before, save when the great winter whales washed up, and I was more than a little frightened by the way it tossed its head and stamped its feet and snorted. The man who rode it chuckled and spoke to it, and told me to hold it firm; and then he set a hand on my shoulder, as Thorus had done, and I straightened my back and reminded myself I was a man, and brought it to Robus's little barn, where it became docile as his old nag when I fed it oats and hay and filled the water trough.

The soldier grinned at that, and checked the beast for himself, taking off the high-cantled cavalry saddle, resting his shield and lance against the wall of the pen. I touched the metalled face of the shield with reverent fingers, and studied his sword and axe. Then smiled as he turned to me and asked where he might find food, and ale, and I told him, "Thorym's tavern," and asked, "Shall you fight the Kho'rabi?"

He said, "I think they're likely gone, praise the God," and I wondered why a soldier would be thankful his enemy was not there. I did not understand then.

I brought him to the tavern and fetched him a pot of ale as his fellows gathered. His name was Andyrt, and as luck would have it, he was jennym to the commurmagus, a life-sworn member of the warband, and, I realized, fond of children. At least, he let me crouch by his side and even passed me his helm to hold, bidding the rest be silent when they looked at me askance and some wondered what a child did there, among men.

I bristled at that, and told them I had stood upon the sand with hook in hand, ready to fight, as the Sky Lords passed over. Some laughed then, and some called me liar, but Andyrt bade them silent, and said that he believed me, and that his belief was theirs, else they chose to challenge him. None did, and I saw that they feared him somewhat, or respected him. To me, he was exotic; glamorous and admirable.

I ventured to pluck at his sleeve and ask him what it took to be a warrior and find a place in the warband.

"Well," he said and chuckled, "first you must be strong enough to wield a blade, and skilled enough in its wielding. Save you prefer to slog out your life as a pyke, you must ride a horse. You must be ready to spend long hours bored, and more drinking. To hold your drink. And you must be ready to kill men; and to be, yourself, killed."

"I am," I said, thinking of the beach, and the airboat; and Andyrt said, "It is not so easy, to put a blade into a man. Harder still to take his in you."

"I'd kill Kho'rabi," I told him firmly. "I'd give my life to defend Kellambek."

He touched my cheek then, gently, as sometimes my father did, and said, "That's an easy thing to say, boy. The doing of it is far harder. Better you pray our God grants strength to the Sentinels, and there's no Coming in your life-time."

"You fight them," I said. "You're a warrior."

He nodded at that. I remember a shadow passing across his face, like the cold penumbra of the Sky Lords' boat. He said, "I'm life-sworn, boy; I know no other way."

I opened my mouth to question him further, to argue, but just then the commur-magus entered the tavern, our mantis on her heels, like a plump and fussing hen, and a silence fell.

Andyrt began to rise, sinking back on the sorcerer's gesture. The black-clad woman approached our table and two of the warband sprang to their feet, relinquishing their places. I found myself crouched between Andyrt and the commur-magus, who asked mildly, "Who's this?"

Andyrt said, grinning, "A young warrior, by all accounts. He stood firm when the skyboat came."

The mantis said, "His name is Daviot, eldest son of Aditus and Donia. I understand he did, indeed, run back to join his father on the beach."

The commur-magus raised blue-black brows at that, and her fine lips curved in a smile. I stood upright, shoulders squared, and looked her in the eye. Had I not, after all, proved myself? Was I not, after all, intent on becoming a warrior?

"So," she said, her voice soft and not at all mocking, "Whitefish village breeds its share of men."

That was fine as Thorus's praise; as good as my father's hand on my shoulder. I nodded, modestly. The commur-magus continued to study me, not even turning when she was passed a mug of ale and a fresh plate of fried fish and bread. She waved regal thanks; her eyes did not leave my face, as if she saw there things I did not know about myself.

"You stood upon the beach?" she said, her voice gentle; speculative as her gaze. "Were you not afraid?"

I began to shake my head, but there was a power in her eyes that compelled truth, that brought back memory. I set Andyrt's helm carefully down on the cleanest patch of dirt between the chairs and nodded.

"Tell me," she said.

I looked awhile at her face. It was dark as Andyrt's, which is to say lighter than any in the village, but unmarked by scars. I thought her beautiful; nor was she very old. Her eyes were green, and as I looked into them, they seemed to obscure the men around her, to send the confines of the tavern into shadow, to absorb the morning light.

I told her everything.

When I was done she nodded and said, "You saw the cats and dogs—the gulls, even—were gone?"

"Then," I told her, and frowned as an unrecognized memory came back. "But this morning the dogs were awake again, and the cats were on the beach. And the gulls," I pointed sea-ward, at the shapes wheeling and squalling against the new-formed blue, "they're back."

"Think you they fled the Coming?" she asked.

"They were not there then," I said. "The sky was empty, save for the boat. I think they must have."

"Why?" she asked me; and I said, "I suppose they were frightened. Or they felt the power of the Sky Lords. But they *were* gone, then."

She sipped a mouthful of ale; chewed a mouthful of fish and bread, still staring at me. I watched her face, wondering what she made of me: what she wanted of me. I felt I was tested and judged. I tried to find Andyrt's eyes, but could not: it was as though the mage's compelling gaze sunk fish hooks in my mind, in my attention, locking me to her as soundly as the lures of the surf-trollers locked the autumnal grylle to their barbed baits.

She turned then to the mantis and my attention was unlocked, as if I were a fish loosed from the net. I looked to Andyrt, who smiled reassuringly and shrugged, motioning for me to be silent and wait. I did: nervous and impatient. The commur-magus said to the mantis, "He's talents, think you?"

The mantis favored me with a look I thought sad, and ducked his head. "He's a memory," he agreed—though then I was unaware of what, exactly, he meant—and added, "Of all my pupils he's the best-schooled in the liturgics: he can repeat them back, word for word."

"As he did this Coming," said the commur-magus, and turned to me again, though now without that draining gaze.

"You brought Andyrt's horse to stable, no? Tell me about his horse and his kit."

"It was brown," I said, confused. "A light brown, with golden hair in its mane and tail. Its hooves were black, but the right foreleg was patched with white, and the hoof there was shaded pale. The saddle was dark with sweat, and the bucket where the lance rests was stitched with black. The stirrups were leather, with dull metal inside. There were two bags behind the saddle, brown, with golden buckles. When he took it off, the horse's hide was pale and sweaty. It was glad to be rid of the weight. It was a gelding, and it snorted when he took off the bridle, and flicked its tail as it began to eat the oats I brought it."

The commur-magus clapped a hand across my eyes then, the other behind my head, so that I could not move, startling me, and said, "What weapons does Andyrt carry?"

"A lance," I told her, for all I was suddenly terrified. "That he left in Robus's stable. Twice a man's height, of black wood, with a long, soft-curved blade. Not like a fishing hook. Also, a sword, an axe and a small knife."

The hands went away from my face and I saw the commur-magus smiling, Andyrt grinning approvingly. The mantis looked less pleased. The others seated around the table seemed wonderstruck: I wondered why, for it seemed entirely natural to me to recall such simple things in their entirety.

"He's the knack, I think," the commur-magus said.

And the mantis nodded and said, "I'd wondered. I'd thought of sending word to Cambar."

"You should have," said the commur-magus.

Andyrt looked at me with something I can now, older, recognize as awe in his eyes. Then, only a decade of my life gone by, I preened myself, aware that I was, somehow, special; that I had passed a test of some kind.

"Are his parents agreeable, he should go to Durbrecht," the commur-magus said. "This one is a natural."

A natural *what*, I did not know; nor what or where Durbrecht was. I frowned and said, "I'd be a soldier."

"There are other callings," said the commur-magus,

and smiled a small apology to Andyrt. "Some higher than the warband."

"Like yours?" I asked, emboldened by her friendly manner. "Do I have magic in me, then?"

She chuckled at that, though not in an unkind way, and shook her head. "Not mine," she advised me. "And I am only a lowly commur-magus, who rides on my lord's word. No, Daviot, you've not my kind of magic in you; you've the magic of your memory."

I frowned anew at that: what magic was there in memory? I remembered things—was that unusual?—I always had. Everyone in Whitefish village knew that. Folk came to me, asking dates, confirmation of things said, and I told them: it was entirely natural to me, and not at all magical.

"He's but twelve years old," I heard the mantis say; and saw the commur-magus nod, and heard her answer, "Then on his manhood. I'd speak with his parents now, however."

The mantis rose, like a plump soldier attending an order, and went bustling from the tavern. I shifted awhile from foot to foot, more than a little disconcerted, and finally asked, "What's Durbrecht?"

"A place," the commur-magus said, "a city and a college, the two the same. Do you know what a storyman is?"

"Yes," I told her, and could not resist demonstrating my powers of recall, boasting. "One came to the village a year ago. He was old—his hair was white and he wore a beard—he rode a mule. He told stories of Gahan's coronation, and of the Comings. His name was . . ." I paused an instant, the old man's face vivid in the eye of my mind; I smelled again the garlic that edged his breath, and the faint odor of sweat that soured his grubby white shirt. ". . . Callum."

The commur-magus ducked her head solemnly, her face grave now, and said, "Callum learned to use his art in Durbrecht. He memorized the old tales there, under the Mnemonikos."

"Nuh . . . moni . . . kos?" I struggled to fit my tongue around the unfamiliar word.

"The Mnemonikos," the commur-magus nodded. "The

Rememberers; those who keep all our history in their heads. Without them, our past should be forgotten; without them, we should have no history."

"Is that important?" I wondered, sensing that my soldierly ambitions were somehow, subtly, defeated.

"If we cannot remember the past," the commur-magus said, "then we must forever repeat our mistakes. If we forget what we were, and what we have done, then we go blind into our future, like untaught children."

I thought awhile on that, scarcely aware that she spoke to me as to a man, struggling as hard with the concept as I had struggled to pronounce the word, the name: Mnemonikos. At last I nodded with all the gravity of my single decade and said, "Yes, I think I see it. If my grandfather's father had not told him about the tides and the seasons of the fish, then he could not have told my father, and then he should have needed to learn all that for himself."

"And if *he* did not remember, then he could not pass on that knowledge to you," said the commur-magus.

"No," I allowed, "but I want to be a soldier."

"But," said the commur-magus, gently, "you see the importance of remembering."

I agreed; a trifle reluctantly, for I felt that she steered our conversation toward a harbor that should render me swordless, bereft of my recently-found ambition. I looked to Andyrt for support, but his scarred face was bland and he hid it behind his cup.

"The Mnemonikos hold all our history in their heads," the commur-magus said softly. "All the tales of the Comings; all the tales of the land. They know of the Kho'rabi; of the Sky Lords and the Dragonmasters: all of it. Without them, we should have no past. The swords they bear never rust or break or blunt . . ."

"They bear swords?" I interrupted eagerly, finding these mysterious Rememberers suddenly more interesting. "They're warriors, then?"

I blushed (and pouted, I think) as the commur-magus smiled and chuckled and shook her head. She said: "Not swords as you mean, Daviot. I mean the blade that finds it scabbard here," she tapped her forehead, "in the mind. And that—my word on it!—is the sharpest blade of all.

Think you this," she tapped the shortsword on her hip now, "is a greater weapon than what I wear here?" She tapped her head again. "No! The blade is for carving flesh, when needs must. The knowledge here," again she touched her skull, "is what can defeat the magic of the Sky Lords."

"I'll face a Kho'rabi knight," Andyrt said, "and trade him blow for blow. I'd not assume to trust steel against their mages, though—that's a fight for your kind, Rekyn: magic against magic."

It was the first time I had heard the commur-magus referred to by name. I watched her nod and smile, and heard her say, "Aye—to each his own talent. Do you understand, Daviot? You've the strength of memory," Rekyn said. "All I've heard from you this day tells me that—and that's a terrible strength, my friend. It's the strength of things past, recalled; it's the strength of time, of history. It's the strength of *knowing*, of knowledge. It's the strength that binds the land, the people. Listen to me! In four years you become a man, and when you do, I'd ask that you go to Durbrecht and hone that blade you carry in your head."

So intense was her voice, her expression—though she used no magic on me then—that I heard proud clarions, a summons to battle; and, still, confusion.

"Is Durbrecht far?" I asked.

"Leagues distant," she answered. "You should have to quit this village, your parents."

"How should I live?" I asked—I was a fisherman's child: I had acquired a measure of practicality.

And she laughed and said, "Be you accepted by the college, all will be paid for you. You'd have board and lodging, and a stipend for pleasure while you learn."

A stipend for pleasure—that had a distinct appeal.

"But how," I wondered, "should I earn all that?"

"By learning," she said, solemnly and urgently. "By learning to use that memory of yours, and by learning our history."

"Not work?" I asked, not quite understanding: to be fed and bedded without labor? How could that be for a boy from Whitefish village?

"Only at learning," she replied.

I pondered awhile, more than a little confused. I looked to where Andyrt's helm lay, observing the dented steel, the sweaty stains on the leather straps, the sheen of oil that overlay the beginnings of rust. I looked at the jennym's sword hilt, leather-wrapped and indented with the familiar pressure of his fingers. I looked at his face and found no answer there. I said, "Is Durbrecht very big?" I asked; and she answered, "Bigger than Cambar."

"Have you been there?" I demanded.

"I was trained there," she said. "I was sent by my village mantis when I came of age. There is a sorcerous college there, too, besides that of the Mnemonikos. I learnt to use my talent there, and then was sent to Cambar."

I scuffed my feet awhile in the dirt of Thorym's tavern, aware that I contemplated my future. Then I looked her in the eye again and asked, "If I do not like it? May I come back?"

"If you do not like it," she said, "or they do not like you, then you come back. In the first year they test you, and then—be you unfit; or they for you—you come back to Whitefish village."

"Or to Cambar Keep," said Andyrt. "To be a soldier, if you still so wish."

That seemed to me a reasonable enough compromise. What was a year? A spring, a summer, an autumn, and a winter: not much time, then. But sufficient enough that I might see something of the world beyond Whitefish village. See this wondrous city of Durbrecht; learn there to use this thing Rekyn saw in me, and—more important then, when I was young—learn the martial arts. And if it did not suit me, or me it, then I could ride out from Cambar Keep with Andyrt and his squadron.

It seemed an opportunity no boy could, in his right mind, refuse. "Yes," I said.

LORDS OF THE SKY

Coming soon wherever Bantam Spectra books are sold.